100%: The Story of a Patriot

Scenes from a Courtesan's Life

Honoré de Balzac

MINT EDITIONS

Scenes from a Courtesan's Life was first published in 1838.

This edition published by Mint Editions 2020.

ISBN 9781513280301 | E-ISBN 9781513285320

Published by Mint Editions®

 MINT
EDITIONS
minteditionbooks.com

Publishing Director: Jennifer Newens
Design & Production: Rachel Lopez Metzger
Project Manager: Micaela Clark
Translated by James Waring
Typesetting: Westchester Publishing Services

100%: The Story of a Patriot

Upton Sinclair

MINT EDITIONS

100%: The Story of a Patriot was first published in 1920.

This edition published by Mint Editions 2020.

ISBN 9781513269887 | E-ISBN 9781513274881

Published by Mint Editions®

MINT
EDITIONS

minteditionbooks.com

Publishing Director: Jennifer Newens
Design & Production: Rachel Lopez Metzger
Project Manager: Micaela Clark
Typesetting: Westchester Publishing Services

Section 1

N ow and then it occurs to one to reflect upon what slender threads
of accident depend the most important circumstances of his
life; to look back and shudder, realizing how close to the edge of
nothingness his being has come. A young man is walking down the
street, quite casually, with an empty mind and no set purpose; he comes
to a crossing, and for no reason that he could tell he takes the right
hand turn instead of the left; and so it happens that he encounters a
blue-eyed girl, who sets his heart to beating. He meets the girl, marries
her—and she became your mother. But now, suppose the young man
had taken the left hand turn instead of the right, and had never met the
blue-eyed girl; where would you be now, and what would have become
of those qualities of mind which you consider of importance to the
world, and those grave affairs of business to which your time is devoted?

Something like that it was which befell Peter Gudge; just such an
accident, changing the whole current of his life, and making the series
of events with which this story deals. Peter was walking down the
street one afternoon, when a woman approached and held out to him a
printed leaflet. "Read this, please," she said.

And Peter, who was hungry, and at odds with the world, answered
gruffly: "I got no money." He thought it was an advertising dodger, and
he said: "I can't buy nothin'."

"It isn't anything for sale," answered the woman. "It's a message."

"Religion?" said Peter. "I just got kicked out of a church."

"No, not a church," said the woman. "It's something different; put
it in your pocket." She was an elderly woman with gray hair, and she
followed along, smiling pleasantly at this frail, poor-looking stranger,
but nagging at him. "Read it some time when you've nothing else to do."
And so Peter, just to get rid of her, took the leaflet and thrust it into his
pocket, and went on, and in a minute or two had forgotten all about it.

Peter was thinking—or rather Peter's stomach was thinking for him;
for when you have had nothing to eat all day, and nothing on the day
before but a cup of coffee and one sandwich, your thought-centers are
transferred from the top to the middle of you. Peter was thinking that
this was a hell of a life. Who could have foreseen that just because he
had stolen one miserable fried doughnut, he would lose his easy job and
his chance of rising in the world? Peter's whole being was concentrated

on the effort to rise in the world; to get success, which means money, which means ease and pleasure—the magic names which lure all human creatures.

But who could have foreseen that Mrs. Smithers would have kept count of those fried doughnuts every time anybody passed thru her pantry? And it was only that one ridiculous circumstance which had brought Peter to his present misery. But for that he might have had his lunch of bread and dried herring and weak tea in the home of the shoe-maker's wife, and might have still been busy with his job of stirring up dissension in the First Apostolic Church, otherwise known as the Holy Rollers, and of getting the Rev. Gamaliel Lunk turned out, and Shoemaker Smithers established at the job of pastor, with Peter Gudge as his right hand man.

Always it had been like that, thru Peter's twenty years of life. Time after time he would get his feeble clutch fixed upon the ladder of prosperity, and then something would happen—some wretched thing like the stealing of a fried doughnut—to pry him loose and tumble him down again into the pit of misery.

So Peter walked along, with his belt drawn tight, and his restless blue eyes wandering here and there, looking for a place to get a meal. There were jobs to be had, but they were hard jobs, and Peter wanted an easy one. There are people in this world who live by their muscles, and others who live by their wits; Peter belonged to the latter class; and had missed many a meal rather than descend in the social scale.

Peter looked into the faces of everyone he passed, searching for a possible opening. Some returned his glance, but never for more than a second, for they saw an insignificant looking man, undersized, undernourished, and with one shoulder higher than the other, a weak chin and mouth, crooked teeth, and a brown moustache too feeble to hold itself up at the corners. Peters' straw hat had many straws missing, his second-hand brown suit was become third-hand, and his shoes were turning over at the sides. In a city where everybody was "hustling," everybody, as they phrased it, "on the make," why should anyone take a second glance at Peter Gudge? Why should anyone care about the restless soul hidden inside him, or dream that Peter was, in his own obscure way, a sort of genius? No one did care; no one did dream.

It was about two o'clock of an afternoon in July, and the sun beat down upon the streets of American City. There were crowds upon the streets, and Peter noticed that everywhere were flags and bunting. Once or twice he heard the strains of distant music, and wondered what was "up." Peter had not been reading the newspapers; all his attention had been taken up by the quarrels of the Smithers faction and the Lunk faction in the First Apostolic Church, otherwise known as the Holy Rollers, and great events that had been happening in the world outside were of no concern to him. Peter knew vaguely that on the other side of the world half a dozen mighty nations were locked together in a grip of death; the whole earth was shaken with their struggles, and Peter had felt a bit of the trembling now and then. But Peter did not know that his own country had anything to do with this European quarrel, and did not know that certain great interests thruout the country had set themselves to rouse the public to action.

This movement had reached American City, and the streets had broken out in a blaze of patriotic display. In all the windows of the stores there were signs: "Wake up, America!" Across the broad Main Street there were banners: "America Prepare!" Down in the square at one end of the street a small army was gathering—old veterans of the Civil War, and middle-aged veterans of the Spanish War, and regiments of the state militia, and brigades of marines and sailors from the ships in the harbor, and members of fraternal lodges with their Lord High Chief Grand Marshals on horseback with gold sashes and waving white plumes, and all the notables of the city in carriages, and a score of bands to stir their feet and ten thousand flags waving above their heads. "Wake up America!" And here was Peter Gudge, with an empty stomach, coming suddenly upon the swarming crowds in Main Street, and having no remotest idea what it was all about.

A crowd suggested one thing to Peter. For seven years of his young life he had been assistant to Pericles Priam, and had traveled over America selling Priam's Peerless Pain Paralyzer; they had ridden in an automobile, and wherever there was a fair or a convention or an excursion or a picnic, they were on hand, and Pericles Priam would stop at a place where the crowds were thickest, and ring a dinner bell, and deliver his super-eloquent message to humanity—the elixir of life revealed, suffering banished from the earth, and all inconveniences of this mortal state brought to an end for one dollar per bottle of fifteen per cent opium. It had been Peter's job to handle the bottles and take in the coin; and so now, when he saw the crowd, he looked about him eagerly. Perhaps there might be here some vender of corn-plasters or ink-stain removers, or some three card monte man to whom Peter could attach himself for the price of a sandwich.

Peter wormed his way thru the crowd for two or three blocks, but saw nothing more promising than venders of American flags on little sticks, and of patriotic buttons with "Wake up America!" But then, on the other side of the street at one of the crossings Peter saw a man standing on a truck making a speech, and he dug his way thru the crowd, elbowing, sliding this way and that, begging everybody's pardon—until at last he was out of the crowd, and standing in the open way which had been cleared for the procession, a seemingly endless road lined with solid walls of human beings, with blue-uniformed policemen holding them back. Peter started to run across—and at that same instant came the end of the world.

Section 2

O ne who seeks to tell about events in words comes occasionally upon a fundamental difficulty. An event of colossal and overwhelming significance may happen all at once, but the words which describe it have to come one by one in a long chain. The event may reveal itself without a moment's warning; but if one is to give a sense of it in words, one must prepare for it, build up to it, awaken anticipation, establish a climax. If the description of this event which fate sprung upon Peter Gudge as he was crossing the street were limited to the one word "Bang" in letters a couple of inches high across the page, the impression would hardly be adequate.

The end of the world, it seemed to Peter, when he was able to collect enough of his terrified wits to think about it. But at first there was no thinking; there was only sensation—a terrific roar, as if the whole universe had suddenly turned to sound; a blinding white glare, as of all the lightnings of the heavens; a blow that picked him up as if he had been a piece of thistledown, and flung him across the street and against the side of a building. Peter fell upon the sidewalk in a heap, deafened, blinded, stunned; and there he lay—he had no idea how long-until gradually his senses began to return to him, and from the confusion certain factors began to stand out: a faint gray smoke that seemed to lie upon the ground, a bitter odor that stung the nostrils and tongue, and screams of people, moaning and sobbing and general uproar. Something lay across Peter's chest, and he felt that he was suffocating, and struggled convulsively to push it away; the hands with which he pushed felt something hot and wet and slimy, and the horrified Peter realized that it was half the body of a mangled human being.

Yes, it was the end of the world. Only a couple of days previously Peter Gudge had been a devout member of the First Apostolic Church, otherwise known as the Holy Rollers, and had listened at prayer-meetings to soul-shaking imaginings out of the Book of Revelations. So Peter knew that this was it; and having many sins upon his conscience, and being in no way eager to confront his God, he looked out over the bodies of the dead and the writhing wounded, and saw a row of boxes standing against the building, having been placed there by people who wished to see over the heads of the crowd. Peter started to crawl, and found that he was able to do so, and wormed his way behind one of these packing-boxes, and got inside and lay hidden from his God.

There was blood on him, and he did not know whether it was his own or other peoples'. He was trembling with fright, his crooked teeth were hammering together like those of an angry woodchuck. But the effects of the shock continued to pass away, and his wits to come back to him, and at last Peter realized that he never had taken seriously the ideas of the First Apostolic Church of American City. He listened to the moans of the wounded, and to the shouts and uproar of the crowd, and began seriously figuring out what could have happened. There had once been an earthquake in American City; could this be another one? Or had a volcano opened up in the midst of Main Street? Or could it have been a gas-main? And was this the end, or would it explode some more? Would the volcano go on erupting, and blow Peter and his frail packing-box thru the walls of Guggenheim's Department-store?

So Peter waited, and listened to the horrible sounds of people in agony, and pleading with others to put them out of it. Peter heard voices of men giving orders, and realized that these must be policemen, and that no doubt there would be ambulances coming. Maybe there was something the matter with him, and he ought to crawl out and get himself taken care of. All of a sudden Peter remembered his stomach; and his wits, which had been sharpened by twenty years' struggle against a hostile world, realized in a flash the opportunity which fate had brought to him. He must pretend to be wounded, badly wounded; he must be unconscious, suffering from shock and shattered nerves; then they would take him to the hospital and put him in a soft bed and give him things to eat—maybe he might stay there for weeks, and they might give him money when he came out.

Or perhaps he might get a job in the hospital, something that was easy, and required only alert intelligence. Perhaps the head doctor in the hospital might want somebody to watch the other doctors, to see if they were neglecting the patients, or perhaps flirting with some of the nurses—there was sure to be something like that going on. It had been that way in the orphans' home where Peter had spent a part of his childhood till he ran away. It had been that way again in the great Temple of Jimjambo, conducted by Pashtian el Kalandra, Chief Magistrian of Eleutherinian Exoticism. Peter had worked as scullion in the kitchen in that mystic institution, and had worked his way upward until he possessed the confidence of Tushbar Akrogas, major-domo and right hand man of the Prophet himself.

Wherever there was a group of people, and a treasure to be

administered, there Peter knew was backbiting and scandal and intriguing and spying, and a chance for somebody whose brains were "all there." It might seem strange that Peter should think about such things, just then when the earth had opened up in front of him and the air had turned to roaring noise and blinding white flame, and had hurled him against the side of a building and dropped the bleeding half of a woman's body across his chest; but Peter had lived from earliest childhood by his wits and by nothing else, and such a fellow has to learn to use his wits under any and all circumstances, no matter how bewildering. Peter's training covered almost every emergency one could think of; he had even at times occupied himself by imagining what he would do if the Holy Rollers should turn out to be right, and if suddenly Gabriel's trumpet were to blow, and he were to find himself confronting Jesus in a long white night-gown.

Section 3

Peter's imaginings were brought to an end by the packing-box being pulled out from the wall. "Hello!" said a voice.

Peter groaned, but did not look up. The box was pulled out further, and a face peered in. "What you hidin' in there for?"

Peter stammered feebly: "Wh-wh-what?"

"You hurt?" demanded the voice.

"I dunno," moaned Peter.

The box was pulled out further, and its occupant slid out. Peter looked up, and saw three or four policemen bending over him; he moaned again.

"How did you get in there?" asked one.

"I crawled in."

"What for?"

"To g-g-get away from the—what was it?"

"Bomb," said one of the policemen; and Peter was astounded that for a moment he forgot to be a nervous wreck.

"Bomb!" he cried; and at the same moment one of the policemen lifted him to his feet.

"Can you stand up?" he demanded; and Peter tried, and found that he could, and forgot that he couldn't. He was covered with blood and dirt, and was an unpresentable object, but he was really relieved to discover that his limbs were intact.

"What's your name?" demanded one of the policemen, and when Peter answered, he asked, "Where do you work?"

"I got no job," replied Peter.

"Where'd you work last?" And then another broke in, "What did you crawl in there for?"

"My God!" cried Peter. "I wanted to get away!"

The policemen seemed to find it suspicious that he had stayed hidden so long. They were in a state of excitement themselves, it appeared; a terrible crime had been committed, and they were hunting for any trace of the criminal. Another man came up, not dressed in uniform, but evidently having authority, and he fell onto Peter, demanding to know who he was, and where he had come from, and what he had been doing in that crowd. And of course Peter had no very satisfactory answers to give to any of these questions. His occupations had been unusual, and not entirely credible, and his purposes were hard to explain to a suspicious questioner. The man was big and burly, at least a foot taller than Peter, and as he talked he stooped down and stared into Peter's eyes as if he were looking for dark secrets hidden back in the depths of Peter's skull. Peter remembered that he was supposed to be sick, and his eyelids drooped and he reeled slightly, so that the policemen had to hold him up.

"I want to talk to that fellow," said the questioner. "Take him inside." One of the officers took Peter under one arm, and the other under the other arm, and they half walked and half carried him across the street and into a building.

Section 4

I t was a big store which the police had opened up. Inside there were wounded people lying on the floor, with doctors and others attending them. Peter was marched down the corridor, and into a room where sat or stood several other men, more or less in a state of collapse like himself; people who had failed to satisfy the police, and were being held under guard.

Peter's two policemen backed him against the wall and proceeded to go thru his pockets, producing the shameful contents—a soiled rag, and two cigarette butts picked up on the street, and a broken pipe, and a watch which had once cost a dollar, but was now out of order, and too badly damaged to be pawned. That was all they had any right to find, so far as Peter knew. But there came forth one thing more—the printed circular which Peter had thrust into his pocket. The policeman who pulled it out took a glance at it, and then cried, "Good God!" He stared at Peter, then he stared at the other policeman and handed him the paper.

At that moment the man not in uniform entered the room. "Mr. Guffey!" cried the policeman. "See this!" The man took the paper, and glanced at it, and Peter, watching with bewildered and fascinated eyes, saw a most terrifying sight. It was as if the man went suddenly out of his mind. He glared at Peter, and under his black eyebrows the big staring eyes seemed ready to jump out of his head.

"Aha!" he exclaimed; and then, "So I've got you!" The hand that held the paper was trembling, and the other hand reached out like a great claw, and fastened itself in the neck of Peter's coat, and drew it together until Peter was squeezed tight. "You threw that bomb!" hissed the man.

"Wh-what?" gasped Peter, his voice almost fainting. "B-b-bomb?"

"Out with it!" cried the man, and his face came close to Peter's, his teeth gleaming as if he were going to bite off Peter's nose. "Out with it! Quick! Who helped you?"

"My G-God!" said Peter. "I d-dunno what you mean."

"You dare lie to me?" roared the man; and he shook Peter as if he meant to jar his teeth out. "No nonsense now! Who helped you make that bomb?"

Peter's voice rose to a scream of terror: "I never saw no bomb! I dunno what you're talkin' about!"

"You, come this way," said the man, and started suddenly toward the door. It might have been more convenient if he had turned Peter around, and got him by the back of his coat-collar; but he evidently held Peter's physical being as a thing too slight for consideration—he just kept his grip in the bosom of Peter's jacket, and half lifted him and half shoved him back out of the room, and down a long passage to the back part of the building. And all the time he was hissing into Peter's face: "I'll have it out of you! Don't think you can lie to me! Make up your mind to it, you're going to come thru!"

The man opened a door. It was some kind of storeroom, and he walked Peter inside and slammed the door behind him. "Now, out with it!" he said. The man thrust into his pocket the printed circular, or whatever it was—Peter never saw it again, and never found out what was printed on it. With his free hand the man grabbed one of Peter's hands, or rather one finger of Peter's hand, and bent it suddenly backward with terrible violence. "Oh!" screamed Peter. "Stop!" And then, with a wild shriek, "You'll break it."

"I mean to break it! mean to break every bone in your body! I'll tear your finger-nails out; I'll tear the eyes out of your head, if I have to! You tell me who helped you make that bomb!"

Peter broke out in a storm of agonized protest; he had never heard of any bomb, he didn't know what the man was talking about; he writhed and twisted and doubled himself over backward, trying to evade the frightful pain of that pressure on his finger.

"You're lying!" insisted Guffey. "I know you're lying. You're one of that crowd."

"What crowd? Ouch! I dunno what you mean!"

"You're one of them Reds, aint you?"

"Reds? What are Reds?"

"You want to tell me you don't know what a Red is? Aint you been giving out them circulars on the street?"

"I never seen the circular!" repeated Peter. "I never seen a word in it; I dunno what it is."

"You try to stuff me with that?"

"Some woman gimme that circular on the street! Ouch! Stop! Jesus! I tell you I never looked at the circular!"

"You dare go on lying?" shouted the man, with fresh access of rage. "And when I seen you with them Reds? I know about your plots, I'm going to get it out of you." He grabbed Peter's wrist and began to twist it, and Peter half turned over in the effort to save himself, and shrieked again, in more piercing tones, "I dunno! I dunno!"

"What's them fellows done for you that you protect them?" demanded the other. "What good'll it do you if we hang you and let them escape?"

But Peter only screamed and wept the louder.

"They'll have time to get out of town," persisted the other. "If you speak quick we can nab them all, and then I'll let you go. You understand, we won't do a thing to you, if you'll come thru and tell us who put you up to this. We know it wasn't you that planned it; it's the big fellows we want."

He began to wheedle and coax Peter; but then, when Peter answered again with his provoking "I dunno," he would give another twist to Peter's wrist, and Peter would yell, almost incoherent with terror and pain—but still declaring that he could tell nothing, he knew nothing about any bomb.

So at last Guffey wearied of this futile inquisition; or perhaps it occurred to him that this was too public a place for the prosecution of a "third degree"—there might be some one listening outside the door. He stopped twisting Peter's wrist, and tilted back Peter's head so that Peter's frightened eyes were staring into his.

"Now, young fellow," he said, "look here. I got no time for you just now, but you're going to jail, you're my prisoner, and make up your mind to it, sooner or later I'm going to get it out of you. It may take a day, or it may take a month, but you're going to tell me about this bomb plot, and who printed this here circular opposed to Preparedness, and all about these Reds you work with. I'm telling you now—so you think it over; and meantime, you hold your mouth, don't say a word to a living soul, or if you do I'll tear your tongue out of your throat."

Then, paying no attention to Peter's wailings, he took him by the back of the collar and marched him down the hall again, and turned him over to one of the policemen. "Take this man to the city jail," he said, "and put him in the hole, and keep him there until I come, and don't let him speak a word to anybody. If he tries it, mash his mouth for him." So the policeman took poor sobbing Peter by the arm and marched him out of the building.

Section 5

The police had got the crowds driven back by now, and had ropes across the street to hold them, and inside the roped space were several ambulances and a couple of patrol-wagons. Peter was shoved into one of these latter, and a policeman sat by his side, and the bell clanged, and the patrol-wagon forced its way slowly thru the struggling crowd. Half an hour later they arrived at the huge stone jail, and Peter was marched inside. There were no formalities, they did not enter Peter on the books, or take his name or his finger prints; some higher power had spoken, and Peter's fate was already determined. He was taken into an elevator, and down into a basement, and then down a flight of stone steps into a deeper basement, and there was an iron door with a tiny slit an inch wide and six inches long near the top. This was the "hole," and the door was opened and Peter shoved inside into utter darkness. The door banged, and the bolts rattled; and then silence. Peter sank upon a cold stone floor, a bundle of abject and hideous misery.

These events had happened with such terrifying rapidity that Peter Gudge had hardly time to keep track of them. But now he had plenty of time, he had nothing but time. He could think the whole thing out, and realize the ghastly trick which fate had played upon him. He lay there, and time passed; he had no way of measuring it, no idea whether it was hours or days. It was cold and clammy in the stone cell; they called it the "cooler," and used it to reduce the temperature of the violent and intractable. It was a trouble-saving device; they just left the man there and forgot him, and his own tormented mind did the rest.

And surely no more tormented mind than the mind of Peter Gudge had ever been put in that black hole. It was the more terrible, because so utterly undeserved, so preposterous. For such a thing to happen to him, Peter Gudge, of all people—who took such pains to avoid discomfort in life, who was always ready to oblige anybody, to do anything he was told to do, so as to have'an easy time, a sufficiency of food, and a warm corner to crawl into! What could have persuaded fate to pick him for the victim of this cruel prank; to put him into this position, where he could not avoid suffering, no matter what he did? They wanted him to tell something, and Peter would have been perfectly willing to tell anything—but how could he tell it when he did not know it?

The more Peter thought about it, the more outraged he became. It was monstrous! He sat up and glared into the black darkness. He talked to himself, he talked to the world outside, to the universe which had forgotten his existence. He stormed, he wept. He got on his feet and flung himself about the cell, which was six feet square, and barely tall enough for him to stand erect. He pounded on the door with his one hand which Guffey had not lamed, he kicked, and he shouted. But there was no answer, and so far as he could tell, there was no one to hear.

When he had exhausted himself, he sank down, and fell into a haunted sleep; and then he wakened again, to a reality worse than any nightmare. That awful man was coming after him again! He was going to torture him, to make him tell what he did not know! All the ogres and all the demons that had ever been invented to frighten the imagination of children were as nothing compared to the image of the man called Guffey, as Peter thought of him.

Several ages after Peter had been locked up, he heard sounds outside, and the door was opened. Peter was cowering in the corner, thinking that Guffey had come. There was a scraping on the floor, and then the door was banged again, and silence fell. Peter investigated and discovered that they had put in a chunk of bread and a pan of water.

Then more ages passed, and Peter's impotent ragings were repeated; then once more they brought bread and water, and Peter wondered, was it twice a day they brought it, or was this a new day? And how long did they mean to keep him here? Did they mean to drive him mad? He asked these questions of the man who brought the bread and water, but the man made no answer, he never at any time spoke a word. Peter had no company in that "hole" but his God; and Peter was not well acquainted with his God, and did not enjoy a tete-a-tete with Him.

What troubled Peter most was the cold; it got into his bones, and his teeth were chattering all the time. Despite all his moving about, he could not keep warm. When the man opened the door, he cried out to him, begging for a blanket; each time the man came, Peter begged more frantically than ever. He was ill, he had been injured in the explosion, he needed a doctor, he was going to die! But there was never any answer. Peter would lie there and shiver and weep, and writhe, and babble, and lose consciousness for a while, and not know whether he was awake or asleep, whether he was living or dead. He was becoming delirious, and the things that were happening to him, the people who were tormenting him, became monsters and fiends who carried him away upon far journeys, and plunged him thru abysses of terror and torment.

And yet, many and strange as were the phantoms which Peter's sick imagination conjured up, there was no one of them as terrible as the reality which prevailed just then in the life of American City, and was determining the destiny of a poor little man by the name of Peter Gudge. There lived in American City a group of men who had taken possession of its industries and dominated the lives of its population. This group, intrenched in power in the city's business and also in its government, were facing the opposition of a new and rapidly rising power, that of organized labor, determined to break the oligarchy of business and take over its powers. The struggle of these two groups was coming to its culmination. They were like two mighty wrestlers, locked in a grip of death; two giants in combat, who tear up trees by the roots and break off fragments of cliffs from the mountains to smash in each other's skulls. And poor Peter—what was he? An ant which happened to come blundering across the ground where these combatants met. The earth was shaken with their trampling, the dirt was kicked this way and that, and the unhappy ant was knocked about, tumbled head over heels, buried in the debris; and suddenly—Smash!—a giant foot came down upon the place where he was struggling and gasping!

Section 6

P eter had been in the "hole" perhaps three days, perhaps a week—he did not know, and no one ever told him. The door was opened again, and for the first time he heard a voice, "Come out here."

Peter had been longing to hear a voice; but now he shrunk terrified into a corner. The voice was the voice of Guffey, and Peter knew what it meant. His teeth began to rattle again, and he wailed, "I dunno anything! I can't tell anything!"

A hand reached in and took him by the collar, and he found himself walking down the corridor in front of Guffey. "Shut up!" said the man, in answer to all his wailings, and took him into a room and threw him into a chair as if he had been a bundle of bedding, and pulled up another chair and sat down in front of Peter.

"Now look here," he said. "I want to have an understanding with you. Do you want to go back into that hole again?"

"N-n-no," moaned Peter.

"Well, I want you to know that you'll spend the rest of your life in that hole, except when you're talking to me. And when you're talking to me you'll be having your arms twisted off you, and splinters driven into your finger nails, and your skin burned with matches—until you tell me what I want to know. Nobody's going to help you, nobody's going to know about it. You're going to stay here with me until you come across."

Peter could only sob and moan.

"Now," continued Guffey, "I been finding out all about you, I got your life story from the day you were born, and there's no use your trying to hide anything. I know your part in this here bomb plot, and I can send you to the gallows without any trouble whatever. But there's some things I can't prove on the other fellows. They're the big ones, the real devils, and they're the ones I want, so you've got a chance to save yourself, and you better be thankful for it."

Peter went on moaning and sobbing.

"Shut up!" cried the man. And then, fixing Peter's frightened gaze with his own, he continued, "Understand, you got a chance to save yourself. All you got to do is to tell what you know. Then you can come out and you won't have any more trouble. We'll take good care of you; everything'll be easy for you."

Peter continued to gaze like a fascinated rabbit. And such a longing as surged up in his soul—to be free, and out of trouble, and taken care of! If only he had known anything to tell; if only there was some way he could find out something to tell!

Section 7

S uddenly the man reached out and grasped one of Peter's hands. He twisted the wrist again, the sore wrist which still ached from the torture. "Will you tell?"

"I'd tell if I could!" screamed Peter. "My God, how can I?"

"Don't lie to me," hissed the man. "I know about it now, you can't fool me. You know Jim Goober."

"I never heard of him!" wailed Peter.

"You lie!" declared the other, and he gave Peter's wrist a twist.

"Yes, yes, I know him!" shrieked Peter.

"Oh, that's more like it!" said the other. "Of course you know him. What sort of a looking man is he?"

"I—I dunno. He's a big man."

"You lie! You know he's a medium-sized man!"

"He's a medium-sized man."

"A dark man?"

"Yes, a dark man."

"And you know Mrs. Goober, the music teacher?"

"Yes, I know her."

"And you've been to her house?"

"Yes, I've been to her house."

"Where is their house?"

"I dunno—that is—"

"It's on Fourth Street?"

"Yes, it's on Fourth Street."

"And he hired you to carry that suit-case with the bombs in it, didn't he?"

"Yes, he hired me."

"And he told you what was in it, didn't he?"

"He—he—that is—I dunno."

"You don't know whether he told you?"

"Y-y-yes, he told me."

"You knew all about the plot, didn't you?"

"Y-y-yes, I knew."

"And you know Isaacs, the Jew?"

"Y-y-yes, I know him."

"He was the fellow that drove the jitney, wasn't he?"

"Y-y-yes, he drove the jitney."

"Where did he drive it?"

"H-h-he drove it everywhere."

"He drove it over here with the suit-case, didn't he?"

"Yes, he did."

"And you know Biddle, and you know what he did, don't you?"

"Yes, I know."

"And you're willing to tell all you know about it, are you?"

"Yes, I'll tell it all. I'll tell whatever you—"

"You'll tell whatever you know, will you?"

"Y-y-yes, sir."

"And you'll stand by it? You'll not try to back out? You don't want to go back into the hole?"

"No, sir."

And suddenly Guffey pulled from his pocket a paper folded up. It was several typewritten sheets. "Peter Gudge," he said, "I been looking up your record, and I've found out what you did in this case. You'll see when you read how perfectly I've got it. You won't find a single mistake in it." Guffey meant this for wit, but poor Peter was too far gone with terror to have any idea that there was such a thing as a smile in the world.

"This is your story, d'you see?" continued Guffey. "Now take it and read it."

So Peter took the paper in his trembling hand, the one which had not been twisted lame. He tried to read it, but his hand shook so that he had to put it on his knee, and then he discovered that his eyes had not yet got used to the light. He could not see the print. "I c-c-can't," he wailed.

And the other man took the paper from him. "I'll read it to you," he said. "Now you listen, and put your mind on it, and make sure I've got it all right."

And so Guffey started to read an elaborate legal document: "I, Peter Gudge, being duly sworn do depose and declare—" and so on. It was an elaborate and detailed story about a man named Jim Goober, and his wife and three other men, and how they had employed Peter to buy for them certain materials to make bombs, and how Peter had helped them to make the bombs in a certain room at a certain given address, and how they had put the bombs in a suit-case, with a time clock to set them off, and how Isaacs, the jitney driver, had driven them to a certain corner on Main Street, and how they had left the suit-case with the bombs on the street in front of the Preparedness Day parade.

It was very simple and clear, and Peter, as he listened, was almost ready to cry with delight, realizing that this was all he had to do to escape from his horrible predicament. He knew now what he was supposed to know; and he knew it. Why had not Guffey told him long ago, so that he might have known it without having his fingers bent out of place and his wrist twisted off?

"Now then," said Guffey, "that's your confession, is it?"

"Y-y-yes," said Peter.

"And you'll stand by it to the end?"

"Y-y-yes, sir."

"We can count on you now? No more nonsense?"

"Y-y-yes, sir."

"You swear it's all true?"

"I do."

"And you won't let anybody persuade you to go back on it—no matter what they say to you?"

"N-n-no, sir," said Peter.

"All right," said Guffey; and his voice showed the relief of a business man who has closed an important deal. He became almost human as lie went on. "Now, Peter," he said, "you're our man, and we're going to count on you. You understand, of course, that we have to hold you as a witness, but you're not to be a prisoner, and we're going to treat you well. We'll put you in the hospital part of the jail, and you'll have good grub and nothing to do. In a week or so, we'll want you to appear before the grand jury. Meantime, you understand—not a word to a soul! People may try to worm something out of you, but don't you open your mouth about this case except to me. I'm your boss, and I'll tell you what to do, and I'll take care of you all the way. You got that all straight?"

"Y-y-yes, sir," said Peter.

Section 8

There was once, so legend declares, a darky who said that he liked to stub his toe because it felt so good when it stopped hurting. On this same principle Peter had a happy time in the hospital of the American City jail. He had a comfortable bed, and plenty to eat, and absolutely nothing to do. His sore joints became gradually healed, and he gained half a pound a day in weight, and his busy mind set to work to study the circumstances about him, to find out how he could perpetuate these comfortable conditions, and add to them the little luxuries which make life really worth living.

In charge of this hospital was an old man by the name of Doobman. He had been appointed because he was the uncle of an alderman, and he had held the job for the last six years, and during that time had gained weight almost as rapidly as Peter was gaining. He had now come to a condition where he did not like to get out of his armchair if it could be avoided. Peter discovered this, and so found it possible to make himself useful in small ways. Also Mr. Doobman had a secret vice; he took snuff, and for the sake of discipline he did not want this dreadful fact to become known. Therefore he would wait until everybody's back was turned before he took a pinch of snuff; and Peter learned this, and would tactfully turn his back.

Everybody in this hospital had some secret vice, and it was Mr. Doobman's duty to repress the vices of the others. The inmates of the hospital included many of the prisoners who had money, and could pay to make themselves comfortable. They wanted tobacco, whiskey, cocaine and other drugs, and some of them wanted a chance to practice unnamable horrors. All the money they could smuggle in they were ready to spend for license to indulge themselves. As for the attendants in the hospital, they were all political appointees, derelicts who had been unable to hold a job in the commercial world, and had sought an easy berth, like Peter himself. They took bribes, and were prepared to bribe Peter to outwit Mr. Doobman; Mr. Doobman, on the other hand, was prepared to reward Peter with many favors, if Peter would consent to bring him secret information. In such a situation it was possible for a man with his wits about him to accumulate quite a little capital.

For the most part Peter stuck by Doobman; having learned by bitter experience that in the long run it pays to be honest. Doobman was referred to by the other attendants as the "Old Man"; and always in Peter's life, from the very dawn of childhood, there had been some such "Old Man," the fountain-head of authority, the dispenser of creature comforts. First had been "Old Man" Drubb, who from early morning until late at night wore green spectacles, and a sign across his chest, "I am blind," and made a weary little child lead him thru the streets by the hand. At night, when they got home to their garret-room, "Old Man" Drubb would take off his green goggles, and was perfectly able to see Peter, and if Peter had made the slightest mistake during the day he would beat him.

When Drubb was arrested, Peter was taken to the orphan asylum, and there was another "Old Man," and the same harsh lesson of subservience to be learned. Peter had run away from the asylum; and then had come Pericles Priam with his Pain Paralyzer, and Peter had studied his whims and served his interests. When Pericles had married a rich widow and she had kicked Peter out, there had come the Temple of Jimjambo, where the "Old Man" had been Tushbar Akrogas, the major-domo—terrible when he was thwarted, but a generous dispenser of favors when once you had learned to flatter him, to play upon his weaknesses, to smooth the path of his pleasures. All these years Peter had been forced to "crook the pregnant hinges of the knee"; it had become an instinct with him—an instinct that went back far behind the twenty years of his conscious life, that went back twenty thousand years, perhaps ten times twenty thousand years, to a time when Peter had chipped flint spear-heads at the mouth of some cave, and broiled marrow-bones for some "Old Man" of the borde, and seen rebellious young fellows cast out to fall prey to the sabre-tooth tiger.

Section 9

Peter found that he was something of a personality in this hospital. He was the "star" witness in the sensational Goober case, about which the whole city, and in fact the whole country was talking. It was known that he had "turned State's"; but just what he knew and what he had told was a mighty secret, and Peter "held his mouth" and looked portentous, and enjoyed thrills of self-importance.

But meantime there was no reason why he should not listen to others talk; no reason why he should not inform himself fully about this case, so that in future he might be able to take care of himself. He listened to what "Old Man" Doobman had to say, and to what Jan Christian, his Swedish assistant had to say, and to what Gerald Leslie, the "coke" fiend, had to say. All these, and others, had friends on the outside, people who were "in the know." Some told one thing, and others told exactly the opposite; but Peter put this and that together, and used his own intrigue-sharpened wits upon it, and before long he was satisfied that he had got the facts.

Jim Goober was a prominent labor leader. He had organized the employees of the Traction Trust, and had called and led a tremendous strike. Also he had called building strikes, and some people said he had used dynamite upon uncompleted buildings, and made a joke of it. Anyhow, the business men of the city wanted to put him where he could no longer trouble them; and when some maniac unknown had flung a dynamite bomb into the path of the Preparedness parade, the big fellows of the city had decided that now was the opportunity they were seeking. Guffey, the man who had taken charge of Peter, was head of the secret service of the Traction Trust, and the big fellows had put him in complete charge. They wanted action, and would take no chances with the graft-ridden and incompetent police of the city. They had Goober in jail, with his wife and three of his gang, and thru the newspapers of the city they were carrying on a propaganda to prepare the public for the hanging of all five.

And that was all right, of course; Jim Goober was only a name to Peter, and of less importance than a single one of Peter's meals. Peter understood what Guffey had done, and his only grudge was because Guffey had not had the sense to tell him his story at the beginning, instead of first nearly twisting his arm off. However, Peter reflected, no doubt Guffey had meant to teach him a lesson, to make sure of him. Peter had learned the lesson, and his purpose now was to make this clear to Guffey and to Doobman.

"Hold your mouth," Guffey had said, and Peter never once said a word about the Goober case. But, of course, he talked about other matters. A fellow could not go around like a mummy all day long, and it was Peter's weakness that he liked to tell about his exploits, the clever devices by which he had outwitted his last "Old Man." So to Gerald Leslie, the "coke" fiend, he told the story of Pericles Priam, and how many thousands of dollars he had helped to wheedle out of the public, and how twice he and Pericles had been arrested for swindling. Also he told about the Temple of Jimjambo, and all the strange and incredible things that had gone on there. Pashtian el Kalandra, who called himself the Chief Magistrian of Eleutherinian Exoticism, gave himself out to his followers to be eighty years of age, but as a matter of fact he was less than forty. He was supposed to be a Persian prince, but had been born in a small town in Indiana, and had begun life as a grocer-boy. He was supposed to live upon a handful of fruit, but every day it had been Peter's job to assist in the preparation of a large beef-steak or a roast chicken. These were "for sacrificial purposes," so the prophet explained to his attendants; and Peter would get the remains of the sacrificial beef-steaks and chickens, and would sacrificially devour them behind the pantry door. That had been one of his private grafts, which he got in return for keeping secret from the prophet some of the stealings of Tushbar Akrogas, the major-domo.

A wonderful place had been this Temple of Jimjambo. There were mystic altars with seven veils before them, and thru these the Chief Magistrian would appear, clad in a long cream-colored robe with gold and purple borders, and with pink embroidered slippers and symbolic head-dress. His lectures and religious rites had been attended by hundreds—many of them rich society women, who came rolling up to the temple in their limousines. Also there had been a school, where children had been initiated into the mystic rites of the cult. The prophet would take these children into his private apartments, and there were awful rumors—which had ended in the raiding of the temple by the police, and the flight of the prophet, and likewise of the majordomo, and of Peter Gudge, his scullion and confederate.

Also, Peter thought it was fun to tell Gerald Leslie about his adventures with the Holy Rollers, into whose church he had drifted during his search for a job. Peter had taken up with this sect, and learned the art of "talking in tongues," and how to fall over the back of your chair in convulsions of celestial glory. Peter had gained the confidence of the Rev. Gamaliel Lunk, and had been secretly employed by him to carry on a propaganda among the congregation to obtain a raise in salary for the underpaid convulsionist. But certain things which Peter had learned had caused him to go over to the faction of Shoemaker Smithers, who was trying to persuade the congregation that he could roll harder and faster than the Rev. Gamaliel. Peter had only held this latter job a few days before he had been fired for stealing the fried doughnut.

Section 10

All these things and more Peter told; thinking that he was safe now, under the protection of authority. But after he had spent about two months in the hospital, he was summoned one day into the office, and there stood Guffey, glowering at him in a black fury. "You damned fool!" were Guffey's first words.

Peter's knees went weak and his teeth began to chatter again. "Wh-wh-what?" he cried.

"Didn't I tell you to hold your mouth?" And Guffey looked as if he were going to twist Peter's wrist again.

"Mr. Guffey, I ain't told a soul! I ain't said one word about the Goober case, not one word!"

Peter rushed on, pouring out protests. But Guffey cut him short. "Shut up, you nut! Maybe you didn't talk about the Goober case, but you talked about yourself. Didn't you tell somebody you'd worked with that fellow Kalandra?"

"Y-y-yes, sir."

"And you knew the police were after him, and after you, too?"

"Y-y-yes, sir."

"And you said you'd been arrested selling fake patent medicines?"

"Y-y-yes, sir."

"Christ almighty!" cried Guffey. "And what kind of a witness do you think you'll make?"

"But," cried Peter in despair, "I didn't tell anybody that would matter. I only—"

"What do you know what would matter?" roared the detective, adding a stream of furious oaths. "The Goober people have got spies on us; they've got somebody right here in this jail. Anyhow, they've found out about you and your record. You've gone and ruined us with your blabbing mouth!"

"My Lord!" whispered Peter, his voice dying away.

"Look at yourself on a witness-stand! Look at what they'll do to you before a jury! Traveling over the country, swindling people with patent medicines—and getting in jail for it! Working for that hell-blasted scoundrel Kalandra—" and Guffey added some dreadful words, descriptive of the loathsome vices of which the Chief Magistrian had been accused. "And you mixed up in that kind of thing!"

"I never done anything like that!" cried Peter wildly. "I didn't even know for sure."

"Tell that to the jury!" sneered Guffey. "Why, they've even been to that Shoemaker Smithers, and they'll put his wife on the stand to prove you a sneak thief, and tell how she kicked you out. And all because you couldn't hold your mouth as I told you to!"

Peter burst into tears. He fell down on his knees, pleading that he hadn't meant any harm; he hadn't had any idea that he was not supposed to talk about his past life; he hadn't realized what a witness was, or what he was supposed to do. All he had been told was to keep quiet about the Goober case, and he had kept quiet. So Peter sobbed and pleaded—but in vain. Guffey ordered him back to the hole, declaring his intention to prove that Peter was the one who had thrown the bomb, and that Peter, instead of Jim Goober, had been the head and front of the conspiracy. Hadn't Peter signed a confession that he had helped to make the bomb?

Section 11

Again Peter did not know how long he lay shivering in the black dungeon. He only knew that they brought him bread and water three times, before Guffey came again and summoned him forth. Peter now sat huddled into a chair, twisting his trembling hands together, while the chief detective of the Traction Trust explained to him his new program. Peter was permanently ruined as a witness in the case. The labor conspirators had raised huge sums for their defense; they had all the labor unions of the city, and in fact of the entire country behind them, and they were hiring spies and informers, and trying to find out all they could about the prosecution, the evidence it had collected and the moves it was preparing. Guffey did not say that he had been afraid to kick Peter out because of the possibility that Peter might go over to the Goober side and tell all he knew; but Peter guessed this while he sat listening to Guffey's explanation, and realized with a thrill of excitement that at last he had really got a hold upon the ladder of prosperity. Not in vain had his finger been almost broken and his wrist almost dislocated!

"Now," said Guffey, "here's my idea: As a witness you're on the bum, but as a spy, you're it. They know that you blabbed, and that I know it; they know I've had you in the hole. So now what I want to do is to make a martyr of you. D'you see?"

Peter nodded; yes, he saw. It was his specialty, seeing things like that.

"You're an honest witness, you understand? I tried to get you to lie, and you wouldn't, so now you go over to the other side, and they take you in, and you find out all you can, and from time to time you meet somebody as I'll arrange it, and send me word what you've learned. You get me?"

"I get you," said Peter, eagerly. No words could portray his relief. He had a real job now! He was going to be a sleuth, like Guffey himself.

"Now," said Guffey, "the first thing I want to know is, who's blabbing in this jail; we can't do anything but they get tipped off. I've got witnesses that I want kept hidden, and I don't dare put them here for fear of the Goober crowd. I want to know who are the traitors. I want to know a lot of things that I'll tell you from time to time. I want you to get next to these Reds, and learn about their ideas, so you can talk their lingo."

"Sure," said Peter. He could not help smiling a little. He was supposed to be a "Red" already, to have been one of their leading conspirators.

But Guffey had abandoned that pretence—or perhaps had forgotten about it!

It was really an easy job that Peter had set before him. He did not have to pretend to be anything different from what he was. He would call himself a victim of circumstances, and would be honestly indignant against those who had sought to use him in a frame-up against Jim Goober. The rest would follow naturally. He would get the confidence of the labor people, and Guffey would tell him what to do next.

"We'll put you in one of the cells of this jail," said the chief detective, "and we'll pretend to give you a 'third degree.' You'll holler and make a fuss, and say you won't tell, and finally we'll give up and kick you out. And then all you have to do is just hang around. They'll come after you, or I miss my guess."

So the little comedy was arranged and played thru. Guffey took Peter by the collar and led him out into the main part of the jail, and locked him in one of a row of open cells. He grabbed Peter by the wrist and pretended to twist it, and Peter pretended to protest. He did not have to draw on his imagination; he knew how it felt, and how he was supposed to act, and he acted. He sobbed and screamed, and again and again he vowed that he had told the truth, that he knew nothing else than what he had told, and that nothing could make him tell any more. Guffey left him there until late the next afternoon, and then came again, and took him by the collar, and led him out to the steps of the jail, and gave him a parting kick.

Peter was free! What a wonderful sensation—freedom! God! Had there ever been anything like it? He wanted to shout and howl with joy. But instead he staggered along the street, and sank down upon a stone coping, sobbing, with his head clasped in his hands, waiting for something to happen. And sure enough, it happened. Perhaps an hour passed, when he was touched lightly on the shoulder. "Comrade," said a soft voice, and Peter, looking between his fingers, saw the skirts of a girl. A folded slip of paper was pressed into his hand and the soft voice said: "Come to this address." The girl walked on, and Peter's heart leaped with excitement. Peter was a sleuth at last!

Section 12

P eter waited until after dark, in order to indulge his sense of the romantic; also he flattered his self-importance by looking carefully about him as he walked down the street. He did not know just who would be shadowing him, but Peter wanted to be sleuthy.

Also he had a bit of genuine anxiety. He had told the truth when he said to Guffey that he didn't know what a "Red" was; but since then he had been making in quiries, and now he knew. A "Red" was a fellow who sympathized with labor unions and with strikes; who wanted to murder the rich and divide their property, and believed that the quickest way to do the dividing was by means of dynamite. All "Reds" made bombs, and carried concealed weapons, and perhaps secret poisons—who could tell? And now Peter was going among them, he was going to become one of them! It was almost too interesting, for a fellow who aimed above everything to be comfortable. Something in him whispered, "Why not skip; get out of town and be done with it?" But then he thought of the rewards and honors that Guffey had promised him. Also there was the spirit of curiosity; he might skip at any time, but first he would like to know a bit more about being a "dick."

He came to the number which had been given him, a tiny bungalow in a poor neighborhood, and rang the doorbell. It was answered by a girl, and at a glance Peter saw that it was the girl who had spoken to him. She did not wait for him to announce himself, but cried impulsively, "Mr. Gudge! Oh, I'm so glad you've come!" She added, "Comrade!"—just as if Peter were a well-known friend. And then, "But *are* you a comrade?"

"How do you mean?" asked Peter.

"You're not a Socialist? Well, we'll make one of you." She brought him in and showed him to a chair, saying, "I know what they did to you; and you stood out against them! Oh, you were wonderful! Wonderful!"

Peter was at a loss what to say. There was in this girl's voice a note of affection, as well as of admiration; and Peter in his hard life had had little experience with emotions of this sort. Peter had watched the gushings and excitements of girls who were seeking flirtations; but this girl's attitude he felt at once was not flirtatious. Her voice tho soft, was just a trifle too solemn for a young girl; her deep-set, wistful grey eyes rested on Peter with the solicitude of a mother whose child has just escaped a danger.

She called: "Sadie, here's Mr. Gudge." And there entered another girl, older, taller, but thin and pale like her sister. Jennie and Sadie Todd were their names, Peter learned; the older was a stenographer, and supported the family. The two girls were in a state of intense concern. They started to question Peter about his experiences, but he had only talked for a minute or two before the elder went to the telephone. There were various people who must see Peter at once, important people who were to be notified as soon as he turned up. She spent some time at the phone, and the people she talked with must have phoned to others, because for the next hour or two there was a constant stream of visitors coming in, and Peter had to tell his story over and over again.

The first to come was a giant of a man with tight-set mouth and so powerful a voice that it frightened Peter. He was not surprised to learn that this man was the leader of one of the most radical of the city's big labor unions, the seamen's. Yes, he was a "Red," all right; he corresponded to Peter's imaginings—a grim, dangerous man, to be pictured like Samson, seizing the pillars of society and pulling them down upon his head. "They've got you scared, my boy," he said, noting Peter's hesitating answers to his questions. "Well, they've had me scared for forty-five years, but I've never let them know it yet." Then, in order to cheer Peter up and strengthen his nerves, he told how he, a runaway seaman, had been hunted thru the Everglades of Florida with bloodhounds, and tied to a tree and beaten into insensibility.

Then came David Andrews, whom Peter had heard of as one of the lawyers in the Goober case, a tall, distinguished-looking man with keen, alert features. What was such a man doing among these outcasts? Peter decided that he must be one of the shrewd ones who made money out of inciting the discontented. Then came a young girl, frail and sensitive, slightly crippled. As she crossed the room to shake his hand tears rolled down her cheeks, and Peter stood embarrassed, wondering if she had just lost a near relative, and what was he to say about it. From her first words he gathered, to his great consternation, that she had been moved to tears by the story of what he himself had endured.

Ada Ruth was a poet, and this was a new type for Peter; after much groping in his mind he set her down for one of the dupes of the movement—a poor little sentimental child, with no idea of the wickedness by which she was surrounded. With her came a Quaker boy with pale, ascetic face and black locks which he had to shake back from his eyes every now and then; he wore a Windsor tie, and a black felt hat, and other marks of eccentricity and from his speeches Peter gathered that he was ready to blow up all the governments of the world in the interests of Pacificism. The same was true of McCormick, an I. W. W. leader who had just served sixty days in jail, a silent young Irishman with drawn lips and restless black eyes, who made Peter uneasy by watching him closely and saying scarcely a word.

Section 13

They continued to come, one at a time or in groups; old women and young women, old men and young men, fanatics and dreamers, agitators who could hardly open their mouths without some white-hot words escaping, revealing a blaze of passion smouldering in the deeps of them. Peter became more and more uneasy, realizing that he was actually in the midst of all the most dangerous "Reds" of American City. They it was whom our law-abiding citizens dreaded, who were the objects of more concern to the police than all the plain, everyday burglars and bandits. Peter now could see the reason—he had not dreamed that such angry and hate-tormented people existed in the world. Such people would be capable of anything! He sat, with his restless eyes wandering from one face to another. Which one of this crowd had helped to set off the bomb? And would they boast about it to him this evening?

Peter half expected this; but then again, he wondered. They were such strange criminals! They called him "Comrade"; and they spoke with that same affection that had so bewildered him in little Jennie. Was this just a ruse to get his confidence, or did these people really think that they loved him—Peter Gudge, a stranger and a secret enemy? Peter had been at great pains to fool them; but they seemed to him so easy to fool that his pains were wasted. He despised them for this, and all the while he listened to them he was saying to himself, "The poor nuts!"

They had come to hear his story, and they plied him with questions, and made him tell over and over again every detail. Peter, of course, had been carefully instructed; he was not to mention the elaborate confession he had been made to sign; that would be giving too dangerous a weapon to these enemies of law and order. He must tell as brief a story as possible; how he had happened to be near the scene of the explosion, and how the police had tried to force him to admit that he knew something about the case. Peter told this, according to orders; but he had not been prepared for the minute questioning to which he was subjected by Andrews, the lawyer, aided by old John Durand, the leader of the seamen. They wanted to know everything that had been done to him, and who had done it, and how and when and where and why. Peter had a sense of the dramatic, and enjoyed being the center of attention and admiration, even tho it was from a roomful of criminal "Reds." So he told all the picturesque details of how Guffey had twisted his wrist and shut him in a dungeon; the memory of the pain was still poignant, and came out of him now, with a realism that would have moved a colder group.

So pretty soon here were all these women sobbing and raging. Little Ada Ruth became inspired, and began reciting a poem—or was she composing it right here, before his eyes? She seemed entranced with indignation. It was something about the workers arising—the outcry of a mob—

> *"No further patience with a heedless foe—*
> *Get off our backs, or else to hell you go!"*

Peter listened, and thought to himself, "The poor nut!" And then Donald Gordon, the Quaker boy, took the floor, and began shaking his long black locks, and composing a speech, it seemed. And Peter listened, and thought again, "The poor nut!" Then another man, the editor of a labor journal, revealed the fact that he was composing an editorial; he knew Guffey, and was going to publish Guffey's picture, and brand him as an "Inquisitionist." He asked for Peter's picture, and Peter agreed to have one taken, and to be headlined as "The Inquisitionist's Victim." Peter had no idea what the long word meant; but he assented, and thought again, "The poor nut!" All of them were "nuts"—taking other people's troubles with such excitement!

But Peter was frightened, too; he couldn't altogether enjoy being a hero, in this vivid and startling fashion; having his name and fame spread from one end of the country to the other, so that organized labor might know the methods which the great traction interests of American City were employing to send a well-known labor leader to the gallows! The thing seemed to grow and grow before Peter's frightened eyes. Peter, the ant, felt the earth shaking, and got a sudden sense of the mountain size of the mighty giants who were stamping in combat over his head. Peter wondered, had Guffey realized what a stir his story would make, what a powerful weapon he was giving to his enemies? What could Guffey expect to get from Peter, to compensate for this damage to his own case? Peter, as he listened to the stormy oratory in the crowded little room, found himself thinking again and again of running away. He had never seen anything like the rage into which these people worked themselves, the terrible things they said, the denunciations, not merely of the police of American City, but of the courts and the newspapers, the churches and the colleges, everything that seemed respectable and sacred to law-abiding citizens like Peter Gudge.

Peter's fright became apparent. But why shouldn't he be frightened? Andrews, the lawyer, offered to take him away and hide him, lest the opposition should try to make way with him. Peter would be a most important witness for the Goober defense, and they must take good care of him. But Peter recovered his self-possession, and took up his noble role. No, he would take his chances with the rest of them, he was not too much afraid.

Sadie Todd, the stenographer, rewarded him for his heroism. They had a spare bedroom in their little home, and if Peter cared to stay with them for a while, they would try to make him comfortable. Peter accepted this invitation, and at a late hour in the evening the gathering broke up. The various groups of "Reds" went their way, their hands clenched and their faces portraying a grim resolve to make out of Peter's story a means of lashing discontented labor to new frenzies of excitement. The men clasped Peter's hand cordially; the ladies gazed at him with soulful eyes, and whispered their admiration for his brave course, their hope, indeed their conviction, that he would stand by the truth to the end, and would study their ideas and join their "movement." All the while Peter watched them, and continued saying to himself: "The poor nuts!"

Section 14

The respectable newspapers of American City of course did not waste their space upon fantastic accusations brought by radicals, charging the police authorities with using torture upon witnesses. But there was a Socialist paper published every week in American City, and this paper had a long account of Peter's experiences on the front page, together with his picture. Also there were three labor papers which carried the story, and the Goober Defense Committee prepared a circular about it and mailed out thousands of copies all over the country. This circular was written by Donald Gordon, the Quaker boy. He brought Peter a proof of it, to make sure that he had got all the details right, and Peter read it, and really could not help being thrilled to discover what a hero he was. Peter had not said anything about his early career, and whoever among the Goober Defense Committee had learned those details chose to be diplomatically silent. Peter smiled to himself as he thought about that. They were foxy, these people! They were playing their hand for all it was worth—and Peter admired them for that. In Donald Gordon's narrative Peter appeared as a poor workingman; and Peter grinned. He was used to the word "working," but when he talked about "working people," he meant something different from what these Socialists meant.

The story went out, and of course all sorts of people wanted to meet Peter, and came to the home of the Todd girls. So Peter settled down to his job of finding out all he could about these visitors, their names and occupations, their relations to the radical movement. Guffey had advised him not to make notes, for fear of detection, but Peter could not carry all this in his head, so he would retire to his room and make minute notes on slips of paper, and carefully sew these up in the lining of his coat, with a thrill of mystery.

Except for this note-taking, however, Peter's sleuthing was easy work, for these people all seemed eager to talk about what they were doing; sometimes it frightened Peter—they were so open and defiant! Not merely did they express their ideas to one another and to him, they were expressing them on public platforms, and in their publications, in pamphlets and in leaflets—what they called "literature." Peter had had no idea their "movement" was so widespread or so powerful. He had expected to unearth a secret conspiracy, and perhaps a dynamite-bomb or two; instead of which, apparently, he was unearthing a volcano!

However, Peter did the best he could. He got the names and details about some forty or fifty people of all classes; obscure workingmen and women, Jewish tailors, Russian and Italian cigar-workers, American-born machinists and printers; also some "parlor Reds"—large, immaculate and shining ladies who came rolling up to the little bungalow in large, immaculate and shining automobiles, and left their uniformed chauffeurs outside for hours at a time while they listened to Peter's story of his "third degree." One benevolent lady with a flowing gray veil, who wafted a sweet perfume about the room, suggested that Peter might be in need, and pressed a twenty dollar bill into his hand. Peter, thrilled, but also bewildered, got a new sense of the wonders of this thing called "the movement," and decided that when Guffey got thru with him he might turn into a "Red" in earnest for a while.

Meantime he settled down to make himself comfortable with the Todd sisters. Sadie went off to her work before eight o'clock every morning, and that was before Peter got up; but Jennie stayed at home, and fixed his breakfast, and opened the door for his visitors, and in general played the hostess for him. She was a confirmed invalid; twice a week she went off to a doctor to have something done to her spine, and the balance of the time she was supposed to be resting, but Peter very seldom saw her doing this. She was always addressing circulars, or writing letters for the "cause," or going off to sell literature and take up collections at meetings. When she was not so employed, she was arguing with somebody—frequently with Peter—trying to make him think as she did.

Poor kid, she was all wrought up over the notions she had got about the wrongs of the working classes. She gave herself no peace about it, day or night, and this, of course, was a bore to Peter, who wanted peace above all things. Over in Europe millions of men were organized in armies, engaged in slaughtering one another. That, of course, was, very terrible, but what was the good of thinking about it? There was no way to stop it, and it certainly wasn't Peter's fault. But this poor, deluded child was acting all the time as if she were to blame for this European conflict, and had the job of bringing it to a close. The tears would come into her deep-set grey eyes, and her soft chin would quiver with pain whenever she talked about it; and it seemed to Peter she was talking about it all the time. It was her idea that the war must be stopped by uprisings on the part of the working people in Europe. Apparently she thought this might be hastened if the working people of American City would rise up and set an example!

Section 15

Jennie talked about this plan quite openly; she would put a red ribbon in her hair, and pin a red badge on her bosom, and go into meeting-places and sell little pamphlets with red covers. So, of course, it would be Peter's duty to report her to the head of the secret service of the Traction Trust. Peter regretted this, and was ashamed of having to do it; she was a nice little girl, and pretty, too, and a fellow might have had some fun with her if she had not been in such a hysterical state. He would sit and look at her, as she sat bent over her typewriter. She had soft, fluffy hair, the color of twilight, and even white teeth, and a faint flush that came and went in her cheeks—yes, she would not be bad looking at all, if only she would straighten up, and spend a little time on her looks, as other girls did.

But no, she was always in a tension, and the devil of it was, she was trying to get Peter into the same state. She was absolutely determined that Peter must get wrought up over the wrongs of the working classes. She took it for granted that he would, when he was instructed. She would tell him harrowing stories, and it was his duty to be duly harrowed; he must be continually acting an emotional part. She would give him some of her "literature" to read, and then she would pin him down and make sure that he had read it. He knew how to read—Pericles Priam had seen to that, because he wanted him to attend to the printing of his circulars and his advertisements in the country newspapers where he was traveling. So now Peter was penned in a corner and compelled to fix his attention upon "The A. B. C. of Socialism," or "Capital and Proletariat," or "The Path to Power."

Peter told himself that it was part of his job to acquire this information. He was going to be a "Red," and he must learn their lingo; but he found it awfully tiresome, full of long technical words which he had never heard before. Why couldn't these fellows at least talk American? He had known that there were Socialists, and also "Arnychists," as he called them, and he thought they were all alike. But now he learned, not merely about Socialists and "Arnychists," but about State Socialists and Communist Anarchists, and Communist Syndicalists and Syndicalist Anarchists and Socialist Syndicalists, and Reformist Socialists and Guild Socialists, to say nothing about Single Taxers and Liberals and Progressives and numerous other varieties, whom he had to meet and classify and listen to respectfully and sympathetically. Each particular group insisted upon the distinctions which made it different, and each insisted that it had the really, truly truth; and Peter became desperately bored with their everlasting talk—how much more simple to lump them all together, as did Guffey and McGivney, calling them all "Reds!"

Peter had got it clearly fixed in his mind that what these "Reds" wanted was to divide up the property of the rich. Everyone he had questioned about them had said this. But now he learned that this wasn't it exactly. What they wanted was to have the State take over the industries, or to have the labor unions do it, or to have the working people in general do it. They pointed to the post office and the army and the navy, as examples of how the State could run things. Wasn't that all right? demanded Jennie. And Peter said Yes, that was all right; but hidden back in Peter's soul all the time was a whisper that it wouldn't make a damn bit of difference. There was a sucker born every minute, and you might be sure that no matter how they fixed it up, there would always be some that would find it easy to live off the rest. This poor kid, for example, who was ready to throw herself away for any fool notion, or for anybody that came along and told her a hard-luck story—would there ever be a state of society in which she wouldn't be a juicy morsel to be gobbled up by some fellow with a normal appetite?

She was alone in the house all day with Peter, and she got to seem more and more pretty as he got to know her better. Also it was evident that she liked Peter more and more as Peter played his game. Peter revealed himself as deeply sympathetic, and a quick convert to the cause; he saw everything that Jennie explained to him, he was horrified at the horrible stories, he was ready to help her end the European war by starting a revolution among the working people of American City. Also, he told her about himself, and awakened her sympathy for his harsh life, his twenty years of privation and servitude; and when she wept over this, Peter liked it. It was fine, somehow, to have her so sorry for him; it helped to compensate him for the boredom of hearing her be sorry for the whole working class.

Peter didn't know whether Jennie had learned about his bad record, but he took no chances—he told her everything, and thus took the sting out of it. Yes, he had been trapped into evil ways, but it wasn't his fault, he hadn't known any better, he had been a pitiful victim of circumstances. He told how he had been starved and driven about and beaten by "Old Man" Drubb, and the tears glistened in Jennie's grey eyes and stole down her cheeks. He told about loneliness and heartsickness and misery in the orphan asylum. And how could he, poor lad, realize that it was wrong to help Pericles Priam sell his Peerless Pain Paralyzer? How could he know whether the medicine was any good or not—he didn't even know now, as a matter of fact. As for the Temple of Jimjambo, all that Peter had done was to wash dishes and work as a kitchen slave, as in any hotel or restaurant.

It was a story easy to fix up, and especially easy because the first article in the creed of Socialist Jennie was that economic circumstances were to blame for human frailties. That opened the door for all varieties of grafters, and made the child such an easy mark that Peter would have been ashamed to make a victim of her, had it not been that she happened to stand in the path of his higher purposes—and also that she happened to be young, only seventeen, with tender grey eyes, and tempting, sweet lips, alone there in the house all day.

Section 16

Peter's adventures in love had so far been pretty much of a piece with the rest of his life experiences; there had been hopes, and wonderful dreams, but very few realizations. Peter knew a lot about such matters; in the orphan asylum there were few vicious practices which he did not witness, few obscene imaginings with which he was not made familiar. Also, Pericles Priam had been a man like the traditional sailor, with a girl in every port; and generally in these towns and villages there had been no place for Peter to go save where Pericles went, so Peter had been the witness of many of his master's amours and the recipient of his confidences. But none of these girls and women had paid any attention to Peter. Peter was only a "kid"; and when he grew up and was no longer a kid, but a youth tormented with sharp desires, they still paid no attention to him—why should they? Peter was nothing; he had no position, no money, no charms; he was frail and undersized, his teeth were crooked, and one shoulder higher than the other. What could he expect from women and girls but laughter and rebuffs?

Then Peter moved on to the Temple of Jimjambo, and there a devastating experience befell him—he tumbled head over heels and agonizingly in love. There was a chambermaid in the institution, a radiant creature from the Emerald Isles with hair like sunrise and cheeks like apples, and a laugh that shook the dish-pans on the kitchen walls. She laughed at Peter, she laughed at the major-domo, she laughed at all the men in the place who tried to catch her round the waist. Once or twice a month perhaps she would let them succeed, just to keep them interested, and to keep herself in practice.

The only one she really favored was the laundry deliveryman, and Peter soon realized why. This laundry fellow had the use of an automobile on Sundays, and Nell would dress herself up to kill, and roll away in state with him. He would spend all his week's earnings entertaining her at the beach; Peter knew, because she would tell the whole establishment on Monday morning. "Gee, but I had a swell time!" she would say; and would count the ice-creams and the merry-go-rounds and the whirly-gigs and all the whang-doodle things. She would tell about the tattooed men and the five-legged calf and the woman who was half man, and all the while she would make the dishpans rattle.

Yes, she was a marvelous creature, and Peter suddenly realized that his ultimate desire in life was to possess a "swell lady-friend" like Nell. He realized that there was one essential prerequisite, and that was money. None of them would look at you without money. Nell had gone out with him only once, and that was upon the savings of six months, and Peter had not been able to conceal the effort it cost him to spend it all. So he had been set down as a "tight-wad," and had made no headway.

Nell had disappeared, along with everybody else when the police raided the Temple. Peter never knew what had become of her, but the old longings still haunted him, and he would find himself imagining—suppose the police had got her; suppose she were in jail, and he with his new "pull" were able to get her out, and carry her away and keep her hid from the laundry man!

These were dreams; but meantime here was reality, here was a new world. Peter had settled down in the home of the Todd sisters; and what was their attitude toward these awful mysteries of love?

Section 17

It had been arranged with Guffey that at the end of a week Peter was to have a secret meeting with one of the chief detective's men. So Peter told the girls that he was tired of being a prisoner in the house and must get some fresh air.

"Oh please, Mr. Gudge, don't take such a chance!" cried Sadie, her thin, anxious face suddenly growing more anxious and thin. "Don't you know this house is being watched? They are just hoping to catch you out alone. It would be the last of you."

"I'm not so important as that," said Peter; but she insisted that he was, and Peter was pleased, in spite of his boredom, he liked to hear her insist upon his importance.

"Oh!" she cried. "Don't you know yet how much depends on you as a witness for the Goober defense? This case is of concern to millions of people all over the world! It is a test case, Mr. Gudge—are they to be allowed to murder the leaders of the working class without a struggle? No, we must show them that there is a great movement, a world-wide awakening of the workers, a struggle for freedom for the wage slaves—"

But Peter could stand no more of this. "All right," he said, suddenly interrupting Sadie's eloquence. "I suppose it's my duty to stay, even if I die of consumption, being shut up without any fresh air." He would play the martyr; which was not so hard, for he was one, and looked like one, with his thin, one-sided little figure, and his shabby clothes. Both Sadie and Jennie gazed at him with admiration, and sighed with relief.

But later on, Peter thought of an idea. He could go out at night, he told Sadie, and slip out the back way, so that no one would see him; he would not go into crowds or brightly lighted streets, so there would be no chance of his being recognized. There was a fellow he absolutely had to see, who owed him some money; it was way over on the other side of the city—that was why he rejected Jennie's offer to accompany him.

So that evening Peter climbed a back fence and stole thru a neighbor's chicken-yard and got away. He had a fine time ducking and dodging in the crowds, making sure that no one was trailing him to his secret rendezvous—no "Red" who might chance to be suspicious of his "comradeship." It was in the "American House," an obscure hotel, and Peter was to take the elevator to the fourth floor, without speaking to any one, and to tap three times on the door of Room 427. Peter did so, and the door opened, and he slipped in, and there he met Jerry McGivney, with the face of a rat.

"Well, what have you got?" demanded McGivney; and Peter sat down and started to tell. With eager fingers he undid the amateur sewing in the lining of his coat, and pulled out his notes with the names and descriptions of people who had come to see him.

McGivney glanced over them quickly. "Jesus!" he said, "What's the good of all this?"

"Well, but they're Reds!" exclaimed Peter.

"I know," said the other, "but what of that? We can go hear them spout at meetings any night. We got membership lists of these different organizations. But what about the Goober case?"

"Well," said Peter, "they're agitating about it all the time; they've been printing stuff about me."

"Sure, we know that," said McGivney. "And the hell of a fine story you gave them; you must have enjoyed hearing yourself talk. But what good does that do us?"

"But what do you want to know?" cried Peter, in dismay.

"We want to know their secret plans," said the other. "We want to know what they're doing to get our witnesses; we want to know who it is that is selling us out, who's the spy in the jail. Didn't you find that out?"

"N-no," said Peter. "Nobody said anything about it."

"Good God!" said the detective. "D'you expect them to bring you things on a silver tray?" He began turning over Peter's notes again, and finally threw them on the bed in disgust. He began questioning Peter, and Peter's dismay turned to despair. He had not got a single thing that McGivney wanted. His whole week of "sleuthing" had been wasted!

The detective did not mince words. "It's plain that you're a boob," he said. "But such as you are, we've got to do the best we can with you. Now, put your mind on it and get it straight: we know who these Reds are, and we know what they're teaching; we can't send 'em to jail for that. What we want you to find out is the name of their spy, and who are their witnesses in the Goober case, and what they're going to say."

"But how can I find out things like that?" cried Peter.

"You've got to use your wits," said McGivney. "But I'll give you one tip; get yourself a girl."

"A girl?" cried Peter, in wonder.

"Sure thing," said the other. "That's the way we always work. Guffey

UPTON SINCLAIR

says there's just three times when people tell their secrets: The first is when they're drunk, and the second is when they're in love—"

Then McGivney stopped. Peter, who wanted to complete his education, inquired, "And the third?"

"The third is when they're both drunk and in love," was the reply. And Peter was silent, smitten with admiration. This business of sleuthing was revealing itself as more complicated and more fascinating all the time.

"Ain't you seen any girl you fancy in that crowd?" demanded the other.

"Well—it might be—" said Peter, shyly.

"It ought to be easy," continued the detective. "Them Reds are all free lovers, you know."

"Free lovers!" exclaimed Peter. "How do you mean?"

"Didn't you know about that?" laughed the other.

Peter sat staring at him. All the women that Peter had ever known or heard of took money for their love. They either took it directly, or they took it in the form of automobile rides and flowers and candy and tickets to the whang-doodle things. Could it be that there were women who did not take money in either form, but whose love was entirely free?

The detective assured him that such was the case. "They boast about it," said he. "They think it's right." And to Peter that seemed the most shocking thing he had yet heard about the Reds.

To be sure, when he thought it over, he could see that it had some redeeming points; it was decidedly convenient from the point of view of the man; it was so much money in his pocket. If women chose to be that silly—and Peter found himself suddenly thinking about little Jennie Todd. Yes, she would be that silly, it was plain to see. She gave away everything she had; so of course she would be a "free lover!"

Peter went away from his rendezvous with McGivney, thrilling with a new and wonderful idea. You couldn't have got him to give up his job now. This sleuthing business was the real thing!

It was late when Peter got home, but the two girls were sitting up for him, and their relief at his safe return was evident. He noticed that Jennie's face expressed deeper concern than her sister's, and this gave him a sudden new emotion. Jennie's breath came and went more swiftly because he had entered the room; and this affected his own breath in the same way. He had a swift impulse towards her, an entirely unselfish desire to reassure her and relieve her anxiety; but with an instinctive understanding of the sex game which he had not before known he possessed, he checked this impulse and turned instead to the older sister, assuring her that nobody had followed him. He told an elaborate story, prepared on the way; he had worked for ten days for a fellow at sawing wood—hard work, you bet, and then the fellow had tried to get out of paying him! Peter had caught him at his home that evening, and had succeeded in getting five dollars out of him, and a promise of a few dollars more every week. That was to cover future visits to McGivney.

Section 18

Peter lay awake a good part of the night, thinking over this new job—that of getting himself a girl. He realized that for some time he had been falling in love with little Jennie; but he wanted to be sane and practical, he wanted to use his mind in choosing a girl. He was after information, first of all. And who had the most to give him? He thought of Miss Nebbins, who was secretary to Andrews, the lawyer; she would surely know more secrets than anyone else; but then, Miss Nebbins was an old maid, who wore spectacles and broad-toed shoes, and was evidently out of the question for love-making. Then he thought of Miss Standish, a tall, blond beauty who worked in an insurance office and belonged to the Socialist Party. She was a "swell dresser," and Peter would have been glad to have something like that to show off to McGivney and the rest of Guffey's men; but with the best efforts of his self-esteem, Peter could not imagine himself persuading Miss Standish to look at him. There was a Miss Yankovich, one of the real Reds, who trained with the I. W. W.; but she was a Jewess, with sharp, black eyes that clearly indicated a temper, and frightened Peter. Also, he had a suspicion that she was interested in McCormick—tho of course with these "free lovers" you could never tell.

But one girl Peter was quite sure about, and that was little Jennie; he didn't know if Jennie knew many secrets, but surely she could find some out for him. Once he got her for his own, he could use her to question others. And so Peter began to picture what love with Jennie would be like. She wasn't exactly what you would call "swell," but there was something about her that made him sure he needn't be ashamed of her. With some new clothes she would be pretty, and she had grand manners—she had not shown the least fear of the rich ladies who came to the house in their automobiles; also she knew an awful lot for a girl—even if most of what she knew wasn't so!

Peter lost no time in setting to work at his new job. In the papers next morning appeared the usual details from Flanders; thousands of men being shot to pieces almost every hour of the day and night, a million men on each side locked in a ferocious combat that had lasted for weeks, that might last for months. And sentimental little Jennie sat there with brimming eyes, talking about it while Peter ate his oatmeal and thin milk. And Peter talked about it too; how wicked it was, and how they must stop it, he and Jennie together. He agreed with her now; he was a Socialist, he called her "Comrade," and told her she had converted him. Her eyes lighted up with joy, as if she had really done something to end the war.

They were sitting on the sofa, looking at the paper, and they were alone in the house. Peter suddenly looked up from the reading and said, very much embarrassed, "But Comrade Jennie—"

"Yes," she said, and looked at him with her frank grey eyes. Peter was shy, truly a little frightened, this kind of detective business being new to him.

"Comrade Jennie," he said, "I—I—don't know just how to say it, but I'm afraid I'm falling a little in love."

Jennie drew back her hands, and Peter heard her breath come quickly. "Oh, Mr. Gudge!" she exclaimed.

"I—I don't know—" stammered Peter. "I hope you won't mind."

"Oh, don't let's do that!" she cried.

"Why not, Comrade Jennie?" And he added, "I don't know as I can help it."

"Oh, we were having such a happy time, Mr. Gudge! I thought we were going to work for the cause!"

"Well, but it won't interfere—"

"Oh, but it does, it does; it makes people unhappy!"

"Then—" and Peter's voice trembled—"then you don't care the least bit for me, Comrade Jennie?"

She hesitated a moment. "I don't know," she said. "I hadn't thought—"

And Peter's heart gave a leap inside him. It was the first time that any girl had ever had to hesitate in answering that question for Peter. Something prompted him—just as if he had been doing this kind of "sleuthing" all his life. He reached over, and very gently took her hand. "You do care just a little for me?" he whispered.

"Oh, Comrade Gudge," she answered, and Peter said, "Call me 'Peter.' Please, please do."

"Comrade Peter," she said, and there was a little catch in her throat, and Peter, looking at her, saw that her eyes were cast down.

"I know I'm not very much to love," he pleaded. "I'm poor and obscure—I'm not good looking—"

"Oh, it isn't that!" she cried, "Oh, no, no! Why should I think about such things? You are a comrade!"

Peter had known, of course, just how she would take this line of talk. "Nobody has ever loved me," he said, sadly. "Nobody cares anything about you, when you are poor, and have nothing to offer—"

"I tell you, that isn't it!" she insisted. "Please don't think that! You are a hero. You have sacrificed for the cause, and you are going on and become a leader."

"I hope so," said Peter, modestly. "But then, what is it, Comrade Jennie? Why don't you care for me?"

She looked up at him, and their eyes met, and with a little sob in her voice she answered, "I'm not well, Comrade Peter. I'm of no use; it would be wicked for me to marry."

Somewhere back in the depths of Peter, where his inner self was crouching, it was as if a sudden douche of ice-cold water were let down on him. "Marry!" Who had said anything about marrying? Peter's reaction fitted the stock-phrase of the comic papers: "This is so sudden!"

But Peter was too clever to reveal such dismay. He humored little Jennie, saying, "We don't have to marry right away. I could wait, if only I knew that you cared for me; and some day, when you get well—"

She shook her head sadly. "I'm afraid I'll never get really well. And besides, neither of us have any money, Comrade Peter."

Ah, there it was! Money, always money! This "free love" was nothing but a dream.

"I could get a job," said Peter—just like any other tame and conventional wooer.

"But you couldn't earn enough for two of us," protested the girl; and suddenly she sprang up. "Oh, Comrade Peter, let's not fall in love with each other! Let's not make ourselves unhappy, let's work for the cause! Promise me that you will!"

Peter promised; but of course he had no remotest intention of keeping the promise. He was not only a detective, he was a man—and in both capacities he wanted Comrade Jennie. He had all the rest of the day, and over the addressing of envelopes which he undertook with her, he would now and then steal love-glances; and Jennie knew now what these looks meant, and the faint flush would creep over her cheeks and down into her neck and throat. She was really very pretty when she was falling in love, and Peter found his new job the most delightful one of his lifetime. He watched carefully, and noted the signs, and was sure he was making no mistake; before Sadie came back at supper-time he had his arms about Comrade Jennie, and was pressing kisses upon the lovely white throat; and Comrade Jennie was sobbing softly, and her pleading with him to stop had grown faint and unconvincing.

Section 19

T here was the question of Sadie to be settled. There was a certain severe look that sometimes came about Sadie's lips, and that caused Peter to feel absolutely certain that Comrade Sadie had no sympathy with "free love," and very little sympathy with any love save her own for Jennie. She had nursed her "little sister" and tended her like a mother for many years; she took the food out of her mouth to give to Jennie—and Jennie in turn gave it to any wandering agitator who came along and hung around until mealtime. Peter didn't want Sadie to know what had been going on in her absence, and yet he was afraid to suggest to Jennie that she should deceive her sister.

He managed it very tactfully. Jennie began pleading again: "We ought not to do this, Comrade Peter!" And so Peter agreed, perhaps they oughtn't, and they wouldn't any more. So Jennie put her hair in order, and straightened her blouse, and her lover could see that she wasn't going to tell Sadie.

And the next day they were kissing again and agreeing again that they mustn't do it; and so once more Jennie didn't tell Sadie. Before long Peter had managed to whisper the suggestion that their love was their own affair, and they ought not to tell anybody for the present; they would keep the delicious secret, and it would do no one any harm. Jennie had read somewhere about a woman poet by the name of Mrs. Browning, who had been an invalid all her life, and whose health had been completely restored by a great and wonderful love. Such a love had now come to her; only Sadie might not understand, Sadie might think they did not know each other well enough, and that they ought to wait. They knew, of course, that they really did know each other perfectly, so there was no reason for uncertainty or fear. Peter managed deftly to put these suggestions into Jennie's mind as if they were her own.

And all the time he was making ardent love to her; all day long, while he was helping her address envelopes and mail out circulars for the Goober Defense Committee. He really did work hard; he didn't mind working, when he had Jennie at the table beside him, and could reach over and hold her hand every now and then, or catch her in his arms and murmur passionate words. Delicious thrills and raptures possessed him; his hopes would rise like a flood-tide—but then, alas, only to ebb again! He would get so far, and every time it would be as if he had run into a stone wall. No farther!

Peter realized that McGivney's "free love" talk had been a cruel mistake. Little Jennie was like all the other women—her love wasn't going to be "free." Little Jennie wanted a husband, and every time you kissed her, she began right away to talk about marriage, and you dared not hint at anything else because you knew it would spoil everything. So Peter was thrown back upon devices older than the teachings of any "Reds." He went after little Jennie, not in the way of "free lovers," but in the way of a man alone in the house with a girl of seventeen, and wishing to seduce her. He vowed that he loved her with an overwhelming and eternal love. He vowed that he would get a job and take care of her. And then he let her discover that he was suffering torments; he could not live without her. He played upon her sympathy, he played upon her childish innocence, he played upon that pitiful, weak sentimentality which caused her to believe in pacifism and altruism and socialism and all the other "isms" that were jumbled up in her head.

And so in a couple of weeks Peter had succeeded in his purpose of carrying little Jennie by storm. And then, how enraptured he was! Peter, with his first girl, decided that being a detective was the job for him! Peter knew that he was a real detective now, using the real inside methods, and on the trail of the real secrets of the Goober case!

And sure enough, he began at once to get them. Jennie was in love; Jennie was, as you might say, "drunk with love," and so she fulfilled both the conditions which Guffey had laid down. So Jennie told the truth! Sitting on Peter's knee, with her arms clasped about him, and talking about her girlhood, the happy days before her mother and father had been killed in the factory where they worked, little Jennie mentioned the name of a young man, Ibbetts.

"Ibbetts?" said Peter. It was a peculiar name, and sounded familiar.

"A cousin of ours," said Jennie.

"Have I met him?" asked Peter, groping in his mind.

"No, he hasn't been here."

"Ibbetts?" he repeated, still groping; and suddenly he remembered. "Isn't his name Jack?"

Jennie did not answer for a moment. He looked at her, and their eyes met, and he saw that she was frightened. "Oh, Peter!" she whispered. "I wasn't to tell! I wasn't to tell a soul!"

Inside Peter, something was shouting with delight. To hide his emotion he had to bury his face in the soft white throat. "Sweetheart!" he whispered. "Darling!"

"Uh, Peter!" she cried. "You know—don't you?"

"Of course!" he laughed. "But I won't tell. You needn't mind trusting me."

"Oh, but Mr. Andrews was so insistent!" said Jennie, "He made Sadie and me swear that we wouldn't breathe it to a soul."

"Well, you didn't tell," said Peter. "I found it out by accident. Don't mention it, and nobody will be any the wiser. If they should find out that I know, they wouldn't blame you; they'd understand that I know Jack Ibbetts—me being in jail so long."

So Jennie forgot all about the matter, and Peter went on with the kisses, making her happy, as a means of concealing his own exultation. He had done the job for which Guffey had sent him! He had solved the first great mystery of the Goober case! The spy in the jail of American City, who was carrying out news to the Defense Committee, was Jack Ibbetts, one of the keepers in the jail, and a cousin of the Todd sisters!

Section 20

It was fortunate that this was the day of Peter's meeting with McGivney. He could really not have kept this wonderful secret to himself over night. He made excuses to the girls, and dodged thru the chicken-yard as before, and made his way to the American House. As he walked, Peter's mind was working busily. He had really got his grip on the ladder of prosperity now; he must not fail to tighten it.

McGivney saw right away from Peter's face that something had happened. "Well?" he inquired.

"I've got it!" exclaimed Peter.

"Got what?"

"The name of the spy in the jail."

"Christ! You don't mean it!" cried the other.

"No doubt about it," answered Peter.

"Who is he?"

Peter clenched his hands and summoned his resolution. "First," he said, "you and me got to have an understanding. Mr. Guffey said I was to be paid, but he didn't say how much, or when."

"Oh, hell!" said McGivney. "If you've got the name of that spy, you don't need to worry about your reward."

"Well, that's all right," said Peter, "but I'd like to know what I'm to get and how I'm to get it."

"How much do you want?" demanded the man with the face of a rat. Rat-like, he was retreating into a corner, his sharp black eyes watching his enemy. "How much?" he repeated.

Peter had tried his best to rise to this occasion. Was he not working for the greatest and richest concern in American City, the Traction Trust? Tens and hundreds of millions of dollars they were worth—he had no idea how much, but he knew they could afford to pay for his secret. "I think it ought to be worth two hundred dollars," he said.

"Sure," said McGivney, "that's all right. We'll pay you that."

And straightway Peter's heart sank. What a fool he had been! Why hadn't he had more courage, and asked for five hundred dollars? He might even have asked a thousand, and made himself independent for life!

"Well," said McGivney, "who's the spy?"

Peter made an agonizing, effort, and summoned yet more nerve. "First, I got to know, when do I get that money?"

"Oh, good God!" said McGivney. "You give us the information, and you'll get your money all right. What kind of cheap skates do you take us for?"

"Well, that's all right," said Peter. "But you know, Mr. Guffey didn't give me any reason to think he loved me. I still can hardly use this wrist like I used to."

"Well, he was trying to get some information out of you," said McGivney. "He thought you were one of them dynamiters—how could you blame him? You give me the name of that spy, and I'll see you get your money."

But still Peter wouldn't yield. He was afraid of the rat-faced McGivney, and his heart was thumping fast, but he stood his ground. "I think I ought to see that money," he said, doggedly.

"Say, what the hell do you take me for?" demanded the detective. "D'you suppose I'm going to give you two hundred dollars and then have you give me some fake name and skip?"

"Oh, I wouldn't do that!" cried Peter.

"How do I know you wouldn't?"

"Well, I want to go on working for you."

"Sure, and we want you to go on working for us. This ain't the last secret we'll get from you, and you'll find we play straight with our people—how'd we ever get anywheres otherwise? There's a million dollars been put up to hang that Goober crowd, and if you deliver the goods, you'll get your share, and get it right on time."

He spoke with conviction, and Peter was partly persuaded. But most of Peter's lifetime had been spent in watching people bargaining with one another—watching scoundrels trying to outwit one another—and when it was a question of some money to be got, Peter was like a bulldog that has got his teeth fixed tight in another dog's nose; he doesn't consider the other dog's feelings, nor does he consider whether the other dog admires him or not.

"On time?" said Peter. "What do you mean by 'on time'?"

"Oh, my God!" said McGivney, in disgust.

"Well, but I want to know," said Peter. "D'you mean when I give the name, or d'you mean after you've gone and found out whether he really is the spy or not?"

So they worried back and forth, these snarling bulldogs, growing more and more angry. But Peter was the one who had got his teeth in, and Peter hung on. Once McGivney hinted quite plainly that the great

Traction Trust had had power enough to shut Peter in the "hole" on two occasions and keep him there, and it might have power enough to do it a third time. Peter's heart failed with terror, but all the same, he hung on to McGivney's nose.

"All right," said the rat-faced man, at last. He said it in a tone of wearied scorn; but that didn't worry Peter a particle. "All right, I'll take a chance with you." And he reached into his pocket and pulled out a roll of bills—twenty dollar bills they were, and he counted out ten of them. Peter saw that there was still a lot left to the roll, and knew that he hadn't asked as much money as McGivney had been prepared to have him ask; so his heart was sick within him. At the same time his heart was leaping with exultation—such a strange thing is the human heart!

Section 21

M cGivney laid the money on the bed. "There it is," he said, "and if you give me the name of the spy you can take it. But you'd better take my advice and not spend it, because if it turns out that you haven't got the spy, by God, I believe Ed Guffey'd twist the arms out of you!"

Peter was easy about that. "I know he's the spy all right."

"Well, who is he?"

"He's Jack Ibbetts."

"The devil you say!" cried McGivney, incredulously.

"Jack Ibbetts, one of the night keepers in the jail."

"I know him," said the other. "But what put that notion into your head?"

"He's a cousin of the Todd sisters."

"Who are the Todd sisters?"

"Jennie Todd is my girl," said Peter.

"Girl!" echoed the other; he stared at Peter, and a grin spread over his face. "You got a girl in two weeks? I didn't know you had it in you!"

It was a doubtful compliment, but Peter's smile was no less expansive, and showed all his crooked teeth. "I got her all right," he said, "and she blabbed it out the first thing—that Ibbetts was her cousin. And then she was scared, because Andrews, the lawyer, had made her and her sister swear they wouldn't mention his name to a soul. So you see, they're using him for a spy—there ain't a particle of doubt about it."

"Good God!" said McGivney, and there was genuine dismay in his tone. "Who'd think it possible? Why, Ibbetts is as decent a fellow as ever you talked to—and him a Red, and a traitor at that! You know, that's what makes it the devil trying to handle these Reds—you never can tell who they'll get; you never know who to trust. How, d'you suppose they manage it?"

"I dunno," said Peter. "There's a sucker born every minute, you know!"

"Well, anyhow, I see you ain't one of 'em," said the rat-faced man, as he watched Peter take the roll of bills from the bed and tuck them away in an inside pocket.

Section 22

P eter was warned by the rat-faced man that he must be careful how he spent any of that money. Nothing would be more certain to bring suspicion on him than to have it whispered about that he was "in funds." He must be able to show how he had come honestly by everything he had. And Peter agreed to that; he would hide the money away in a safe place until he was thru with his job.

Then he in turn proceeded to warn McGivney. If they were to fire Ibbetts from his job, it would certainly cause talk, and might direct suspicion against Peter. McGivney answered with a smile that he wasn't born yesterday. They would "promote" Jack Ibbetts, giving him some job where he couldn't get any news about the Goober case; then, after a bit, they would catch him up on some mistake, or get him into some trouble, and fire him.

At this meeting, and at later meetings, Peter and the rat-faced man talked out every aspect of the Goober case, which was becoming more and more complicated, and bigger as a public issue. New people were continually being involved, and new problems continually arising; it was more fascinating than a game of chess. McGivney had spoken the literal truth when he said that the big business interests of American City had put up a million dollars to hang Goober and his crowd. At the very beginning there had been offered seventeen thousand dollars in rewards for information, and these rewards naturally had many claimants. The trouble was that people who wanted this money generally had records that wouldn't go well before a jury; the women nearly always turned out to be prostitutes, and the men to be ex-convicts, forgers, gamblers, or what not. Sometimes they didn't tell their past records until the other side unearthed them, and then it was necessary to doctor court records, and pull wires all over the country.

There were a dozen such witnesses as this in the Goober case. They had told their stories before the grand jury, and innumerable flaws and discrepancies had been discovered, which made more work and trouble for Guffey and his lieutenants. Thru a miserable mischance it happened that Jim Goober and his wife had been watching the parade from the roof of a building a couple of miles away, at the very hour when they were accused of having planted the suit-case with the bomb in it. Somebody had taken a photograph of the parade from this roof, which showed both Goober and his wife looking over, and also a big clock in front of a jewelry store, plainly indicating the very minute. Fortunately the prosecution got hold of this photograph first; but now the defense had learned of its existence, and was trying to get a look at it. The prosecution didn't dare destroy it, because its existence could be proven; but they had photographed the photograph, and re-photographed that, until they had the face of the clock so dim that the time could not be seen. Now the defense was trying to get evidence that this trick had been worked.

Then there were all the witnesses for the defense. Thru another mischance it had happened that half a dozen different people had seen the bomb thrown from the roof of Guggenheim's Department Store; which entirely contradicted the suit-case theory upon which the prosecution was based. So now it was necessary to "reach" these various witnesses. One perhaps had a mortgage on his home which could be bought and foreclosed; another perhaps had a wife who wanted to divorce him, and could be persuaded to help get him into trouble. Or perhaps he was engaged in an intrigue with some other man's wife; or perhaps some woman could be sent to draw him into an intrigue.

Then again, it appeared that very soon after the explosion some of Guffey's men had taken a sledge hammer and smashed the sidewalk, also the wall of the building where the explosion had taken place. This was to fit in with the theory of the suit-case bomb, and they had taken a number of photographs of the damage. But now it transpired that somebody had taken a photograph of the spot before this extra damage had been done, and that the defense was in possession of this photograph. Who had taken this photograph, and how could he be "fixed"? If Peter could help in such matters, he would come out of the Goober case a rich man.

Peter would go away from these meetings with McGivney with his head full of visions, and would concentrate all his faculties upon the collecting of information. He and Jennie and Sadie talked about the case incessantly, and Jennie and Sadie would tell freely everything they had heard outside. Others would come in—young McCormick, and Miriam Yankovitch, and Miss Nebbins, the secretary to Andrews, and they would tell what they had learned and what they suspected, and what the defense was hoping to find out. They got hold of a cousin of the man who had taken the photograph on the roof; they were working on him, to get him to persuade the photographer to tell the truth. Next day Donald Gordon would come in, cast down with despair, because it had been learned that one of the most valuable witnesses of the defense, a groceryman, had once pleaded guilty to selling spoilt cheese! Thus every evening, before he went to sleep, Peter would jot down notes, and sew them up inside his jacket, and once a week he would go to the meeting with McGivney, and the two would argue and bargain over the value of Peter's news.

Section 23

I t had become a fascinating game, and Peter would never have tired of it, but for the fact that he had to stay all day in the house with little Jennie. A honeymoon is all right for a few weeks, but no man can stand it forever. Little Jennie apparently never tired of being kissed, and never seemed satisfied that Peter thoroughly loved her. A man got thru with his love-making after awhile, but a woman, it appeared, never knew how to drop the subject; she was always looking before and after, and figuring consequences and responsibilities, her duty and her reputation and all the rest of it. Which, of course, was a bore.

Jennie was unhappy because she was deceiving Sadie; she wanted to tell Sadie, and yet somehow it was easier to go on concealing than admit that one had concealed. Peter didn't see why Sadie had to be told at all; he didn't see why things couldn't stay just as they were, and why he and his sweetheart couldn't have some fun now and then, instead of always being sentimental, always having agonies over the class war, to say nothing of the world war, and the prospects of America becoming involved in it.

This did not mean that Peter was hard and feelingless. No, when Peter clasped trembling little Jennie in his arms he was very deeply moved; he had a real sense of what a gentle and good little soul she was. He would have been glad to help her—but what could he do about it? The situation was such that he could not plead with her, he could not try to change her; he had to give himself up to all her crazy whims and pretend to agree with her. Little Jennie was by her weakness marked for destruction, and what good would it do for him to go to destruction along with her?

Peter understood clearly that there are two kinds of people in the world, those who eat, and those who are eaten; and it was his intention to stay among the former, group. Peter had come in his twenty years of life to a definite understanding of the things called "ideas" and "causes" and "religions." They were bait to catch suckers; and there is a continual competition between the suckers, who of course don't want to be caught, and those people of superior wits who want to catch them, and therefore are continually inventing new and more plausible and alluring kinds of bait. Peter had by now heard enough of the jargon of the "comrades" to realize that theirs was an especially effective kind;

and here was poor little Jennie, stuck fast on the hook, and what could Peter do about it?

Yet, this was Peter's first love, and when he was deeply thrilled, he understood the truth of Guffey's saying that a man in love wants to tell the truth. Peter would have the impulse to say to her: "Oh, drop all that preaching, and give yourself a rest! Let's you and me enjoy life a bit."

Yes, it would be all he could do to keep from saying this—despite the fact that he knew it would ruin everything. Once little Jennie appeared in a new silk dress, brought to her by one of the rich ladies whose heart was touched by her dowdy appearance. It was of soft grey silk—cheap silk, but fresh and new, and Peter had never had anything so fine in his arms before. It matched Jennie's grey eyes, and its freshness gave her a pink glow; or was it that Peter admired her, and loved her more, and so brought the blood to her cheeks? Peter had an impulse to take her out and show her off, and he pressed his face into the soft folds of the dress and whispered, "Say kid, some day you an me got to cut all this hard luck business for a bit!"

He felt little Jennie stiffen, and draw away from him; so quickly he had to set to work to patch up the damage. "I want you to get well," he pleaded. "You're so good to everybody—you treat everybody well but yourself!"

It had been something in his tone rather than his actual words that had frightened the girl. "Oh Peter!" she cried. "What does it matter about me, or about any other one person, when millions of young men are being shot to fragments, and millions of women and children are starving to death!"

So there they were, fighting the war again; Peter had to take up her burden, be a hero, and a martyr, and a "Red." That same afternoon, as fate willed it, three "wobblies" out of a job came to call; and oh, how tired Peter was of these wandering agitators—insufferable "grouches!" Peter would want to say: "Oh, cut it out! What you call your 'cause' is nothing but your scheme to work with your tongues instead of with a pick and a shovel." And this would start an imaginary quarrel in Peter's mind. He would hear one of the fellows demanding, "How much pick and shovel work you ever done?" Another saying, "Looks to me like you been finding the easy jobs wherever you go!" The fact that this was true did not make Peter's irritation any less, did not make it easier for him to meet with Comrade Smith, and Brother Jones, and Fellow-worker Brown just out of jail, and listen to their hard-luck stories, and watch them take from the table food that Peter wanted, and—the bitterest pill of all—let them think that they were fooling him with their patter!

The time came when Peter wasn't able to stand it any longer. Shut up in the house all day, he was becoming as irritable as a chained dog. Unless he could get out in the world again, he would surely give himself away. He pleaded that the doctors had warned him that his health would not stand indoor life; he must get some fresh air. So he got away by himself, and after that he found things much easier. He could spend a little of his money; he could find a quiet corner in a restaurant and get himself a beefsteak, and eat all he wanted of it, without feeling the eyes of any "comrades" resting upon him reprovingly. Peter had lived in a jail, and in an orphan asylum, and in the home of Shoemaker Smithers, but nowhere had he fared so meagerly as in the home of the Todd sisters, who were contributing nearly everything they owned to the Goober defense, and to the "Clarion," the Socialist paper of American City.

Section 24

Peter went to see Andrews, the lawyer, and asked for a job; he wanted to be active in the case, he said, so he was set to work in the offices of the Defense Committee, where he heard people talking about the case all day, and he could pick up no end of valuable tips. He made himself agreeable and gained friends; before long he was intimate with one of the best witnesses of the defense, and discovered that this man had once been named as co-respondent in a divorce case. Peter found out the name of the woman, and Guffey set to work to bring her to American City. The job was to be done cleverly, without the woman's even knowing that she was being used. She would have a little holiday, and the spell of old love would reassert itself, and Guffey would have a half dozen men to spring the trap—and there would be a star witness of the Goober defense clean down and out! "There's always something you can get them on!" said McGivney, and cheerfully paid Peter Gudge five hundred dollars for the information he had brought.

Peter would have been wildly happy, but just at this moment a dreadful calamity befell him. Jennie had been talking about marriage more and more, and now she revealed to him a reason which made marriage imperative. She revealed it with downcast eyes, with blushes and trembling; and Peter was so overcome with consternation that he could not play the part that was expected of him. Hitherto in these love crises he had caught Jennie in his arms and comforted her; but now for a moment he let her see his real emotions.

Jennie promptly had a fit. What was the matter with him? Didn't he mean to marry her, as he had promised? Surely he must realize now that they could no longer delay! And Peter, who was not familiar with the symptoms of hysterics, lost his head completely and could think of nothing to do but rush out of the house and slam the door.

The more he considered it, the more clearly he realized that he was in the devil of a predicament. As a servant of the Traction Trust, he had taken it for granted that he was immune to all legal penalties and obligations; but here, he had a feeling, was a trouble from which the powerful ones of the city would be unable to shield their agent. Were they able to arrange it so that one could marry a girl, and then get out of it when one's job was done?

Peter was so uneasy that he had to call up the office of Guffey and get hold of McGivney. This was dangerous, because the prosecution was tapping telephone wires, and they feared the defense might be doing the same. But Peter took a chance; he told McGivney to come and meet him at the usual place; and there they argued the matter out, and Peter's worst fears were confirmed. When he put the proposition up to McGivney, the rat-faced man guffawed in his face. He found it so funny that he did not stop laughing until he saw that he was putting his spy into a rage.

"What's the joke?" demanded Peter. "If I'm ruined, where'll you get any more information?"

"But, my God!" said McGivney. "What did you have to go and get that kind of a girl for?"

"I had to take what I could," answered Peter. "Besides, they're all alike—they get into trouble, and you can't help it."

"Sure, you can help it!" said McGivney. "Why didn't you ask long ago? Now if you've got yourself tied up with a marrying proposition, it's your own lookout; you can't put it off on me."

They argued back and forth. The rat-faced man was positive that there was no way Peter could pretend to marry Jennie and not have the marriage count. He might get himself into no end of trouble and certainly he would be ruined as a spy. What he must do was to pay the girl some money and send her somewhere to get fixed up. McGivney would find out the name of a doctor to do the job.

"Yes, but what excuse can I give her?" cried Peter. "I mean, why I don't marry her!"

"Make something up," said McGivney. "Why not have a wife already?" Then, seeing Peter's look of dismay: "Sure, you can fix that. I'll get you one, if you need her. But you won't have to take that trouble—just tell your girl a hard luck story. You've got a wife, you thought you could get free from her, but now you find you can't; your wife's got wind of what you're doing here, and she's trying to blackmail you. Fix it up so your girl can't do anything on account of hurting the Goober defense. If she's really sincere about it, she won't disgrace you; maybe she won't even tell her sister."

Peter hated to do anything like that. He had a vision of little Jennie lying on the sofa in hysterics as he had left her, and he dreaded the long emotional scene that would be necessary. However, it seemed that he must go thru with it; there was no better way that he could think of. Also, he must be quick, because in a couple of hours Sadie would be coming home from work, and it might be too late.

Section 25

Peter hurried back to the Todd home, and there was white-faced little Jennie lying on the bed, still sobbing. One would think she might have used up her surplus stock of emotions; but no, there is never any limit to the emotions a woman can pour out. As soon as Peter had got fairly started on the humiliating confession that he had a wife, little Jennie sprang up from the bed with a terrified shriek, and confronted him with a face like the ghost of an escaped lunatic. Peter tried to explain that it wasn't his fault, he had really expected to be free any day. But Jennie only clasped her hands to her forehead and screamed: "You have deceived me! You have betrayed me!" It was just like a scene in the movies, the bored little devil inside Peter was whispering.

He tried to take her hand and reason with her, but she sprang away from him, she rushed to the other side of the room and stood there, staring at him as if she were some wild thing that he had in a corner and was threatening to kill. She made so much noise that he was afraid that she would bring the neighbors in; he had to point out to her that if this matter became public he would be ruined forever as a witness, and thus she might be the means of sending Jim Goober to the gallows.

Thereupon Jennie fell silent, and it was possible for Peter to get in a word. He told her of the intrigues against him; the other side had sent somebody to him and offered him ten thousand dollars if he would sell out the Goober defense. Now, since he had refused, they were trying to blackmail him, using his wife. They had somehow come to suspect that he was involved in a love affair, and this was to be the means of ruining him.

Jennie still would not let Peter touch, her, but she consented to sit down quietly in a chair, and figure out what they were going to do. Whatever happened, she said, they must do no harm to the Goober case. Peter had done her a monstrous wrong in keeping the truth from her, but she would suffer the penalty, whatever it might be; she would never involve him.

Peter started to explain; perhaps it wasn't so serious as she feared. He had been thinking things over; he knew where Pericles Priam, his old employer, was living, and Pericles was rich now, and Peter felt sure that he could borrow two hundred dollars, and there were places where little Jennie could go—there were ways to get out of this trouble—

But little Jennie stopped him. She was only a child in some ways, but in others she was a mature woman. She had strange fixed ideas, and when you ran into them it was like running into a stone wall. She would not hear of the idea Peter suggested; it would be murder.

"Nonsense," said Peter, echoing McGivney. "It's nothing; everybody does it." But Jennie was apparently not listening. She sat staring with her wild, terrified eyes, and pulling at her dress with her fingers. Peter got to watching these fingers, and they got on his nerves. They behaved like insane fingers; they manifested all the emotions which the rest of little Jennie was choking back and repressing.

"If you would only not take it so seriously!" Peter pleaded. "It's a miserable accident, but it's happened, and now we've got to make the best of it. Some day I'll get free; some day I'll marry you."

"Stop, Peter!" the girl whispered, in her tense voice. "I don't want to talk to you any more, if that's all you have to say. I don't know that I'd be willing to marry you—now that I know you could deceive me—that you could go on deceiving me day after day for months."

Peter thought she was going to break out into hysterics again, and he was frightened. He tried to plead with her, but suddenly she sprang up. "Go away!" she exclaimed. "Please go away and let me alone. I'll think it over and decide what to do myself. Whatever I do, I won't disgrace you, so leave me alone, go quickly!"

Section 26

S he drove him out of the house, and Peter went, though with many misgivings. He wandered about the streets, not knowing what to do with himself, looking back over the blunders he had made and tormenting himself with that most tormenting of all thoughts: how different my life might have been, if only I had had sense enough to do this, or not to do that! Dinner time came, and Peter blew himself to a square meal, but even that did not comfort him entirely. He pictured Sadie coming home at this hour. Was Jennie telling her or not?

There was a big mass meeting called by the Goober Defense Committee that evening, and Peter attended, and it proved to be the worst thing he could have done. His mind was in no condition to encounter the fierce passions of this crowded assemblage. Peter had the picture of himself being exposed and denounced; he wasn't sure yet that it mightn't happen to him. And here was this meeting—thousands of workingmen, horny handed blacksmiths, longshoremen with shoulders like barns and truckmen with fists like battering rams, long-haired radicals of a hundred dangerous varieties, women who waved red handkerchiefs and shrieked until to Peter they seemed like gorgons with snakes instead of hair.

Such were the mob-frenzies engendered by the Goober case; and Peter knew, of course, that to all these people he was a traitor, a poisonous worm, a snake in the grass. If ever they were to find out what he was doing—if for instance, someone were to rise up and expose him to this crowd—they would seize him and tear him to pieces. And maybe, right now, little Jennie was telling Sadie; and Sadie would tell Andrews, and Andrews would become suspicious, and set spies on Peter Gudge! Maybe they had spies on him already, and knew of his meetings with McGivney!

Haunted by such terrors, Peter had to listen to the tirades of Donald Gordon, of John Durand, and of Sorensen, the longshoremen's leader. He had to listen to exposure after exposure of the tricks which Guffey had played; he had to hear the district attorney of the county denounced as a suborner of perjury, and his agents as blackmailers and forgers. Peter couldn't understand why such things should be permitted—why these speakers were not all clapped into jail. But instead, he had to sit there and listen; he even had to applaud and pretend to approve!

All the other secret operatives of the Traction Trust and of the district attorney's office had to listen and pretend to approve! In the hall Peter had met Miriam Yankovich, and was sitting next to her. "Look," she said, "there's a couple of dicks over there. Look at the mugs on them!"

"Which?" said Peter.

And she answered: "That fellow that looks like a bruiser, and that one next to him, with the face of a rat." Peter looked, and saw that it was McGivney; and McGivney looked at Peter, but gave no sign.

The meeting lasted until nearly midnight. It subscribed several thousand dollars to the Goober defense fund, and adopted ferocious resolutions which it ordered printed and sent to every local of every labor union in the country. Peter got out before it was over, because he could no longer stand the strain of his own fears and anxieties. He pushed his way thru the crowd, and in the lobby he ran into Pat McCormick, the I. W. W. leader.

There was more excitement in this boy's grim face than Peter had ever seen there before. Peter thought it was the meeting, but the other rushed up to him, exclaiming: "Have you heard the news?"

"What news?"

"Little Jennie Todd has killed herself!"

"My God!" gasped Peter, starting back.

"Ada Ruth just told me. Sadie found a note when she got home. Jennie had left—she was going to drown herself."

"But what—why?" cried Peter, in horror.

"She was suffering so, her health was so wretched, she begs Sadie not to look for her body, not to make a fuss—they'll never find her."

And horrified and stunned as Peter was, there was something inside him that drew a deep breath of relief. Little Jennie had kept her promise! Peter was, safe!

Section 27

Yes, Peter was safe, but it had been a close call, and he still had painful scenes to play his part in. He had to go back to the Todd home and meet the frantic Sadie, and weep and be horrified with the rest of them. It would have been suspicious if he had not done this; the "comrades" would never have forgiven him. Then to his dismay, he found that Sadie had somehow come to a positive conviction as to Jennie's trouble. She penned Peter up in a corner and accused him of being responsible; and there was poor Peter, protesting vehemently that he was innocent, and wishing that the floor would open up and swallow him.

In the midst of his protestations a clever scheme occurred to him. He lowered his voice in shame. There was a man, a young man, who used to come to see Jennie off and on. "Jennie asked me not to tell." Peter hesitated a moment, and added his master-stroke. "Jennie explained to me that she was a free-lover; she told me all about free love. I told her I didn't believe in it, but you know, Sadie, when Jennie believed in anything, she would stand by it and act on it. So I felt certain it wouldn't do any good for me to butt in."

Sadie almost went out of her mind at this. She glared at Peter. "Slanderer! Devil!" she cried. "Who was this man?"

Peter answered, "He went by the name of Ned. That's what Jennie called him. It wasn't my business to pin her down about him."

"It wasn't your business to look out for an innocent child?"

"Jennie herself said she wasn't an innocent child, she knew exactly what she was doing—all Socialists did it." And to this parting shot he added that he hadn't thought it was decent, when he was a guest in a home, to spy on the morals of the people in it. When Sadie persisted in doubting him, and even in calling him names, he took the easiest way out of the difficulty—fell into a rage and stormed out of the house.

Peter felt pretty certain that Sadie would not spread the story very far; it was too disgraceful to her sister and to herself; and maybe when she had thought it over she might come to believe Peter's story; maybe she herself was a "free lover." McGivney had certainly said that all Socialists were, and he had been studying them a lot. Anyhow, Sadie would have to think first of the Goober case, just as little Jennie had done. Peter had them there all right, and realized that he could afford to be forgiving, so he went to the telephone and called up Sadie and said: "I want you to know that I'm not going to say anything about this story; it won't become known except thru you."

There were half a dozen people whom Sadie must have told. Miss Nebbins was icy-cold to Peter the next time he came in to see Mr. Andrews; also Miriam Yankovich lost her former cordiality, and several other women treated him with studied reserve. But the only person who spoke about the matter was Pat McCormick, the I. W. W. boy who had given Peter the news of little Jennie's suicide. Perhaps Peter hadn't been able to act satisfactorily on that occasion; or perhaps the young fellow had observed something for himself, some love-glances between Peter and Jennie. Peter had never felt comfortable in the presence of this silent Irish boy, whose dark eyes would roam from one person to another in the room, and seemed to be probing your most secret thoughts.

Now Peter's worst fears were justified. "Mac" got him off in a corner, and put his fist under his nose, and told him that he was "a dirty hound," and if it hadn't been for the Goober case, he, "Mac," would kill him without a moment's concern.

And Peter did not dare open his mouth; the look on the Irishman's face was so fierce that he was really afraid for his life. God, what a hateful lot these Reds were! And now here was Peter with the worst one of all against him! From now on his life would be in danger from this maniac Irishman! Peter hated him—so heartily and genuinely that it served to divert his thoughts from little Jennie, and to make him regard himself as a victim.

Yes, in the midnight hours when Jennie's gentle little face haunted him and his conscience attacked him, Peter looked back upon the tangled web of events, and saw quite clearly how inevitable this tragedy had been, how naturally it had grown out of circumstances beyond his control. The fearful labor struggle in American City was surely not Peter's fault; nor was it his fault that he had been drawn into it, and forced to act first as an unwilling witness, and then as a secret agent. Peter read the American City "Times" every morning, and knew that the cause of Goober was the cause of anarchy and riot, while the cause of the district attorney and of Guffey's secret service was the cause of law and order. Peter was doing his best in this great cause, he was following the instructions of those above him, and how could he be blamed because one poor weakling of a girl had got in the way of the great chariot of the law?

Peter knew that it wasn't his fault; and yet grief and terror gnawed at him. For one thing, he missed little Jennie, he missed her by day and he missed her by night. He missed her gentle voice, her fluffy soft hair, her body in his empty arms. She was his first love, and she was gone, and it is human weakness to appreciate things most when they have been lost.

Peter aspired to be a strong man, a "he-man," according to the slang that was coming into fashion; he now tried to live up to that role. He didn't want to go mooning about over this accident; yet Jennie's face stayed with him—sometimes wild, as he had seen it at their last meeting, sometimes gentle and reproachful. Peter would remember how good she had been, how tender, how never-failing in instant response to an advance of love on his part. Where would he ever find another girl like that?

Another thing troubled him especially—a strange, inexplicable thing, for which Peter had no words, and about which he found himself frequently thinking. This weak, frail slip of a girl had deliberately given her life for her convictions; she had died, in order that he might be saved as a witness for the Goobers! Of course Peter had known all along that little Jennie was doomed, that she was throwing herself away, that nothing could save her. But somehow, it does frighten the strongest heart when people are so fanatical as to throw away their very lives for a cause. Peter found himself regarding the ideas of these Reds from a new angle; before this they had been just a bunch of "nuts," but now they seemed to him creatures of monstrous deformity, products of the devil, or of a God gone insane.

Section 28

There was only one person whom Peter could take into his confidence, and that was McGivney. Peter could not conceal from McGivney the fact that he was troubled over his bereavement; and so McGivney took him in hand and gave him a "jacking up." It was dangerous work, this of holding down the Reds; dangerous, because their doctrines were so insidious, they were so devilishly cunning in their working upon people's minds. McGivney had seen more than one fellow start fooling with their ideas and turn into one himself. Peter must guard against that danger.

"It ain't that," Peter explained. "It ain't their ideas. It's just that I was soft on that kid."

"Well, it comes to the same thing," said McGivney. "You get sorry for them, and the first thing you know, you're listening to their arguments. Now, Peter, you're one of the best men I've got on this case—and that's saying a good deal, because I've got charge of seventeen." The rat-faced man was watching Peter, and saw Peter flush with pleasure. Yes, he continued, Peter had a future before him, he would make all kinds of money, he would be given responsibility, a permanent position. But he might throw it all away if he got to fooling with these Red doctrines. And also, he ought to understand, he could never fool McGivney; because McGivney had spies on him!

So Peter clenched his hands and braced himself up. Peter was a real "he-man," and wasn't going to waste himself. "It's just that I can't help missing the girl!" he explained; to which the other answered: "Well, that's only natural. What you want to do is to get yourself another one."

Peter went on with his work in the office of the Goober Defense Committee. The time for the trial had come, and the struggle between the two giants had reached its climax. The district attorney, who was prosecuting the case, and who was expecting to become governor of the state on the strength of it, had the backing of half a dozen of the shrewdest lawyers in the city, their expenses being paid by the big business men. A small army of detectives were at work, and the court where the trial took place was swarming with spies and agents. Every one of the hundreds of prospective jurors had been investigated and card-cataloged, his every weakness and every prejudice recorded; not merely had his psychology been studied, but his financial status, and that of his relatives and friends. Peter had met half a dozen other agents beside McGivney, men who had come to question him about this or that detail; and from the conversation of these men he got glimpses of the endless ramifications of the case. It seemed to him that the whole of American City had been hired to help send Jim Goober to the gallows.

Peter was now getting fifty dollars a week and expenses, in addition to special tips for valuable bits of news. Hardly a day passed that he didn't get wind of some important development, and every night he would have to communicate with McGivney. The prosecution had a secret office, where there was a telephone operator on duty, and couriers traveling to the district attorney's office and to Guffey's office—all this to forestall telephone tapping. Peter would go from the headquarters of the Goober Defense Committee to a telephone-booth in some hotel, and there he would give the secret number, and then his own number, which was six forty-two. Everybody concerned was known by numbers, the principal people, both of the prosecution and of the defense; the name "Goober" was never spoken over the phone.

After the trial had got started it was hard to get anybody to work in the office of the Defense Committee—everybody wanted to be in court! Someone would come in every few minutes, with the latest reports of sensational developments. The prosecution had succeeded in making away with the police court records, proving the conviction of its star witness of having kept a brothel for negroes. The prosecution had introduced various articles alleged to have been found on the street by the police after the explosion; one was a spring, supposed to have been part of a bomb—but it turned out to be a part of a telephone! Also they had introduced parts of a clock—but it appeared that in their super-zeal they had introduced the parts of *two* clocks! There was some excitement like this every day.

Section 29

T he time came when the prosecution closed its case, and Peter was summoned to the office of Andrews, to be coached in his part as a witness. He would be wanted in two or three days, the lawyers told him.

Now Peter had never intended to appear as a witness; he had been fooling the defense all this time—"stringing them along," as he phrased it, so as to keep in favor with them to the end. Meantime he had been figuring out how to justify his final refusal. Peter was eating his lunch when this plan occurred to him, and he was so much excited that he swallowed a piece of pie the wrong way, and had to jump up and run out of the lunch-room. It was his first stroke of genius; hitherto it was McGivney who had thought these things out, but now Peter was on the way to becoming his own boss! Why should he go on taking orders, when he had such brains of his own? He took the plan to McGivney, and McGivney called it a "peach," and Peter was so proud he asked for a raise, and got it.

This plan had the double advantage that not merely would it save Peter's prestige and reputation, among the Reds, it would ruin McCormick, who was one of the hardest workers for the defense, and one of the most dangerous Reds in American City, as well as being a personal enemy of Peter's. McGivney pulled some of his secret wires, and the American City "Times," in the course of its accounts of the case, mentioned a rumor that the defense proposed to put on the stand a man who claimed to have been tortured in the city jail, in an effort to make him give false testimony against Goober; the prosecution had investigated this man's record and discovered that only recently he had seduced a young girl, and she had killed herself because of his refusal to marry her. Peter took this copy of the American City "Times" to the office of David Andrews, and insisted upon seeing the lawyer before he went to court; he laid the item on the desk, and declared that there was his finish as a witness in the Goober case. "It's a cowardly, dirty lie!" he declared. "And the man responsible for circulating it is Pat McCormick."

Such are the burdens that fall upon the shoulders of lawyers in hard-fought criminal trials! Poor Andrews did his best to patch things up; he pleaded with Peter—if the story was false, Peter ought to be glad of a chance to answer his slanderers. The defense would put witnesses on the stand to deny it. They would produce Sadie Todd to deny it.

"But Sadie told me she suspected me!"

"Yes," said Andrews, "but she told me recently she wasn't sure."

"Much good that'll do me!" retorted Peter. "They'll ask me if anybody ever accused me, and who, and I'll have to say McCormick, and if they put him on the stand, will he deny that he accused me?"

Peter flew into a rage against McCormick; a fine sort of radical he was, pretending to be devoted to the cause, and having no better sense than to repeat a cruel slander against a comrade! Here Peter had been working on this case for nearly six months, working for barely enough to keep body and soul together, and now they expected him to go on the and have a story like that brought out in the papers, and have the prosecution hiring witnesses to prove him a villain. "No, sir!" said Peter. "I'm thru with this case right now. You put McCormick on the witness stand and let him save Goober's life. You can't use me, I'm out!" And shutting his ears to the lawyer's pleading, he stormed out of the office, and over to the office of the Goober Defense Committee, where he repeated the same scene.

Section 30

Thus Peter was done with the Goober case, and mighty glad of it he was. He was tired of the strain, he needed a rest and a little pleasure. He had his pockets stuffed with money, and a good fat bank account, and proposed to take things easy for the first time in his hard and lonely life.

The opportunity was at hand: for he had taken McGivney's advise and got himself another girl. It was a little romance, very worldly and delightful. To understand it, you must know that in the judicial procedure of American City they used both men and women jurors; and because busy men of affairs did not want to waste their time in the jury-box, nor to have the time of their clerks and workingmen wasted, there had gradually grown up a class of men and women who made their living by working as jurors. They hung around the courthouse and were summoned on panel after panel, being paid six dollars a day, with numerous opportunities to make money on the side if they were clever.

Among this group of professional jurors, there was the keenest competition to get into the jury-box of the Goober case. It was to be a long and hard-fought case, there would be a good deal of prestige attached to it, and also there were numerous sums of money floating round. Anybody who got in, and who voted right, might be sure of an income for life, to say nothing of a life-job as a juror if he wanted it.

Peter happened to be in court while the talesmen were being questioned. A very charming and petite brunette—what Peter described as a "swell dresser"—was on the stand, and was cleverly trying to satisfy both sides. She knew nothing about the case, she had never read anything about it, she knew nothing and cared nothing about social problems; so she was accepted by the prosecution. But then the defense took her in hand, and it appeared that once upon a time she had been so indiscreet as to declare to somebody her conviction that all labor leaders ought to be stood up against the wall and filled with lead; so she was challenged by the defense, and very much chagrined she came down from the stand, and took a seat in the courtroom next to Peter. He saw a trace of tears in her eyes, and realizing her disappointment, ventured a word of sympathy. The acquaintance grew, and they went out to lunch together.

Mrs. James was her name, and she was a widow, a grass widow as she archly mentioned. She was quick and lively, with brilliant white teeth, and cheeks with the glow of health in them; this glow came out of a little bottle, but Peter never guessed it. Peter had got himself a good suit of clothes now, and made bold to spend some money on the lunch. As it happened, both he and Mrs. James were thru with the Goober case; both were tired and wanted a change, and Peter, blushing shyly, suggested that a sojourn at the beach might be fun. Mrs. James agreed immediately, and the matter was arranged.

Peter had seen enough of the detective business by this time to know what you can safely do, and what you had better not do. He didn't travel with his grass widow, he didn't pay her car-fare, nor do anything else to constitute her a "white slave." He simply went to the beach and engaged himself a comfortable apartment; and next day, strolling on the board walk, he happened to meet the widow.

So for a couple of months Peter and Mrs. James set up housekeeping together. It was a wonderful experience for the former, because Mrs. James was what is called a "lady," she had rich relatives, and took pains to let Peter know that she had lived in luxury before her husband had run away to Paris with a tight-rope walker. She taught Peter all those worldly arts which one misses when one is brought up in an orphan asylum, and on the road with a patent medicine vender. Tactfully, and without hurting his feelings, she taught him how to hold a knife and fork, and what color tie to select. At the same time she managed to conduct a propaganda which caused him to regard himself as the most favored of mankind; he was overwhelmed with gratitude for every single kiss from the lips of his grass widow. Of course he could not expect such extraordinary favors of fortune without paying for them; he had learned by now that there was no such thing as "free love." So he paid, hand over fist; he not only paid all the expenses of the unregistered honeymoon, he bought numerous expensive presents at the lady's tactful suggestion. She was always so vivacious and affectionate when Peter had given her a present! Peter lived in a kind of dream, his money seemed to go out of his pockets without his having to touch it.

Meantime great events were rolling by, unheeded by Peter and his grass widow who never read the newspapers. For one thing Jim Goober was convicted and sentenced to die on the gallows, and Jim Goober's associate, Biddle, was found guilty, and sentenced to prison for life. Also, America entered the war, and a wave of patriotic excitement swept like a prairie fire over the country. Peter could not help hearing about this; his attention was attracted to one aspect of the matter—Congress was about to pass a conscription act. And Peter was within the age limit; Peter would almost certainly be drafted into the army!

No terror that he had ever felt in his life was equal to this terror. He had tried to forget the horrible pictures of battle and slaughter, of machine-guns and hand-grenades and torpedoes and poison gas, with which little Jennie had filled his imagination; but now these imaginings came crowding back upon him, now for the first time they concerned him. From that time on his honeymoon was spoiled. Peter and his grass widow were like a party of picnickers who are far away in the wilderness, and see a black thunder-storm come rolling up the sky!

Also, Peter's bank account was running low. Peter had had no conception how much money you could spend on a grass widow who is a "swell dresser" and understands what is "proper." He was overwhelmed with embarrassment; he put off telling Mrs. James until the last moment—in fact, until he wasn't quite sure whether he had enough money in bank to meet the last check he had given to the landlady. Then, realizing that the game was up, he told.

He was surprised to see how charmingly a grass widow of "good breeding" could take bad tidings. Evidently it wasn't the first time that Mrs. James had been to the beach. She smiled cheerfully, and said that it was the jury-box for her once more. She gave Peter her card, and told him she would be glad to have him call upon her again—when he had restored his fortunes. She packed up her suit-case and her new trunk full of Peter's presents, and departed with the most perfect sweetness and good taste.

Section 31

S o there was Peter, down and out once more. But fate was kind to him. That very day came a letter signed "Two forty-three," which meant McGivney. "Two forty-three" had some important work for Peter, so would he please call at once? Peter pawned his last bit of jewelry for his fare to American City, and met McGivney at the usual rendezvous.

THE PURPOSE OF THE MEETING was quickly explained. America was now at war, and the time had come when the mouths of these Reds were to be stopped for good. You could do things in war-time that you couldn't do in peace-time, and one of the things you were going to do was to put an end to the agitation against property. Peter licked his lips, metaphorically speaking. It was something he had many times told McGivney ought to be done. Pat McCormick especially ought to be put away for good. These were a dangerous bunch, these Reds, and Mac was the worst of all. It was every man's duty to help, and what could Peter do?

McGivney answered that the authorities were making a complete list of all the radical organizations and their members, getting evidence preliminary to arrests. Guffey was in charge of the job; as in the Goober case, the big business interests of the city were going ahead while the government was still wiping the sleep out of its eyes. Would Peter take a job spying upon the Reds in American City?

"I can't!" exclaimed Peter. "They're all sore at me because I didn't testify in the Goober case."

"We can easily fix that up," answered the rat-faced man. "It may mean a little inconvenience for you. You may have to go to jail for a few days."

"To jail!" cried Peter, in dismay.

"Yes," said the other, "you'll have to get arrested, and made into a martyr. Then, you see, they'll all be sure you're straight, and they'll take you back again and welcome you."

Peter didn't like the idea of going to jail; his memories of the jail in American City were especially painful. But McGivney explained that this was a time when men couldn't consider their own feelings; the country was in danger, public safety must be protected, and it was up to everybody to make some patriotic sacrifice. The rich men were all subscribing to liberty bonds; the poor men were going to give their lives; and what was Peter Gudge going to give? "Maybe I'll be drafted into the army," Peter remarked.

"No, you won't—not if you take this job," said McGivney. "We can fix that. A man like you, who has special abilities, is too precious to be wasted." Peter decided forthwith that he would accept the proposition. It was much more sensible to spend a few days in jail than to spend a few years in the trenches, and maybe the balance of eternity under the sod of France.

Matters were quickly arranged. Peter took off his good clothes, and dressed himself as became a workingman, and went into the eating-room where Donald Gordon, the Quaker boy, always got his lunch. Peter was quite sure that Donald would be one of the leading agitators against the draft, and in this he was not mistaken.

Donald was decidedly uncordial in his welcoming of Peter; without saying a word the young Quaker made Peter aware that he was a renegade, a coward who had "thrown down" the Goober defense. But Peter was patient and tactful; he did not try to defend himself, nor did he ask any questions about Donald and Donald's activities. He simply announced that he had been studying the subject of militarism, and had come to a definite point of view. He was a Socialist and an Internationalist; he considered America's entry into the war a crime, and he was willing to do his part in agitating against it. He was going to take his stand as a conscientious objector; they might send him to jail if they pleased, or even stand him against a wall and shoot him, but they would never get him to put on a uniform.

It was impossible for Donald Gordon to hold out against a man who talked like that; a man who looked him in the eye and expressed his convictions so simply and honestly. And that evening Peter went to a meeting of Local American City of the Socialist Party, and renewed his acquaintance with all the comrades. He didn't make a speech or do anything conspicuous, but simply got into the spirit of things; and next day he managed to meet some of the members, and whenever and wherever he was asked, he expressed his convictions as a conscientious objector. So before a week had passed Peter found that he was being tolerated, that nobody was going to denounce him as a traitor, or kick him out of the room.

At the next weekly meeting of Local American City, Peter ventured to say a few words. It was a red-hot meeting, at which the war and the draft were the sole subjects of discussion. There were some Germans in the local, some Irishmen, and one or two Hindoos; they, naturally, were all ardent pacifists. Also there were agitators of what was coming to be called the "left wing"; the group within the party who considered it too conservative, and were always clamoring for more radical declarations, for "mass action" and general strikes and appeals to the proletariat to rise forthwith and break their chains. These were days of great events; the Russian revolution had electrified the world, and these comrades of the "left wing" felt themselves lifted upon pinions of hope.

Peter spoke as one who had been out on the road, meeting the rank and file; he could speak for the men on the job. What was the use of opposing the draft here in a hall, where nobody but party members were present? What was wanted was for them to lift up their voices on the street, to awaken the people before it was too late! Was there anybody in this gathering bold enough to organize a street meeting?

There were some who could not resist this challenge, and in a few minutes Peter had secured the pledges of half a dozen young hot-heads, Donald Gordon among them. Before the evening was past it had been arranged that these would-be-martyrs should hire a truck, and make their debut on Main Street the very next evening. Old hands in the movement warned them that they would only get their heads cracked by the police. But the answer to that was obvious—they might as well get their heads cracked by the police as get them blown to pieces by German artillery.

Section 32

Peter reported to McGivney what was planned, and McGivney promised that the police would be on hand. Peter warned him to be careful and have the police be gentle; at which McGivney grinned, and answered that he would see to that.

It was all very simple, and took less than ten minutes of time. The truck drew up on Main Street, and a young orator stepped forward and announced to his fellow citizens that the time had come for the workers to make known their true feelings about the draft. Never would free Americans permit themselves to be herded into armies and shipped over seas and be slaughtered for the benefit of international bankers. Thus far the orator had got, when a policeman stepped forward and ordered him to shut up. When he refused, the policeman tapped on the sidewalk with his stick, and a squad of eight or ten came round the corner, and the orator was informed that he was under arrest. Another orator stepped forward and took up the harangue, and when he also had been put under arrest, another, and another, until the whole six of them, including Peter, were in hand.

The crowd had had no time to work up any interest one way or the other, A patrol-wagon was waiting, and the orators were bundled in and driven to the station-house, and next morning they were haled before a magistrate and sentenced each to fifteen days. As they had been expecting to get six months, they were a happy bunch of "left wingers."

And they were still happier when they saw how they were to be treated in jail. Ordinarily it was the custom of the police to inflict all possible pain and humiliation upon the Reds. They would put them in the revolving tank, a huge steel structure of many cells which was turned round and round by a crank. In order to get into any cell, the whole tank had to be turned until that particular cell was opposite the entrance, which meant that everybody in the tank got a free ride, accompanied by endless groaning and scraping of rusty machinery; also it meant that nobody got any consecutive sleep. The tank was dark, too dark to read, even if they had had books or papers. There was nothing to do save to smoke cigarettes and shoot craps, and listen to the smutty stories of the criminals, and plot revenge against society when they got out again. But up in the new wing of the jail were some cells which were clean and bright and airy, being only three or four feet from a row of windows.

In these cells they generally put the higher class of criminals—women who had cut the throats of their sweethearts, and burglars who had got away with the swag, and bankers who had plundered whole communities. But now, to the great surprise of five out of the six anti-militarists, the entire party was put in one of these big cells, and allowed the privilege of having reading matter and of paying for their own food. Under these circumstances martyrdom became a joke, and the little party settled down to enjoy life. It never once occurred to them to think of Peter Gudge as the source of this bounty. They attributed it, as the French say, "to their beautiful eyes."

There was Donald Gordon, who was the son of a well-to-do business man, and had been to college, until he was expelled for taking the doctrines of Christianity too literally and expounding them too persistently on the college campus. There was a big, brawny lumber-jack from the North, Jim Henderson by name, who had been driven out of the camps for the same reason, and had appalling stories to tell of the cruelties and hardships of the life of a logger. There was a Swedish sailor by the name of Gus, who had visited every port in the world, and a young Jewish cigar-worker who had never been outside of American City, but had travelled even more widely in his mind.

The sixth man was the strangest character of all to Peter; a shy, dreamy fellow with eyes so full of pain and a face so altogether mournful that it hurt to look at him. Duggan was his name, and he was known in the movement as the "hobo poet." He wrote verses, endless verses about the lives of society's outcasts; he would get himself a pencil and paper and sit off in the corner of the cell by the hour, and the rest of the fellows, respecting his work, would talk in whispers so as not to disturb him. He wrote all the time while the others slept, it seemed to Peter. He wrote verses about the adventures of his fellow-prisoners, and presently he was writing verses about the jailers, and about other prisoners in this part of the jail. He would have moods of inspiration, and would make up topical verses as he went along; then again he would sink back into his despair, and say that life was hell, and making rhymes about it was childishness.

There was no part of America that Tom Duggan hadn't visited, no tragedy of the life of outcasts that he hadn't seen. He was so saturated with it that he couldn't think of anything else. He would tell about men who had perished of thirst in the desert, about miners sealed up for weeks in an exploded mine, about matchmakers poisoned until their teeth fell out, and their finger nails and even their eyes. Peter could see no excuse for such morbidness, such endless harping upon the horrible things of life. It spoiled all his happiness in the jail—it was worse than little Jennie's talking about the war!

Section 33

One of Duggan's poems had to do with a poor devil named Slim, who was a "snow-eater," that is to say, a cocaine victim. This Slim wandered about the streets of New York in the winter-time without any shelter, and would get into an office building late in the afternoon, and hide in one of the lavatories to spend the night. If he lay down, he would be seen and thrown out, so his only chance was to sit up; but when he fell asleep, he would fall off the seat—therefore he carried a rope in his pocket, and would tie himself in a sitting position.

Now what was the use of a story like that? Peter didn't want to hear about such people! He wanted to express his disgust; but he knew, of course, that he must hide it. He laughed as he exclaimed, "Christ Almighty, Duggan, can't you give us something with a smile? You don't think it's the job of Socialists to find a cure for the dope habit, do you? That's sure one thing that ain't caused by the profit system."

Duggan smiled his bitterest smile. "If there's any misery in the world today that ain't kept alive by the profit system, I'd like to see it! D'you think dope sells itself? If there wasn't a profit in it, would it be sold to any one but doctors? Where'd you get your Socialism, anyhow?"

So Peter beat a hasty retreat. "Oh, sure, I know all that. But here you're shut up in jail because you want to change things. Ain't you got a right to give yourself a rest while you're in?"

The poet looked at him, as solemn as an owl. He shook his head. "No," he said. "Just because we're fixed up nice and comfortable in jail, have we got the right to forget the misery of those outside?"

The others laughed; but Duggan did not mean to be funny at all. He rose slowly to his feet and with his arms outstretched, in the manner of one offering himself as a sacrifice, he proclaimed:

"While there is a lower class, I am in it.

"While there is a criminal element, I am of it.

"While there is a soul in jail, I am not free."

Then he sat down and buried his face in his hands. The group of rough fellows sat in solemn silence. Presently Gus, the Swedish sailor, feeling perhaps that the rebuke to Peter had been too severe, spoke timidly: "Comrade Gudge, he ban in jail twice already."

So the poet looked up again. He held out his hand to Peter. "Sure, I know that!" he said, clasping Peter in the grip of comradeship. And then he added: "I'll tell you a story with a smile!"

Once upon a time, it appeared, Duggan had been working in a moving picture studio, where they needed tramps and outcasts and all sorts of people for crowds. They had been making a "Preparedness" picture, and wanted to show the agitators and trouble-makers, mobbing the palace of a banker. They got two hundred bums and hoboes, and took them in trucks to the palace of a real banker, and on the front lawn the director made a speech to the crowd, explaining his ideas. "Now," said he, "remember, the guy that owns this house is the guy that's got all the wealth that you fellows have produced. You are down and out, and you know that he's robbed you, so you hate him. You gather on his lawn and you're going to mob his home; if you can get hold of him, you're going to tear him to bits for what he's done to you." So the director went on, until finally Duggan interrupted: "Say, boss, you don't have to teach us. This is a real palace, and we're real bums!"

Apparently the others saw the "smile" in this story, for they chuckled for some time over it. But it only added to Peter's hatred of these Reds; it made him realize more than ever that they were a bunch of "sore heads," they were green and yellow with jealousy. Everybody that had succeeded in the world they hated—just because they had succeeded! Well, *they* would never succeed; they could go on forever with their grouching, but the mass of the workers in America had a normal attitude toward the big man, who could do things. They did not want to wreck his palace; they admired him for having it, and they followed his leadership gladly.

It seemed as if Henderson, the lumber-jack, had read Peter's thought. "My God!" he said. "What a job it is to make the workers class-conscious!" He sat on the edge of his cot, with his broad shoulders bowed and his heavy brows knit in thought over the problem of how to increase the world's discontent. He told of one camp where he had worked—so hard and dangerous was the toil that seven men had given up their lives in the course of one winter. The man who owned this tract, and was exploiting it, had gotten the land by the rankest kind of public frauds; there were filthy bunk-houses, vermin, rotten food, poor wages and incessant abuse. And yet, in the spring-time, here came the young son of this owner, on a honeymoon trip with his bride. "And Jesus," said Henderson, "if you could have seen those stiffs turn out and cheer to split their throats! They really meant it, you know; they just loved that pair of idle, good-for-nothing kids!"

Gus, the sailor, spoke up, his broad, good-natured face wearing a grin which showed where three of his front teeth had been knocked out with a belaying pin. It was exactly the same with the seamen, he declared. They never saw the ship-owners, they didn't know even the names of the people who were getting the profit of their toil, but they had a crazy loyalty to their ship, Some old tanker would be sent out to sea on purpose to be sunk, so that the owners might get the insurance. But the poor A. Bs. would love that old tub so that they would go down to the bottom with her—or perhaps they would save her, to the owners great disgust!

Thus, for hours on end, Peter had to sit listening to this ding donging about the wrongs of the poor and the crimes of the rich. Here he had been sentenced for fifteen days and nights to listen to Socialist wrangles! Every one of these fellows had a different idea of how he wanted the world to be run, and every one had a different idea of how to bring about the change. Life was an endless struggle between the haves and the have-nots, and the question of how the have-nots were to turn out the haves was called "tactics." When you talked about "tactics" you used long technical terms which made your conversation unintelligible to a plain, ordinary mortal. It seemed to Peter that every time he fell asleep it was to the music of proletariat and surplus value and unearned increment, possibilism and impossibilism, political action, direct action, mass action, and the perpetual circle of Syndicalist-Anarchist, Anarchist-Communist, Communist-Socialist and Socialist-Syndicalist.

I n company such as this Peter's education for the role of detective was completed by force, as it were. He listened to everything, and while he did not dare make any notes, he stored away treasures in his mind, and when he came out of the jail he was able to give McGivney a pretty complete picture of the various radical organizations in American City, and the attitude of each one toward the war.

Peter found that McGivney's device had worked perfectly. Peter was now a martyr and a hero; his position as one of the "left wingers" was definitely established, and anyone who ventured to say a word against him would be indignantly rebuked. As a matter of fact, no one desired to say much. Pat McCormick, Peter's enemy, was out on an organizing trip among the oil workers.

Duggan had apparently taken a fancy to Peter, and took him to meet some of his friends, who lived in an old, deserted warehouse, which happened to have skylights in the roof; this constituted each room a "studio," and various radicals rented the rooms, and lived here a sort of picnic existence which Peter learned was called "Bohemian." They were young people, most of them, with one or two old fellows, derelicts; they wore flannel shirts, and soft ties, or no ties at all, and their fingers were always smeared with paint. Their life requirements were simple; all they wanted was an unlimited quantity of canvas and paint, some cigarettes, and at long intervals a pickle or some sauer-kraut and a bottle of beer. They would sit all day in front of an easel, painting the most inconceivable pictures—pink skies and green-faced women and purple grass and fantastic splurges of color which they would call anything from "The Woman with a Mustard Pot" to "A Nude Coming Downstairs." And there would be others, like Duggan, writing verses all day; pounding away on a typewriter, if they could manage to rent or borrow one. There were several who sang, and one who played the flute and caused all the others to tear their hair. There was a boy fresh from the country, who declared that he had run away from home because the family sang hymns all day Sunday, and never sang in tune.

From people such as these you would hear the most revolutionary utterances; but Peter soon realized that it was mostly just talk with them. They would work off their frenzies with a few dashes of paint or some ferocious chords on the piano. The really dangerous ones were not here; they were hidden away in offices or dens of their own, where they were prompting strikes and labor agitations, and preparing incendiary literature to be circulated among the poor.

You met such people in the Socialist local, and in the I. W. W. headquarters, and in numerous clubs and propaganda societies which Peter investigated, and to which he was welcomed as a member. In the Socialist local there was a fierce struggle going on over the war. What should be the attitude of the party? There was a group, a comparatively small group, which believed that the interests of Socialism would best be served by helping the Allies to the overthrow of the Kaiser. There was another group, larger and still more determined, which believed that the war was a conspiracy of allied capitalism to rivet its power upon the world, and this group wanted the party to stake its existence upon a struggle against American participation. These two groups contested for the minds of the rank and file of the members, who seemed to be bewildered by the magnitude of the issue and the complexity of the arguments. Peter's orders were to go with the extreme anti-militarists; they were the ones whose confidence he wished to gain, also they were the trouble-makers of the movement, and McGivney's instructions were to make all the trouble possible.

Over at the I. W. W. headquarters was another group whose members were debating their attitude to the war. Should they call strikes and try to cripple the leading industries of the country? Or should they go quietly on with their organization work, certain that in the end the workers would sicken of the military adventure into which they were being snared? Some of these "wobblies" were Socialist party members also, and were active in both gatherings; two of them, Henderson, the lumber-jack, and Gus Lindstrom, the sailor, had been in jail with Peter, and had been among his intimates ever since.

Also Peter met the Pacifists; the "Peoples' Council," as they called themselves. Many of these were religious people, two or three clergymen, and Donald Gordon, the Quaker, and a varied assortment of women— sentimental young girls who shrunk from the thought of bloodshed, and mothers with tear-stained cheeks who did not want their darlings to be drafted. Peter saw right away that these mothers had no "conscientious objections." Each mother was thinking about her own son and about nothing else. Peter was irritated at this, and took it for his special job to see that those mother's darlings did their duty.

He attended a gathering of Pacifists in the home of a school-teacher. They made heart-breaking speeches, and finally little Ada Ruth, the poetess, got up and wanted to know, was it all to end in talk, or would they organize and prepare to take some action against the draft? Would they not at least go out on the street, get up a parade with banners of protest, and go to jail as Comrade Peter Gudge had so nobly done?

Comrade Peter was called on for "a few words." Comrade Peter explained that he was no speaker; after all, actions spoke louder than words, and he had tried to show what he believed. The others were made ashamed by this, and decided for a bold stand at once. Ada Ruth became president and Donald Gordon secretary of the "Anti-conscription League"—a list of whose charter members was turned over to McGivney the same evening.

Section 35

All this time the country had been going to war. The huge military machine was getting under way, the storm of public feeling was rising. Congress had voted a huge loan, a country-wide machine of propaganda was being organized, and the oratory of Four Minute Men was echoing from Maine to California. Peter read the American City "Times" every morning, and here were speeches of statesmen and sermons of clergymen, here were cartoons and editorials, all burning with the fervor's of patriotism. Peter absorbed these, and his soul became transfigured. Hitherto Peter had been living for himself; but there comes a time in the life of every man who can use his brain at all when he realizes that he is not the one thing of importance in the universe, the one end to be served. Peter very often suffered from qualms of conscience, waves of doubt as to his own righteousness. Peter, like every other soul that ever lived, needed a religion, an ideal.

The Reds had a religion, as you might call it; but this religion had failed to attract Peter. In the first place it was low; its devotees were wholly lacking in the graces of life, in prestige, and that ease which comes with assurance of power. They were noisy in their fervors, and repelled Peter as much as the Holy Rollers. Also, they were always harping upon the sordid and painful facts of life; who but a pervert would listen to "sob stories," when he might have all the things that are glorious and shining and splendid in the world?

But now here was the religion Peter wanted. These clergymen in their robes of snow white linen, preaching in churches with golden altars and stained-glass windows; these statesmen who wore the halo of fame, and went about with the cheering of thousands in their ears; these mighty captains of industry whose very names were magic—with power, when written on pieces of paper, to cause cities to rise in the desert, and then to fall again beneath a rain of shells and poison gas; these editors and cartoonists of the American City "Times," with all their wit and learning—these people all combined to construct for Peter a religion and an ideal, and to hand it out to him, ready-made and precisely fitted to his understanding. Peter would go right on doing the things he had been doing before; but he would no longer do them in the name of Peter Gudge, the ant, he would do them in the name of a mighty nation of a hundred and ten million people, with all its priceless memories of the past and its infinite hopes for the future; he would do them in the sacred name of patriotism, and the still more sacred name of democracy. And—most convenient of circumstances—the big business men of American City, who had established a secret service bureau with Guffey in charge of it, would go right on putting up their funds, and paying Peter fifty dollars a week and expenses while he served the holy cause!

It was the fashion these days for orators and public men to vie with one another in expressing the extremes of patriotism, and Peter would read these phrases, and cherish them; they came to seem a part of him, he felt as if he had invented them. He became greedy for more and yet more of this soul-food; and there was always more to be had—until Peter's soul was become swollen, puffed up as with a bellows. Peter became a patriot of patriots, a super-patriot; Peter was a red-blooded American and no mollycoddle; Peter was a "he-American," a 100% American—and if there could have been such a thing as a 101% American, Peter would have been that. Peter was so much of an American that the very sight of a foreigner filled him with a fighting impulse. As for the Reds—well, Peter groped for quite a time before he finally came upon a formula which expressed his feelings. It was a famous clergyman who achieved it for him—saying that if he could have his way he would take all the Reds, and put them in a ship of stone with sails of lead, and send them forth with hell for their destination.

So Peter chafed more and more at his inability to get action. How much more evidence did the secret service of the Traction Trust require? Peter would ask this question of McGivney again and again, and McGivney would answer: "Keep your shirt on. You're getting your pay every week. What's the matter with you?"

"The matter is, I'm tired of listening to these fellows ranting," Peter would say. "I want to stop their mouths."

Yes, Peter had come to take it as a personal affront that these radicals should go on denouncing the cause which Peter had espoused. They all thought of Peter as a comrade, they were most friendly to him; but Peter had the knowledge of how they would regard him when they knew the real truth, and this imagined contempt burned him like an acid. Sometimes there would be talk about spies and informers, and then these people would exhaust their vocabulary of abuse, and Peter, of course, would apply every word of it to himself and become wild with anger. He would long to answer back; he was waiting for the day when he might vindicate himself and his cause by smashing these Reds in the mouth.

Section 36

"Well," said McGivney one day, "I've got something interesting for you now. You're going into high society for a while!"

And the rat-faced man explained that there was a young man in a neighboring city, reputed to be a multi-millionaire, who had written a book against the war, and was the financial source of much pacificism and sedition. "These people are spending lots of money for printing," said McGivney, "and we hear this fellow Lackman is putting it up. We've learned that he is to be in town tomorrow, and we want you to find out all about his affairs."

So Peter was to meet a millionaire! Peter had never known one of these fortunate beings, but he was for them—he had always been for them. Ever since he had learned to read, he had liked to find stories about them in the newspapers, with pictures of them and their palaces. He had read these stories as a child reads fairy tales. They were his creatures of dreams, belonging to a world above reality, above pain and inconvenience.

And then in the days when Peter had been a servant in the Temple of Jimjambo, devoted to the cult of Eleutherinian Exoticism, he had found hanging in the main assembly room a picture labelled, "Mount Olympus," showing a dozen gods and goddesses reclining at ease on silken couches, sipping nectar from golden goblets and gazing down upon the far-off troubles of the world. Peter would peer from behind the curtains and see the Chief Magistrian emerging from behind the seven mystic veils, lifting his rolling voice and in a kind of chant expounding life to his flock of adoring society ladies. He would point to the picture and explain those golden, Olympian days when the Eleutherinian cult had originated. The world had changed much since then, and for the worse; those who had power must take it as their task to restore beauty and splendor to the world, and to develop the gracious possibilities of being.

Peter, of course, hadn't really believed in anything that went on in the Temple of Jimjambo; and yet he had been awed by its richness, and by the undoubtedly exclusive character of its worshippers; he had got the idea definitely fixed in his head that there really had been a Mount Olympus, and when he tried to imagine the millionaires and their ways, it was these gods and goddesses, reclining on silken couches and sipping nectar, that came to his mind!

Now since Peter had come to know the Reds, who wanted to blow up the palaces of the millionaires, he was more than ever on the side of his gods and goddesses. His fervors for them increased every time he heard them assailed; he wanted to meet some of them, and passionately, yet respectfully, pour out to them his allegiance. A glow of satisfaction came over him as he pictured himself in some palace, lounging upon a silken conch and explaining to a millionaire his understanding of the value of beauty and splendor in the world.

And now he was to meet one; it was to be a part of his job to cultivate one! True, there was something wrong with this particular millionaire—he was one of those freaks who for some reason beyond imagining gave their sympathy to the dynamiters and assassins. Peter had met "Parlor Reds" at the home of the Todd sisters; the large shining ladies who came in large shining cars to hear him tell of his jail experiences. But he hadn't been sure as to whether they were really millionaires or not, and Sadie, when he had inquired particularly, had answered vaguely that every one in the radical movement who could afford an automobile or a dress-suit was called a millionaire by the newspapers.

But young Lackman was a real millionaire, McGivney positively assured him; and so Peter was free to admire him in spite of all his freak ideas, which the rat-faced man explained with intense amusement. Young Lackman conducted a school for boys, and when one of the boys did wrong, the teacher would punish himself instead of the boy! Peter must pretend to be interested in this kind of "education," said McGivney, and he must learn at least the names of Lackman's books.

"But will he pay any attention to me?" demanded Peter.

"Sure, he will," said McGivney. "That's the point—you've been in jail, you've really done something as a pacifist. What you want to do is to try to interest him in your Anti-conscription League. Tell him you want to make it into a national organization, you want to get something done besides talking."

The address of young Lackman was the Hotel de Soto; and as he heard this, Peter's heart gave a leap. The Hotel de Soto was the Mount Olympus of American City! Peter had walked by the vast white structure, and seen the bronze doors swing outward, and the favored ones of the earth emerging to their magic chariots; but never had it occurred to him that he might pass thru those bronze doors, and gaze upon those hidden mysteries!

"Will they let me in?" he asked McGivney, and the other laughed.

"Just walk in as if you owned the place," he said. "Hold up your head, and pretend you've lived there all your life."

That was easy for McGivney to say, but not so easy for Peter to imagine. However, he would try it; McGivney must be right, for it was the same thing Mrs. James had impressed upon him many times. You must watch what other people did, and practice by yourself, and then go in and do it as if you had never done anything else. All life was a gigantic bluff, and you encouraged yourself in your bluffing by the certainty that everybody else was bluffing just as hard.

At seven o'clock that evening Peter strolled up to the magic bronze doors, and touched them; and sure enough, the blue-uniformed guardians drew them back without a word, and the tiny brass-button imps never even glanced at Peter as he strode up to the desk and asked for Mr. Lackman.

The haughty clerk passed him on to a still more haughty telephone operator, who condescended to speak into her trumpet, and then informed him that Mr. Lackman was out; he had left word that he would return at eight. Peter was about to go out and wander about the streets for an hour, when he suddenly remembered that everybody else was bluffing; so he marched across the lobby and seated himself in one of the huge leather arm-chairs, big enough to hold three of him. There he sat, and continued to sit—and nobody said a word!

Section 37

Yes, this was Mount Olympus, and here were the gods: the female ones in a state of divine semi-nudity, the male ones mostly clad in black coats with pleated shirt-fronts puffing out. Every time one of them moved up to the desk Peter would watch and wonder, was this Mr. Lackman? He might have been able to pick out a millionaire from an ordinary crowd; but here every male god was got up for the precise purpose of looking like a millionaire, so Peter's job was an impossible one.

In front of him across the lobby floor there arose a ten-foot pillar to a far-distant roof. This pillar was of pale, green-streaked marble, and Peter's eyes followed it to the top, where it exploded in a snow-white cloud-burst, full of fascination. There were four cornucopias, one at each corner, and out of each cornucopia came tangled ropes of roses, and out of these roses came other ropes, with what appeared to be apples and leaves, and still more roses, and still more emerging ropes, spreading in a tangle over the ceiling. Here and there, in the midst of all this splendor, was the large, placidly smiling face of a boy angel; four of these placidly smiling boy angels gazed from the four sides of the snow-white cloud-burst, and Peter's eye roamed from one to another, fascinated by the mathematics of this architectural marvel. There were fourteen columns in a row, and four such rows in the lobby. That made fifty-six columns in all, or two hundred and twenty-four boy angels' heads. How many cornucopias and how many roses and how many apples it meant, defied all calculation. The boy angels' heads were exactly alike, every head with the same size and quality of smile; and Peter marvelled—how many days would it take a sculptor to carve the details of two hundred and twenty-four boy angel smiles?

All over the Hotel de Soto was this same kind of sumptuous magnificence; and Peter experienced the mental effect which it was contrived to produce upon him—a sense of bedazzlement and awe, a realization that those who dwelt in the midst of this splendor were people to whom money was nothing, who could pour out treasures in a never-ceasing flood. And everything else about the place was of the same character, contrived for the same effect—even the gods and the goddesses! One would sweep by with a tiara of jewels in her hair; you might amuse yourself by figuring out the number of the jewels, as you had figured out the number of the boy angels' heads. Or you might take her gown of black lace, embroidered with golden butterflies, every one patiently done by hand; you might figure—so many yards of material, and so many golden butterflies to the yard! You might count the number of sparkling points upon her jet slippers, or trace the intricate designs upon her almost transparent stockings—only there was an inch or two of the stockings which you could not see.

Peter watched these gorgeous divinities emerge from the elevators, and sweep their way into the dining-room beyond. Some people might have been shocked by their costumes; but to Peter, who had the picture of Mount Olympus in mind, they seemed most proper. It all depended on the point of view: whether you thought of a goddess as fully clothed from chin to toes, and proceeded with a pair of shears to cut away so much of her costume, or whether you imagined the goddess in a state of nature, and proceeded to put veils of gauze about her, and a ribbon over each shoulder to hold the veils in place.

Twice Peter went to the desk, to inquire if Mr. Lackman had come in yet; but still he had not come; and Peter—growing bolder, like the fox who spoke to the lion—strolled about the lobby, gazing at the groups of gods at ease. He had noticed a great balcony around all four sides of this lobby, the "mezzanine floor," as it was called; he decided he would see what was up there, and climbed the white marble stairs, and beheld more rows of chairs and couches, done in dark grey velvet. Here, evidently, was where the female gods came to linger, and Peter seated himself as unobtrusively as possible, and watched.

Directly in front of him sat a divinity, lolling on a velvet couch with one bare white arm stretched out. It was a large stout arm, and the possessor was large and stout, with pale golden hair and many sparkling jewels. Her glance roamed lazily from place to place. It rested for an instant on Peter, and then moved on, and Peter felt the comment upon his own insignificance.

Nevertheless, he continued to steal glances now and then, and presently saw an interesting sight. In her lap this Juno had a gold-embroidered bag, and she opened it, disclosing a collection of mysterious apparatus of which she proceeded to make use: first a little gold hand-mirror, in which she studied her charms; then a little white powder-puff with which she deftly tapped her nose and cheeks; then some kind of red pencil with which she proceeded to rub her lips; then a golden pencil with which she lightly touched her eyebrows. Then it seemed as if she must have discovered a little hair which had grown since she left her dressing-room. Peter couldn't be sure, but she had a little pair of tweezers, and seemed to pull something out of her chin. She went on with quite an elaborate and complicated toilet, paying meantime not the slightest attention to the people passing by.

Peter looked farther, and saw that just as when one person sneezes or yawns everybody else in the room is irresistibly impelled to sneeze or yawn, so all these Dianas and Junos and Hebes on the "mezzanine floor" had suddenly remembered their little gold or silver hand-mirrors, their powder-puffs and red or golden or black pencils. One after another, the little vanity-bags came forth, and Peter, gazing in wonder, thought that Mount Olympus had turned into a beauty parlor.

Peter rose again and strolled and watched the goddesses, big and little, old and young, fat and thin, pretty and ugly—and it seemed to him the fatter and older and uglier they were, the more intently they gazed into the little hand-mirrors. He watched them with hungry eyes, for he knew that here he was in the midst of high life, the real thing, the utmost glory to which man could ever hope to attain, and he wanted to know all there was to know about it. He strolled on, innocent and unsuspecting, and the two hundred and twenty-four white boy angels in the ceiling smiled their bland and placid smiles at him, and Peter knew no more than they what complications fate had prepared for him on that mezzanine floor!

On one of the big lounges there sat a girl, a radiant creature from the Emerald Isles, with hair like sunrise and cheeks like apples. Peter took one glance at her, and his heart missed three successive beats, and then, to make up for lost time, began leaping like a runaway race-horse. He could hardly believe what his eyes told him; but his eyes insisted, his eyes knew; yes, his eyes had gazed for hours and hours on end upon that hair like sunrise and those cheeks like apples. The girl was Nell, the chambermaid of the Temple of Jimjambo!

She had not looked Peter's way, so there was time for him to start back and hide himself behind a pillar; there he stood, peering out and watching her profile, still arguing with his eyes. It couldn't be Nell; and yet it was! Nell transfigured, Nell translated to Olympus, turned into a goddess with a pale grey band about her middle, and a pale grey ribbon over each shoulder to hold it in place! Nell reclining at ease and chatting vivaciously to a young man with the face of a bulldog and the dinner-jacket of a magazine advertisement!

Peter gazed and waited, while his heart went on misbehaving. Peter learned in those few fearful minutes what real love is, a most devastating force. Little Jennie was forgotten, Mrs. James, the grass widow was forgotten, and Peter knew that he had never really admired but one woman in the world, and that was Nell, the Irish chambermaid of the Temple of Jimjambo. The poets have seen fit to represent young love as a mischievous little archer with a sharp and penetrating arrow, and now Peter understood what they had meant; that arrow had pierced him thru, and he had to hold on to the column to keep himself from falling.

Section 38

Presently the couple rose and strolled away to the elevator, and Peter followed. He did not dare get into the elevator with them, for he had suddenly become accutely aware of the costume he was wearing in his role of proletarian anti-militarist! But Peter was certain that Nell and her escort were not going out of the building, for they had no hats or wraps; so he went downstairs and hunted thru the lobby and the dining-room, and then thru the basement, from which he heard strains of music. Here was another vast room, got up in mystic oriental fashion, with electric lights hidden in bunches of imitation flowers on each table. This room was called the "grill," and part of it was bare for dancing, and on a little platform sat a band playing music.

The strangest music that ever assailed human ears! If Peter had heard it before seeing Nell, he would not have understood it, but now its weird rhythms fitted exactly to the moods which were tormenting him. This music would groan, it would rattle and squeak; it would make noises like swiftly torn canvas, or like a steam siren in a hurry. It would climb up to the heavens and come banging down to hell. And every thing with queer, tormenting motions, gliding and writhing, wriggling, jerking, jumping. Peter would never have known what to make of such music, if he had not had it here made visible before his eyes, in the behavior of the half-naked goddesses and the black-coated gods on this dancing floor. These celestial ones came sliding across the floor like skaters, they came writhing like serpents, they came strutting like turkeys, jumping like rabbits, stalking solemnly like giraffes. They came clamped in one another's arms like bears trying to hug each other to death; they came contorting themselves as if they were boa-constrictors trying to swallow each other. And Peter, watching them and listening to their music, made a curious discovery about himself. Deeply buried in Peter's soul were the ghosts of all sorts of animals; Peter had once been a boa-constrictor, Peter had once been a bear, Peter had once been a rabbit and a giraffe, a turkey and a fox; and now under the spell of this weird music these dead creatures came to life in his soul. So Peter discovered the meaning of "jazz," in all its weirdly named and incredible varieties.

Also Peter discovered that he had once been a caveman, and had hit his rival over the head with a stone axe and carried off his girl by the hair. All this he discovered while he stood in the doorway of the Hotel de Soto grill, and watched Nell, the ex-chambermaid of the Temple of Jimjambo, doing the turkey-trot and the fox-trot and the grizzly-bear and the bunny-hug in the arms of a young man with the face of a bulldog.

Peter stood for a long while in a daze. Nell and the young man sat down at one of the tables to have a meal, but still Peter stood watching and trying to figure out what to do. He knew that he must not speak to her in his present costume; there would be no way to make her understand that he was only playing a role—that he who looked like a "dead one" was really a prosperous man of important affairs, a 100% red-blooded patriot disguised as a proletarian pacifist. No, he must wait, he must get into his best before he spoke to her. But meantime, she might go away, and he might not be able to find her again in this huge city!

After an hour or two he succeeded in figuring out a way, and hurried upstairs to the writing-room and penned a note:

"Nell: This is your old friend Peter Gudge. I have struck it rich and have important news for you. Be sure to send word to me. Peter." To this he added his address, and sealed it in an envelope to "Miss Nell Doolin."

Then he went out into the lobby, and signalled to one of the brass-button imps who went about the place calling names in shrill sing-song; he got this youngster off in a corner and pressed a dollar bill into his hand. There was a young lady in the grill who was to have this note at once. It was very important. Would the brass-button imp do it?

The imp said sure, and Peter stood in the doorway and watched him walk back and forth thru the aisles of the grill, calling in his shrill sing-song, "Miss Nell Doolin! Miss Nell Doolin!" He walked right by the table where Nell sat eating; he sang right into her face, it seemed to Peter; but she never gave a sign.

Peter did not know what to make of it, but he was bound to get that note to Nell. So when the imp returned, he pointed her out, and the imp went again and handed the note to her. Peter saw her take it—then he darted away; and remembering suddenly that he was supposed to be on duty, he rushed back to the office and inquired for Mr. Lackman. To his horror he learned that Mr. Lackman had returned, paid his bill, and departed with his suitcase to a destination unknown!

Section 39

P eter had a midnight appointment with McGivney, and now had
to go and admit this humiliating failure. He had done his best, he
declared; he had inquired at the desk, and waited and waited, but the
hotel people had failed to notify him of Lackman's arrival. All this was
strictly true; but it did not pacify McGivney, who was in a black fury. "It
might have been worth thousands of dollars to you!" he declared. "He's
the biggest fish we'll ever get on our hook."

"Won't he come again?" asked grief-stricken Peter.

"No," declared the other. "They'll get him at his home city."

"But won't that do?" asked Peter, naively.

"You damned fool!" was McGivney's response. "We wanted to get
him here, where we could pluck him ourselves."

The rat-faced man hadn't intended to tell Peter so much, but in his
rage he let it out. He and a couple of his friends had planned to "get
something" on this young millionaire, and scare the wits out of him,
with the idea that he would put up a good many thousand dollars to be
let off. Peter might have had his share of this—only he had been fool
enough to let the bird get out of his net!

Peter offered to follow the young man to his home city, and find
some way to lure him back into McGivney's power. After McGivney
had stormed for a while, he decided that this might be possible. He
would talk it over with the others, and let Peter know. But alas, when
Peter picked up an afternoon newspaper next day, he read on the front
page how young Lackman, stepping off the train in his home city that
morning, had been placed under arrest; his school had been raided, and
half a dozen of the teachers were in jail, and a ton of Red literature had
been confiscated, and a swarm of dire conspiracies against the safety of
the country had been laid bare!

Peter read this news, and knew that he was in for another stormy
hour with his boss. But he hardly gave a thought to it, because of
something which had happened a few minutes before, something of
so much greater importance. A messenger had brought him a special
delivery letter, and with thumping heart he had torn it open and read:

"All right. Meet me in the waiting-room of Guggenheim's
Department Store at two o'clock this afternoon. But for God's sake
forget Nell Doolin. Yours, Edythe Eustace."

So here was Peter dressed in his best clothes, as for his temporary honeymoon with the grass widow, and on the way to the rendezvous an hour ahead of time. And here came Nell, also dressed, every garment so contrived that a single glance would tell the beholder that their owner was moving in the highest circles, and regardless of expense. Nell glanced over her shoulder now and then as she talked, and explained that Ted Crothers, the man with the bulldog face, was a terror, and it was hard to get away from him, because he had nothing to do all day.

The waiting-room of a big department-store was not the place Peter would have selected for the pouring out of his heart; but he had to make the best of it, so he told Nell that he loved her, that he would never be able to love anybody else, and that he had made piles of money now, he was high up on the ladder of prosperity. Nell did not laugh at him, as she had laughed in the Temple of Jimjambo, for it was easily to be seen that Peter Gudge was no longer a scullion, but a man of the world with a fascinating air of mystery. Nell wanted to know forthwith what was he doing; he answered that he could not tell, it was a secret of the most desperate import; he was under oath. These were the days of German spies and bomb-plots, when kings and kaisers and emperors and tsars were pouring treasures into America for all kinds of melodramatic purposes; also the days of government contracts and secret deals, when in the lobbies and private meeting-places of hotels like the de Soto there were fortunes made and unmade every hour. So it was easy for Nell to believe in a real secret, and being a woman, she put all her faculties upon the job of guessing it.

She did not again ask Peter to tell her; but she let him talk, and tactfully guided the conversation, and before long she knew that Peter was intimate with a great many of the most desperate Reds, and likewise that he knew all about the insides of the Goober case, and about the great men of American City who had put up a million dollars for the purpose of hanging Goober, and about the various ways in which this money had been spent and wires had been pulled to secure a conviction. Nell put two and two together, and before long she figured out that the total was four; she suddenly confronted Peter with this total, and Peter was dumb with consternation, and broke down and confessed everything, and told Nell all about his schemes and his achievements and his adventures—omitting only little Jennie and the grass widow.

He told about the sums he had been making and was expecting to make; he told about Lackman, and showed Nell the newspaper with pictures of the young millionaire and his school. "What a handsome fellow!" said Nell. "It's a shame!"

"How do you mean?" asked Peter, a little puzzled. Could it be that Nell had any sympathy for these Reds?

"I mean," she answered, "that he'd have been worth more to you than all the rest put together."

Nell was a woman, and her mind ran to the practical aspect of things. "Look here, Peter," she said, "you've been letting those 'dicks' work you. They're getting the swag, and just giving you tips. What you need is somebody to take care of you."

Peter's heart leaped. "Will you do it?" he cried.

"I've got Ted on my hands," said the girl. "He'd cut my throat, and yours too, if he knew I was here. But I'll try to get myself free, and then maybe—I won't promise, but I'll think over your problem, Peter, and I'll certainly try to help, so that McGivney and Guffey and those fellows can't play you for a sucker any longer."

She must have time to think it over, she said, and to make inquiries about the people involved—some of whom apparently she knew. She would meet Peter again the next day, and in a more private place than here. She named a spot in the city park which would be easy to find, and yet sufficiently remote for a quiet conference.

Section 40

Peter had been made so bold by Nell's flattery and what she had said about his importance, that he did not go back to McGivney to take his second scolding about the Lackman case. He was getting tired of McGivney's scoldings; if McGivney didn't like his work, let McGivney go and be a Red for a while himself. Peter walked the streets all day and a part of the night, thinking about Nell, and thrilling over the half promises she had made him.

They met next day in the park. No one was following them, and they found a solitary place, and Nell let him kiss her several times, and in between the kisses she unfolded to him a terrifying plan. Peter had thought that he was something of an intriguer, but his self-esteem shriveled to nothingness in the presence of the superb conception which had come to ripeness in the space of twenty-four hours in the brain of Nell Doolin, alias Edythe Eustace.

Peter had been doing the hard work, and these big fellows had been using him, handing him a tip now and then, and making fortunes out of the information he brought them. McGivney had let the cat out of the bag in this case of Lackman; you might be sure they had been making money, big money, out of all the other cases. What Peter must do was to work up something of his own, and get the real money, and make himself one of the big fellows. Peter had the facts, he knew the people; he had watched in the Goober case exactly how a "frame-up" was made, and now he must make one for himself, and one that would pay. It was a matter of duty to rid the country of all these Reds; but why should he not have the money as well?

Nell had spent the night figuring over it, trying to pick out the right person. She had hit on old "Nelse" Ackerman, the banker. Ackerman was enormously and incredibly wealthy; he was called the financial king of American City. Also he was old, and Nell happened to know he was a coward; he was sick in bed just now, and when a man is sick he is still more of a coward. What Peter must do was to discover some kind of a bomb-plot against old "Nelse" Ackerman. Peter might talk up the idea among some of his Reds and get them interested in it, or he might frame up some letters to be found upon them, and hide some dynamite in their rooms. When the plot was discovered, it would make a frightful uproar, needless to say; the king would hear of it, and of Peter's part as the discoverer of it, and he would unquestionably reward Peter. Perhaps Peter might arrange to be retained as a secret agent to protect the king from the Reds. Thus Peter would be in touch with real money, and might hire Guffey and McGivney, instead of their hiring him.

If Peter had stood alone, would he have dared so perilous a dream as this? Or was he a "piker"; a little fellow, the victim of his own fears and vanities? Anyhow, Peter was not alone; he had Nell, and it was necessary that he should pose before Nell as a bold and desperate blade. Just as in the old days in the Temple, it was necessary that Peter should get plenty of money, in order to take Nell away from another man. So he said all right, he would go in on that plan; and proceeded to discuss with Nell the various personalities he might use.

The most likely was Pat McCormick. "Mac," with his grim, set face and his silent, secretive habits, fitted perfectly to Peter's conception of a dynamiter. Also "Mac" was Peter's personal enemy; "Mac" had just returned from his organizing trip in the oil fields, and had been denouncing Peter and gossiping about him in the various radical groups. "Mac" was the most dangerous Red of them all! He must surely be one of the dynamiters!

Another likely one was Joe Angell, whom Peter had met at a recent gathering of Ada Ruth's "Anti-conscription League." People made jokes about this chap's name because he looked the part, with his bright blue eyes that seemed to have come out of heaven, and his bright golden hair, and even the memory of dimples in his cheeks. But when Joe opened his lips, you discovered that he was an angel from the nether regions. He was the boldest and most defiant of all the Reds that Peter had yet come upon. He had laughed at Ada Ruth and her sentimental literary attitude toward the subject of the draft. It wasn't writing poems and passing resolutions that was wanted; it wasn't even men who would refuse to put on the uniform, but men who would take the guns that were offered to them, and drill themselves, and at the proper time face about and use the guns in the other direction. Agitating and organizing were all right in their place, but now, when the government dared challenge the workers and force them into the army, it was men of action that were needed in the radical movement.

Joe Angell had been up in the lumber country, and could tell what was the mood of the real workers, the "huskies" of the timberlands. Those fellows weren't doing any more talking; they had their secret committees that were ready to take charge of things as soon as they had put the capitalists and their governments out of business. Meantime, if there was a sheriff or prosecuting attorney that got too gay, they would "bump him off." This was a favorite phrase of "Blue-eyed Angell." He would use it every half hour or so as he told about his adventures. "Yes," he would say; "he got gay, but we bumped him off all right."

Section 41

S o Nell and Peter settled down to work out the details of their "frame-up" on Joe Angell and Pat McCormick. Peter must get a bunch of them together and get them to talking about bombs and killing people; and then he must slip a note into the pockets of all who showed interest, calling them to meet for a real conspiracy. Nell would write the notes, so that no one could fasten the job onto Peter. She pulled out a pencil and a little pad from her handbag, and began: "If you really believe in a bold stroke for the workers' rights, meet me—" And then she stopped. "Where?"

"In the studios," put in Peter.

And Nell wrote, "In the studios. Is that enough?"

"Room 17." Peter knew that this was the room of Nikitin, a Russian painter who called himself an Anarchist.

So Nell wrote "Room 17," and after further discussion she added: "Tomorrow morning at eight o'clock. No names and no talk. Action!" This time was set because Peter recollected that there was to be a gathering of the "wobblies" in their headquarters this very evening. It was to be a business meeting, but of course these fellows never got together very long without starting the subject of "tactics." There was a considerable element among them who were dissatisfied with what they called the "supine attitude" of the organization, and were always arguing for action. Peter was sure he would be able to get some of them interested in the idea of a dynamite conspiracy.

As it turned out, Peter had no trouble at all; the subject was started without his having to put in a word. Were the workers to be driven like sheep to the slaughter, and the "wobblies" not to make one move? So asked the "Blue-eyed Angell," vehemently, and added that if they were going to move, American City was as good a place as any. He had talked with enough of the rank and file to realize that they were ready for action; all they needed was a battle-cry and an organization to guide them.

Henderson, the big lumber-jack, spoke up. That was just the trouble; you couldn't get an organization for such a purpose. The authorities would get spies among you, they would find out what you were doing, and drive you underground.

"Well," cried Joe, "we'll go underground!"

"Yes," agreed the other, "but then your organization goes bust. Nobody knows who to trust, everybody's accusing the rest of being a spy."

"Hell!" said Joe Angell. "I've been in jail for the movement, I'll take my chances of anybody's calling me a spy. What I'm not going to do is to sit down and see the workers driven to hell, because I'm so damn careful about my precious organization."

When others objected, Angell rushed on still more vehemently. Suppose they did fail in a mass-uprising, suppose they were driven to assassination and terrorism? At least they would teach the exploiters a lesson, and take a little of the joy out of their lives.

Peter thought it would be a good idea for him to pose as a conservative just now. "Do you really think the capitalists would give up from fear?" he asked.

And the other answered: "You bet I do! I tell you if we'd made it understood that every congressman who voted this country into war would be sent to the front trenches, our country would still be at peace."

"But," put in Peter, deftly, "it ain't the congressmen. It's people higher up than them."

"You bet," put in Gus, the Swedish sailor. "You bet you! I name you one dozen big fellows in dis country—you make it clear if we don't get peace dey all get killed—we get peace all right!"

So Peter had things where he wanted them. "Who are those fellows?" he asked, and got the crowd arguing over names. Of course they didn't argue very long before somebody mentioned "Nelse" Ackerman, who was venomously hated by the Reds because he had put up a hundred thousand dollars of the Anti-Goober fund. Peter pretended not to know about Nelse; and Jerry Rudd, a "blanket-stiff" whose head was still sore from being cracked open in a recent harvesters' strike, remarked that by Jesus, if they'd put a few fellows like that in the trenches, there'd be some pacifists in Ameriky sure enough all right.

IT SEEMED ALMOST AS IF Joe Angell had come there to back up Peter's purpose. "What we want," said he, "is a few fellows to fight as hard for themselves as they fight for the capitalists."

"Yes," assented Henderson, grimly. "We're all so good—we wait till our masters tell us we can kill."

That was the end of the discussion; but it seemed quite enough to Peter. He watched his chance, and one by one he managed to slip his little notes into the coat-pockets of Joe Angell, Jerry Rudd, Henderson, and Gus, the sailor. And then Peter made his escape, trembling with excitement. The great dynamite conspiracy was on! "They must be got rid of!" he was whispering to himself. "They must be got rid of by any means! It's my duty I'm doing."

Section 42

Peter had an appointment to meet Nell on a street corner at eleven o'clock that same night, and when she stepped off the street-car, Peter saw that she was carrying a suit-case. "Did you get your job done?" she asked quickly, and when Peter answered in the affirmative, she added: "Here's your bomb!"

Peter's jaw fell. He looked so frightened that she hastened to reassure him. It wouldn't go off; it was only the makings of a bomb, three sticks of dynamite and some fuses and part of a clock. The dynamite was wrapped carefully, and there was no chance of its exploding—if he didn't drop it! But Peter wasn't much consoled. He had had no idea that Nell would go so far, or that he would actually have to handle dynamite. He wondered where and how she had got it, and wished to God he was out of this thing.

But it was too late now, of course. Said Nell: "You've got to get this suit-case into the headquarters, and you've got to get it there without anybody seeing you. They'll be shut up pretty soon, won't they?"

"We locked up when we left," said Peter.

"And who has the key?"

"Grady, the secretary."

"There's no way you can get it?"

"I can get into the room," said Peter, quickly. "There's a fire escape, and the window isn't tight. Some of us that know about it have got in that way when the place was locked."

"All right," said Nell. "We'll wait a bit; we mustn't take chances of anyone coming back."

They started to stroll along the street, Nell still carrying the suit-case, as if distrusting the state of Peter's nerves, Meantime she explained, "I've got two pieces of paper that we've got to plant in the room. One's to be torn up and thrown into the trash-basket. It's supposed to be part of a letter about some big plan that's to be pulled off, and it's signed 'Mac.' That's for McCormick, of course. I had to type it, not having any sample of his handwriting. The other piece is a drawing; there's no marks to show what it is, but of course the police'll soon find out. It's a plan of old Ackerman's home, and there's a cross mark showing his sleeping-porch. Now, what we want to do is to fix this on McCormick. Is there anything in the room that belongs to him?"

Peter thought, and at last remembered that in the bookshelves were some books which had been donated by McCormick, and which had his name written in. That was the trick! exclaimed Nell. They would hide the paper in one of these books, and when the police made a thorough search they would find it. Nell asked what was in these books, and Peter thought, and remembered that one was a book on sabotage. "Put the paper in that," said Nell. "When the police find it, the newspapers'll print the whole book."

Peter's knees were trembling so that he could hardly walk, but he kept reminding himself that he was a "he-man," a 100% American, and that in these times of war every patriot must do his part. His part was to help rid the country of these Reds, and he must not flinch. They made their way to the old building in which the I. W. W. headquarters were located, and Peter climbed up on the fence and swung over to the fire-escape, and Nell very carefully handed the suit-case to him, and Peter opened the damaged window and slipped into the room.

He knew just where the cupboard was, and quickly stored the suit-case in the corner, and piled some odds and ends of stuff in front of it, and threw an old piece of canvas over it. He took out of his right-hand pocket a typewritten letter, and tore it into small pieces and threw them into the trash-basket. Then he took out of his left-hand pocket the other paper, with the drawing of Ackerman's house. He went to the bookcase and with shaking fingers struck a match, picked out the little redbound book entitled "Sabotage," and stuck the paper inside, and put the book back in place. Then he climbed out on the fire-escape and dropped to the ground, jumped over the fence, and hurried down the alley to where Nell was waiting for him.

"It's for my country!" he was whispering to himself.

Section 43

The job was now complete, except for getting McCormick to the rendezvous next morning. Nell had prepared and would mail in the postoffice a special delivery letter addressed to McCormick's home. This would be delivered about seven o'clock in the morning, and inside was a typewritten note, as follows:

"Mac: Come to Room 17 of the studios at eight in the morning. Very important. Our plan is all ready, my part is done. Joe."

Nell figured that McCormick would take this to be a message from Angell. He wouldn't know what it was about, but he'd be all the more certain to come and find out. The essential thing was that the raid by the detectives must occur the very minute the conspirators got together, for as soon as they compared notes they would become suspicious, and might scatter at once. McGivney must have his men ready; he must be notified and have plenty of time to get them ready.

But there was a serious objection to this—if McGivney had time, he would demand a talk with Peter, and Nell was sure that Peter couldn't stand a cross-questioning at McGivney's hands. Peter, needless to say, agreed with her; his heart threatened to collapse at the thought of such an ordeal. What Peter really wanted to do was to quit the whole thing right there and then; but he dared not say so, he dared not face the withering scorn of his confederate. Peter clenched his hands and set his teeth, and when he passed a street light he turned his face away, so that Nell might not read the humiliating terror written there. But Nell read it all the same; Nell believed that she was dealing with a quivering, pasty-faced coward, and proceeded on that basis; she worked out the plans, she gave Peter his orders, and she stuck by him to see that he carried them out.

Peter had McGivney's home telephone number, which he was only supposed to use in the most desperate emergency. He was to use it now, and tell McGivney that he had just caught some members of the I. W. W., with Pat McCormick as their leader, preparing to blow up some people with dynamite bombs. They had some bombs in a suitcase in their headquarters, and were just starting out with other bombs in their pockets. Peter must follow them, otherwise he would lose them, and some crime might be committed before he could interfere. McGivney must have his agents ready with automobiles to swoop down upon any place that Peter indicated. Peter would follow up the conspirators, and phone McGivney again at the first opportunity he could find.

Nell was especially insistent that when Peter spoke to McGivney he must have only a moment to spare, no time for questions, and he must not stop to answer any. He must be in a state of trembling excitement; and Peter was sure that would be very easy! He rehearsed over to Nell every word he must say, and just how he was to cut short the conversation and hang up the receiver. Then he went into an all night drug-store just around the corner from the headquarters, and from a telephone booth called McGivney's home.

It was an apartment house, and after some delay Peter heard the voice of his employer, surly with sleep. But Peter waked him up quickly. "Mr. McGivney, there's a dynamite plot!"

"*What?*"

"I. W. W. They've got bombs in a suit-case! They're starting off to blow somebody up tonight."

"By God! What do you mean? Who?"

"I dunno yet. I only heard part of it, and I've got to go. They're starting, I've got to follow them. I may lose them and it'll be too late. You hear me, I've got to follow them!"

"I hear you. What do you want me to do?"

"I'll phone you again the first chance I get. You have your men ready, a dozen of them! Have automobiles, so you can come quick. You get me?"

"Yes, but—"

"I can't talk any more, I may lose them, I haven't a second! You be at your phone, and have your men ready—everything ready. You get me?"

"Yes, but listen, man! You sure you're not mistaken?"

"Yes, yes, I'm sure!" cried Peter, his voice mounting in excitement. "They've got the dynamite, I tell you—everything! It's a man named Nelse."

"Nelse what?"

"The man they're going to kill. I've got to go now, you get ready. Good-bye!" And Peter hung up the receiver. He had got so excited over the part he was playing that he sprang up and ran out of the drug-store, as if he really had to catch up with some I. W. W. conspirators carrying a dynamite bomb!

But there was Nell, and they strolled down the street again. They came to a small park, and sat on one of the benches, because Peter's legs would no longer hold him up. Nell walked about to make sure there was no one on any of the other benches; then she came back and rehearsed the next scene with Peter. They must go over it most carefully, because before long the time was coming when Peter wouldn't have Nell to coach him, and must be prepared to stand on his own legs. Peter knew that, and his legs failed him. He wanted to back down, and declare that he couldn't go ahead with it; he wanted to go to McGivney and confess everything. Nell divined what was going on in his soul, and wished to save him the humiliation of having it known. She sat close to him on the bench, and put her hand on his as she talked to him, and presently Peter felt a magic thrill stealing over him. He ventured to put his arm about Nell, to get still more of this delicious sensation; and Nell permitted the embraces, for the first time she even encouraged them. Peter was a hero now, he was undertaking a bold and desperate venture; he was going to put it thru like a man, and win Nell's real admiration. "Our country's at war!" she exclaimed. "And these devils are stopping it!"

So pretty soon Peter was ready to face the whole world; Peter was ready to go himself and blow up the king of American City with a dynamite bomb! In that mood he stayed thru the small hours of the morning, sitting on the bench clasping his girl in his arms, and wishing she would give a little more time to heeding his love-making, and less to making him recite his lessons.

Section 44

S o the day began to break and the birds to sing. The sun rose on Peter's face gray with exhaustion and the Irish apples in Nell's cheeks badly faded. But the time for action had come, and Peter went off to watch McCormick's home until seven o'clock, when the special delivery letter was due to arrive.

It came on time, and Peter saw McCormick come out of the house and set forth in the direction of the studios. It was too early for the meeting, so Peter figured that he would stop to get his breakfast; and sure enough "Mac" turned into, a little dairy lunch, and Peter hastened to the nearest telephone and called his boss.

"Mr. McGivney," he said, "I lost those fellows last night, but now I got them again. They decided not to do anything till today. They're having a meeting this morning and we've a chance to nab them all."

"Where?" demanded McGivney.

"Room seventeen in the studios; but don't let any of your men go near there, till I make sure the right fellows are in."

"Listen here, Peter Gudge!" cried McGivney. "Is this straight goods?"

"My God!" cried Peter. "What do you take me for? I tell you they've got loads of dynamite."

"What have they done with it?"

"They've got some in their headquarters. About the rest I dunno. They carried it off and I lost them last night. But then I found a note in my pocket—they were inviting me to come in."

"By God!" exclaimed the rat-faced man.

"We've got the whole thing, I tell you! Have you got your men ready?"

"Yes."

"Well then, have them come to the corner of Seventh and Washington Streets, and you come to Eighth and Washington. Meet me there just as quick as you can."

"I get you," was the answer, and Peter hung up, and rushed off to the appointed rendezvous. He was so nervous that he had to sit on the steps of a building. As time passed and McGivney didn't appear, wild imaginings began to torment him. Maybe McGivney hadn't understood him correctly! Or maybe his automobile might break down! Or his telephone might have got out of order at precisely the critical moment! He and his men would arrive too late, they would find the trap sprung, and the prey escaped.

Ten minutes passed, fifteen minutes, twenty minutes. At last an automobile rushed up the street, and McGivney stepped out, and the automobile sped on. Peter got McGivney's eye, and then stepped back into the shelter of a doorway. McGivney followed. "Have you got them?" he cried.

"I d-d-dunno!" chattered Peter. "They s-s-said they were c-coming at eight!"

"Let me see that note!" commanded McGivney; so Peter pulled out one of Nell's notes which he had saved for himself:

"If you really believe in a bold stroke for the workers' rights, meet me in the studios, Room 17, tomorrow morning at eight o'clock. No names and no talk. Action!"

"You found that in your pocket?" demanded the other.

"Y-yes, sir."

"And you've no idea who put it there."

"N-no, but I think Joe Angell—"

McGivney looked at his watch. "You've got twenty minutes yet," be said.

"You got the dicks?" asked Peter.

"A dozen of them. What's your idea now?"

Peter stammered out his suggestions. There was a little grocery store just across the street from the entrance to the studio building. Peter would go in there, and pretend to get something to eat, and would watch thru the window, and the moment he saw the right men come in, he would hurry out and signal to McGivney, who would be in a drugstore at the next corner. McGivney must keep out of sight himself, because the "Reds" knew him as one of Guffey's agents.

It wasn't necessary to repeat anything twice. McGivney was keyed up and ready for business, and Peter hurried down the street, and stepped into the little grocery store without being observed by anyone. He ordered some crackers and cheese, and seated himself on a box by the window and pretended to eat. But his hands were trembling so that he could hardly get the food into his mouth; and this was just as well, because his mouth was dry with fright, and crackers and cheese are articles of diet not adapted to such a condition.

He kept his eyes glued on the dingy doorway of the old studio building, and presently—hurrah!—he saw McCormick coming down the street! The Irish boy turned into the building, and a couple of minutes later came Gus the sailor, and before another five minutes had passed here came Joe Angell and Henderson. They were walking quickly, absorbed in conversation, and Peter could imagine he heard them talking about those mysterious notes, and who could be the writer, and what the devil could they mean?

Peter was now wild with nervousness; he was afraid somebody in the grocery store would notice him, and he made desperate efforts to eat the crackers and cheese, and scattered the crumbs all over himself and over the floor. Should he wait for Jerry Rudd, or should he take those he had already? He had got up and started for the door, when he saw the last of his victims coming down the street. Jerry was walking slowly, and Peter couldn't wait until he got inside. A car was passing, and Peter took the chance to slip out and bolt for the drug store. Before he had got half way there McGivney had seen him, and was on the run to the next corner.

Peter waited only long enough to see a couple of automobiles come whirling down the street, packed solid with husky detectives. Then he turned off and hurried down a side street. He managed to get a couple of blocks away, and then his nerves gave way entirely, and he sat down on the curbstone and began to cry—just the way little Jennie had cried when he told her he couldn't marry her! People stopped to stare at him, and one benevolent old gentleman came up and tapped him on the shoulder and asked what was the trouble. Peter, between his tear-stained fingers, gasped: "My m-m-mother died!" And so they let him alone, and after a while he got up and hurried off again.

Section 45

P eter was now in a state of utter funk. He knew that he would have
to face McGivney, and he just couldn't do it. All he wanted was
Nell; and Nell, knowing that he would want her, had agreed to be in the
park at half past eight. She had warned him not to talk to a soul until
he had talked to her. Meantime she had gone home and renewed her
Irish roses with French rouge, and restored her energy with coffee and
cigarettes, and now she was waiting for him, smiling serenely, as fresh
as any bird or flower in the park that summer morning. She asked him
in even tones how things had gone, and when Peter began to stammer
that he didn't think he could face McGivney, she proceeded to build up
his courage once more. She let him put his arms about her, even there
in broad daylight; she whispered to him to get himself together, to be a
man, and worthy of her.

What had he to be afraid of, anyway? They hadn't a single thing on
him, and there was no possible way they could get anything. His hands
were clean all the way thru, and all he had to do was to stick it out; he
must make up his mind in advance, that no matter what happened, he
would never break down, he would never vary from the story he had
rehearsed with her. She made him go over the story again; how on the
previous evening, at the gathering in the I. W. W. headquarters, they
had talked about killing Nelse Ackerman as a means of bringing the war
to an end. And after the talk he had heard Joe Angell whisper to Jerry
Rudd that he had the makings of a bomb already; he had a suit-case
full of dynamite stored there in the closet, and he and Pat McCormick
had been planning to pull off something that very night. Peter had gone
out, but had watched outside, and had seen Angell, Henderson, Rudd
and Gus come out. Peter had noticed that Angell's pockets were stuffed,
and had assumed that they were going to do their dynamiting, so he
had phoned to McGivney from the drug-store. By this phoning he had
missed the crowd, and then he had been ashamed and afraid to tell
McGivney, and had spent the night wandering in the park. But early in
the morning he had found the note, and had understood that it must
have been slipped into his pocket, and that the conspirators wanted
him to come in on their scheme. That was all, except for three or four
sentences or fragments of sentences which Peter had overheard between
Joe Angell and Jerry Rudd. Nell made him learn these sentences by

heart, and she insisted that he must not under any circumstances try to remember or be persuaded to remember anything further.

At last Peter was adjudged ready for the ordeal, and went to Room 427 in the American House, and threw himself on the bed. He was so exhausted that once or twice he dozed; but then he would think of some new question that McGivney might ask him, and would start into wakefulness. At last he heard a key turn, and started up. There entered one of the detectives, a man named Hammett. "Hello, Gudge," said he. "The boss wants you to get arrested."

"Arrested!" exclaimed Peter. "Good Lord!" He had a sudden swift vision of himself shut up in a cell with those Reds, and forced to listen to "hard luck stories."

"Well," said Hammett, "we're arresting all the Reds, and if we skip you, they'll be suspicious. You better go somewhere right away and get caught."

Peter saw the wisdom of this, and after a little thought he chose the home of Miriam Yankovitch. She was a real Red, and didn't like him; but if he was arrested in her home, she would have to like him, and it would tend to make him "solid" with the "left wingers." He gave the address to Hammett, and added, "You better come as soon as you can, because she may kick me out of the house."

"That's all right," replied the other, with a laugh. "Tell her the police are after you, and ask her to hide you."

So Peter hurried over to the Jewish quarter of the city, and knocked on a door in the top story of a tenement house. The door was opened by a stout woman with her sleeves rolled up and her arms covered with soap-suds. Yes, Miriam was in. She was out of a job just now, said Mrs. Yankovitch. They had fired her because she talked Socialism. Miriam entered the room, giving the unexpected visitor a cold stare that said as plain as words: "Jennie Todd!"

But this changed at once when Peter told her that he had been to I. W. W. headquarters and found the police in charge. They had made a raid, and claimed to have discovered some kind of plot; fortunately Peter had seen the crowd outside, and had got away. Miriam took him into an inside room and asked him a hundred questions which he could not answer. He knew nothing, except that he had been to a meeting at headquarters the night before, and this morning he had gone there to get a book, and had seen the crowd and run.

Half an hour later came a bang on the door, and Peter dived under the bed. The door was burst open, and he heard angry voices commanding, and vehement protests from Miriam and her mother. To judge from the sounds, the men began throwing the furniture this way and that; suddenly a hand came under the bed, and Peter was grabbed by the ankle, and hauled forth to confront four policemen in uniform.

It was an awkward situation, because apparently these policemen hadn't been told that Peter was a spy; the boobs thought they were getting a real dynamiter! One grabbed each of Peter's wrists, and another kept him and Miriam covered with a revolver, while the fourth proceeded to go thru his pockets, looking for bombs. When they didn't find any, they seemed vexed, and shook him and hustled him about, and made clear they would be glad of some pretext to batter in his head. Peter was careful not to give them such a pretext; he was frightened and humble, and kept declaring that he didn't know anything, he hadn't done any harm.

"We'll see about that, young fellow!" said the officer, as he snapped the handcuffs on Peter's wrists. Then, while one of them remained on guard with the revolver, the other three proceeded to ransack the place, pulling out the bureau-drawers and kicking the contents this way and that, grabbing every scrap of writing they could find and jamming it into a couple of suit-cases. There were books with red bindings and terrifying titles, but no bombs, and no weapons more dangerous than a carving knife and Miriam's tongue. The girl stood there with her black eyes flashing lightnings, and told the police exactly what she thought of them. She didn't know what had happened in the I. W. W. headquarters, but she knew that whatever it was, it was a frame-up, and she dared them to arrest her, and almost succeeded in her fierce purpose. However, the police contented themselves with kicking over the washtub and its contents, and took their departure, leaving Mrs. Yankovitch screaming in the midst of a flood.

Section 46

They dragged Peter out thru a swarming tenement crowd, and clapped him into an automobile, and whirled him away to police headquarters, where they entered him in due form and put him in a cell. He was uneasy right away, because he had failed to arrange with Hammett how long he was to stay locked up. But barely an hour had passed before a jailer came, and took him to a private room, where he found himself confronted by McGivney and Hammett, also the Chief of Police of the city, a deputy district attorney, and last but most important of all—Guffey. It was the head detective of the Traction Trust who took Peter in charge.

"Now, Gudge," said he, "what's this job you've been putting up on us?"

It struck Peter like a blow in the face. His heart went down, his jaw dropped, he stared like an idiot. Good God!

But he remembered Nell's last solemn words: "Stick it out, Peter; stick it out!" So he cried: "What do you mean, Mr. Guffey?"

"Sit down in that chair there," said Guffey. "Now, tell us what you know about this whole business. Begin at the beginning and tell us everything—every word." So Peter began. He had been at a meeting at the I. W. W. headquarters the previous evening. There had been a long talk about the inactivity of the organization, and what could be done to oppose the draft. Peter detailed the arguments, the discussion of violence, of dynamite and killing, the mention of Nelse Ackerman and the other capitalists who were to be put out of the way. He embellished all this, and exaggerated it greatly—it being the one place where Nell had said he could do no harm by exaggerating.

Then he told how after the meeting had broken up he had noticed several of the men whispering among themselves. By pretending to be getting a book from the bookcase he had got close to Joe Angell and Jerry Rudd; he had heard various words and fragments of sentences, "dynamite," "suit-case in the cupboard," "Nelse," and so on. And when the crowd went out he noticed that Angell's pockets were bulging, and assumed that he had the bombs, and that they were going to do the job. He rushed to the drug-store and phoned McGivney. It took a long time to get McGivney, and when he had given his message and run out again, the crowd was out of sight. Peter was in despair, he was ashamed to confront McGivney, he wandered about the streets for hours looking for the crowd. He spent the rest of the night in the park. But then in the morning he discovered the piece of paper in his pocket, and understood that somebody had slipped it to him, intending to invite him to the conspiracy; so he had notified McGivney, and that was all he knew.

McGivney began to cross-question him. He had heard Joe Angell talking to Jerry Rudd; had he heard him talking to anybody else? Had he heard any of the others talking? Just what had he heard Joe Angell say? Peter must repeat every word all over. This time, as instructed by Nell, he remembered one sentence more, and repeated this sentence: "Mac put it in the 'sab-cat.'" He saw the others exchange glances. "That's just what I heard," said Peter—"just those words. I couldn't figure out what they meant?"

"Sab-cat?" said the Chief of Police, a burly figure with a brown moustache and a quid of tobacco tucked in the corner of his mouth. "That means 'sabotage,' don't it?"

"Yes," said the rat-faced man.

"Do you know anything in the office that has to do with sabotage?" demanded Guffey of Peter.

And Peter thought. "No, I don't," he said.

They talked among themselves for a minute or two. The Chief said they had got all McCormick's things out of his room, and might find some clue to the mystery in these. Guffey went to the telephone, and gave a number with which Peter was familiar—that of I. W. W. headquarters. "That you, Al?" he said. "We're trying to find if there's something in those rooms that has to do with sabotage. Have you found anything— any apparatus or pictures, or writing—anything?" Evidently the answer was in the negative, for Guffey said: "Go ahead, look farther; if you get anything, call me at the chief's office quick. It may give us a lead."

Then Guffey hung up the receiver and turned to Peter. "Now Gudge," he said, "that's all your story, is it; that's all you got to tell us?"

"Yes, sir."

"Well then, you might as well quit your fooling right away. We understand that you framed this thing up, and we're not going to be taken in."

Peter stared at Guffey, speechless; and Guffey, for his part, took a couple of steps toward Peter, his brows gathering into a terrible frown, and his fists clenched. In a wave of sickening horror Peter remembered the scenes after the Preparedness Day explosion. Were they going to put him thru that again?

"We'll have a show-down, Gudge, right here," the head detective continued. "You tell us all this stuff about Angell—his talk with Jerry Rudd, and his pockets stuffed with bombs and all the rest of it—and he denies every word of it."

"But, m-m-my God! Mr. Guffey," gasped Peter. "Of *course* he'll deny it!" Peter could hardly believe his ears—that they were taking seriously the denial of a dynamiter, and quoting it to him!

"Yes, Gudge," responded Guffey, "but you might as well know the truth now as later—Angell is one of our men; we've had him planted on these 'wobblies' for the last year."

The bottom fell out of Peter's world; Peter went tumbling heels over head—down, down into infinite abysses of horror and despair. Joe Angell was a secret agent like himself! The Blue-eyed Angell, who talked dynamite and assassination at a hundred radical gatherings, who shocked the boldest revolutionists by his reckless language—Angell a spy, and Peter had proceeded to plant a "frame-up" on him!

Section 47

It was all up with Peter. He would go back into the hole! He would be tortured for the balance of his days! In his ears rang the shrieks of ten thousand lost souls and the clang of ten thousand trumpets of doom; and yet, in the midst of all the noise and confusion, Peter managed somehow to hear the voice of Nell, whispering over and over again: "Stick it out, Peter; stick it out!"

He flung out his hands and started toward his accuser. "Mr. Guffey, as God is my witness, I don't know a thing about it but what I've told you. That's what happened, and if Joe Angell tells you anything different he's lying."

"But why should he lie?"

"I don't know why; I don't know anything about it!"

Here was where Peter reaped the advantage of his lifelong training as an intriguer. In the midst of all his fright and his despair, Peter's subconscious mind was working, thinking of schemes. "Maybe Angell was framing something up on you! Maybe he was fixing some plan of his own, and I come along and spoiled it; I sprung it too soon. But I tell you it's straight goods I've given you." And Peter's very anguish gave him the vehemence to check Guffey's certainty. As he rushed on, Peter could read in the eyes of the detective that he wasn't really as sure as he talked.

"Did you see that suit-case?" he demanded.

"No, I didn't see no suit-case!" answered Peter. "I don't even know if there was a suit-case. I only know I heard Joe Angell say 'suit-case,' and I heard him say 'dynamite.'"

"Did you see anybody writing anything in the place?"

"No, I didn't," said Peter. "But I seen Henderson sitting at the table working at some papers he had in his pocket, and I seen him tear something up and throw it into the trash-basket." Peter saw the others look at one another, and he knew that he was beginning to make headway.

A moment later came a diversion that helped to save him. The telephone rang, and the Chief of Police answered and nodded to Guffey, who came and took the receiver. "A book?" he cried, with excitement in his tone. "What sort of a plan? Well, tell one of your men to take the car and bring that book and the plan here to the chief's office as quick as he can move; don't lose a moment, everything may depend on it."

And then Guffey turned to the others. "He says they found a book on sabotage in the book-case, and in it there's some kind of a drawing of a house. The book has McCormick's name in it."

There were many exclamations over this, and Peter had time to think before the company turned upon him again. The Chief of Police now questioned him, and then the deputy of the district attorney questioned him; still he stuck to his story. "My God!" he cried. "Would you think I'd be mad enough to frame up a job like this? Where'd I get all that stuff? Where'd I get that dynamite?"—Peter almost bit off his tongue as he realized the dreadful slip he had made. No one had ever told him that the suit-case actually contained dynamite! How had he known there was dynamite in it? He was desperately trying to think of some way he could have heard; but, as it happened, no one of the five men caught him up. They all knew that there was dynamite in the suit-case; they knew it with overwhelming and tremendous certainty, and they overlooked entirely the fact that Peter wasn't supposed to know it. So close to the edge of ruin can a man come and yet escape!

Peter made haste to get away from that danger-spot. "Does Joe Angell deny that he was whispering to Jerry Rudd?"

"He doesn't remember that," said Guffey. "He may have talked with him apart, but nothing special, there wasn't any conspiracy."

"Does he deny that he talked about dynamite?"

"They may have talked about it in the general discussion, but he didn't whisper anything."

"But I heard him!" cried Peter, whose quick wits had thought up a way of escape, "I know what I heard! It was just before they were leaving, and somebody had turned out some of the lights. He was standing with his back to me, and I went over to the book-case right behind him."

Here the deputy district attorney put in. He was a young man, a trifle easier to fool than the others. "Are you sure it was Joe Angell?" he demanded.

"My God! Of course it was!" said Peter. "I couldn't have been mistaken." But he let his voice die away, and a note of bewilderment be heard in it.

"You say he was whispering?"

"Yes, he was whispering."

"But mightn't it have been somebody else?"

"Why, I don't know what to say," said Peter. "I thought for sure it was Joe Angell; but I had my back turned, I'd been talking to Grady, the secretary, and then I turned around and moved over to the book-case."

"How many men were there in the room?"

"About twenty, I guess."

"Were the lights turned off before you turned around, or after?"

"I don't remember that; it might have been after." And suddenly poor bewildered Peter cried: "It makes me feel like a fool. Of course I ought to have talked to the fellow, and made sure it was Joe Angell before I turned away again; but I thought sure it was him. The idea it could be anybody else never crossed my mind."

"But you're sure it was Jerry Rudd that was talking to him?"

"Yes, it was Jerry Rudd, because his face was toward me."

"Was it Rudd or was it the other fellow that made the reply about the 'sab-cat'?" And then Peter was bewildered and tied himself up, and led them into a long process of cross-questioning; and in the middle of it came the detective, bringing the book on sabotage with McCormick's name written in the fly-leaf, and with the ground plan of a house between the pages.

They all crowded around to look at the plan, and the idea occurred to several of them at once: Could it be Nelse Ackerman's house? The Chief of Police turned to his phone, and called up the great banker's secretary. Would he please describe Mr. Ackerman's house; and the chief listened to the description. "There's a cross mark on this plan—the north side of the house, a little to the west of the center. What could that be?" Then, "My God!" And then, "Will you come down here to my office right away and bring the architect's plan of the house so we can compare them?" The Chief turned to the others, and said, "That cross mark in the house is the sleeping porch on the second floor where Mr. Ackerman sleeps!"

So then they forgot for a while their doubts about Peter. It was fascinating, this work of tracing out the details of the conspiracy, and fitting them together like a picture puzzle. It seemed quite certain to all of them that this insignificant and scared little man whom they had been examining could never have prepared so ingenious and intricate a design. No, it must really be that some master mind, some devilish intriguer was at work to spread red ruin in American City!

They dismissed Peter for the present, sending him back to his cell. He stayed there for two days with no one to advise him, and no hint as to his fate. They did not allow newspapers in the jail, but they had left Peter his money, and so on the second day he succeeded in bribing one of his keepers and obtaining a copy of the American City "Times," with all the details of the amazing sensation spread out on the front page.

For thirty years the "Times" had been standing for law and order against all the forces of red riot and revolution; for thirty years the "Times" had been declaring that labor leaders and walking delegates and Socialists and Anarchists were all one and the same thing, and all placed their reliance fundamentally upon one instrument, the dynamite bomb. Here at last the "Times" was vindicated, this was the "Times" great day! They had made the most of it, not merely on the front page, but on two other pages, with pictures of all the conspicuous conspirators, including Peter, and pictures of the I. W. W. headquarters, and the suit-case, and the sticks of dynamite and the fuses and the clock; also of the "studio" in which the Reds had been trapped, and of Nikitin, the Russian anarchist who owned this den. Also there were columns of speculation about the case, signed statements and interviews with leading clergymen and bankers, the president of the Chamber of Commerce and the secretary of the Real Estate Exchange. Also there was a two-column, double-leaded editorial, pointing out how the "Times" had been saying this for thirty years, and not failing to connect up the case with the Goober case, and the Lackman case, and the case of three pacifist clergymen who had been arrested several days before for attempting to read the Sermon on the Mount at a public meeting.

And Peter knew that he, Peter Gudge, had done all this! The forces of law and order owed it all to one obscure little secret service agent! Peter would get no credit, of course; the Chief of Police and the district attorney were issuing solemn statements, taking the honors to themselves, and with never one hint that they owed anything to the secret service department of the Traction Trust. That was necessary, of course; for the sake of appearances it had to be pretended that the public authorities were doing the work, exercising their legal functions in due and regular form. It would never do to have the mob suspect that these activities were being financed and directed by the big business interests of the city. But all the same, it made Peter sore! He and McGivney and the rest of Guffey's men had a contempt for the public officials, whom they regarded as "pikers"; the officials had very little money to spend, and very little power. If you really wanted to get anything done in America, you didn't go to any public official, you went to the big men of affairs, the ones who had the "stuff," and were used to doing things quickly and efficiently. It was the same in this business of spying as in everything else.

Now and then Peter would realize how close he had come to ghastly ruin. He would have qualms of terror, picturing himself shut up in the hole, and Guffey proceeding to torture the truth out of him. But he was able to calm these fears. He was sure this dynamite conspiracy would prove too big a temptation for the authorities; it would sweep them away in spite of themselves. They would have to go thru with it, they would have to stand by Peter.

And sure enough, on the evening of the second day a jailer came and said: "You're to be let out." And Peter was ushered thru the barred doors and turned loose without another word.

Section 49

Peter went to Room 427 of the American House and there was McGivney waiting for him. McGivney said nothing about any suspicion of Peter, nor did Peter say anything—he understood that by-gones were to be by-gones. The authorities were going to take this gift which the fates had handed to them on a silver platter. For years they had been wanting to get these Reds, and now magically and incredibly, they had got them!

"Now, Gudge," said McGivney, "here's your story. You've been arrested on suspicion, you've been cross-questioned and put thru the third degree, but you succeeded in satisfying the police that you didn't know anything about it, and they've released you. We've released a couple of others at the same time, so's to cover you all right; and now you're to go back and find out all you can about the Reds, and what they're doing, and what they're planning. They're shouting, of course, that this is a 'frame-up.' You must find out what they know. You must be careful, of course—watch every step you take, because they'll be suspicious for a while. We've been to your room and turned things upside down a bit, so that will help to make it look all right."

Peter sallied forth; but he did not go to see the Reds immediately. He spent an hour dodging about the city to make sure no one was shadowing him; then he called up Nell at a telephone number she had given him, and an hour later they met in the park, and she flew to his arms and kissed him with rapturous delight. He had to tell her everything, of course; and when she learned that Joe Angell was a secret agent, she first stared at him in horror, and then she laughed until she almost cried. When Peter told how he had met that situation and got away with it, for the first time he was sure that he had won her love.

"Now, Peter," she said, when they were calm again, we've got to get action at once. The papers are full of it, and old Nelse Ackerman must be scared out of his life. Here's a letter I'm going to mail tonight—you notice I've used a different typewriter from the one I used last time. I went into a typewriter store, and paid them to let me use one for a few minutes, so they can never trace this letter to me.

The letter was addressed to Nelson Ackerman at his home, and marked "Personal." Peter read:

"This is a message from a friend. The Reds had an agent in your home. They drew a plan of your house. The police are hiding things from you, because they can't get the truth, and don't want you to know they are incompetent. There is a man who discovered all this plot, and you should see him. They won't let you see him if they can help it. You should demand to see him. But do not mention this letter. If you do not get to the right man, I will write you again. If you keep this a secret, you may trust me to help you to the end. If you tell anybody, I will be unable to help you."

"Now," said Nell, "when he gets that letter he'll get busy, and you've got to know what to do, because of course everything depends on that." So Nell proceeded to drill Peter for his meeting with the King of American City. Peter now stood in such awe of her judgment that he learned his lessons quite patiently, and promised solemnly that he would do exactly what she said and nothing else. He reaped his reward of kisses, and went home to sleep the sleep of the just.

Next morning Peter set out to do some of his work for McGivney, so that McGivney would have no ground for complaint. He went to see Miriam Yankovich, and this time Miriam caught him by his two hands and wrung them, and Peter knew that he had atoned for his crime against little Jennie. Peter was a martyr once more. He told how he had been put thru the third degree; and she told how the water from the washtub had leaked thru the ceiling, and the plaster had fallen, and ruined the dinner of a poor workingman's family.

Also, she told him all about the frame-up as the Reds saw it. Andrews, the lawyer, was demanding the right to see the prisoners, but this was refused, and they were all being held without bail. On the previous evening Miriam had attended a gathering at Andrews' home, at which the case was talked out. All the I. W. W.'s declared that the thing was the rankest kind of frame-up; the notes were obviously fake, and the dynamite had undoubtedly been planted by the police. They had used it as a pretext to shut up the I. W. W. headquarters, and to arrest a score of radicals. Worst of all, of course, was the propaganda; the hideous stories with which they were filling the papers. Had Peter seen this morning's "Times?" A perfectly unmistakable incitement to mobs to gather and lynch the Reds!

Section 50

From Miriam's, Peter went back to Room 427. It was Nell's idea that Nelse Ackerman would not lose a minute next morning; and sure enough, Peter found a note on the dressing-table: "Wait for me, I want to see you."

Peter waited, and before long McGivney came in and sat down in front of him, and began very solemnly: "Now Peter Gudge, you know I'm your friend."

"Yes, of course."

"I've stood by you," said McGivney. "If it hadn't been for me, the boss would have had you in the hole right now, trying to sweat you into confessing you planted that dynamite. I want you to know that, and I want you to know that I'm going to stand by you, and I expect you to stand by me and give me a square deal."

"Why, sure!" said Peter. "What is it?" Then McGivney proceeded to explain: Old Nelse Ackerman had got the idea that the police were holding back something from him. He was scared out of his wits about this case, of course. He had himself shut up in a cupboard at night, and made his wife pull down the curtains of her limousine when she went driving. And now he was insisting that he must have a talk with the man who had discovered this plot against him. McGivney hated to take the risk of having Peter become acquainted with anybody, but Nelse Ackerman was a man whose word was law. Really, he was Peter's employer; he had put up a lot of the money for the secret service work which Guffey was conducting, and neither Guffey or any of the city authorities dared try to fool him.

"Well, that's all right," said Peter; "it won't hurt for me to see him."

"He's going to question you about this case," said McGivney. "He's going to try to find out everything he can. So you got to protect us; you got to make him understand that we've done everything possible. You got to put us right with him."

Peter promised solemnly he would do so; but McGivney wasn't satisfied. He was in a state of trepidation, and proceeded to hammer and hammer at Peter, impressing upon him the importance of solidarity, of keeping faith with his fellows. It sounded exactly like some of the I. W. W.'s talking among themselves!

"You may think, here's a chance to jump on us and climb out on top, but don't you forget it, Peter Gudge, we've got a machine, and in the long run it's the machine that wins. We've broken many a fellow that's tried to play tricks on us, and we'll break you. Old Nelse will get what he wants out of you; he'll offer you a big price, no doubt—but before long he'll be thru with you, and then you'll come back to us, and I give you fair warning, by God, if you play us dirty, Guffey will have you in the hole in a month or two, and you'll come out on a stretcher."

So Peter pledged his faith again; but, seeing his chance, he added: "Don't you think Mr. Guffey ought to do something for me, because of that plot I discovered?"

"Yes, I think that," said McGivney; "that's only fair."

And so they proceeded to bargain. Peter pointed out all the dangers he had run, and all the credit which the others had got. Guffey hadn't got credit in the papers, but he had got it with his employers, all right, and he would get still more if Peter stood by him with the king of American City. Peter said it ought to be worth a thousand dollars, and he said he ought to have it right away, before he went to see the king. At which Guffey scowled ferociously. "Look here, Gudge! you got the nerve to charge us such a price for standing by your frame-up?"

McGivney generally treated Peter as a coward and a feeble bluffer; but he had learned also that there was one time when the little man completely changed his nature, and that was when it was a question of getting hold of some cash. That was the question now; and Peter met McGivney scowl for scowl. "If you don't like my frame-up," he snarled, "you go kick to the newspapers about it!"

Peter was the bulldog again, and had got his teeth in the other bulldog's nose, and he hung right there. He had seen the rat-faced man pull money out of his clothes before this, and he knew that this time, above all other times, McGivney would come prepared. So he insisted—a thousand or nothing; and as before, his heart went down into his boots when McGivney produced his wad, and revealed that there was more in the wad than Peter had demanded!

However, Peter consoled himself with the reflection that a thousand dollars was a tidy sum of money, and he set out for the home of Nelse Ackerman in a jovial frame of mind. Incidentally he decided that it might be the part of wisdom not to say anything to Nell about this extra thousand. When women found out that you had money, they'd never rest till they had got every cent of it, or at least had made you spend it on them!

Section 51

Nelse Ackerman's home was far out in the suburbs of the city, upon a knoll surrounded by forest. It was a couple of miles from the nearest trolley line, which forced Peter to take a hot walk in the sun. Apparently the great banker, in selecting the site of his residence, had never once thought that anybody might want to get to it without an automobile. Peter reflected as he walked that if he continued to move in these higher circles, he too would have to join the motor-driving class.

About the estate there ran a great bronze fence, ten feet high, with sharp, inhospitable spikes pointing outwards. Peter had read about this fence a long time ago in the American City "Times"; it was so and so many thousand yards long, and had so and so many spikes, and had cost so and so many tens of thousands of dollars. There were big bronze gates locked tight, and a sign that said: "Beware the dogs!" Inside the gates were three guards carrying rifles and walking up and down; they were a consequence of the recent dynamite conspiracy, but Peter did not realize this, he took them for a regular institution, and a symbol of the importance of the man he was to visit.

He pressed a button by the side of the gate, and a lodgekeeper came out, and Peter, according to orders, gave the name "Arthur G. McGillicuddy." The lodge-keeper went inside and telephoned, and then came back and opened the gate, just enough to admit Peter. "You're to be searched," said the lodge-keeper; and Peter, who had been arrested many times, took no offense at this procedure, but found it one more evidence of the importance of Nelse Ackerman. The guards went thru his pockets, and felt him all over, and then one of them marched him up the long gravel avenue thru the forest, climbed a flight of marble steps to the palace on the knoll, and turned him over to a Chinese butler who walked on padded slippers.

If Peter had not known that this was a private home he would have thought it was an art gallery. There were great marble columns, and paintings bigger than Peter, and tapestries with life-size horses; there were men in armor, and battle axes and Japanese dancing devils, and many other strange sights. Ordinarily Peter would have been interested in learning how a great millionaire decorated his house, and would have drunk deep of the joy of being amid such luxury. But now all his thoughts were taken up with his dangerous business. Nell had told him what to look for, and he looked. Mounting the velvet-carpeted staircase, he noted a curtain behind which a man might hide, and a painting of a Spanish cavalier on the wall just opposite. He would make use of these two sights.

They went down a hall, like a corridor in the Hotel de Soto, and at the end of it the butler tapped softly upon a door, and Peter was ushered into a big apartment in semi-darkness. The butler retired without a sound, closing the door behind him and Peter stood hesitating, looking about to get his bearings. From the other side of the room he heard three faint coughs, suggesting a sick man. There was a four-poster bed of some dark wood, with a canopy over it and draperies at the side, and a man in the bed, sitting propped up with pillows. There were more coughs, and then a faint whisper, "This way." So Peter crossed over and stood about ten feet from the bed, holding his hat in his hands; he was not able to see very much of the occupant of the bed, nor was he sure it would be respectful for him to try to see.

"So you're—(cough) what's your name?"

"Gudge," said Peter.

"You are the man—(cough) that knows about the Reds?"

"Yes, sir."

The occupant of the bed coughed every two or three minutes thru the conversation that followed, and each time Peter noticed that he put his hand up to his mouth as if he were ashamed of the noise. Gradually Peter got used to the twilight, and could see that Nelse Ackerman was an old man with puffy, droopy cheeks and chin, and dark puffy crescents under his eyes. He was quite bald, and had on his head a skull cap of embroidered black silk, and a short, embroidered jacket over his night shirt. Beside the bed stood a table covered with glasses and bottles and pill-boxes, and also a telephone. Every few minutes this telephone would ring, and Peter would wait patiently while Mr. Ackerman settled some complex problem of business. "I've told them my terms," he would say with irritation, and then he would cough; and Peter, who was sharply watching every detail of the conduct of the rich, noted that he was too polite even to cough into the telephone. "If they will pay a hundred and twenty-five thousand dollars on account, I will wait, but not a cent less," Nelse Ackerman would say. And Peter, awe-stricken, realized that he had now reached the very top of Mount Olympus, he was at the highest point he could hope to reach until he went to heaven.

The old man fixed his dark eyes on his visitor. "Who wrote me that letter?" whispered the husky voice.

Peter had been expecting this. "What letter, sir?"

"A letter telling me to see you."

"I don't know anything about it, sir."

"You mean—(cough) you didn't write me an anonynious letter?"

"No, sir, I didn't."

"Then some friend of yours must have written it."

"I dunno that. It might have been some enemy of the police."

"Well, now, what's this about the Reds having an agent in my home?"

"Did the letter say that?"

"It did."

"Well, sir, that's putting it too strong. I ain't sure, it's just an idea I've had. It'll need a lot of explaining."

"You're the man who discovered this plot, I understand?"

"Yes, sir."

"Well, take a chair, there," said the banker. There was a chair near the bedside, but it seemed to Peter too close to be respectful, so he pulled it a little farther away, and sat down on the front six inches of it, still holding his hat in his hands and twisting it nervously. "Put down that hat," said the old man, irritably. So Peter stuck the hat under his chair, and said: "I beg pardon, sir."

Section 52

The old plutocrat was feeble and sick, but his mind was all there, and his eyes seemed to be boring Peter through. Peter realized that he would have to be very careful—the least little slip would be fatal here.

"Now, Gudge," the old man began, "I want you to tell me all about it. To begin with, how did you come to be among these Reds? Begin at the beginning."

So Peter told how he had happened to get interested in the radical movement, laying particular stress upon the dangerousness of these Reds, and his own loyalty to the class which stood for order and progress and culture in the country. "It ought to be stopped, Mr. Ackerman!" he exclaimed, with a fine show of feeling; and the old banker nodded. Yes, yes, it ought to be stopped!

"Well," said Peter, "I said to myself, 'I'm going to find out about them fellows.' I went to their meetings, and little by little I pretended to get converted, and I tell you, Mr. Ackerman, our police are asleep; they don't know what these agitators are doing, what they're preaching. They don't know what a hold they've got on the mobs of the discontented!"

Peter went on to tell in detail about the propaganda of social revolution, and about conspiracies against law and order, and the property and even the lives of the rich. Peter noticed that when the old man took a sip of water his hand trembled so that he could hardly keep the water from spilling; and presently, when the phone rang again, his voice became shrill and imperious. "I understand they're applying for bail for those men. Now Angus, that's an outrage! We'll not hear to anything like that! I want you to see the judge at once, and make absolutely certain that those men are held in jail."

Then again the old banker had a coughing fit. "Now, Gudge," he said, "I know more or less about all that. What I want to know is about this conspiracy against me. Tell me how you came to find out about it."

And Peter told; but of course he embellished it, in so far as it related to Mr. Ackerman—these fellows were talking about Mr. Ackerman all the time, they had a special grudge against him.

"But why?" cried the old man. "Why?"

"They think you're fighting them, Mr. Ackerman."

"But I'm not! That's not true!"

"Well, they say you put up money to hang Goober. They call you—you'll excuse me?"

"Yes, yes, of course."

"They call you the 'head money devil.' They call you the financial king of American City."

"King!" cried the banker. "What rubbish! Why, Gudge, that's fool newspaper talk! I'm a poor man today. There are two dozen men in this city richer than I am, and who have more power. Why—" But the old man fell to coughing and became so exhausted that he sank back into his pillows until he recovered his breath. Peter waited respectfully; but of course he wasn't fooled. Peter had carried on bargaining many times in his life, and had heard people proclaim their poverty and impotence.

"Now, Gudge," the old man resumed. "I don't want to be killed; I tell you I don't want to be killed."

"No, of course not," said Peter. It was perfectly comprehensible to him that Mr. Ackerman didn't want to be killed. But Mr. Ackerman seemed to think it necessary to impress the idea upon him; in the course of the conversation he came back to it a number of times, and each time he said it with the same solemn assurance, as if it were a brand new idea, and a very unusual and startling idea. "I don't want to be killed, Gudge; I tell you I don't want to let those fellows get me. No, no; we've got to circumvent them, we've got to take precautions—every precaution—I tell you every possible precaution."

"I'm here for that purpose, Mr. Ackerman," said Peter, solemnly. "I'll do everything. We'll do everything, I'm sure."

"What's this about the police?" demanded the banker. "What's this about Guffey's bureau? You say they're not competent?"

"Well now, I'll tell you, Mr. Ackerman," said Peter, "It's a little embarrassing. You see, they employ me—"

"Nonsense!" exclaimed the other. "*I* employ you! I'm putting up the money for this work, and I want the facts!—I want them all."

"Well," said Peter, "they've been very decent to me—"

"I say tell me everything!" exclaimed the old man. He was a most irritable old man, and couldn't stand for a minute not having what he asked for. "What's the matter with them?"

Peter answered, as humbly as he could: "I could tell you a great deal that'd be of use to you, Mr. Ackerman, but you got to keep it between you and me."

"All right!" said the other, quickly. "What is it?"

"If you give a hint of it to anybody else," persisted Peter, "then I'll get fired."

"You'll not get fired, I'll see to that. If necessary I'll hire you direct."

"Ah, but you don't understand, Mr. Ackerman. It's a machine, and you can't run against it; you gotta understand it, you gotta handle it right. I'd like to help you, and I know I can help you, but you gotta let me explain it, and you gotta understand some things."

"All right," said the old man. "Go ahead, what is it?"

"Now," said Peter, "it's like this. These police and all these fellows mean well, but they don't understand; it's too complicated, they ain't been in this movement long enough. They're used to dealing with criminals; but these Reds, you see, are cranks. Criminals ain't organized, at least they don't stand together; but these Reds do, and if you fight 'em, they fight back, and they make what they call 'propaganda.' And that propaganda is dangerous—if you make a wrong move, you may find you've made 'em stronger than they were before."

"Yes, I see that," said the old man. "Well?"

"Then again, the police dunno how dangerous they are. You try to tell them things, they won't really believe you. I've known for a long time there was a group of these people getting together to kill off all the rich men, the big men all over the country. They've been spying on these rich men, getting ready to kill them. They know a lot about them that you can't explain their knowing. That's how I got the idea they had somebody in your house, Mr. Ackerman."

"Tell me what you mean. Tell me at once."

"Well, sir, every once in a while I pick up scraps of conversation. One day I heard Mac—"

"Mac?"

"That's McCormick, the one who's in jail. He's an I. W. W. leader, and I think the most dangerous of all. I heard him whispering to another fellow, and it scared me, because it had to do with killing a rich man. He'd been watching this rich man, and said he was going to shoot him down right in his own house! I didn't hear the name of the man—I walked away, because I didn't want him to think I was trying to listen in. They're awful suspicious, these fellows; if you watch Mac you see him looking around over his shoulder every minute or two. So I strolled off, and then I strolled back again, and he was laughing about something, and I heard him say these words; I heard him say, 'I was hiding behind the curtain, and there was a Spanish fellow painted on the wall, and every time I peeked out that bugger was looking at me, and I wondered if he wasn't going to give me away.'"

And Peter stopped. His eyes had got used to the twilight now, and he could see the old banker's eyes starting out from the crescents of dark, puffy flesh underneath. "My God!" whispered Nelse Ackerman.

"Now, that was all I heard," said Peter. "And I didn't know what it meant. But when I learned about that drawing that Mac had made of your house, I thought to myself, Jesus, I bet that was Mr. Ackerman he was waiting to shoot!"

"Good God! Good God!" whispered the old man; and his trembling fingers pulled at the embroidery on the coverlet. The telephone rang, and he took up the receiver, and told somebody he was too busy now to talk; they would have to call him later. He had another coughing spell, so that Peter thought he was going to choke, and had to help him get some medicine down his throat. Peter was a little bit shocked to see such obvious and abject fear in one of the gods. After all, they were just men, these Olympians, as much subject to pain and death as Peter Gudge himself!

Also Peter was surprised to find how "easy" Mr. Ackerman was. He made no lofty pretence of being indifferent to the Reds. He put himself at Peter's mercy, to be milked at Peter's convenience. And Peter would make the most of this opportunity.

"Now, Mr. Ackerman," he began, "You can see it wouldn't be any use to tell things like that to the police. They dunno how to handle such a situation; the honest truth is, they don't take these Reds serious. They'll spend ten times as much money to catch a plain burglar as they will to watch a whole gang like this."

"How can they have got into my home?" cried the old man.

"They get in by ways you'd never dream of, Mr. Ackerman. They have people who agree with them. Why, you got no idea, there's some preachers that are Reds, and some college teachers, and some rich men like yourself."

"I know, I know," said Ackerman. "But surely—"

"How can you tell? You may have a traitor right in your own family."

So Peter went on, spreading the Red Terror in the soul of this old millionaire who did not want to be killed. He said again that he did not want to be killed, and explained his reluctance in some detail. So many people were dependent upon him for their livings, Peter could have no conception of it! There were probably a hundred thousand men with their families right here in American City, whose jobs depended upon plans which Ackerman was carrying, and which nobody but Ackerman could possibly carry. Widows and orphans looked to him for protection of their funds; a vast net-work of responsibilities required his daily, even his hourly decisions. And sure enough, the telephone rang, and Peter heard Nelse Ackerman declare that the Amalgamated Securities Company would have to put off a decision about its dividends until tomorrow, because he was too busy to sign certain papers just then. He hung up the receiver and said: "You see, you see! I tell you, Gudge, we must not let them get me!"

They came down to the question of practical plans, and Peter was ready with suggestions. In the first place, Mr. Ackerman must give no hint either to the police authorities or to Guffey that he was dissatisfied with their efforts. He must simply provide for an interview with Peter now and then, and he and Peter, quite privately, must take certain steps to get Mr. Ackerman that protection which his importance to the community made necessary. The first thing was to find out whether or not there was a traitor in Mr. Ackerman's home, and for that purpose there must be a spy, a first-class detective working in some capacity or other. The only trouble was, there were so few detectives you could trust; they were nearly all scoundrels, and if they weren't scoundrels, it was because they didn't have sense enough to be—they were boobs, and any Red could see thru them in five minutes.

"But I tell you," said Peter, "what I've thought. I've got a wife that's a wonder, and just now while we were talking about it, I thought, if I could only get Edythe in here for a few days, I'd find out everything about all the people in your home, your relatives as well as your servants."

"Is she a professional detective?" asked the banker.

"Why no, sir," said Peter. "She was an actress, her name was Edythe Eustace; perhaps you might have heard of her on the stage."

"No, I'm too busy for the theatre," said Mr. Ackerman.

"Of course," said Peter. "Well, I dunno whether she'd be willing to do it; she don't like having me mix up with these Reds, and she's been begging me to quit for a long time, and I'd just about promised her I would. But if I tell her about your trouble maybe she might, just as a favor."

But how could Peter's wife be introduced into the Ackerman household without attracting suspicion? Peter raised this question, pointing out that his wife was a person of too high a social class to come as a servant. Mr. Ackerman added that he had nothing to do with engaging his servants, any more than with engaging the bookkeepers in his bank. It would look suspicious for him to make a suggestion to his housekeeper. But finally he remarked that he had a niece who sometimes came to visit him, and would come at once if requested, and would bring Edythe Eustace as her maid. Peter was sure that Edythe would be able to learn this part quickly, she had acted it many times on the stage, in fact, it had been her favorite role. Mr. Ackerman promised to get word to his niece, and have her meet Edythe at the Hotel de Soto that same afternoon.

Then the old banker pledged his word most solemnly that he would not whisper a hint about this matter except to his niece. Peter was most urgent and emphatic; he specified that the police were not to be told, that no member of the household was to be told, not even Mr. Ackerman's private secretary. After Mr. Ackerman had had this duly impressed upon him, he proceeded in turn to impress upon Peter the idea which he considered of most importance in the world: "I don't want to be killed, Gudge, I tell you I don't want to be killed!" And Peter solemnly promised to make it his business to listen to all conversations of the Reds in so far as they might bear upon Mr. Ackerman.

When he rose to take his departure, Mr. Ackerman slipped his trembling fingers into the pocket of his jacket, and pulled out a crisp and shiny note. He unfolded it, and Peter saw that it was a five hundred dollar bill, fresh from the First National Bank of American City, of which Mr. Ackerman was chairman of the board of directors. "Here's a little present for you, Gudge," he said. "I want you to understand that if you protect me from these villains, I'll see that you are well taken care of. From now on I want you to be my man."

"Yes, sir," said Peter, "I'll be it, sir. I thank you very much, sir." And he thrust the bill into his pocket, and bowed himself step by step backwards toward the door. "You're forgetting your hat," said the banker.

"Why, yes," said the trembling Peter, and he came forward again, and got his hat from under the chair, and bowed himself backward again.

"And remember, Gudge," said the old man, "I don't want to be killed! I don't want them to get me!"

Section 54

Peter's first care when he got back into the city was to go to Mr. Ackerman's bank and change that five hundred dollar bill. The cashier gazed at him sternly, and scrutinized the bill carefully, but he gave Peter five one hundred dollar bills without comment. Peter tucked three of them away in a safe hiding-place, and put the other two in his pocketbook, and went to keep his appointment with Nell.

He told her all that had happened, and where she was to meet Mr. Ackerman's niece. "What did he give you?" Nell demanded, at once, and when Peter produced the two bills, she exclaimed, "My God! the old skint-flint!" "He said there'd be more," remarked Peter.

"It didn't cost him anything to say that," was Nell's answer. "We'll have to put the screws on him." Then she added, "You'd better let me take care of this money for you, Peter."

"Well," said Peter, "I have to have some for my own expenses, you know."

"You've got your salary, haven't you?"

"Yes, that's true, but—"

"I can keep it safe for you," said Nell, "and some day when you need it you'll be glad to have it. You've never saved anything yourself; that's a woman's job."

Peter tried to haggle with her, but it wasn't the same as haggling with McGivney; she looked at him with her melting glances, and it made Peter's head swim, and automatically he put out his hand and let her take the two bills. Then she smiled, so tenderly that he made bold to remind her, "You know, Nell, you're my wife now!"

"Yes, yes," she answered, "of course. But we've got to get rid of Ted Crothers somehow. He watches me all the time, and I have no end of trouble making excuses and getting away."

"How're you're going to get rid of him?" asked Peter, hungrily.

"We'll have to skip," she answered; "just as soon as we have pulled off our new frame-up—"

"Another one?" gasped Peter, in dismay.

And the girl laughed. "You wait!" she said. "I'm going to pull some real money out of Nelse Ackerman this time! Then when we've made our killing, we'll skip, and be fixed for life. You wait—and don't talk love to me now, because my mind is all taken up with my plans, and I can't think about anything else."

So they parted, and Peter went to see McGivney in the American House. "Stand up to him!" Nell had said. But it was not easy to do, for McGivney pulled and hauled him and turned him about, upside down and inside outwards, to know every single thing that had happened between him and Nelse Ackerman. Lord, how these fellows did hang on to their sources of graft! Peter repeated and insisted that he really had played entirely fair—he hadn't told Nelse Ackerman a thing except just the truth as he had told it to Guffey and McGivney. He had said that the police were all right, and that Guffey's bureau was stepping right on the tail of the Reds all the time.

"And what does he want you to do?" demanded the rat-faced man.

Peter answered, "He just wanted to make sure that he was learning everything of importance, and he wanted me to promise him that he would get every scrap of information that I collected about the plot against him; and of course I promised him that we'd bring it all to him."

"You going to see him any more?" demanded McGivney.

"He didn't say anything about that."

"Did he get your address?"

"No, I suppose if he wants me he'll let you know, the same as before."

"All right," said McGivney. "Did he give you any money?"

"Yes," said Peter, "he gave me two hundred dollars, and he said there was plenty more where that came from, so that we'd work hard to help him. He said he didn't want to get killed; he said that a couple of dozen times, I guess. He spent more time saying that than anything else. He's sick, and he's scared out of his wits."

So at last McGivney condescended to thank Peter for his faithfulness, and went on to give him further orders.

The Reds were raising an awful howl. Andrews, the lawyer, had succeeded in getting a court order to see the arrested men, and of course the prisoners had all declared that the case was a put-up job. Now the Reds were preparing to send out a circular to their fellow Reds all over the country, appealing for publicity, and for funds to fight the "frame-up."

They were very secret about it, and McGivney wanted to know where they were getting their money. He wanted a copy of the circular they were printing, and to know where and when the circulars were to be mailed. Guffey had been to see the post office authorities, and they were going to confiscate the circulars and destroy them all without letting the Reds know it.

Peter rubbed his hands with glee. That was the real business! That was going after these criminals in the way Peter had been urging! The rat-faced man answered that it was nothing to what they were going to do in a few days. Let Peter keep on his job, and he would see! Now, when the public was wrought up over this dynamite conspiracy, was the time to get things done.

Section 55

Peter took a street car to the home of Miriam Yankovitch, and on the way he read the afternoon edition of the American City "Times." The editors of this paper were certainly after the Reds, and no mistake! They had taken McCormick's book on Sabotage, just as Nell had predicted, and printed whole chapters from it, with the most menacing sentences in big type, and some boxed up in little frames and scattered here and there over the page so that no one could possibly miss them. They had a picture of McCormick taken in the jail; he hadn't had a chance to shave for several days, and probably hadn't felt pleasant about having his picture taken—anyhow, he looked ferocious enough to frighten the most skeptical, and Peter was confirmed in his opinion that Mac was the most dangerous Red of them all.

Columns and columns of material this paper published about the case, subtly linking it up with all the other dynamitings and assassinations in American history, and with German spy plots and bomb plots. There was a nation-wide organization of these assassins, so the paper said; they published hundreds of papers, with millions of readers, all financed by German gold. Also, there was a double-leaded editorial calling on the citizens to arise and save the republic, and put an end to the Red menace once for all. Peter read this, and like every other good American, he believed every word that he read in his newspaper, and boiled with hatred of the Reds.

He found Miriam Yankovitch away from home. Her mother was in a state of excitement, because Miriam had got word that the police were giving the prisoners the "third degree," and she had gone to the offices of the Peoples' Council to get the radicals together and try to take some immediate action. So Peter hurried over to these offices, where he found some twenty-five Reds and Pacifists assembled, all in the same state of excitement. Miriam was walking up and down the room, clasping and unclasping her hands, and her eyes looked as if she had been crying all day. Peter remembered his suspicion that Miriam and Mac were lovers. He questioned her. They had put Mac in the "hole," and Henderson, the lumber-jack, was laid up in the hospital as a result of the ordeal he had undergone.

The Jewish girl went into details, and Peter found himself shuddering—he had such a vivid memory of the third degree himself!

He did not try to stop his shuddering, but took to pacing up and down the room like Miriam, and told them how it felt to have your wrists twisted and your fingers bent backward, and how damp and horrible it was in the "hole." So he helped to work them into a state of hysteria, hoping that they would commit some overt action, as McGivney wanted. Why not storm the jail and set free the prisoners?

Little Ada Ruth said that was nonsense; but might they not get banners, and parade up and down in front of the jail, protesting against this torturing of men who had not been convicted of any crime? The police would fall on them, of course, the crowds would mob them and probably tear them to pieces, but they must do something. Donald Gordon answered that this would only make them impotent to keep up the agitation. What they must try to get was a strike of labor. They must send telegrams to the radical press, and go out and raise money, and call a mass-meeting three days from date. Also, they must appeal to all the labor unions, and see if it was possible to work up sentiment for a general strike.

Peter, somewhat disappointed, went back and reported to McGivney this rather tame outcome. But McGivney said that was all right, he had something that would fix them; and he revealed to Peter a startling bit of news. Peter had been reading in the papers about German spies, but he had only half taken it seriously; the war was a long way off, and Peter had never seen any of that German gold that they talked so much about—in fact, the Reds were in a state of perpetual poverty, one and all of them stinting himself eternally to put up some portion of his scant earnings to pay for pamphlets and circulars and postage and defence funds, and all the expenses of an active propaganda organization. But now, McGivney declared, there was a real, sure-enough agent of the Kaiser in American City! The government had pretty nearly got him in his nets, and one of the things McGivney wanted to do before the fellow was arrested was to get him to contribute some money to the radical cause.

It wasn't necessary to point out to Peter the importance of this. If the authorities could show that the agitation on behalf of McCormick and the rest had been financed by German money, the public would justify any measures taken to bring it to an end. Could Peter suggest to McGivney the name of a German Socialist who might be persuaded to approach this agent of the Kaiser, and get him to contribute money for the purpose of having a general strike called in American City? Several of the city's big manufacturing plants were being made over for war purposes, and obviously the enemy had much to gain by strikes and labor discontent. Guffey's men had been trying for a long time to get Germans to contribute to the Goober Defense fund, but here was an even better opportunity.

Peter thought of Comrade Apfel, who was one of the extreme Socialists, and a temporary Pacifist like most Germans. Apfel worked in a bakery, and his face was as pasty as the dough he kneaded, but it would show a tinge of color when he rose in the local to denounce the "social patriots," those party members who were lending their aid to British plans for world domination. McGivney said he would send somebody to Apfel at once, and give him the name of the Kaiser's agent as one who might be induced to contribute to the radical defense fund. Apfel would, of course, have no idea that the man was a German agent; he would go to see him, and ask him for money, and McGivney and his fellow-sleuths would do the rest. Peter said that was fine, and offered to go to Apfel himself; but the rat-faced man answered no, Peter was too precious, and no chance must be taken of directing Apfel's suspicions against him.

Section 56

Peter had received a brief scrawl from Nell, telling him that it was all right, she had gone to her new job, and would soon have results. So Peter went cheerfully about his own duties of trying to hold down the protest campaign of the radicals. It was really quite terrifying, the success they were having, in spite of all the best efforts of the authorities. Bundles of circulars appeared at their gatherings as if by magic, and were carried away and distributed before the authorities could make any move. Every night at the Labor Temple, where the workers gathered, there were agitators howling their heads off about the McCormick case. To make matters worse, there was an obscure one cent evening paper in American City which catered to working-class readers, and persisted in publishing evidence tending to prove that the case was a "frame-up." The Reds had found out that their mail was being interfered with, and were raising a terrific howl about that—pretending, of course, that it was "free speech" they cared about!

The mass meeting was due for that evening, and Peter read an indignant editorial in the American City "Times," calling upon the authorities to suppress it. "Down with the Red Flag!" the editorial was headed; and Peter couldn't see how any red-blooded, 100% American could read it, and not be moved to do something.

Peter said that to McGivney, who answered: "We're going to do something; you wait!" And sure enough, that afternoon the papers carried the news that the mayor of American City had notified the owners of the Auditorium that they would be held strictly responsible under the law for all incendiary and seditious utterances at this meeting; thereupon, the owners of the Auditorium had cancelled the contract. Furthermore, the mayor declared that no crowds should be gathered on the street, and that the police would be there to see to it, and to protect law and order. Peter hurried to the rooms of the Peoples' Council, and found the radicals scurrying about, trying to find some other hall; every now and then Peter would go to the telephone, and let McGivney know what hall they were trying to get, and McGivney would communicate with Guffey, and Guffey would communicate with the secretary of the Chamber of Commerce, and the owner of this hall would be called up and warned by the president of the bank which held a mortgage on the hall, or by the chairman of the board of directors of the Philharmonic Orchestra which gave concerts there.

So there was no Red mass meeting that night—and none for many a night thereafter in American City! Guffey's office had got its German spy story ready, and next morning, here was the entire front page of the American City "Times" given up to the amazing revelation that Karl von Stroeme, agent of the German government, and reputed to be a nephew of the German Vice-chancellor, had been arrested in American City, posing as a Swedish sewing-machine agent, but in reality having been occupied in financing the planting of dynamite bombs in the buildings of the Pioneer Foundry Company, now being equipped for the manufacture of machine-guns. Three of von Stroeme's confederates had been nabbed at the same time, and a mass of papers full of important revelations—not the least important among them being the fact that only yesterday von Stroeme had been caught dealing with a German Socialist of the ultra-Red variety, an official of the Bread and Cake-Makers' Union Number 479, by the name of Ernst Apfel. The government had a dictagraph record of conversations in which von Stroeme had contributed one hundred dollars to the Liberty Defense League, an organization which the Reds had got up for the purpose of carrying on agitation for the release of the I. W. W.s arrested in the dynamite plot against the life of Nelse Ackerman. Moreover it was proven that Apfel had taken this money and distributed it among several German Reds, who had turned it in to the defense fund, or used it in paying for circulars calling for a general strike.

Peter's heart was leaping with excitement; and it leaped even faster when he had got his breakfast and was walking down Main Street. He saw crowds gathered, and American flags flying from all the buildings, just as on the day of the Preparedness parade. It caused Peter to feet queer spasms of fright; he imagined another bomb, but he couldn't resist the crowds with their eager faces and contagious enthusiasm. Presently here came a band, with magnificent martial music, and here came soldiers marching—tramp, tramp, tramp—line after line of khaki-clad boys with heavy packs upon their backs and shiny new rifles. Our boys! Our boys! God bless them!

It was three regiments of the 223rd Division, coming from Camp Lincoln to be entrained for the war. They might better have been entrained at the camp, of course, but everyone had been clamoring for some glimpse of the soldiers, and here they were with their music and their flags, and their crowds of flushed, excited admirers—two endless lines of people, wild with patriotic fervor, shouting, singing, waving hats and handkerchiefs, until the whole street became a blur, a mad delirium. Peter saw these closely pressed lines, straight and true, and the legs that moved like clock-work, and the feet that shook the ground like thunder. He saw the fresh, boyish faces, grimly set and proud, with eyes fixed ahead, never turning, even tho they realized that this might be their last glimpse of their home city, that they might never come back from this journey. Our boys! Our boys! God bless them! Peter felt a choking in his throat, and a thrill of gratitude to the boys who were protecting him and his country; he clenched his hands and set his teeth, with fresh determination to punish the evil men and women—draft-dodgers, slackers, pacifists and seditionists—who were failing to take their part in this glorious emprise.

Section 57

Peter went to the American House and met McGivney, and was put to work on a job that precisely suited his mood. The time had come for action, said the rat-faced man. The executive committee of the I. W. W. local had been drafting an appeal to the main organization for help, and the executive committee was to meet that evening; Peter was to get in touch with the secretary, Grady, and find out where this meeting was to be, and make the suggestion that all the membership be gathered, and other Reds also. The business men of the city were going to pull off their big stroke that night, said McGivney; the younger members of the Chamber of Commerce and the Merchants' and Manufacturers' Association had got together and worked out a secret plan, and all they wanted was to have the Reds collected in one place.

So Peter set out and found Shawn Grady, the young Irish boy who kept the membership lists and other papers of the organization, in a place so secret that not even Peter had been able to find them. Peter brought the latest news about the sufferings of Mac in the "hole," and how Gus, the sailor, had joined Henderson in the hospital. He was so eloquent in his indignation that presently Grady told him about the meeting for that evening, and about the place, and Peter said they really ought to get some of their friends together, and work out some way to get their protest literature distributed quickly, because it was evident they could no longer use the mails. What was the use of resolutions of executive committees, when what was wanted was action by the entire membership? Grady said all right, they would notify the active members and sympathizers, and he gave Peter the job of telephoning and travelling about town getting word to a dozen people.

At six o'clock that evening Peter reported the results to McGivney, and then he got a shock. "You must go to that meeting yourself," said the rat-faced man. "You mustn't take any chance of their suspecting you."

"But, my God!" cried Peter. "What's going to happen there?"

"You don't need to worry about that," answered the other. "I'll see that you're protected."

The gathering was to take place at the home of Ada Ruth, the poetess, and McGivney had Peter describe this home to him. Beyond the living-room was a hallway, and in this hallway was a big clothes closet. At the first alarm Peter must make for this place. He must get into the closet, and McGivney would be on hand, and they would pen Peter up and pretend to club him, but in reality would protect him from whatever happened to the rest. Peter's knees began to tremble, and he denounced the idea indignantly; what would happen to him if anything were to happen to McGivney, or to his automobile, and were to fail to get there in time? McGivney declared that Peter need not worry—he was too valuable a man for them to take any chances with. McGivney would be there, and all Peter would have to do was to scream and raise a rumpus, and finally fall unconscious, and McGivney and Hammett and Cummings would carry him out to their automobile and take him away!

Peter was so frightened that he couldn't eat any dinner, but wandered about the street talking to himself and screwing up his courage. He had to stop and look at the American flags, still waving from the buildings, and read the evening edition of the American City "Times," in order to work up his patriotic fervor again. As he set out for the home of the little cripple who wrote pacifist poetry, he really felt like the soldier boys marching away to war.

Ada Ruth was there, and her mother, a dried-up old lady who knew nothing about all these dreadful world movements, but whose pleadings had no effect upon her inspired daughter; also Ada's cousin, a lean old-maid school teacher, secretary of the Peoples' Council; also Miriam Yankovitch, and Sadie Todd, and Donald Gordon. On the way Peter had met Tom Duggan, and the mournful poet revealed that he had composed a new poem about Mac in the "hole." Immediately afterwards came Grady, the secretary, his pockets stuffed with his papers. Grady, a tall, dark-eyed, impulsive-tempered Irish boy, was what the Socialists called a "Jimmie Higgins," that is, one of the fellows who did the hard and dreary work of the movement, who were always on hand no matter what happened, always ready to have some new responsibility put upon their shoulders. Grady had no use for the Socialists, being only interested in "industrial action," but he was willing to be called a "Jimmie Higgins"; he had said that Peter was one too, and Peter had smiled to himself, thinking that a "Jimmie Higgins" was about the last thing in the world he ever would be. Peter was on the way to independence and prosperity, and it did not occur to him to reflect that he might be a "Jimmie Higgins" to the "Whites" instead of to the Reds!

Grady now pulled out his papers, and began to talk over with Donald Gordon the proceedings of the evening. He had had a telegram from the national headquarters of the I. W. W., promising support, and his thin, hungry face lighted up with pride as he showed this. Then he announced that "Bud" Connor was to be present—a well-known organizer, who had been up in the oil country with McCormick, and brought news that the workers there were on the verge of a big strike. Then came Mrs. Jennings, a poor, tormented little woman who was slowly dying of a cancer, and whose husband was suing her for divorce because she had given money to the I. W. W. With her, and helping her along, came "Andy" Adams, a big machinist, who had been kicked out of his lodge for talking too much "direct action." He pulled from his pocket a copy of the "Evening Telegraph," and read a few lines from an editorial, denouncing "direct action" as meaning dynamiting, which it didn't, of course, and asking how long it would be before the friends of law and order in American City would use a little "direct action" of their own.

Section 58

So they gathered, until about thirty were present, and then the meeting speedily got down to business. It was evident, said Grady, that the authorities had deliberately framed-up the dynamite conspiracy, in order to have an excuse for wiping out the I. W. W. organization; they had closed the hall, and confiscated everything, typewriters and office furniture and books—including a book on Sabotage which they had turned over to the editor of the "Evening Times"! There was a hiss of anger at this. Also, they had taken to interfering with the mail of the organization; the I. W. W. were having to get out their literature by express. They were fighting for their existence, and they must find some way of getting the truth to people. If anybody had any suggestions to make, now was the time.

There came one suggestion after another; and meantime Peter sat as if his chair were full of pins. Why didn't they come—the younger members of the Chamber of Commerce and the Merchants' and Manufacturers' Association—and do what they were going to do without any further delay? Did they expect Peter to sit there all night, trembling with alarm—and he not having any dinner besides?

Suddenly Peter gave a jump. Outside came a yell, and Donald Gordon, who was making a speech, stopped suddenly, and the members of the company stared at one another, and some sprang to their feet. There were more yells, rising to screams, and some of the company made for the front doors, and some for the back doors, and yet others for the windows and the staircase. Peter wasted no time, but dived into the clothes closet in the hallway back of the living-room, and got into the farthest corner of this closet, and pulled some of the clothes on top of him; and then, to make him safer yet, came several other people piling on top of him.

From his place of refuge he listened to the confusion that reigned. The place was a bedlam of women's shrieks, and the curses of fighting men, and the crash of overturning furniture, and of clubs and monkey-wrenches on human heads. The younger members of the Chamber of Commerce and the Merchants' and Manufacturers' Association had come in sufficient force to make sure of their purpose. There were enough to crowd the room full, and to pack all the doorways, and two or three to guard each window, and a flying squadron to keep watch for anybody who jumped from the roof or tried to hide in the trees of the garden.

Peter cowered, and listened to the furious uproar, and presently he heard the cries of those on top of him, and realized that they were being pulled off and clubbed; he felt hands reach down and grab him, and he cringed and cried in terror; but nothing happened to him, and presently he glanced up and he saw a man wearing a black mask, but easily to be recognized as McGivney. Never in all his life had Peter been gladder to see a human face than he was to see that masked face of a rat! McGivney had a club in his hand, and was dealing ferocious blows to the clothes heaped around Peter. Behind McGivney were Hammett and Cummings, covering the proceedings, and now and then carefully putting in a blow of their own.

Most of the fighting inside the house and outside came quickly to an end, because everybody who fought was laid out or overpowered. Then several of the agents of Guffey, who had been studying these Reds for a year or two and knew them all, went about picking out the ones who were especially wanted, and searching them for arms, and then handcuffing them. One of these men approached Peter, who instantly fell unconscious, and closed his eyes; then Hammett caught him under the armpits and Cummings by the feet, and McGivney walked alongside as a bodyguard, remarking now and then, "We want this fellow, we'll take care of him."

They carried Peter outside, and in the darkness he opened his eyes just enough to see that the street was lined with automobiles, and that the Reds were being loaded aboard. Peter's friends carried him to one car and drove him away, and then Peter returned to consciousness, and the four of them sat up and laughed to split their sides, and slapped one another on the back, and mentioned the satisfactory things they had seen. Had Hammett noticed that slice Grady had got over the eyes, and the way the blood had run all over him? Well, he wanted to be a Red— they had helped him be one—inside and out! Had McGivney noticed how "Buck" Ellis, one of their men, had put the nose of the hobo poet out of joint? And young Ogden, son of the president of the Chamber of Commerce, had certainly managed to show how he felt about these cattle, the female ones as well as the males; when that Yankovich slut had slapped his face, he had caught her by the breasts and nearly twisted them off, and she had screamed and fainted!

Yes, they had cleaned them out. But that wasn't all of it, they were going to finish the job tonight, by God! They were going to give these pacifists a taste of the war, they were going to put an end to the Red Terror in American City! Peter might go along if he liked and see the good work; they were going into the country, and it would be dark, and if he kept a mask on he would be quite safe. And Peter said yes; his blood was up, he was full of the spirit of the hunt, he wanted to be in at the death, regardless of everything.

Section 59

The motor purred softly, and the car sped as if upon wings thru the suburbs of American City, and to the country beyond. There were cars in front, and other cars behind, a long stream of white lights flying out into the country. They came to a grove of big pine trees, which rose two or three feet thick, like church arches, and covered the ground beneath them with a soft, brown carpet. It was a well-known picnic place, and here all the cars were gathering by appointment. Evidently it had all been pre-arranged, with that efficiency which is the pride of 100% Americans. A man with a black mask over his face stood in the center of the grove, and shouted his directions thru a megaphone, and each car as it swept in ranged itself alongside the next car in a broad circle, more than a hundred feet across. These cars of the younger members of the Chamber of Commerce and the Merchants' and Manufacturers' Association were well behaved—they were accustomed to sliding precisely into place according to orders of a megaphone man, when receptions were being given, or when the younger members and their wives and fiancees, clad in soft silks and satins, came rolling up to their dinner-parties and dances.

The cars came and came, until there was just room enough for the last one to slide in. Then at a shouted command, "Number one!" a group of men stepped out of one of the cars, dragging a handcuffed prisoner. It was Michael Dubin, the young Jewish tailor who had spent fifteen days in jail with Peter. Michael was a student and dreamer, and not used to scenes of violence; also, he belonged to a race which expresses its emotions, and consequently is offensive to 100% Americans. He screamed and moaned while the masked men un-handcuffed him, and took off his coat and tore his shirt in the back. They dragged him to a tree in the center of the ring, a somewhat smaller tree, just right for his wrists to meet around and be handcuffed again. There he stood in the blinding glare of thirty or forty cars, writhing and moaning, while one of the black-masked men stripped off his coat and got ready for action. He produced a long black-snake whip, and stood poised for a moment; then in a booming voice the man with the megaphone shouted, "Go!" and the whip whistled thru the air and was laid across the back of Michael, and tore into the flesh so that the blood leaped into sight. There was a scream of anguish, and the victim began to twist and turn and kick about as if in his death-throes. Again the whip whistled, and again you heard the thud as it tore into the flesh, and another red stripe leaped to view.

Now the younger members of the Chamber of Commerce and the Merchants' and Manufacturers' Association were in excellent condition for this evening's labor. They were not pale and thin, underfed and overworked, as were their prisoners; they were sleek and rosy, and ashine with health. It was as if long years ago their fathers had foreseen the Red menace, and the steps that would have to be taken to preserve 100% Americanism; the fathers had imported a game which consisted of knocking little white balls around a field with various styles and sizes of clubs. They had built magnificent club-houses out here in the suburbs, and had many hundreds of acres of ground laid out for this game, and would leave their occupations of merchanting and manufacturing early in the afternoon, in order to repair to these fields and keep their muscles in condition. They would hold tournaments, and vie with one another, and tell over the stories of the mighty strokes which they had made with their clubs, and of the hundreds of strokes they had made in a single afternoon. So the man with the black-snake whip was "fit," and didn't need to stop for breath. Stroke after stroke he laid on, with a splendid rhythmic motion; he kept it up easily, on and on. Had he forgotten?

Did he think this was a little white ball he was swinging down upon? He kept on and on, until you could no longer count the welts, until the whole back of Michael Dubin was a mass of raw and bleeding flesh. The screams of Michael Dubin died away, and his convulsive struggling ceased, and his head hung limp, and he sunk lower and lower upon the tree.

At last the master of ceremonies stepped forward and ordered a halt, and the man with the whip wiped the sweat from his forehead with his shirt-sleeve, and the other men unchained the body of Michael Dubin, and dragged it a few feet to one side and dumped it face downward in the pine-leaves.

"Number two!" called the master of ceremonies, in a clear, compelling voice, as if he were calling the figures of a quadrille; and from another car another set of men emerged, dragging another prisoner. It was Bert Glikas, a "blanket-stiff" who was a member of the I. W. W.'s executive committee, and had had two teeth knocked out in a harvest-strike only a couple of weeks previously. While they were getting off his coat, he managed to get one hand free, and he shook it at the spectators behind the white lights of the automobiles. "God damn you!" he yelled; and so they tied him up, and a fresh man stepped forward and picked up the whip, and spit on his hands for good luck, and laid on with a double will; and at every stroke Glikas yelled a fresh curse; first in English, and then, as if he were delirious, in some foreign language. But at last his curses died away, and he too sank insensible, and was unhitched and dragged away and dumped down beside the first man. "Number three!" called the master of ceremonies.

Section 60

N ow Peter was sitting in the back seat of his car, wearing the mask which McGivney had given him, a piece of cloth with two holes for his eyes and another hole for him to breathe thru. Peter hated these Reds, and wanted them punished, but he was not used to bloody sights, and was finding this endless thud, thud of the whip on human flesh rather more than he could stand. Why had he come? This wasn't his part of the job of saving his country from the Red menace. He had done his share in pointing out the dangerous ones; he was a man of brains, not a man of violence. Peter saw that the next victim was Tom Duggan with his broken and bloody nose, and in spite of himself, Peter started with dismay. He realized that without intending it he had become a little fond of Tom Duggan. For all his queerness, Duggan was loyal, he was a good fellow when you had got underneath his surly manners. He had never done anything except just to grumble, and to put his grumbles into verses; they were making a mistake in whipping him, and for a moment Peter had a crazy impulse to interfere and tell them so.

The poet never made a sound. Peter got one glimpse of his face in the blazing white light, and in spite of the fact that it was smashed and bloody, Peter read Tom Duggan's resolve—he would die before they would get a moan out of him. Each time the lash fell you could see a quiver all over his form; but there was never a sound, and he stood, hugging the tree in a convulsive grip. They lashed him until the whip was spattering blood all over them, until blood was running to the ground. They had taken the precaution to bring along a doctor with a little black case, and he now stepped up and whispered to the master of ceremonies. They unfastened Duggan, and broke the grip of his arms about the tree, and dumped him down beside Glikas.

Next came the turn of Donald Gordon, the Socialist Quaker, which brought a bit of cheap drama. Donald took his religion seriously; he was always shouting his anti-war sentiments in the name of Jesus, which made him especially obnoxious. Now he saw a chance to get off one of his theatrical stunts; he raised his two manacled hands into the air as if he were praying, and shouted in piercing tones: "Father, forgive them, for they know not what they do!"

A murmur started in the crowd; you could hear it mounting to a roar. "Blasphemy!" they cried. "Stop his dirty mouth!" It was the same mouth that had been heard on a hundred platforms, denouncing the war and those who made money out of the war. They were here now, the men who had been denounced, the younger members of the Chamber of Commerce and the Merchants' and Manufacturers' Association, the best people of the city, those who were saving the country, and charging no more than the service was worth. So they roared with fury at this sacreligious upstart. A man whose mask was a joke, because he was so burly and hearty that everybody in the crowd knew him, took up the bloody whip. It was Billy Nash, secretary of the "Improve America League," and the crowd shouted, "Go to it, Billy! Good eye, old boy!" Donald Gordon might tell God that Billy Nash didn't know what he was doing, but Billy thought that he knew, and he meant before he got thru to convince Donald that he knew. It didn't take very long, because there was nothing much to the young Quaker but voice, and he fainted at the fourth or fifth stroke, and after the twentieth stroke the doctor interfered.

Then came the turn of Grady, secretary of the I. W. W., and here a terrible thing happened. Grady, watching this scene from one of the cars, had grown desperate, and when they loosed the handcuffs to get off his coat, he gave a sudden wrench and broke free, striking down one man after another. He had been brought up in the lumber country, and his strength was amazing, and before the crowd quite realized it, he was leaping between two of the cars. A dozen men sprang upon him from a dozen directions, and he went down in the midst of a wild melee. They pinned him with his face mashed into the dirt, and from the crowd there rose a roar as from wild beasts in the night-time,

"String him up! String him up!" One man came running with a rope, shouting, "Hang him!"

The master of ceremonies tried to protest thru his megaphone, but the instrument was knocked out of his hands, and he was hauled to one side, and presently there was a man climbing up the pine tree and hanging the rope over a limb. You could not see Grady for the jostling throng about him, but suddenly there was a yell from the crowd, and you saw him quite plainly—he shot high up into the air, with the rope about his neck and his feet kicking wildly. Underneath, men danced about and yelled and waved their hats in the air, and one man leaped up and caught one of the kicking feet and hung onto it.

Then, above all the din, a voice was heard thru the megaphone, "Let him down a bit! Let me get at him!" And those who held the rope gave way, and the body came down toward the ground, still kicking, and a man took out a clasp-knife, and cut the clothing away from the body, and cut off something from the body; there was another yell from the crowd, and the men in the automobiles slapped their knees and shrieked with satisfaction. Those in the car with Peter whispered that it was Ogden, son of the president of the Chamber of Commerce; and all over town next day and for weeks thereafter men would nudge one another, and whisper about what Bob Ogden had done to the body of Shawn Grady, secretary of the "damned wobblies." And every one who nudged and whispered about it felt certain that by this means the Red Terror had been forever suppressed, and 100% Americanism vindicated, and a peaceful solution of the problem of capital and labor made certain.

Strange as it might seem, there was one member of the I. W. W. who agreed with them. One of the victims of that night had learned his lesson! When Tom Duggan was able to sit up again, which was six weeks later, he wrote an article about his experience, which was published in an I. W. W. paper, and afterwards in pamphlet form was read by many hundreds of thousands of workingmen. In it the poet said:

"The preamble of the I. W. W. opens with the statement that the employing class and the working class have nothing in common; but on this occasion I learned that the preamble is mistaken. On this occasion I saw one thing in common between the employing class and the working class, and that thing was a black-snake whip. The butt end of the whip was in the hands of the employing class, and the lash of the whip was on the backs of the working class, and thus to all eternity was symbolized the truth about the relationship of the classes!"

Section 61

Peter awoke next morning with a vivid sense of the pain and terror of life. He had been clamoring to have those Reds punished; but somehow or other he had thought of this punishment in an abstract way, a thing you could attend to by a wave of the hand. He hadn't quite realized the physical side of it, what a messy and bloody job it would prove. Two hours and more he had listened to the thud of a whip on human flesh, and each separate stroke had been a blow upon his own nerves. Peter had an overdose of vengeance; and now, the morning after, his conscience was gnawing at him. He had known every one of those boys, and their faces rose up to haunt him. What had any of them done to deserve such treatment? Could he say that he had ever known a single one of them to do anything as violent as the thing they had all suffered?

But more than anything else Peter was troubled by fear. Peter, the ant, perceived the conflict of the giants becoming more ferocious, and realized the precariousness of his position under the giants' feet. The passions of both sides were mounting, and the fiercer their hate became, the greater the chance of Peter's being discovered, the more dreadful his fate if he were discovered. It was all very well for McGivney to assure him that only four of Guffey's men knew the truth, and that all these might be trusted to the death. Peter remembered a remark he had heard Shawn Grady make, and which had caused him to lose his appetite for more than one meal. "They've got spies among us," the young Irishman had said. "Well, sooner or later we'll do a bit of spying of our own!"

And now these words came back to Peter like a voice from the grave. Suppose one of the Reds who had money were to hire somebody to get a job in Guffey's office! Suppose some Red girl were to try Peter's device, and seduce one of Guffey's men—by no means a difficult task! The man mightn't even mean to reveal that Peter Gudge was a secret agent; he might just let it slip, as little Jennie had let slip the truth about Jack Ibbetts! Thus Mac would know who had framed him up; and what would Mac do to Peter when he got out on bail? When Peter thought of things like that he realized what it meant to go to war; he saw that he had gained nothing by staying at home, he might as well have been in the front-line trenches! After all, this was war, class-war; and in all war the penalty for spying is death.

Also Peter was worried about Nell. She had been in her new position for nearly a week, and he hadn't heard a word from her. She had forbidden him to write, for fear he might write something injudicious. Let him just wait, Edythe Eustace would know how to take care of herself. And that was all right, Peter had no doubt about the ability of Edythe Eustace to take care of herself. What troubled him was the knowledge that she was working on another "frame-up," and he stood in fear of the exuberance of her imagination. The last time that imagination had been pregnant, it had presented him with a suit-case full of dynamite. What it might bring forth next time he did not know, and was afraid to think. Nell might cause him to be found out by Guffey; and that would be nearly as horrible as to be found out by Mac!

Peter got his morning "Times," and found a whole page about the whipping of the Reds, portraying the job as a patriotic duty heroically performed; and that naturally cheered Peter up considerably. He turned to the editorial page, and read a two column "leader" that was one whoop of exultation. It served still more to cure Peter's ache of conscience; and when he read on and found a series of interviews with leading citizens, giving cordial endorsement to the acts of the "vigilantes," Peter became ashamed of his weakness, and glad that he had not revealed it to anyone. Peter was trying his best to become a real "he-man," a 100% red-blooded American, and he had the "Times" twice each day, morning and evening, to guide, sustain and inspire him.

Peter had been told by McGivney to fix himself up and pose as one of the martyrs of the night's affair, and this appealed to his sense of humor. He cut off the hair from a part of his head, and stuck some raw cotton on top, and plastered it over with surgical tape. He stuck another big wad of surgical tape across his forehead, and a criss-cross of it on his cheek, and tied up his wrist in an excellent imitation of a sprain. Thus rigged out he repaired to the American House, and McGivney rewarded him with a hearty laugh, and then proceeded to give some instructions which, entirely restored Peter's usual freshness of soul. Peter was going up on Mount Olympus again!

The rat-faced man explained in detail. There was a lady of great wealth—indeed, she was said to be several times a millionaire—who was an openly avowed Red, a pacifist of the most malignant variety. Since the arrest of young Lackman she had come forward and put up funds to finance the "People's Council," and the "Anti-Conscription League," and all the other activities which for the sake of convenience were described by the term "pro-German." The only trouble was this lady was so extremely wealthy it was hard to do anything to her. Her husband was a director in a couple of Nelse Ackerman's banks, and had other powerful connections. The husband was a violent, anti-Socialist, and a buyer of liberty bonds; he quarrelled with his wife, but nevertheless he did not want to see her in jail, and this made an embarrassing situation for the police and the district attorney's office, and even for the Federal authorities, who naturally did not want to trouble one of the courtiers of the king of American City. "But something's got to be done," said McGivney. "This camouflaged German propaganda can't go on." So Peter was to try to draw Mrs. Godd into some kind of "overt action."

"Mrs. Godd?" said Peter. It seemed to him a singular coincidence that one of the dwellers on Mount Olympus should bear that name. The great lady lived on a hilltop out in the suburbs, not so far from the hilltop of Nelse Ackerman. One of the adventures looked forward to by Reds and pacifists in distress was to make a pilgrimage to this palace and obtain some long, green plasters to put over their wounds. Now was the time at all times for Peter to go, said McGivney. Peter had many wounds to be plastered, and Mrs. Godd would be indignant at the proceedings of last night, and would no doubt express herself without restraint.

Section 62

Peter hadn't been so excited since the time when he had waited to meet young Lackman. He had never quite forgiven himself for this costly failure, and now he was to have another chance. He took a trolley ride out into the country, and walked a couple of miles to the palace on the hilltop, and mounted thru a grove of trees and magnificent Italian gardens. According to McGivney's injunctions, he summoned his courage, and went to the front door of the stately mansion and rang the bell.

Peter was hot and dusty from his long walk, the sweat had made streaks down his face and marred the pristine whiteness of his plasters. He was never a distinguished-looking person at best, and now, holding his damaged straw hat in his hands, he looked not so far from a hobo. However, the French maid who came to the door was evidently accustomed to strange-looking visitors. She didn't order Peter to the servant's entrance, nor threaten him with the dogs; she merely said, "Be seated, please. I will tell madame"—putting the accent on the second syllable, where Peter had never heard it before.

And presently here came Mrs. Godd in her cloud of Olympian beneficence; a large and ample lady, especially built for the role of divinity. Peter felt suddenly awe-stricken. How had he dared come here? Neither in the Hotel de Soto, with its many divinities, nor in the palace of Nelse Ackerman, the king, had he felt such a sense of his own lowliness as the sight of this calm, slow-moving great lady inspired. She was the embodiment of opulence, she was "the real thing." Despite the look of kindliness in her wide-open blue eyes, she impressed him with a feeling of her overwhelming superiority. He did not know it was his duty as a gentleman to rise from his chair when a lady entered, but some instinct brought him to his feet and caused him to stand blinking as she crossed to him from the opposite end of the big room.

"How do you do?" she said in a low, full voice, gazing at him steadily out of the kind, wide-open blue eyes. Peter stammered, "How d-dy do, M—Mrs. Godd."

In truth, Peter was almost dumb with bewilderment. Could it really, possibly be that this grand personage was a Red? One of the things that had most offended him about all radicals was their noisiness, their aggressiveness; but here was a grand serenity of looks and manner, a soft, slow voice—here was beauty, too, a skin unlined, despite middle years, and glowing with health and a fine cleanness. Nell Doolin had had a glowing complexion, but there was always a lot of powder stuck on, and when you investigated closely, as Peter had done, you discovered muddy spots in the edges of her hair and on her throat. But Mrs. Godd's skin shone just as the skin of a goddess would be expected to shine, and everything about her was of a divine and compelling opulence. Peter could not have explained just what it was that gave this last impression so overwhelmingly. It was not that she wore many jewels, or large ones, for Mrs. James had beaten her at that; it was not her delicate perfume, for Nell Doolin scattered more sweetness on the air; yet somehow even poor, ignorant Peter felt the difference—it seemed to him that none of Mrs. Godd's costly garments had ever been worn before, that the costly rugs on the floor had never been stepped on before, the very chair on which he sat had never been sat on before!

Little Ada Ruth had called Mrs. Godd "the mother of all the world;" and now suddenly she became the mother of Peter Gudge. She had read the papers that morning, she had received a half dozen telephone calls from horrified and indignant Reds, and so a few words sufficed to explain to her the meaning of Peter's bandages and plasters. She held out to him a beautiful cool hand, and quite without warning, tears sprang into the great blue eyes.

"Oh, you are one of those poor boys! Thank God they did not kill you!" And she led him to a soft couch and made him lie down amid silken pillows. Peter's dream of Mount Olympus had come literally true! It occurred to him that if Mrs. Godd were willing to play permanently the role of mother to Peter Gudge, he would be willing to give up his role of anti-Red agent with its perils and its nervous strains; he would forget duty, forget the world's strife and care; he would join the lotus-eaters, the sippers of nectar on Mount Olympus!

She sat and talked to him in the soft, gentle voice, and the kind blue eyes watched him, and Peter thought that never in all his life had he encountered such heavenly emotions. To be sure, when he had gone to see Miriam Yankovich, old Mrs. Yankovich had been just as kind, and tears of sympathy had come into her eyes just the same. But then, Mrs. Yankovich was nothing but a fat old Jewess, who lived in a tenement and smelt of laundry soap and partly completed washing; her hands had been hot and slimy, and so Peter had not been in the least grateful for her kindness. But to encounter tender emotions in these celestial regions, to be talked to maternally and confidentially by this wonderful Mrs. Godd in soft white chiffons just out of a band-box *this* was quite another matter!

Section 63

Peter did not want to set traps for this mother of Mount Olympus, he didn't want to worm any secrets from her. And as it happened, he found that he did not have to, because she told him everything right away, and without the slightest hesitation. She talked just as the "wobblies" had talked in their headquarters; and Peter, when he thought it over, realized that there are two kinds of people who can afford to be frank in their utterance—those who have nothing to lose, and those who have so much to lose that they cannot possibly lose it.

Mrs. Godd said that what had been done to those men last night was a crime, and it ought to be punished if ever a crime was punished, and that she would like to engage detectives and get evidence against the guilty ones. She said furthermore that she sympathized with the Reds of the very reddest shade, and if there were any color redder than Red she would be of that color. She said all this in her quiet, soft voice. Tears came into her eyes now and then, but they were well-behaved tears, they disappeared of their own accord, and without any injury to Mrs. Godd's complexion, or any apparent effect upon her self-possession.

Mrs. Godd said that she didn't see how anybody could fail to be a Red who thought about the injustices of present-day society. Only a few days before she had been in to see the district attorney, and had tried to make a Red out of him! Then she told Peter how there had come to see her a man who had pretended to be a radical, but she had realized that he didn't know anything about radicalism, and had told him she was sure he was a government agent. The man had finally admitted it, and showed her his gold star—and then Mrs. Godd had set to work to convert him! She had argued with him for an hour or two, and then had invited him to go to the opera with her. "And do you know," said Mrs. Godd, in an injured tone, "he wouldn't go! They don't want to be converted, those men; they don't want to listen to reason. I believe the man was actually afraid I might influence him."

"I shouldn't wonder," put in Peter, sympathetically; for he was a tiny bit afraid himself.

"I said to him, 'Here I live in this palace, and back in the industrial quarter of the city are several thousand men and women who slave at machines for me all day, and now, since the war, all night too. I get the profits of these peoples' toil—and what have I done to earn it? Absolutely nothing! I never did a stroke of useful work in my life.' And he said to me, 'Suppose the dividends were to stop, what would you do?' 'I don't know what I'd do,' I answered, 'I'd be miserable, of course, because I hate poverty, I couldn't stand it, it's terrible to think of—not to have comfort and cleanliness and security. I don't see how the working-class stand it—that's exactly why I'm a Red, I know it's wrong for anyone to be poor, and there's no excuse for it. So I shall help to overthrow the capitalist system, even if it means I have to take in washing for my living!"

Peter sat watching her in the crisp freshness of her snowy chiffons. The words brought a horrible image to his mind; he suddenly found himself back in the tenement kitchen, where fat and steaming Mrs. Yankovich was laboring elbow deep in soap-suds. It was on the tip of Peter's tongue to say: "If you really had done a day's washing, Mrs. Godd, you wouldn't talk like that!"

But he remembered that he must play the game, so he said, "They're terrible fellows, them Federal agents. It was two of them pounded me over the head last night." And then he looked faint and pitiful, and Mrs. Godd was sympathetic again, and moved to more recklessness of utterance.

"It's because of this hideous war!" she declared. "We've gone to war to make the world safe for democracy, and meantime we have to sacrifice every bit of democracy at home. They tell you that you must hold your peace while they murder one another, but they may try all they please, they'll never be able to silence me! I know that the Allies are just as much to blame as the Germans, I know that this is a war of profiteers and bankers; they may take my sons and force them into the army, but they cannot take my convictions and force them into their army. I am a pacifist, and I am an internationalist; I want to see the workers arise and turn out of office these capitalist governments, and put an end to this hideous slaughter of human beings. I intend to go on saying that so long as I live." There sat Mrs. Godd, with her lovely firm white hands clasped as if in prayer, one large diamond ring on the left fourth finger shining defiance, and a look of calm, child-like conviction upon her face, confronting in her imagination all the federal agents and district attorneys and capitalist judges and statesmen and generals and drill sergeants in the civilized world.

She went on to tell how she had attended the trial of three pacifist clergymen a week or two previously. How atrocious that Christians in a

Christian country should be sent to prison for trying to repeat the words of Christ! "I was so indignant," declared Mrs. Godd, "that I wrote a letter to the judge. My husband said I would be committing contempt of court by writing to a judge during the trial, but I answered that my contempt for that court was beyond anything I could put into writing. Wait—"

And Mrs. Godd rose gravely from her chair and went over to a desk by the wall, and got a copy of the letter. "I'll read it to you," she said, and Peter listened to a manifesto of Olympian Bolshevism—

To His Honor:

As I entered the sanctuary, I gazed upward to the stained glass dome, upon which were inscribed four words: Peace. Justice. Truth. Law—and I felt hopeful. Before me were men who had violated no constitutional right, who had not the slightest criminal tendency, who, were opposed to violence of every kind.

The trial proceeded. I looked again at the beautiful stained glass dome, and whispered to myself those majestic-sounding words: "Peace. Justice. Truth. Law." I listened to the prosecutors; the Law in their hands was a hard, sharp, cruel blade, seeking insistently, relentlessly for a weak spot in the armor of its victims. I listened to their Truth, and it was Falsehood. Their Peace was a cruel and bloody War. Their justice was a net to catch the victims at any cost—at the cost of all things but the glory of the Prosecutor's office.

I grew sick at heart. I can only ask myself the old, old question: What can we, the people do? How can we bring Peace, justice, Truth and Law to the world? Must we go on bended knees and ask our public servants to see that justice is done to the defenceless, rather than this eternal prosecuting of the world's noblest souls! You will find these men guilty, and sentence them to be shut behind iron bars— which should never be for human beings, no matter what their crime, unless you want to make beasts of them. Is that your object, sir? It would seem so; and so I say that we must overturn the system that is brutalizing, rather than helping and uplifting mankind.

Yours for Peace..Justice..Truth..Law—
Mary Angelica Godd

What were you going to do with such a woman? Peter could understand the bewilderment of His Honor, and of the district attorney's office, and of the secret service department of the Traction Trust—as well as of Mrs. Godd's husband! Peter was bewildered himself; what was the use of his coming out here to get more information, when Mrs. Godd had already committed contempt of court in writing, and had given all the information there was to give to a Federal agent? She had told this man that she had contributed several thousand dollars to the Peoples' Council, and that she intended to contribute more. She had put up bail for a whole bunch of Reds and Pacifists, and she intended to put up bail for McCormick and his friends, just as soon as the corrupt capitalist courts had been forced to admit them to bail. "I know McCormick well, and he's a lovely boy," she said. "I don't believe he had anything more to do with dynamite bombs than I have."

Now all this time Peter had sat there, entirely under the spell of Mrs. Godd's opulence. Peter was dwelling among the lotus-eaters, and forgetting the world's strife and care; he was reclining on a silken couch, sipping nectar with the shining ones of Mount Olympus. But now suddenly, Peter was brought back to duty, as one wakes from a dream to the sound of an alarm-clock. Mrs. Godd was a friend of Mac's, Mrs. Godd proposed to get Mac out on bail! Mac, the most dangerous Red of them all! Peter saw that he must get something on this woman at once!

Section 64

Peter sat up suddenly among his silken cushions, and began to tell Mrs. Godd about the new plan of the Anti-conscription League, to prepare a set of instructions for young conscientious objectors. Peter represented the purpose of these instructions to be the advising of young men as to their legal and constitutional rights. But it was McGivney's idea that Peter should slip into the instructions some phrase advising the young men to refuse military duty; if this were printed and circulated, it would render every member of the Anti-conscription League liable to a sentence of ten or twenty years in jail. McGivney had warned Peter to be very cautious about this, but again Peter found that there was no need of caution. Mrs. Godd was perfectly willing to advise young men to refuse military service. She had advised many such, she said, including her own sons, who unfortunately agreed with their father in being blood-thirsty.

It came to be lunch-time, and Mrs. Godd asked if Peter could sit at table—and Peter's curiosity got the better of all caution. He wanted to see the Godd family sipping their nectar out of golden cups. He wondered, would the disapproving husband and the blood-thirsty sons be present?

There was nobody present but an elderly woman companion, and Peter did not see any golden cups. But he saw some fine china, so fragile that he was afraid to touch it, and he saw a row of silver implements, so heavy that it gave him a surprise each time he picked one up. Also, he saw foods prepared in strange and complicated ways, so chopped up and covered with sauces that it was literally true he couldn't give the name of a single thing he had eaten, except the buttered toast.

He was inwardly quaking with embarrassment during this meal, but he saved himself by Mrs. James's formula, to watch and see what the others were doing and then do likewise. Each time a new course was brought, Peter would wait, and when he saw Mrs. Godd pick up a certain fork or a certain spoon, he would pick up the same one, or as near to it as he could guess. He could put his whole mind on this, because he didn't have to do any talking; Mrs. Godd poured out a steady stream of sedition and high treason, and all Peter had to do was to listen and nod. Mrs. Godd would understand that his mouth was too full for utterance.

After the luncheon they went out on the broad veranda which overlooked a magnificent landscape. The hostess got Peter settled in a soft porch chair with many cushions, and then waved her hand toward the view of the city with its haze of thick black smoke.

"That's where my wage slaves toil to earn my dividends," said she. "They're supposed to stay there—in their 'place,' as it's called, and I stay here in my place. If they want to change places, it's called 'revolution,' and that is 'violence.' What I marvel at is that they use so little violence, and feel so little. Look at those men being tortured in jail! Could anyone blame them if they used violence? Or if they made an effort to escape?"

That suggested a swift, stabbing idea to Peter. Suppose Mrs. Godd could be induced to help in a jail delivery!

"It might be possible to help them to escape," he suggested.

"Do you think so?" asked Mrs. Godd, showing excitement for the first time during that interview.

"It might be," said Peter. "Those jailors are not above taking bribes, you know. I met nearly all of them while I was in that jail, and I think I might get in touch with one or two that could be paid. Would you like me to try it?"

"Well, I don't know—" began the lady, hesitatingly. "Do you really think—"

"You know they never ought to have been put in at all!" Peter interjected.

"That's certainly true!" declared Mrs. Godd.

"And if they could escape without hurting anyone, if they didn't have to fight the jailors, it wouldn't do any real harm—"

That was as far as Peter got with his impromptu conspiracy. Suddenly he heard a voice behind him: "What does this mean?" It was a male voice, fierce and trembling with anger; and Peter started from his silken cushions, and glanced around, thrusting up one arm with the defensive gesture of a person who has been beaten since earliest childhood.

Bearing down on him was a man; possibly he was not an abnormally big man, but certainly he looked so to Peter. His smooth-shaven face was pink with anger, his brows gathered in a terrible frown, and his hands clenched with deadly significance. "You dirty little skunk!" he hissed. "You infernal young sneak!"

"John!" cried Mrs. Godd, imperiously; but she might as well have cried to an advancing thunder-storm. The man made a leap upon Peter, and Peter, who had dodged many hundreds of blows in his lifetime, rolled off the lounging chair, and leaped to his feet, and started for the stairs of the veranda. The man was right behind him, and as Peter reached the first stair the man's foot shot out, and caught Peter fairly in the seat of his trousers, and the first stair was the only one of the ten or twelve stairs of the veranda that Peter touched in his descent.

Landing at the bottom, he did not stop even for a glance; he could hear the snorting of Mr. Godd, it seemed right behind his ear, and Peter ran down the driveway as he had seldom run in his life before. Every now and then Mr. Godd would shoot out another kick, but he had to stop slightly to do this, and Peter gained just enough to keep the kicks from reaching him. So at last the pursuer gave up, and Peter dashed thru the gates of the Godd estate and onto the main highway.

Then he looked over his shoulder, and seeing that Mr. Godd was a safe distance away, he stopped and turned and shook his clenched fist with the menace of a street-rat, shrieking, "Damn you! Damn you!" A whirlwind of impotent rage laid hold upon him. He shouted more curses and menaces, and among them some strange, some almost incredible words. "Yes, I'm a Red, damn your soul, and I'll stay a Red!"

Yes, Peter Gudge, the friend of law and order, Peter Gudge, the little brother to the rich, shouted, "I'm a Red, and what's more, we'll blow you up some day for this—Mac and me'll put a bomb under you!" Mr. Godd turned and stalked with contemptuous dignity back to his own private domestic controversy.

Peter walked off down the road, rubbing his sore trousers and sobbing to himself. Yes, Peter understood now exactly how the Reds felt. Here were these rich parasites, exploiting the labor of working men and living off in palaces by themselves—and what had they done to earn it? What would they ever do for the poor man, except to despise him, and to kick him in the seat of his trousers? They were a set of wilful brutes! Peter suddenly saw the happenings of last night from a new angle, and wished he had all the younger members of the Chamber of Commerce and the Merchants' and Manufacturers' Association right there along with Mr. Godd, so that he could bundle them all off to the devil at once.

And that was no passing mood either. The seat of Peter's trousers hurt so that he could hardly endure the trolley ride home, and all the way Peter was plotting how he could punish Mr. Godd. He remembered suddenly that Mr. Godd was an associate of Nelse Ackerman; and Peter now had a spy in Nelse Ackerman's home, and was preparing some kind of a "frame-up!" Peter would see if he couldn't find some way to start a dynamite conspiracy against Mr. Godd! He would start a campaign against Mr. Godd in the radical movement, and maybe he could find some way to get a bunch of the "wobblies" to carry him off and tie him up and beat him with a black-snake whip!

Section 65

With these reflections Peter went back to the American House, where McGivney had promised to meet him that evening. Peter went to Room 427, and being tired after the previous night's excitement, he lay down and fell fast asleep. And when again he opened his eyes, he wasn't sure whether it was a nightmare, or whether he had died in his sleep and gone to hell with Mr. Godd. Somebody was shaking him, and bidding him in a gruff voice, "Wake up!" Peter opened his eyes, and saw that it was McGivney; and that was all right, it was natural that McGivney should be waking him up. But what was this? McGivney's voice was angry, McGivney's face was dark and glowering, and—most incredible circumstance of all—McGivney had a revolver in his hand, and was pointing it into Peter's face!

It really made it much harder for Peter to get awake, because he couldn't believe that he was awake; also it made it harder for McGivney to get any sense out of him, because his jaw hung down, and he stared with terrified eyes into the muzzle of the revolver.

"M-m-my God, Mr. McGivney! w-w-what's the matter?"

"Get up here!" hissed the rat-faced man, and he added a vile name. He gripped Peter by the lapel of his coat and half jerked him to his feet, still keeping the muzzle of the revolver in Peter's face. And poor Peter, trying desperately to get his wits together, thought of half a dozen wild guesses one after another. Could it be that McGivney had heard him denouncing Mr. Godd and proclaiming himself a Red? Could it be that some of the Reds had framed up something on Peter? Could it be that McGivney had gone just plain crazy; that Peter was in the room with a maniac armed with a revolver?

"Where did you put that money I gave you the other day;" demanded McGivney, and added some more vile names.

Instantly, of course, Peter was on the defensive. No matter how frightened he might be, Peter would never fail to hang on to his money.

"I-I s-s-spent it, Mr. McGivney."

"You're lying to me!"

"N-n-no."

"Tell me where you put that money!" insisted the man, and his face was ugly with anger, and the muzzle of the revolver seemed to be trembling with anger. Peter started to insist that he had spent every cent. "Make him cough up, Hammett!" said McGivney; and Peter for the first time realized that there was another man in the room. His eyes had been so fascinated by the muzzle of the revolver that he hadn't taken a glance about.

Hammett was a big fellow, and he strode up to Peter and grabbed one of Peter's arms, and twisted it around behind Peter's back and up between Peter's shoulders. When Peter started to scream, Hammett clapped his other hand over his mouth, and so Peter knew that it was all up. He could not hold on to money at that cost. When McGivney asked him, "Will you tell me where it is?" Peter nodded, and tried to answer thru his nose.

So Hammett took his hand from his mouth. "Where is it?" And Peter replied, "In my right shoe."

Hammett unlaced the shoe and took it off, and pulled out the inside sole, and underneath was a little flat package wrapped in tissue paper, and inside the tissue paper was the thousand dollars that McGivney had given Peter, and also the three hundred dollars which Peter had saved from Nelse Ackerman's present, and two hundred dollars which he had saved from his salary. Hammett counted the money, and McGivney stuck it into his pocket, and then he commanded Peter to put on his shoe again. Peter obeyed with his trembling fingers, meantime keeping his eye in part on the revolver and in part on the face of the rat.

"W-w-what's the matter, Mr. McGivney?"

"You'll find out in time," was the answer. "Now, you march downstairs, and remember, I've got this gun on you, and there's eight bullets in it, and if you move a finger I'll put them all into you."

So Peter and McGivney and Hammett went down in the elevator of the hotel, and out of doors, and into an automobile. Hammett drove, and Peter sat in the rear seat with McGivney, who had the revolver in his coat pocket, his finger always on the trigger and the muzzle always pointed into Peter's middle. So Peter obeyed all orders promptly, and stopped asking questions because he found he could get no answers.

Meantime he was using his terrified wits on the problem. The best guess he could make was that Guffey had decided to believe Joe Angell's story instead of Peter's. But then, why all this gun-play, this movie stuff? Peter gave up in despair; and it was just as well, for what had happened lay entirely beyond the guessing power of Peter's mind or any other mind.

Section 66

They went to the office of the secret service department of the Traction Trust, a place where Peter had never been allowed to come hitherto. It was on the fourteenth floor of the Merchant's Trust Building, and the sign on the door read: "The American City Land & Investment Company. Walk In." When you walked in, you saw a conventional real estate office, and it was only when you had penetrated several doors that you came to the secret rooms where Guffey and his staff conducted the espionage work of the big business interests of the city.

Peter was hustled into one of these rooms, and there stood Guffey; and the instant Guffey saw him, he bore down upon him, shaking his fist. "You stinking puppy!" he exclaimed. "You miserable little whelp! You dirty, sneaking hound!" He added a number of other descriptive phrases taken from the vocabulary of the kennel.

Peter's knees were shaking, his teeth were chattering, and he watched every motion of Guffey's angry fingers, and every grimace of Guffey's angry features. Peter had been fully prepared for the most horrible torture he had experienced yet; but gradually he realized that he wasn't going to be tortured, he was only going to be scolded and raged at, and no words could describe the wave of relief in his soul. In the course of his street-rat's life Peter had been called more names than Guffey could think of if he spent the next month trying. If all Guffey was going to do was to pace up and down the room, and shake his fist under Peter's nose every time he passed him, and compare him with every kind of a domestic animal, Peter could stand it all night without a murmur.

He stopped trying to find out what it was that had happened, because he saw that this only drove Guffey to fresh fits of exasperation. Guffey didn't want to talk to Peter, he didn't want to hear the sound of Peter's whining gutter-pup's voice. All he wanted was to pour out his rage, and have Peter listen in abject abasement, and this Peter did. But meantime, of course, Peter's wits were working at high speed, he was trying to pick up hints as to what the devil it could mean. One thing was quite clear—the damage, whatever it was, was done; the jig was up, it was all over but the funeral. They had taken Peter's money to pay for the funeral, and that was all they hoped to get out of him.

Gradually came other hints. "So you thought you were going into business on your own!" snarled Guffey, and his fist, which was under Peter's nose, gave an upward poke that almost dislocated Peter's neck.

"Aha!" thought Peter. "Nelse Ackerman has given me away!"

"You thought you were going to make your fortune and retire for life on your income!"

Yes, that was it, surely! But what could Nelse Ackerman have told that was so very bad?

"You were going to have a spy of your own, set up your own bureau, and kick me out, perhaps!"

"My God!" thought Peter. "Who told that?"

Then suddenly Guffey stopped in front of him. "Was that what you thought?" he demanded. He repeated the question, and it appeared that he really wanted an answer, and so Peter stammered, "N-n-no, sir." But evidently the answer didn't suit Guffey, for he grabbed Peter's nose and gave it a tweak that brought the tears into his eyes.

"What was it then?" A nasty sneer came on the head detective's face, and he laughed at Peter with a laugh of venomous contempt. "I suppose you thought she really loved you! Was it that? You thought she really loved you?" And McGivney and Hammett and Guffey ha-ha-ed together, and to Peter it seemed like the mockery of demons in the undermost pit of hell. Those words brought every pillar of Peter's dream castle tumbling in ruins about his ears. Guffey had found out about Nell!

Again and again on the automobile ride to Guffey's office Peter had reminded himself of Nell's command, "Stick it out, Peter! Stick it out!" He had meant to stick it out in spite of everything; but now in a flash he saw that all was lost. How could he stick it out when they knew about Nell, and when Nell, herself, was no longer sticking it out?

Guffey saw these thoughts plainly written in Peter's face, and his sneer turned into a snarl. "So you think you'll tell me the truth now, do you? Well, it happens there's nothing left to tell!"

Again he turned and began pacing up and down the room. The pressure of rage inside him was so great that it took still more time to work it off. But finally the head detective sat down at his desk, and opened the drawer and took out a paper. "I see you're sitting there, trying to think up some new lie to tell me," said he. And Peter did not try to deny it, because any kind of denial only caused a fresh access of rage. "All right," Guffey said, "I'll read you this, and you can see just where you stand, and just how many kinds of a boob you are."

So he started to read the letter; and before Peter had heard one sentence, he knew this was a letter from Nell, and he knew that the castle of his dreams was flat in the dust forever. The ruins of Sargon and Nineveh were not more hopelessly flat!

"Dear Mr. Guffey," read the letter, "I am sorry to throw you down, but fifty thousand dollars is a lot of money, and we all get tired of work and need a rest. This is to tell you that Ted Crothers has just broke into Nelse Ackerman's safe in his home, and we have got some liberty bonds and some jewels which we guess to be worth fifty thousand dollars, and you know Ted is a good judge of jewels.

"Now of course you will find out that I was working in Mr. Ackerman's home and you will be after me hot-foot, so I might as well tell you about it, and tell you it won't do you any good to catch us, because we have got all the inside dope on the Goober frame-up, and everything else your bureau has been pulling off in American City for the last year. You can ask Peter Gudge and he'll tell you. It was Peter and me that fixed up that dynamite conspiracy, but you mustn't blame Peter, because he only did what I told him to do. He hasn't got sense enough to be really dangerous, and he will make you a perfectly good agent if you treat him kind and keep him away from the women. You can do that easy enough if you don't let him get any money, because of course he's nothing much on looks, and the women would never bother with him if you didn't pay him too much.

"Now Peter will tell you how we framed up that dynamite job, and of course you wouldn't want that to get known to the Reds, and you may be sure that if Ted and me get pinched, we'll find some way to let the Reds know all about it. If you keep quiet we'll never say a word, and you've got a perfectly good dynamite conspiracy, with all the evidence you need to put the Reds out of business, and you can just figure it cost you fifty thousand dollars, and it was cheap at the price, because Nelse Ackerman has paid a whole lot more for your work, and you never got anything half as big as this. I know you'll be mad when you read this, but think it over and keep your shirt on. I send it to you by messenger so you can get hold of Nelse Ackerman right quick, and have him not say anything to the police; because you know how it is—if those babies find it out, it will get to the Reds and the newspapers, and it'll be all over town and do a lot of harm to your frame-up. And you know after those Reds have got beaten up and Shawn Grady lynched, you wouldn't like to have any rumor get out that that dynamite was planted by your own people. Ted and me will keep out of sight, and we won't sell the jewels for a while, and everything will be all right.

Yours respectfully,
Edythe

"P. S. It really ain't Peter's fault that he's silly about women, and he would have worked for you all right if it hadn't been for my good looks!"

Section 67

S o there it was. When Peter had heard this letter, he understood
that there was no more to be said, and he said it. His own weight
had suddenly become more than he could support, and he saw a chair
nearby and slipped into it, and sat with eyes of abject misery roaming
from Guffey to McGivney, and from McGivney to Hammett, and then
back to Guffey again.

The head detective, for all his anger, was a practical man; he could not
have managed the very important and confidential work of the Traction
Trust if he had not been. So now he proceeded to get down to business.
Peter would please tell him everything about that dynamite frame-up;
just how they had managed it and just who knew about it. And Peter,
being also a practical man, knew that there was no use trying to hide
anything. He told the story from beginning to end, taking particular
pains to make clear that he and Nell alone were in the secret—except
that beyond doubt Nell had told her lover, Ted Crothers. It was probably
Crothers that got the dynamite. From the conversation that ensued
Peter gathered that this young man with the face of a bull-dog was one
of the very fanciest safecrackers in the country, and no doubt he was
the real brains of the conspiracy; he had put Nell up to it, and managed
every step. Suddenly Peter remembered all the kisses which Nell had
given him in the park, and he found a blush of shame stealing over him.
Yes, there was no doubt about it, he was a boob where women were
concerned!

Peter began to plead for himself, Really it wasn't his fault because
Nell had got a hold on him. In the Temple of Jimjambo, when he was
only a kid, he had been desperately in love with her. She was not only
beautiful, she was so smart; she was the smartest woman he had ever
known. McGivney remarked that she had been playing with Peter even
then—she had been in Guffey's pay at that time, collecting evidence to
put Pashtian el Kalandra in jail and break up the cult of Eleutherinian
Exoticism. She had done many such jobs for the secret service of the
Traction Trust, while Peter was still traveling around with Pericles
Priam selling patent medicine. Nell had been used by Guffey to seduce
a prominent labor leader in American City; she had got him caught in a
hotel room with her, and thus had broken the back of the biggest labor
strike ever known in the city's history.

Peter felt suddenly that he had a good defense. Of course a woman like that had been too much for him! It was Guffey's own fault if he hired people like that and turned them loose! It suddenly dawned on Peter—Nell must have found out that he, Peter, was going to meet young Lackman in the Hotel de Soto, and she must have gone there deliberately to ensnare him. When McGivney admitted that that was possibly true, Peter felt that he had a case, and proceeded to urge it with eloquence. He had been a fool, of course, every kind of fool there was, and he hadn't a word to say for himself; but he had learned his lesson and learned it thoroughly. No more women for him, and no more high life, and if Mr. Guffey would give him another chance—

Guffey, of course, snorted at him. He wouldn't have a pudding-head like Peter Gudge within ten miles of his office! But Peter only pleaded the more abjectly. He really did know the Reds thoroughly, and where could Mr. Guffey find anybody that knew them as well? The Reds all trusted him; he was a real martyr—look at the plasters all over him now! And he had just added another Red laurel to his brow—he had been to see Mrs. Godd, and had had the seat of his trousers kicked by Mr. Godd, and of course he could tell that story, and maybe he could catch some Reds in a conspiracy against Mr. Godd. Anyhow, they had that perfectly good case against McCormick and the rest of the I. W. Ws. And now that things had gone so far, surely they couldn't back down on that case! All that was necessary was to explain matters to Mr. Ackerman—

Peter realized that this was an unfortunate remark. Guffey was on his feet again, pacing up and down the room, calling Peter the names of all the barnyard animals, and incidentally revealing that he had already had an interview with Mr. Ackerman, and that Mr. Ackerman was not disposed to receive amicably the news that the secret service bureau which he had been financing, and which was supposed to be protecting him, had been the means of introducing into his home a couple of high-class criminals who had cracked his safe and made off with jewels that they guessed were worth fifty thousand dollars, but that Mr. Ackerman claimed were worth eighty-five thousand dollars. Peter was informed that he might thank his lucky stars that Guffey didn't shut him in the hole for the balance of his life, or take him into a dungeon and pull him to pieces inch by inch. As it was, all he had to do was to get himself out of Guffey's office, and take himself to hell by the quickest route he could find. "Go on!" said Guffey. "I mean it, get out!"

And so Peter got to his feet and started unsteadily toward the door. He was thinking to himself: "Shall I threaten them? Shall I say I'll go over to the Reds and tell what I know?" No, he had better not do that; the least hint of that might cause Guffey to put him in the hole! But then, how was it possible for Guffey to let him go, to take a chance of his telling? Right now, Guffey must be thinking to himself that Peter might go away, and in a fit of rage or of despair might let out the truth to one of the Reds, and then everything would be ruined forever. No, surely Guffey would not take such a chance! Peter walked very slowly to the door, he opened the door reluctantly, he stood there, holding on as if he were too weak to keep his balance; he waited—waited—

And sure enough, Guffey spoke. "Come back here, you mut!" And Peter turned and started towards the head detective, stretching out his hands in a gesture of submission; if it had been in an Eastern country, he would have fallen on his knees and struck his forehead three times in the dust. "Please, please, Mr. Guffey!" he wailed. "Give me another chance!"

"If I put you to work again," snarled Guffey, "will you do what I tell you, and not what you want to do yourself?"

"Yes, yes, Mr. Guffey."

"You'll do no more frame-ups but my frame-ups?"

"Yes, yes, Mr. Guffey."

"All right, then, I'll give you one more chance. But by God, if I find you so much as winking at another girl, I'll pull your eye teeth out!"

And Peter's heart leaped with relief. "Oh, thank you, thank you, Mr. Guffey!"

"I'll pay you twenty dollars a week, and no more," said Guffey. "You're worth more, but I can't trust you with money, and you can take it or leave it."

"That'll be perfectly satisfactory, Mr. Guffey," said Peter.

Section 68

S
o there was the end of high life for Peter Gudge. He moved no
more in the celestial circles of Mount Olympus. He never again
saw the Chinese butler of Mr. Ackerman, nor the French parlor-maid
of Mrs. Godd. He would no more be smiled at by the two hundred and
twenty-four boy angels of the ceiling of the Hotel de Soto lobby. Peter
would eat his meals now seated on a stool in front of a lunch counter,
he would really be the humble proletarian, the "Jimmie Higgins" of his
role. He put behind him bright dreams of an accumulated competence,
and settled down to the hard day's work of cultivating the acquaintance
of agitators, visiting their homes and watching their activities, getting
samples of the literature they were circulating, stealing their letters and
address-books and note-books, and taking all these to Room 427 of the
American House.

These were busy times just now. In spite of the whippings and the
lynchings and the jailings—or perhaps because of these very things—
the radical movement was seething. The I. W. Ws. had reorganized
secretly, and were accumulating a defense fund for their prisoners;
also, the Socialists of all shades of red and pink were busy, and the
labor men had never ceased their agitation over the Goober case. Just
now they were redoubling their activities, because Mrs. Goober was
being tried for her life. Over in Russia a mob of Anarchists had made
a demonstration in front of the American Legation, because of the
mistreatment of a man they called "Guba." At any rate, that was the way
the news came over the cables, and the news-distributing associations
of the country had been so successful in keeping the Goober case from
becoming known that the editors of the New York papers really did
not know any better, and printed the name as it came, "Guba!" which
of course gave the radicals a fine chance to laugh at them, and say, how
much they cared about labor!

The extreme Reds seemed to have everything their own way in Russia.
Late in the fall they overthrew the Russian government, and took
control of the country, and proceeded to make peace with Germany;
which put the Allies in a frightful predicament, and introduced a new
word into the popular vocabulary, the dread word "Bolshevik." After
that, if a man suggested municipal ownership of ice-wagons, all you had
to do was to call him a "Bolshevik" and he was done for.

However, the extremists replied to this campaign of abuse by taking up the name and wearing it as a badge. The Socialist local of American City adopted amid a storm of applause a resolution to call itself the "Bolshevik local," and the "left-wingers" had everything their own way for a time. The leader in this wing was a man named Herbert Ashton, editor of the American City "Clarion," the party's paper. A newspaperman, lean, sallow, and incredibly bitter, Ashton apparently had spent all his life studying the intrigues of international capital, and one never heard an argument advanced that he was not ready with an answer. He saw the war as a struggle between the old established commercialism of Great Britain, whose government he described as "a gigantic trading corporation," and the newly arisen and more aggressive commercialism of Germany.

Ashton would take the formulas of the war propagandists and treat them as a terrier treats a rat. So this was a war for democracy! The bankers of Paris had for the last twenty years been subsidizing the Russian Tsars, who had shipped a hundred thousand exiles to Siberia to make the world safe for democracy! The British Empire also had gone to war for democracy—first in Ireland, then in India and Egypt, then in the Whitechapel slums! No, said Ashton, the workers were not to be fooled with such bunk. Wall Street had loaned some billions of dollars to the Allied bankers, and now the American people were asked to shed their blood to make the world safe for those loans!

Peter had been urging McGivney to put an end to this sort of agitation, and now the rat-faced man told him that the time for action had come. There was to be a big mass meeting to celebrate the Bolshevik revolution, and McGivney warned Peter to keep out of sight at that meeting, because there might be some clubbing. Peter left off his red badge, and the button with the clasped hands and went up into the gallery and lost himself in the crowd. He saw a great many "bulls" whom he knew scattered thru the audience, and also he saw the Chief of Police and the head of the city's detective bureau. When Herbert Ashton was half way thru his tirade, the Chief strode up to the platform and ordered him under arrest, and a score of policemen put themselves between the prisoner and the howling audience.

Altogether they arrested seven people; and next morning, when they saw how much enthusiasm their action had awakened in the newspapers, they decided to go farther yet. A dozen of Guffey's men, with another dozen from the District Attorney's office, raided the office of Ashton's paper, the

"Clarion," kicked the editorial staff downstairs or threw them out of the windows, and proceeded to smash the typewriters and the printing presses, and to carry off the subscription lists and burn a ton or two of "literature" in the back yard. Also they raided the headquarters of the "Bolshevik local," and placed the seven members of the executive committee under arrest, and the judge fixed the bail of each of them at twenty-five thousand dollars, and every day for a week or two the American City "Times" would send a man around to Guffey's office, and Guffey would furnish him with a mass of material which Peter had prepared, showing that the Socialist program was one of terrorism and murder.

Almost every day now Peter rendered some such service to his country. He discovered where the I. W. W. had hidden a printing press with which they were getting out circulars and leaflets, and this place was raided, and the press confiscated, and half a dozen more agitators thrown into jail. These men declared a hunger strike, and tried to starve themselves to death as a protest against the beatings they got; and then some hysterical women met in the home of Ada Ruth, and drew up a circular of protest, and Peter kept track of the mailing of this circular, and all the copies were confiscated in the post-office, and so one more conspiracy was foiled. They now had several men at work in the post-office, secretly opening the mail of the agitators; and every now and then they would issue an order forbidding mail to be delivered to persons whose ideas were not sound.

Also the post-office department cancelled the second class mailing privileges of the "Clarion," and later it barred the paper from the mails entirely. A couple of "comrades" with automobiles then took up the work of delivering the paper in the nearby towns; so Peter was sent to get acquainted with these fellows, and in the night time some of Guffey's men entered the garage, and fixed one of the cars so that its steering gear went wrong and very nearly broke the driver's neck. So yet another conspiracy was foiled!

Peter was really happy now, because the authorities were thoroughly roused, and when he brought them new facts, he had the satisfaction of seeing something done about it. Ostensibly the action was taken by the Federal agents, or by the District Attorney's office, or by the city police and detectives; but Peter knew that it was always himself and the rest of Guffey's agents, pulling the wires behind the scenes. Guffey had the money, he was working for the men who really counted in American City; Guffey was the real boss. And all over the country it was the same; the Reds were being put out of business by the secret agents of the Chambers of Commerce and the Merchants' and Manufacturers' Associations, and the "Improve America League," and such like camouflaged organizations.

They had everything their own way, because the country was at war, the war excitement was blazing like a prairie fire all over the land, and all you had to do was to call a man a pro-German or a Bolshevik, and to be sufficiently excited about it, and you could get a mob together and go to his home and horsewhip him or tar and feather him or lynch him. For years the big business men had been hating the agitators, and now at last they had their chance, and in every town, in every shop and mill and mine they had some Peter Gudge at work, a "Jimmie Higgins" of the "Whites," engaged in spying and "snooping" upon the "Jimmie Higgins" of the "Reds." Everywhere they had Guffeys and McGivneys to direct these activities, and they had "strong arm men," with guns on their hips and deputy sheriffs' and other badges inside their coats, giving them unlimited right to protect the country from traitors.

There were three or four million men in the training camps, and every week great convoys were sent out from the Eastern ports, loaded with troops for "over there." Billions of dollars worth of munitions and supplies were going, and all the yearnings and patriotic fervors of the country were likewise going "over there." Peter read more speeches and sermons and editorials, and was proud and glad, knowing that he was taking his humble part in the great adventure. When he read that the biggest captains of industry and finance were selling their services to the government for the sum of one dollar a year, how could he complain, who was getting twenty dollars every week? When some of the Reds in their meetings or in their "literature" declared that these captains of industry and finance were the heads of companies which were charging the government enormous prices and making anywhere from three to ten times the profits they had made before the war—then Peter would know that he was listening to an extremely dangerous Bolshevik; he would take the name of the man to McGivney, and McGivney would pull his secret wires, and the man would suddenly find himself out of a job—or maybe being prosecuted by the health department of the city for having set out a garbage can without a cover.

After persistent agitation, the radicals had succeeded in persuading a judge to let out McCormick and the rest of the conspirators on fifty thousand dollars bail apiece. That was most exasperating to Peter, because it was obvious that when you put a Red into jail, you made him a martyr to the rest of the Reds you made him conspicuous to the whole community, and then if you let him out again, his speaking and agitating were ten times as effective as before. Either you ought to keep an agitator in jail for good, or else you ought not put him in at all. But the judges didn't see that—their heads were full of a lot of legal bunk, and they let David Andrews and the other Red lawyers hood-wink them. Herbert Ashton and his Socialist crowd also got out on bail, and the "Clarion" was still published and openly sold on the news-stands. While it didn't dare oppose the war any more, it printed every impolite thing it could possibly collect about the "gigantic trading corporation" known as the British Government, and also about the "French bankers" and the "Italian imperialists." It clamored for democracy for Ireland and Egypt and India, and shamelessly defended the Bolsheviki, those pro-German conspirators and nationalizers of women.

So Peter proceeded to collect more evidence against the "Clarion" staff, and against the I. W. Ws. Presently he read the good news that the government had arrested a couple of hundred of the I. W. W. leaders all over the country, and also the national leaders of the Socialists, and was going to try them all for conspiracy. Then came the trial of McCormick and Henderson and Gus and the rest; and Peter picked up his "Times" one morning, and read on the front page some news that caused him to gasp. Joe Angell, one of the leaders in the dynamite conspiracy, had turned state's evidence! He had revealed to the District Attorney, not only the part which he himself had played in the plan to dynamite Nelse Ackerman's home, but he had told everything that the others had done—just how the dynamite had been got and prepared, and the names of all the leading citizens of the community who were to share Nelse Ackerman's fate! Peter read, on and on, breathless with wonder, and when he got thru with the story he rolled back on his bed and laughed out loud. By heck, that was the limit! Peter had framed a frame-up on Guffey's man, and of course Guffey couldn't send this man to prison; so he had had him turn state's evidence, and was letting him go free, as his reward for telling on the others!

The court calendars were now crowded with "espionage" cases; pacifist clergymen who had tried to preach sermons, and labor leaders who had tried to call strikes; members of the Anti-conscription League and their pupils, the draft-dodgers and slackers; Anarchists and Communists and Quakers, I. W. Ws., and Socialists and "Russellites." There were several trials going on all the time, and in almost every case Peter had a finger, Peter was called on to get this bit of evidence, or to investigate that juror, or to prepare some little job against a witness for the defense. Peter was wrapped up in the fate of each case, and each conviction was a personal triumph. As there was always a conviction, Peter began to swell up again with patriotic fervor, and the memory of Nell Doolin and Ted Crothers slipped far into the background. When "Mac" and his fellow dynamiters were sentenced to twenty years apiece, Peter felt that he had atoned for all his sins, and he ventured timidly to point out to McGivney that the cost of living was going up all the time, and that he had kept his promise not to wink at a woman for six months. McGivney said all right, they would raise him to thirty dollars a week.

Section 70

Of course Peter's statement to McGivney had not been literally true. He had winked at a number of women, but the trouble was none had returned his wink. First he had made friendly advances toward Miriam Yankovich, who was buxom and not bad looking; but Miriam's thoughts were evidently all with McCormick in jail; and then, after her experience with Bob Ogden, Miriam had to go to a hospital, and of course Peter didn't want to fool with an invalid. He made himself agreeable to others of the Red girls, and they seemed to like him; they treated him as a good comrade, but somehow they did not seem to act up to McGivney's theories of "free love." So Peter made up his mind that he would find him a girl who was not a Red. It would give him a little relief now and then, a little fun. The Reds seldom had any fun—their idea of an adventure was to get off in a room by themselves and sing the International or the Red Flag in whispers, so the police couldn't hear them.

It was Saturday afternoon, and Peter went to a clothing store kept by a Socialist, and bought himself a new hat and a new suit of clothes on credit. Then he went out on the street, and saw a neat little girl going into a picture-show, and followed her, and they struck up an acquaintance and had supper together. She was what Peter called a "swell dresser," and it transpired that she worked in a manicure parlor. Her idea of fun corresponded to Peter's, and Peter spent all the money he had that Saturday evening, and made up his mind that if he could get something new on the Reds in the course of the week, he would strike McGivney for forty dollars.

Next morning was Easter Sunday, and Peter met his manicurist by appointment, and they went for a stroll on Park Avenue, which was the aristocratic street of American City and the scene of the "Easter parade." It was war time, and many of the houses had flags out, and many of the men were in uniform, and all of the sermons dealt with martial themes. Christ, it appeared, was risen again to make the world safe for democracy, and to establish self-determination for all people; and Peter and Miss Frisbie both had on their best clothes, and watched the crowds in the "Easter parade," and Miss Frisbie studied the costumes and make-up of the ladies, and picked up scraps of their conversation and whispered them to Peter, and made Peter feel that he was back on Mount Olympus again.

They turned into one of the swell Park Avenue churches; the Church of the Divine Compassion it was called, and it was very "high," with candles and incense—althogh you could hardly smell the incense on this occasion for the scent of the Easter lilies and the ladies. Peter and his friend were escorted to one of the leather covered pews, and they heard the Rev. de Willoughby Stotterbridge, a famous pulpit orator, deliver one of those patriotic sermons which were quoted in the "Times" almost every Monday morning. The Rev. de Willoughby Stotterbridge quoted some Old Testament text about exterminating the enemies of the Lord, and he sang the triumph of American arms, and the overwhelming superiority of American munitions. He denounced the Bolsheviks and all other traitors, and called for their instant suppression; he didn't say that he had actually been among the crowd which had horse-whipped the I. W. Ws. and smashed the printing presses and typewriters of the Socialists, but he made it unmistakably clear that that was what he wanted, and Peter's bosom swelled with happy pride. It was something to a man to know that he was serving his country and keeping the old flag waving; but it was still more to know that he was enlisted in the service of the Almighty, that Heaven and all its hosts were on his side, and that everything he had done had the sanction of the Almighty's divinely ordained minister, speaking in the Almighty's holy temple, in the midst of stained-glass windows and brightly burning candles and the ravishing odor of incense, and of Easter lilies and of mignonette and lavender in the handkerchiefs of delicately gowned and exquisite ladies from Mount Olympus. This, to be sure, was mixing mythologies, but Peter's education had been neglected in his youth, and Peter could not be blamed for taking the great ones of the earth as they were, and believing what they taught him.

The white robed choir marched out, and the music of "Onward Christian Soldiers" faded away, and Peter and his lady went out from the Church of the Divine Compassion, and strolled on the avenue again, and when they had sufficiently filled their nostrils with the sweet odors of snobbery, they turned into the park, where there were places of seclusion for young couples interested in each other. But alas, the fates which dogged Peter in his love-making had prepared an especially cruel prank that morning. At the entrance to the park, whom should Peter meet but Comrade Schnitzelmann, a fat little butcher who belonged to the "Bolshevik local" of American City. Peter tried to look the other way and hurry by, but Comrade Schnitzelmann would not have it so.

He came rushing up with one pudgy hand stretched out, and a beaming smile on his rosy Teutonic countenance. "Ach, Comrade Gudge!" cried he. "Wie geht's mit you dis morning?"

"Very well, thank you," said Peter, coldly, and tried to hurry on.

But Comrade Schnitzelmann held onto his hand. "So! You been seeing dot Easter barade!" said he. "Vot you tink, hey? If we could get all de wage slaves to come und see dot barade, we make dem all Bolsheviks pretty quick! Hey, Comrade Gudge?"

"Yes, I guess so," said Peter, still more coldly.

"We show dem vot de money goes for—hey, Comrade Gudge!" And Comrade Schnitzelmann chuckled, and Peter said, quickly, "Well, good-bye," and without introducing his lady-love took her by the arm and hurried away.

But alas, the damage had been done! They walked for a minute or two amid ominous silence. Then suddenly the manicurist stood still and confronted Peter. "Mr. Gudge," she demanded, "what does that mean?"

And Peter of course could not answer. He did not dare to meet her flashing eyes, but stood digging the toe of his shoe into the path. "I want to know what it means," persisted the girl. "Are you one of those Reds?"

And what could poor Peter say? How could he explain his acquaintance with that Teutonic face and that Teutonic accent?

The girl stamped her foot with impatient anger. "So you're one of those Reds! You're one of those pro-German traitors! You're an imposter, a spy!"

Peter was helpless with embarrassment and dismay. "Miss Frisbie," he began, "I can't explain—"

"*Why* can't you explain? Why can't any honest man explain?"

"But—but—I'm not what you think—it isn't true! I—I—" It was on the tip of Peter's tongue to say, "I'm a patriot! I'm a 100% American, protecting my country against these traitors!" But professional honor sealed his tongue, and the little manicurist stamped her foot again, and her eyes flashed with indignation.

"You dare to seek my acquaintance! You dare to take me to church! Why—if there was a policeman in sight, I'd report you, I'd send you to jail!" And actually she looked around for a policeman! But it is well known that there never is a policeman in sight when you look for one; so Miss Frisbie stamped her foot again and snorted in Peter's face. "Goodbye, *Comrade* Gudge!" The emphasis she put upon that word "comrade" would have frozen the fieriest Red soul; and she turned with a swish of her skirts and strode off, and Peter stood looking mournfully at her little French heels going crunch, crunch, crunch on the gravel path. When the heels were clean gone out of sight, Peter sought out the nearest bench and sat down and buried his face in his hands, a picture of woe. Was there ever in the world a man who had such persistent ill luck with women?

Section 71

These were days of world-agony, when people bought the newspapers several times every day, and when crowds gathered in front of bulletin boards, looking at the big maps with little flags, and speculating, were the Germans going to get to Paris, were they going to get to the Channel and put France out of the war? And then suddenly the Americans struck their first blow, and hurled the Germans back at Chateau-Thierry, and all America rose up with one shout of triumph!

You would think that was a poor time for pacifist agitation; but the members of the Anti-conscription League had so little discretion that they chose this precise moment to publish a pamphlet, describing the torturing of conscientious objectors in military prisons and training camps! Peter had been active in this organization from the beginning, and he had helped to write into the pamphlet a certain crucial phrase which McGivney had suggested. So now here were the pamphlets seized by the Federal government, and all the members of the Anti-conscription League under arrest, including Sadie Todd and little Ada Ruth and Donald Gordon! Peter was sorry about Sadie Todd, in spite of the fact that she had called him names. He couldn't be very sorry about Ada Ruth, because she was obviously a fanatic, bent on getting herself into trouble. As for Donald Gordon, if he hadn't learned his lesson from that whipping, he surely had nobody to blame but himself.

Peter was a member of this Anti-conscription League, so he pretended to be in hiding, and carried on a little comedy with Ada Ruth's cousin, an Englishwoman, who hid him out in her place in the country. Peter had an uncomfortable quarter of an hour when Donald Gordon was released on bail, because the Quaker boy insisted that the crucial phrase which had got them all into trouble had been stricken out of the manuscript before he handed it to Peter Gudge to take to the printer. But Peter insisted that Donald was mistaken, and apparently he succeeded in satisfying the others, and after they were all out on bail, he made bold to come out of his hiding place and to attend one or two protest meetings in private homes.

Then began a new adventure, in some ways the most startling of all. It had to do with another girl, and the beginning was in the home of Ada Ruth, where a few of the most uncompromising of the pacifists gathered to discuss the question of raising money to pay for their legal defense. To this meeting came Miriam Yankovich, pale from an operation for cancer of the breast, but with a heart and mind as Red as ever. Miriam had brought along a friend to help her, because she wasn't strong enough to walk; and it was this friend who started Peter on his new adventure.

Rosie Stern was her name, and she was a solid little Jewish working girl, with bold black eyes, and a mass of shining black hair, and flaming cheeks and a flashing smile. She was dressed as if she knew about her beauty, and really appreciated it; so Peter wasn't surprised when Miriam, introducing her, remarked that Rosie wasn't a Red and didn't like the Reds, but had just come to help her, and to see what a pacifist meeting was like. Perhaps Peter might help to make a Red out of her! And Peter was very glad indeed, for he was never more bored with the whining of pacifists than now when our boys were hurling the Germans back from the Marne and writing their names upon history's most imperishable pages.

Rosie was something new and unforeseen, and Peter went right after her, and presently he realized with delight that she was interested in him. Peter knew, of course, that he was superior to all this crowd, but he wasn't used to having the fact recognized, and as usual when a woman smiled upon him, the pressure of his self-esteem rose beyond the safety point. Rosie was one of those people who take the world as it is and get some fun out of it, so while the pacifist meeting went on, Peter sat over in the corner and told her in whispers his funny adventures with Pericles Priam and in the Temple of Jimjambo. Rosie could hardly repress her laughter, and her black eyes flashed, and before the evening was over their hands had touched several times. Then Peter offered to escort her and Miriam, and needless to say they took Miriam home first. The tenement streets were deserted at this late hour, so they found a chance for swift embraces, and Peter went home with his feet hardly touching the ground.

Rosie worked in a paper-box factory, and next evening Peter took her out to dinner, and their eager flirtation went on. But Rosie showed a tendency to retreat, and when Peter pressed her, she told him the reason. She had no use for Reds; she was sick of the jargon of the Reds, she would never love a Red. Look at Miriam Yankovich—what a wreck she had made of her life! She had been a handsome girl, she might have got a rich husband, but now she had had to be cut to pieces! And look at Sadie Todd, slaving herself to death, and Ada Ruth with her poems that made you tired. Rosie jeered at them all, and riddled them with the arrows of her wit, and of course Peter in his heart agreed with everything she said; yet Peter had to pretend to disagree, and that made Rosie cross and spoiled their fun, and they almost quarreled.

Under these circumstances, naturally it was hard for Peter not to give some hint of his true feeling. After he had spent all of his money on Rosie and a lot of his time and hadn't got anywhere, he decided to make some concession to her—he told her he would give up trying to make a Red out of her. Whereupon Rosie made a face at him. "Very kind indeed of you, Mr. Gudge! But how about my making a 'White' out of you?" And she went on to inform him that she wanted a fellow that could make money and take care of a girl. Peter answered that he was making money all right. Well, how was he making money, asked Rosie. Peter wouldn't tell, but he was making it, and he would prove it by taking her to the theater every night.

So the little duel went on, evening after evening. Peter got more and more crazy about this black-eyed beauty, and she got more and more coquettish, and more and more impatient with his radical leanings. Rosie's father had brought her as a baby from Kisheneff, but she was 100% American all the same, so she told him; those boys in khaki who were over there walloping the Huns were the boys for her, and she was waiting for one of them to come back. What was the matter with Peter that he wasn't doing his part? Was he a draft-dodger? Rosie had never had anything to do with slackers, and wasn't keen for the company of a man who couldn't give an account of himself. Only that day she had been reading in the paper about the atrocities committed by the Huns. How could any man with red blood in his veins sympathize with these pacifists and traitors? And if Peter didn't sympathize with them, why did he travel round with them and give them his moral support? When Peter made a feeble effort at repeating some of the pacifists' arguments, Rosie just said, "Oh, fudge! You've got too much sense to talk that kind of stuff to me." And Peter knew, of course, that he *had* too much sense, and it was hard to keep from letting Rosie see it. He had just lost one girl because of his Red entanglements. Was it up to him to lose another?

For a couple of weeks they sparred and fought. Rosie would let Peter kiss her, and Peter's head would be quite turned with desire. He decided that she was the most wonderful girl he had ever known; even Nell Doolin had nothing on her. But then once more she would pin Peter down on this business of his Redness, and would spurn him, and refuse to see him any more. At last Peter admitted to her that he had lost his sympathy with the Reds, she had converted him, and he despised them. So Rosie replied that she was delighted; they would go at once to see Miriam Yankovich, and Peter would tell her, and try to convert her also. Peter was then in a bad dilemma; he had to insist that Rosie should keep his conversion a secret. But Rosie became indignant, she set her lips and declared that a conversion that had to be kept secret was no conversion at all, it was simply a low sham, and Peter Gudge was a coward, and she was sick of him! So poor Peter went away, heartbroken and bewildered.

Section 72

There was only one way out of this plight for Peter, and that was for him to tell Rosie the truth. And why should he not do it? He was wild about her, and he knew that she was wild about him, and only one thing—his great secret—stood in the way of their perfect bliss. If he told her that great secret, he would be a hero of heroes in her eyes; he would be more wonderful even than the men who were driving back the Germans from the Marne and writing their names upon history's most imperishable pages! So why should he not tell?

He was in her room one evening, and his arms were about her, and she had almost but not quite yielded. "Please, please, Peter," she pleaded, "stop being one of those horrid Reds!" And Peter could stand it no longer. He told her that he really wasn't a Red, but a secret agent employed by the very biggest business men of American City to keep track of the Reds and bring their activities to naught. And when he told this, Rosie stared at him in consternation. She refused to believe him; when he insisted, she laughed at him, and finally became angry. It was a silly yarn, and did he imagine he could string her along like that?

So Peter, irritated, set out to convince her. He told her about Guffey and the American City Land & Investment Company; he told her about McGivney, and how he met McGivney regularly at Room 427 of the American House. He told her about his thirty dollars a week, and how it was soon to be increased to forty, and he would spend it all on her. And perhaps she might pretend to be converted by him, and become a Red also, and if she could satisfy McGivney that she was straight, he would pay her too, and it would be a lot better than working ten and a half hours a day in Isaac & Goldstein's paper box factory.

At last Peter succeeded in convincing the girl. She was subdued and frightened; she hadn't been prepared for anything like that, she said, and would have to have a little time to think it over. Peter then became worried in turn. He hoped she wouldn't mind, he said, and set to work to explain to her how important his work was, how it had the sanction of all the very best people in the city—not merely the great bankers and business men, but mayors and public officials and newspaper editors and college presidents, and great Park Avenue clergymen like the Rev. de Willoughby Stotterbridge of the Church of the Divine Compassion. And Rosie said that was all right, of course, but she was a little scared and would have to think it over. She brought the evening to an abrupt end, and Peter went home much disconcerted.

Perhaps an hour later there came a sharp tap on the door of his lodging-house room, and he went to the door, and found himself confronted by David Andrews, the lawyer, Donald Gordon, and John Durand, the labor giant, president of the Seamen's Union. They never even said, "Howdy do," but stalked into the room, and Durand shut the door behind him, and stood with his back to it, folded his arms and glared at Peter like the stone image of an Aztec chieftain. So before they said a word Peter knew what had happened. He knew that the jig was up for good this time; his career as savior of the nation was at an end. And again it was all on account of a woman—all because he hadn't taken Guffey's advice about winking!

But all other thoughts were driven from Peter's mind by one emotion, which was terror. His teeth began giving their imitation of an angry woodchuck, and his knees refused to hold him; he sat down on the edge of the bed, staring from one to another of these three stone Aztec faces. "Well, Gudge," said Andrews, at last, "so you're the spy we've been looking for all this time!"

Peter remembered Nell's injunction, "Stick it out, Peter! Stick it out!"

"Wh-wh-what do you mean, Mr. Andrews?"

"Forget it, Gudge," said Andrews. "We've just been talking with Rosie, and Rosie was our spy."

"She's been lying to you!" Peter cried.

But Andrews said: "Oh rubbish! We're not that easy! Miriam Yankovich was listening behind the door, and heard your talk."

So then Peter knew that the case was hopeless, and there was nothing left but to ascertain his fate. Had they come just to scold him and appeal to his conscience? Or did they plan to carry him away and strangle him and torture him to death? The latter was the terror that had been haunting Peter from the beginning of his career, and when gradually be made out that the three Aztecs did not intend violence, and that all they hoped for was to get him to admit how much he had told to his employers—then there was laughter inside Peter, and he broke down and wept tears of scalding shame, and said that it had all been because McCormick had told that cruel lie about him and little Jennie Todd. He had resisted the temptation for a year, but then he had been out of a job, and the Goober Defense Committee had refused him any work; he had actually been starving, and so at last he had accepted

McGivney's offer to let him know about the seditious activities of the extreme Reds. But he had never reported anybody who hadn't really broken the law, and he had never told McGivney anything but the truth.

Then Andrews proceeded to examine him. Peter denied that he had ever reported anything about the Goober case. He denied most strenuously that he had ever had anything to do with the McCormick "frame-up." When they tried to pin him down on this case and that, he suddenly summoned his dignity and declared that Andrews had no right to cross-question him, he was a 100%, red-blooded American patriot, and had been saving his country and his God from German agents and Bolshevik traitors.

Donald Gordon almost went wild at that. "What you've been doing was to slip stuff into our pamphlet about conscientious objectors, so as to get us all indicted!"

"That's a lie!" cried Peter. "I never done nothing of the kind!"

"You know perfectly well you rubbed out those pencil marks that I drew through that sentence in the pamphlet."

"I never done it!" cried Peter, again and again.

And suddenly big John Durand clenched his hands, and his face became terrible with his pent-up rage. "You white-livered little sneak!" he hissed. "What we ought to do with you is to pull the lying tongue out of you!" He took a step forward, as if he really meant to do it.

But David Andrews interfered. He was a lawyer, and knew the difference between what he could do and what Guffey's men could do. "No, no, John," he said, "nothing like that. I guess we've got all we can get out of this fellow. We'll leave him to his own conscience and his Jingo God. Come on, Donald." And he took the white-faced Quaker boy with one hand, and the big labor giant with the other, and walked them out of the room, and Peter heard them tramping down the stairs of his lodging house, and he lay on his bed and buried his face in the pillows, and felt utterly wretched, because once more he had been made a fool of, and as usual it was a woman that had done it.

Peter could see it all very clearly when he came to figure over the thing; he could see what a whooping jackass he had been. He might have known that it was up to him to be careful, at this time of all times, when he was suspected of having rubbed out Donald Gordon's pencil marks. They had picked out a girl whom Peter had never seen before, and she had come and posed as Miriam's friend, and had proceeded to take Peter by the nose and lead him to the edge of the precipice and shove him over. And now she would be laughing at him, telling all her friends about her triumph, and about Peter's thirty dollars a week that he would never see again.

Peter spent a good part of the night getting up the story that he was to tell McGivney next morning. He wouldn't mention Rosie Stern, of course; he would say that the Reds had trailed him to Room 427, and it must be they had a spy in Guffey's office. Peter repeated this story quite solemnly, and again realized too late that he had made a fool of himself. It wasn't twenty-four hours before every Red in American City knew the true, inside history of the unveiling of Peter Gudge as a spy of the Traction Trust. The story occupied a couple of pages in that week's issue of the "Clarion," and included Peter's picture, and an account of the part that Peter had played in various frame-ups. It was nearly all true, and the fact that it was guess-work on Donald Gordon's part did not make it any the better for Peter. Of course McGivney and Guffey and all his men read the story, and knew Peter for the whooping jackass that Peter knew himself.

"You go and get yourself a job with a pick and shovel," said McGivney, and Peter sorrowfully took his departure. He had only a few dollars in his pocket, and these did not last very long, and he had got down to his last nickel, and was confronting the wolf of starvation again, when McGivney came to his lodging house room with a new proposition. There was one job left, and Peter might take it if he thought he could stand the gaff.

It was the job of state's witness. Peter had been all thru the Red movement, he knew all these pacifists and Socialists and Syndicalists and I. W. Ws. who were now in jail. In some cases the evidence of the government was far from satisfactory; so Peter might have his salary back again, if he were willing to take the witness stand and tell what he was told to tell, and if he could manage to sit in a courtroom without falling in love with some of the lady jurors, or some of the lady spies of the defense. These deadly shafts of sarcasm Peter did not even feel, because he was so frightened by the proposition which McGivney put up to him. To come out into the open and face the blinding glare of the Red hate! To place himself, the ant, between the smashing fists of the battling giants!

Yes, it might seem dangerous, said McGivney, for a cowardly little whelp like himself; but then a good many men had had the nerve to do it, and none of them had died yet. McGivney himself did not pretend to care very much whether Peter did it or not; he put the matter up to him on Guffey's orders. The job was worth forty dollars a week, and he might take it or leave it.

And there sat Peter, with only a nickel and a couple of pennies in his pocket, and the rent for his room two weeks over-due, and his landlady lying in wait in the hallway like an Indian with a tomahawk. Peter objected, what about all those bad things in his early record, Pericles Priam and the Temple of Jimjambo, which had ruined him as a witness in the Goober case. McGivney answered dryly that he couldn't let himself out with that excuse; he was invited to pose as a reformed "wobbly," and the more crimes and rascalities he had in his record, the more convinced the jury would be that he had been a real "wobbly."

Peter asked, just when would he be expected to appear? And McGivney answered, the very next week. They were trying seventeen of the "wobblies" on a conspiracy charge, and Peter would be expected to take the stand and tell how he had heard them advocate violence, and heard them boast of having set fire to barns and wheat fields, and how they had put phosphorus bombs into haystacks, and copper nails into fruit trees, and spikes into sawmill logs, and emery powder into engine bearings. Peter needn't worry about what he would have to say, McGivney would tell him everything, and would see him thoroughly posted, and he would find himself a hero in the newspapers, which would make clear that he had done everything from the very highest possible motives of 100% Americanism, and that no soldier in the war had been performing a more dangerous service.

To Peter it seemed they might say that without troubling their conscience very much. But McGivney went on to declare that he needn't be afraid; it was no part of Guffey's program to give the Reds the satisfaction of putting his star witness out of business. Peter would be kept in a safe place, and would always have a body-guard. While he was in the city, giving his testimony, they would put him up at the Hotel de Soto.

And that of course settled it. Here was poor Peter, with only a nickel and two coppers in his pocket, and before him stood a chariot of fire with magic steeds, and all he had to do was to step in, and be whirled away to Mount Olympus. Peter stepped in!

Section 74

M cGivney took him to Guffey's office, and Guffey wasted no time upon preliminaries, but turned to his desk, and took out a long typewritten document, a complete account of what the prosecution meant to prove against the seventeen I. W. Ws. First, Peter told what he himself had seen and heard—not very much, but a beginning, a hook to hang his story upon. The I. W. W. hall was the meeting place for the casual and homeless labor of the country, the "bindle-stiffs" who took the hardest of the world's hard knocks, and sometimes returned them. There was no kind of injustice these fellows hadn't experienced, and now and then they had given blow for blow. Also there were loose talkers among them, who worked off their feelings by threats of vengeance upon their enemies. Now and then a real criminal came along, and now and then a paid inciter, a Peter Gudge or a Joe Angell. Peter told the worst that he had heard, and all he knew about the arrested men, and Guffey wrote it all down, and then proceeded to build upon it. This fellow Alf Guinness had had a row with a farmer in Wheatland County; there had been a barn burned nearby, and Guffey would furnish an automobile and a couple of detectives to travel with Peter, and they would visit the scene of that fire and the nearby village, and familiarize themselves with the locality, and Peter would testify how he had been with Guinness when he and a half dozen of the defendants had set fire to that barn.

Peter hadn't intended anything quite so serious as that, but Guffey was so business-like, and took it all so much as a matter of course, that Peter was afraid to show the white feather. After all, this was war-time; hundreds of men were giving up their lives every day in the Argonne, and why shouldn't Peter take a little risk in order to put out of business his country's most dangerous enemies?

So Peter and his two detectives blew themselves to a joy ride in the country. And then Peter was brought back and made comfortable in a room on the twelfth floor of the Hotel de Soto, where he diligently studied the typewritten documents which McGivney brought him, and thoroughly learned the story he was to tell. There was always one of Guffey's men walking up and down in the hallway outside with a gun on his hip, and they brought Peter three meals a day, not forgetting a bottle of beer and a package of cigarettes. Twice a day Peter read in the newspapers about the heroic deeds of our boys over there, and also about the latest bomb plots which had been discovered all over the country, and about various trials under the espionage act.

Also, Peter had the thrill of reading about himself in a real newspaper. Hitherto he had been featured in labor papers, and Socialist papers like the "Clarion," which did not count; but now the American City "Times" came out with a long story of how the district attorney's office had "planted" a secret agent with the I. W. W., and how this man, whose name was Peter Gudge, had been working as one of them for the past two years, and was going to reveal the whole story of I. W. W. infamy on the witness stand.

Two days before the trial Peter was escorted by McGivney and another detective to the district attorney's office, and spent the best part of the day in conference with Mr. Burchard and his deputy, Mr. Stannard, who were to try the case. McGivney had told Peter that the district attorney was not in the secret, he really believed that Peter's story was all true; but Peter suspected that this was camouflage, to save Mr. Burchard's face, and to protect him in case Peter ever tried to "throw him down." Peter noticed that whenever he left any gap in his story, the district attorney and the deputy told him to fill it, and he managed to guess what to fill it with.

Henry Clay Burchard came from the far South, and followed a style of oratory long since gone out of date. He wore his heavy black hair a little long, and when he mounted the platform he would pull out the tremulo stop, stretching out his hands and saying in tones of quivering emotion: "The ladies, God bless them!" Also he would say: "I am a friend of the common man. My heart beats with sympathy for those who constitute the real backbone of America, the toilers of the shop and farm." And then all the banqueters of the Chamber of Commerce and the Merchants' and Manufacturers' Association would applaud, and would send their checks to the campaign fund of this friend of the common man. Mr. Burchard's deputy, Mr. Stannard, was a legal fox who told his chief what to do and how to do it; a dried-up little man who looked like a bookworm, and sat boring you thru with his keen eyes, watching for your weak points and preparing to pierce you thru with one of his legal rapiers. He would be quite friendly about it—he would joke with you in the noon hour, assuming that you would of course understand it was all in the line of business, and no harm meant.

Section 75

The two men heard Peter's story and changed it a little, and then heard him over again and pronounced him all right, and Peter went back to his hotel room and waited in trepidation for his hour in the limelight. When they took him to court his knees were shaking, but also he had a thrill of real importance, for they had provided him with a body-guard of four big huskies; also he saw two "bulls" whom he recognized in the hallway outside the court-room, and many others scattered thru the audience. The place was packed with Red sympathizers, but they had all been searched before they were allowed to enter, and were being watched every moment during the trial.

When Peter stepped into the witness box he felt as Tom Duggan and Donald Gordon must have felt that night when the white glare from thirty or forty automobiles was beating upon them. Peter felt the concentrated Red hate of two or three hundred spectators, and now and then their pent-up fury would break restraint; there would be a murmur of protest, or perhaps a wave of sneering laughter, and the bailiff would bang on the table with his wooden mallet, and the judge would half rise from his seat, and declare that if that happened again he would order the court-room cleared.

Not far in front of Peter at a long table sat the seventeen defendants, looking like trapped rats, and every one of their thirty-four rat eyes were fixed upon Peter's face, and never moved from it. Peter only glanced that way once; they bared their rats' teeth at him, and he quickly looked in another direction. But there also he saw a face that brought him no comfort; there sat Mrs. Godd, in her immaculate white chiffons, her wide-open blue eyes fixed upon his face, her expression full of grief and reproach. "Oh, Mr. Gudge!" she seemed to be saying. "How can you? Mr. Gudge, is this Peace. . . justice. . . Truth. . . Law?" And Peter realized with a pang that he had cut himself off forever from Mount Olympus, and from the porch chair with the soft silken pillows! He turned away toward the box where sat the twelve jurymen and women. One old lady gave him a benevolent smile, and a young farmer gave him a sly wink, so Peter knew that he had friends in that quarter—and after all, they were the ones who really counted in this trial. Mrs. Godd was as helpless as any "wobbly," in the presence of this august court.

Peter told his story, and then came his cross-questioning, and who should rise and start the job but David Andrews, suave and humorous and deadly. Peter had always been afraid of Andrews, and now he winced. Nobody had told him he was to face an ordeal like this! Nobody had told him that Andrews would be allowed to question him about every detail of these crimes which he said he had witnessed, and about all the conversations that had taken place, and who else was present, and what else had been said, and how he had come to be there, and what he had done afterwards, and what he had had to eat for breakfast that morning. Only two things saved Peter, first the constant rapid-fire of objections which Stannard kept making, to give Peter time to think; and second, the cyclone-cellar which Stannard had provided for him in advance. "You can always fail to remember," the deputy had said; "nobody can punish you for forgetting something." So Peter would repeat the minute details of a conversation in which Alf Guinness had told of burning down the barn, but he didn't remember who else had heard the conversation, and he didn't remember what else had been said, nor what was the date of the conversation.

Then came the blessed hour of noon, with a chance for Peter to get fixed up again before the court resumed at two. He was questioned again by Stannard, who patched up all the gaps in his testimony, and then again he failed to remember things, and so avoided the traps which Andrews set for his feet. He was told that he had "done fine," and was escorted back to the Hotel de Soto in triumph, and there for a week he stayed while the defense made a feeble effort to answer his testimony. Peter read in the papers the long speeches in which the district attorney and the deputy acclaimed him as a patriot, protecting his country from its "enemies within;" also he read a brief reference to the "tirade" of David Andrews, who had called him a "rat" and a "slinking Judas." Peter didn't mind that, of course—it was all part of the game, and the calling of names is a pretty sure sign of impotence.

Less easy to accept placidly, however, was something which came to Peter that same day—a letter from Mrs. Godd! It wasn't written to him, but he saw Hammett and another of the "bulls" chuckling together, and he asked what was the joke, and they told him that Mrs. Godd had somehow found out about Guffey, and had written him a letter full of insults, and Guffey was furious. Peter asked what was in it, and they told him, and later on when he insisted, they brought it and showed it to him, and Peter was furious too. On very expensive stationery with a stately crest at the top, the mother of Mount Olympus had written in a large, bland, girlish hand her opinion of "under cover" men and those who hired them:

"You sit like a big spider and weave a net to catch men and destroy them. You destroy alike your victims and your tools. The poor boy, Peter Gudge, whom you sent to my home—my heart bleeds when I think of him, and what you have put him up to! A wretched, feeble-minded victim of greed, who ought to be sent to a hospital for deformed souls, you have taken him and taught him a piece of villainy to recite, so that he may send a group of sincere idealists to prison."

That was enough! Peter put down the letter—he would not dignify such stuff by reading it. He realized that he would have to put his mind on the problem of Mrs. Godd once more. One woman like that, in her position of power, was more dangerous than all the seventeen "wobblies" who had been haled before the court. Peter inquired, and learned that Guffey had already been to see Nelse Ackerman about it, and Mr. Ackerman had been to see Mr. Godd, and Mr. Godd had been to see Mrs. Godd. Also the "Times" had an editorial referring to the "nest of Bolshevism" upon Mount Olympus, and all Mrs. Godd's friends were staying away from her luncheon-parties—so she was being made to suffer for her insolence to Peter Gudge!

"A hospital for deformed souls," indeed! Peter was so upset that his joy in life was not restored even by the news that the jury had found the defendants guilty on the first ballot. He told McGivney that the strain of this trial had been too much for his nerves, and they must take care of him; so an automobile was provided, and Peter was taken to a secret hiding place in the country to recuperate.

Hammett went with him, and Hammett was a first-class gunman, and Peter stayed close by him; in the evening he stayed up in the second story of the farm-house, lest perchance one of the "wobblies" should take too literally the testimony Peter had given concerning their habit of shooting at their enemies out of the darkness. Peter knew how they all must hate him; he read in the paper how the judge summoned the guilty men before him and sentenced them, incidentally forcing them to listen to a scathing address, which was published in full in the "Times." The law provided a penalty of from one to fourteen years, and the judge sentenced sixteen of them to fourteen years, and one to ten years, thus tempering justice with mercy.

Then one day McGivney sent an automobile, and Peter was brought to Guffey's office, and a new plan was unfolded to him. They had arrested another bunch of "wobblies" in the neighboring city of Eldorado, and Peter was wanted there to repeat his testimony. It happened that he knew one of the accused men, and that would be sufficient to get his testimony in—his prize stuff about the burning barns and the phosphorus bombs. He would be taken care of just as thoroughly by the district attorney's office of Eldorado County; or better yet, Guffey would write to his friend Steve Ellman, who did the detective work for the Home and Fireside Association, the big business organization of that city.

Peter hemmed and hawed. This was a pretty hard and dangerous kind of work, it really played the devil with a man's nerves, sitting up there in the hotel room all day, with nothing to do but smoke cigarettes and imagine the "wobblies" throwing bombs at you. Also, it wouldn't last very long; it ought to be better paid. Guffey answered that Peter needn't worry about the job's lasting; if he cared to give this testimony, he might have a joy ride from one end of the country to the other, and everywhere he would live on the fat of the land, and be a hero in the newspapers.

But still Peter hemmed and hawed. He had learned from the American City "Times" how valuable a witness he was, and he ventured to demand his price, even from the terrible Guffey; he stuck it out, in spite of Guffey's frowns, and the upshot was that Guffey said, All right, if Peter would take the trip he might have seventy-five dollars a week and expenses, and Guffey would guarantee to keep him busy for not less than six months.

Section 76

S o Peter went to Eldorado, and helped to send eleven men to the penitentiary for periods varying from three to fourteen years. Then he went to Flagland, and testified in three different trials, and added seven more scalps to his belt. By this time he got to realize that the worst the Reds could do was to make faces at him and show the teeth of trapped rats. He learned to take his profession more easily, and would sometimes venture to go out for an evening's pleasure without his guards. When he was hidden in the country he would take long walks regardless of the thousands of blood-thirsty Reds on his trail.

It was while Peter was testifying in Flagland that a magic word was flashed from Europe, and the whole city went mad with joy. Everyone, from babies to old men, turned out on the streets and waved flags and banged tin cans and shouted for peace with victory. When it was learned that the newspapers had fooled them, they waited three days, and then turned out and went thru the same performance again. Peter was a bit worried at first, for fear the coming of peace might end his job of saving the country; but presently he realized that there was no need for concern, the smashing of the Reds was going on just the same.

They had some raids on the Socialists while Peter was in Flagland, and the detectives told him he might come along for the fun of it. So Peter armed himself with a black-jack and a revolver, and helped to rush the Socialist headquarters. The war was over, but Peter felt just as military as if it were still going on; when he got the little Jewish organizer of the local pent up in a corner behind his desk and proceeded to crack him over the head, Peter understood exactly how our boys had felt in the Argonne. When he discovered the thrill of dancing on typewriter keys with his boots, he even understood how the Huns had felt.

The detectives were joined by a bunch of college boys, who took to that kind of thing with glee. Having got their blood up, they decided they might as well clean out the Red movement entirely, so they rushed a place called the "International Book-Shop," kept by a Hawaiian. The proprietor dodged into the kitchen of a Chinese restaurant next door, and put on an apron; but no one had ever seen a Chinaman with a black mustache, so they fell on him and broke several of the

Chinaman's sauce-pans over his head. They took the contents of the "International Book-Shop" into the back yard and started a bon-fire with it, and detectives and college boys on a lark joined hands and danced an imitation of the Hawaiian hula-hula around the blaze.

So Peter lived a merry life for several months. He had one or two journeys for nothing, because an obstinate judge refused to admit that anything that any I. W. W. had ever said or done anywhere within the last ten years was proper testimony to be introduced against a particular I. W. W. on trial. But most judges were willing to co-operate with the big business men in ridding the country of the Red menace, and Peter's total of scalps amounted to over a hundred before his time was up, and Guffey sent him his last cheek and turned him loose.

That was in the city of Richport, and Peter having in an inside pocket something over a thousand dollars in savings, felt that he had earned a good time. He went for a stroll on the Gay White Way of the city, and in front of a moving picture palace a golden-haired girl smiled at him. This was still in the days of two and three-fourths per cent beer, and Peter invited her into a saloon to have a glass, and when he opened his eyes again it was dark, and he had a splitting headache, and he groped around and discovered that he was lying in a dark corner of an alleyway. Terror gripped his heart, and he clapped his hand to the inside pocket where his wallet had been, and there was nothing but horrible emptiness. So Peter was ruined once again, and as usual it was a woman that had done it!

Peter went to the police-station, but they never found the woman, or if they did, they divided with her and not with Peter. He threw himself on the mercy of the sergeant at the desk, and succeeded in convincing the sergeant that he, Peter, was a part of the machinery of his country's defense, and the sergeant agreed to stand sponsor for ten words to Guffey. So Peter sat himself down with a pencil and paper, and figured over it, and managed to get it into ten words, as follows: "Woman again broke any old job any pay wire fare." And it appeared that Guffey must have sat himself down with a pencil and paper and figured over it also, for the answer came back in ten words, as follows: "Idiot have wired secretary chamber commerce will give you ticket."

So Peter repaired forthwith to the stately offices of the Chamber of Commerce, and the hustling, efficient young business-man secretary sent his clerk to buy Peter a ticket and put him on the train. In a time of need like that Peter realized what it meant to have the backing of a great and powerful organization, with stately offices and money on hand for all emergencies, even when they arose by telegraph. He took a new vow of sobriety and decency, so that he might always have these forces of law and order on his side.

Section 77

Peter was duly scolded, and put to work as an "office man" at his old salary of twenty dollars a week. It was his duty to consult with Guffey's many "operatives," to tell them everything he knew about this individual Red or that organization of Reds. He would use his inside knowledge of personalities and doctrines and movements to help in framing up testimony, and in setting traps for too ardent agitators. He could no longer pose as a Red himself, but sometimes there were cases where he could do detective work without being recognized; when, for example, there was a question of fixing a juror, or of investigating the members of a panel.

The I. W. Ws. had been put out of business in American City, but the Socialists were still active, in spite of prosecutions and convictions. Also there was a new peril looming up; the returned soldiers were coming back, and a lot of them were dissatisfied, presuming to complain of their treatment in the army, and of the lack of good jobs at home, and even of the peace treaty which the President was arranging in Paris. They had fought to make the world safe for democracy, and here, they said, it had been made safe for the profiteers. This was plain Bolshevism, and in its most dangerous form, because these fellows had learned to use guns, and couldn't very well be expected to become pacifists right off the bat.

There had been a great labor shortage during the war, and some of the more powerful unions had taken the general rise in prices as an excuse for demanding higher wages. This naturally had made the members of the Chamber of Commerce and the Merchants' and Manufacturers' Association indignant, and now they saw their chance to use these returned soldiers to smash strikes and to break the organizations of the labor men. They proceeded to organize the soldiers for this purpose; in American City the Chamber of Commerce contributed twenty-five thousand dollars to furnish the club-rooms for them, and when the trolley men went on strike the cars were run by returned soldiers in uniform.

There was one veteran, a fellow by the name of Sydney, who objected to this program. He was publishing a paper, the "Veteran's Friend," and began to use the paper to protest against his comrades acting as what he called "scabs." The secretary of the Merchants' and Manufacturers' Association sent for him and gave him a straight talking to, but he went right ahead with his campaign, and so Guffey's office was assigned the task of shutting him up. Peter, while he could not take an active part in the job, was the one who guided it behind the scenes. They proceeded to plant spies in Sydney's office, and they had so many that it was really a joke; they used to laugh and say that they trod on one another's toes. Sydney was poor, and had not enough money to run his paper, so he accepted any volunteer labor that came along. And Guffey sent him plenty of volunteers—no less than seven operatives—one keeping Sydney's books, another helping with his mailing, two more helping to raise funds among the labor unions, others dropping in every day or two to advise him. Nevertheless Sydney went right ahead with his program of denouncing the Merchants' and Manufacturers' Association, and denouncing the government for its failure to provide farms and jobs for the veterans.

One of Guffey's "under cover operatives"—that was the technical term for the Peter Gudges and Joe Angells—was a man by the name of Jonas. This Jonas called himself a "philosophic anarchist," and posed as the reddest Red in American City; it was his habit to rise up in radical meetings and question the speaker, and try to tempt him to justify violence and insurrection and "mass-action." If he repudiated these ideas, then Jonas would denounce him as a "mollycoddle," a "pink tea Socialist," a "labor faker." Other people in the audience would applaud, and so Guffey's men would find out who were the real Red sympathizers.

Peter had long suspected Jonas, and now he was sent to meet him in Room 427 of the American House, and together they framed up a job on Sydney. Jonas wrote a letter, supposed to come from a German "comrade," giving the names of some papers in Europe to which the editor should send sample copies of his magazine. This letter was mailed to Sydney, and next morning Jonas wandered into the office, and Sydney showed him the letter, and Jonas told him that these were labor papers, and the editors would no doubt be interested to know of the feelings of American soldiers since the war. Sydney sat down to write a letter, and Jonas stood by his side and told him what to write: "To my erstwhile enemies in arms I send fraternal greetings, and welcome you as brothers in the new co-operative commonwealth which is to be"—and so on, the usual Internationalist patter, which all these agitators were spouting day and night, and which ran off the ends of their pens automatically. Sydney mailed these letters, and the sample copies of the magazine, and Guffey's office tipped off the postoffice authorities, who held up the letters. The book-keeper, one of Guffey's operatives, went to the Federal attorney and made affidavit that Sydney had been carrying on a conspiracy with the enemy in war-time, and a warrant was issued, and the offices of the magazine were raided, the subscription-lists confiscated, and everything in the rooms dumped out into the middle of the floor.

So there was a little job all Peter's own; except that Jonas, the scoundrel, claimed it for his, and tried to deprive Peter of the credit! So Peter was glad when the Federal authorities looked the case over and said it was a bum job, and they wouldn't monkey with it. However, the evidence was turned over to District-attorney Burchard, who wasn't quite so fastidious, and his agents made another raid, and smashed up the office again, and threw the returned soldier into jail. The judge fixed the bail at fifteen thousand dollars, and the American City "Times" published the story with scare-headlines all the way across the front page—how the editor of the "Veteran's Friend" had been caught conspiring with the enemy, and here was a photographic copy of his treasonable letter, and a copy of the letter of the mysterious German conspirator with whom he had been in relations! They spent more than a year trying that editor, and although he was out on bail, Guffey saw to it that he could not get a job anywhere in American City; his paper was smashed and his family near to starvation.

Section 78

Peter had now been working faithfully for six or eight months, and all that time he religiously carried out his promise to Guffey and did not wink at a woman. But that is an unnatural life for a man, and Peter was lonely, his dreams were haunted by the faces of Nell Doolin and Rosie Stern, and even of little Jennie Todd. One day another face came back to him, the face of Miss Frisbie, the little manicurist who had spurned him because he was a Red. Now suddenly Peter realized that he was no longer a Red! On the contrary, he was a hero, his picture had been published in the American City "Times," and no doubt Miss Frisbie had seen it. Miss Frisbie was a good girl, a straight girl, and surely all right for him to know!

So Peter went to the manicure parlor, and sure enough, there was the little golden-haired lady; and sure enough, she had read all about him, she had been dreaming that some day she might meet him again—and so Peter invited her to go to a picture show. On the way home they became very chummy, and before a week went by it was as if they had been friends for life. When Peter asked Miss Frisbie if he might kiss her, she answered coyly that he might, but after he had kissed her a few times she explained to him that she was a self-supporting woman, alone and defenseless in the world, and she had nobody to speak for her but herself; she must tell him that she had always been a respectable woman, and that she wanted him to know that before he kissed her any more. And Peter thought it over and decided that he had sowed his full share of wild oats in this life; he was ready to settle down, and the next time he saw Miss Frisbie he told her so, and before the evening was by they were engaged.

Then Peter went to see Guffey, and seated himself on the edge of the chair alongside Guffey's desk, and twisted his hat in his hands, and flushed very red, and began to stammer out his confession. He expected to be received with a gale of ridicule; he was immensely relieved when Guffey said that if Peter had really found a good girl and wanted to marry her, he, Guffey, was for it. There was nothing like the influence of a good woman, and Guffey much preferred his operatives should be married men, living a settled and respectable life. They could be trusted then, and sometimes when a woman operative was needed, they had a partner ready to hand. If Peter had got married long ago, he might have had a good sum of money in the bank by now.

Peter ventured to point out that twenty dollars a week was not exactly a marrying salary, in the face of the present high cost of living. Guffey answered that that was true, and he would raise Peter to thirty dollars right away—only first he demanded the right to talk to Peter's fiancee, and judge for himself whether she was worthy. Peter was delighted, and Miss Frisbie had a private and confidential interview with Peter's boss. But afterwards Peter wasn't quite so delighted, for he realized what Guffey had done. Peter's future wife had been told all about Peter's weakness, and how Peter's boss looked to her to take care of her husband and make him walk the chalkline. So a week after Peter had entered the holy bonds of matrimony, when he and Mrs. Gudge had their first little family tiff, Peter suddenly discovered who was going to be top dog in that family. He was shown his place once for all, and he took it,—alongside that husband who described his domestic arrangements by saying that he and his wife got along beautifully together, they had come to an arrangement by which he was to have his way on all major issues, and she was to have her way on all minor issues, and so far no major issues had arisen.

But really it was a very good thing; for Gladys Frisbie Gudge was an excellent manager, and set to work making herself a nest as busily as any female beaver. She still hung on to her manicurist job, for she had figured it out that the Red movement must be just about destroyed by now, and pretty soon Peter might find himself without work. In the evenings she took to house-hunting, and during her noon hour, without consulting Peter she selected the furniture and the wall-paper, and pretty nearly bought out the stock of a five-and-ten-cent store to equip the beaver's nest.

Gladys Frisbie Gudge was a diligent reader of the fashion magazines, and kept herself right up to the minute with the styles; also she had got herself a book on etiquette, and learned it by heart from cover to cover, and now she took Peter in hand and taught it to him. Why must he always be a "Jimmie Higgins" of the "Whites?" Why should he not acquire the vocabulary of an educated man, the arts and graces of the well-to-do? Gladys knew that it is these subtleties which determine your salary in the long run; so every Sunday morning she would dress him up with a new brown derby and a new pair of brown kid gloves, and take him to the Church of the Divine Compassion, and they would listen to the patriotic sermon of the Rev. de Willoughby Stotterbridge, and Gladys would bow her head in prayer, and out of the corner of her eye would get points on costumes from the lady in the next pew. And afterwards they would join the Sunday parade, and Gladys would point out to Peter the marks of what she called "gentility." In the evenings they would go walking, and she would stop in front of the big shop-windows, or take him into the hotel lobbies where the rich could be seen free of charge. Peter would be hungry, and would want to go to a cheap restaurant and fill himself up with honest grub; but Gladys, who had the appetite of a bird, would insist on marching him into the dining-room of the Hotel de Soto and making a meal upon a cup of broth and some bread and butter—just in order that they might gaze upon a scene of elegance and see bow "genteel" people ate their food.

Section 79

A nd just as ardently as Gladys Frisbie Gudge adored the rich, so ardently did she object to the poor. If you pinned her down to it, she would admit that there had to be poor; there could not be gentility, except on the basis of a large class of ungentility. The poor were all right in their place; what Gladys objected to was their presuming to try to get out of their place, or to criticise their betters. She had a word by which she summed up everything that she despised in the world, and that word was "common;" she used it to describe the sort of people she declined to meet, and she used it in correcting Peter's manners and his taste in hats. To be "common" was to be damned; and when Gladys saw people who were indubitably and inescapably "common," presuming to set themselves up and form standards of their own, she took it as a personal affront, she became vindictive and implacable towards them. Each and every one of them became to her a personal enemy, an enemy to something far more precious than her person, an enemy to the thing she aspired to become, to her ideal.

Peter had once been like that himself, but now he was so comfortable, he had a tendency to become lazy and easy-going. It was well, therefore, that he had Gladys to jack him up, and keep him on his job. Gladys at first did not meet any Reds face to face, she knew them only by the stories that Peter brought home to her when his day's work was done. But each new group that he was hounding became to Gladys an assemblage of incarnate fiends, and while she sat polishing the finger-nails of stout society ladies who were too sleepy to talk, Gladys' busy mind would be working over schemes to foil these fiends.

Sometimes her ideas were quite wonderful. She had a woman's intuition, the knowledge of human foibles, all the intricate subtleties of the emotional life; she would bring to Peter a program for the undoing of some young radical, as complete as if she had known the man or woman all her life. Peter took her ideas to McGivney, and then to Guffey, and the result was that her talents were recognized, and by the lever of a generous salary she was pried loose from the manicure parlor. Guffey sent her to make the acquaintance of the servants in the household of a certain rich man who was continually making contributions to the Direct Primary Association and other semi-Red organizations, and who was believed to have a scandal in his private life. So successful was

Gladys at this job that presently Guffey set her at the still more delicate task of visiting rich ladies, and impressing upon them the seriousness of the Red peril, and persuading them to meet the continually increasing expenses of Guffey's office.

Just now was a busy time in the anti-Red campaign. For nearly two years, ever since the Bolshevik revolution in Russia, there had been gradually developing a split in the Socialist movement, and the "under-cover" operatives of the Traction Trust, as well as those of the district attorney's office and of the Federal government, had been working diligently to widen this split and develop dissensions in the organization. There were some Socialists who believed in politics, and were prepared to devote their lives to the slow and tedious job of building up a party. There were others who were impatient, looking for a short cut, a general strike or a mass insurrection of the workers which would put an end to the slavery of capitalism. The whole game of politics was rotten, these would argue; a politician could find more ways to fool the workers in a minute than the workers could thwart in a year. They pointed to the German Socialists, those betrayers of internationalism. There were people who called themselves Socialists right here in American City who wanted to draw the movement into the same kind of trap!

This debate was not conducted in the realm of abstractions; the two wings of the movement would attack one another with bitterness. The "politicians" would denounce the "impossibilists," calling them "anarchists;" and the other side, thus goaded, would accuse their enemies of being in the hire of the government. Peter would supply McGivney with bits of scandal which the "under cover" men would start going among the "left-wingers;" and in the course of the long wrangles in the local these accusations would come out. Herbert Ashton would mention them with his biting sarcasm, or "Shorty" Gunton would shout them in one of his tirades—"hurling them into his opponents teeth," as he phrased it.

"Shorty" Gunton was a tramp printer, a wandering agitator who was all for direct action, and didn't care a hang who knew it. "Violence?" he would say. "How many thousand years shall we submit to the violence of capitalist governments, and never have the right to reply?" And then again he would say, "Violence? Yes, of course we must repudiate violence—until we get enough of it!" Peter had listened to "Shorty's" railings at the "compromisers" and the "political traders," and had thought him one of the most dangerous men in American City. But later on, after the episode of Joe Angell had opened Peter's eyes, he decided that "Shorty" must also be a secret agent like himself.

Peter was never told definitely, but he picked up a fact here and there, and fitted them together, and before long his suspicion had become certainty. The "left wing" Socialists split off from the party, and called a convention of their own, and this convention in turn split up, one part forming the Communist Party, and another part forming the Communist Labor Party. While these two conventions were in session, McGivney came to Peter, and said that the Federal government had a man on the platform committee of the Communist Party, and they wanted to write in some phrases that would make membership in that party in itself a crime, so that everybody who held a membership card could be sent to prison without further evidence. These phrases must be in the orthodox Communist lingo, and this was where Peter's specialized knowledge was needed.

So Peter wrote the phrases, and a couple of days later he read in the newspapers an account of the convention proceedings. The platform committee had reported, and "Shorty" Gunton had submitted a minority report, and had made a fiery speech in the convention, with the result that his minority report was carried by a narrow margin. This minority report contained all the phrases that Peter had written. A couple of months later, when the government had its case ready, and the wholesale raids upon the Communists took place, "Shorty" Gunton was arrested, but a few days later he made a dramatic escape by sawing his way thru the roof of the jail!

Section 80

The I. W. W. had bobbed up again in American City, and had ventured to open another headquarters. Peter did not dare go to the place himself, but he coached a couple of young fellows whom McGivney brought to him, teaching them the Red lingo, and how to worm their way into the movement. Before long one of them was secretary of the local; and Peter, directing their activities, received reports twice a week of everything the "wobblies" were planning and doing. Peter and Gladys were figuring out another bomb conspiracy to direct attention to these dangerous men, when one day Peter picked up the morning paper and discovered that a kind Providence had delivered the enemy into his hands.

Up in the lumber country of the far Northwest, in a little town called Centralia, the "wobblies" had had their headquarters raided and smashed, just as in American City. They had got themselves another meeting-place, and again the members of the Chamber of Commerce and the Merchants' and Manufacturers' Association had held a secret meeting and resolved to wipe them out. The "wobblies" had appealed to the authorities for protection, and when protection was refused, they had printed a leaflet appealing to the public. But the business men went ahead with their plans. They arranged for a parade of returned soldiers on the anniversary of Armistice Day, and they diverted this parade out of its path so that it would pass in front of the I. W. W. headquarters. Some of the more ardent members carried ropes, symbolic of what they meant to do; and they brought the parade to a halt in front of the headquarters, and set up a yell and started to rush the hall. They battered in the door, and had pushed their way half thru it when the "wobblies" opened fire from inside, killing several of the paraders.

Then, of course, the mob flew into a frenzy of fury. They beat the men in the hall, some of them into insensibility; they flung them into jail, and battered and tortured them, and took one of them out of jail and carried him away in an automobile, and after they had mutilated him as Shawn Grady had been mutilated, they hanged him from a bridge. Of course they saw to it that the newspaper stories which went out from Centralia that night were the right kind of stories; and next morning all America read how a group of "wobblies" had armed themselves with rifles, and concealed themselves on the roof of the

I. W. W. headquarters, and deliberately and in cold blood had opened fire upon a peaceful parade of unarmed war veterans.

Of course the country went wild, and the Guffeys and McGivneys and Gudges all over the United States realized that their chance had come. Peter instructed the secretary of the I. W. W. local of American City to call a meeting for that evening, to adopt a resolution declaring the press stories from Centralia to be lies. At the same time another of Guffey's men, an ex-army officer still wearing his, uniform, caused a meeting of the American Legion to be summoned; he made a furious address to the boys, and at nine o'clock that night some two-score of them set out, armed with big monkey-wrenches from their automobiles, and raided the I. W. W. headquarters, and battered the members over the head with the monkey-wrenches, causing several to leap from the window and break their legs. Next morning the incident was reported in the American City "Times" with shouts of glee, and District-attorney Burchard issued a public statement to the effect that no effort would be made to punish the soldier boys; the "wobblies" had wanted "direct action," and they had got it, and it would be assumed that they were satisfied.

Then the members of the American Legion, encouraged by this applause, and instigated by Guffey's ex-army officer, proceeded to invade and wreck every radical meeting-place in the city. They smashed the "Clarion" office and the Socialist Party headquarters again, and confiscated more tons of literature. They wrecked a couple of book-stores, and then, breaking up into small groups, they inspected all the news-stands in the city, and wherever they found Red magazines like the Nation or the New Republic, they tore up the copies and threatened the agents with arrest. They invaded the rooms of a literary society called the Ruskin Club, frequented mostly by amiable old ladies, and sent some of these elderly dames into hysterics. They discovered the "Russian Peoples' Club," which had hitherto been overlooked because it was an educational organization. But of course no Russian could be trusted these days—all of them were Bolsheviks, or on the way to becoming Bolsheviks, which was the same thing; so Guffey organized a raid on this building, and some two hundred Russians were clubbed and thrown downstairs or out of windows, and an elderly teacher of mathematics had his skull cracked, and a teacher of music had some teeth knocked out.

There were several million young Americans who had been put into military uniform, and had guns put into their hands, and been put thru target practice and bayonet drill, and then had not seen any fighting. These fellows were, as the phrase has it, "spoiling for a fight;" and here was their chance. It was just as much fun as trench warfare, and had the advantage of not being dangerous. When the raiding parties came back, there were no missing members, and no casualties to be telegraphed to heartbroken parents. Some fool women got together and tried to organize a procession to protest against the blockade of Russia; the raiders fell upon these women, and wrecked their banners, and tore their clothing to bits, and the police hustled what was left of them off to jail. It happened that a well-known "sporting man," that is to say a race-track frequenter, came along wearing a red necktie, and the raiders, taking him for a Bolshevik, fell upon him and pretty nearly mauled the life out of him. After that there was protest from people who thought it unwise to break too many laws while defending law and order, so the district attorney's office arranged to take on the young soldier boys as deputy sheriffs, and give them all badges, legal and proper.

Section 81

Peter Gudge often went along on these hunting parties. Peter, curiously enough, discovered in himself the same "complex" as the balked soldier boys. Peter had been reading war news for five years, but had missed the fighting; and now he discovered that he liked to fight. What had kept him from liking to fight in the past was the danger of getting hurt; but now that there was no such danger, he could enjoy it. In past times people had called him a coward, and he had heard it so often that he had come to believe it; but now he realized that it was not true, he was just as brave as anybody else in the crowd.

The truth was that Peter had not had a happy time in his youth, he had never learned, like the younger members of the Chamber of Commerce and the Merchants' and Manufacturers' Association, to knock a little white ball about a field with various shapes and sizes of clubs. Peter was like a business man who has missed his boyhood, and then in later years finds the need of recreation, and takes up some form of sport by the orders of his physician. It became Peter's, form of sport to stick an automatic revolver in his hip-pocket, and take a blackjack in his hand, and rush into a room where thirty or forty Russians or "Sheenies" of all ages and lengths of beard were struggling to learn the intricacies of English spelling. Peter would give a yell, and see this crowd leap and scurry hither and thither, and chase them about and take a whack at a head wherever he saw one, and jump into a crowd who were bunched together like sheep, trying to hide their heads, and pound them over the exposed parts of their anatomy until they scattered into the open again. He liked to get a lot of them started downstairs and send them tumbling heels over head; or if he could get them going out a window, that was more exhilarating yet, and he would yell and whoop at them. He learned some of their cries—outlandish gibberish it was—and he would curse them in their own language. He had a streak of the monkey in him, and as he got to know these people better he would imitate their antics and their gestures of horror, and set a whole room full of the "bulls" laughing to split their sides. There was a famous "movie" comedian with big feet, and Peter would imitate this man, and waddle up to some wretched sweat-shop worker and boot him in the trousers' seat, or step on his toes, or maybe spit in his eye. So he became extremely popular among the "bulls," and they would insist on his going everywhere with them.

Later on, when the government set to work to break up the Communist Party and the Communist Labor Party, Peter's popularity and prestige increased still more. For now, instead of just raiding and smashing, the police and detectives would round up the prisoners and arrest them by hundreds, and carry them off and put them thru "examinations." And Peter was always needed for this; his special knowledge made him indispensable, and he became practically the boss of the proceedings. It had been arranged thru "Shorty" Gunton and the other "under cover" men that the meetings of the Communist and Communist Labor parties should be held on the same night; and all over the country this same thing was done, and next morning the world was electrified by the news that all these meetings had been raided at the same hour, and thousands of Reds placed under arrest. In American City the Federal government had hired a suite of about a dozen rooms adjoining the offices of Guffey, and all night and next morning batches of prisoners were brought in, until there were about four hundred in all. They were crowded into these rooms with barely space to sit down; of course there was an awful uproar, moaning and screaming of people who had been battered, and a smell that beat the monkey cage at the zoological gardens.

The prisoners were kept penned up in this place for several weeks, and all the time more were being brought in; there were so many that the women had to be stored in the toilets. Many of the prisoners fell ill, or pretended to fall ill, and several of them went insane, or pretended to go insane, and several of them died, or pretended to die. And of course the parlor Reds and sympathizers were busy outside making a terrible fuss about it. They had no more papers, and could not hold any more meetings, and when they tried to circulate literature the post-office authorities tied them up; but still somehow they managed to get publicity, and Peter's "under cover" men would report to him who was doing this work, and Peter would arrange to have more raids and more batches of prisoners brought in. In one of the "bomb-plots" which had been unveiled in the East they had discovered some pink paper, used either for printing leaflets, or for wrapping explosives, one could not be sure. Anyhow, the secret agencies with which Guffey was connected had distributed samples of this paper over the country, and any time the police wanted to finish some poor devil, they would find this deadly "pink paper" in his possession, and the newspapers would brand him as one of the group of conspirators who were sending infernal machines thru the mails.

Section 82

Peter was so busy these days that he missed several nights' sleep, and hardly even stopped to eat. He had his own private room, where the prisoners were brought for examination, and he had half a dozen men under his orders to do the "strong arm" work. It was his task to extract from these prisoners admissions which would justify their being sent to prison if they were citizens, or being deported if they were aliens. There was of course seldom any way to distinguish between citizens and aliens; you just had to take a chance on it, proceeding on the certainty that all were dangerous. Many years ago, when Peter had been working for Pericles Priam, they had spent several months in a boarding house, and you could tell when there was going to be beef-steak for dinner, because you heard the cook pounding it with the potato-masher to "tender it up;" and Peter learned this phrase, and now used the process upon his alien Reds. When they came into the room, Peter's men would fall upon them and beat them and cuff them, knocking them about from one fist to another. If they were stubborn and would not "come across," Peter would take them in hand himself, remembering how successful Guffey had been in getting things out of him by the twisting of wrists and the bending back of fingers.

It was amazing how clever and subtle some of these fellows were. They were just lousy foreign laborers, but they spent all their spare time reading; you would find large collections of books in their rooms when you made your raids, and they knew exactly what you wanted, and would parry your questions. Peter would say: "You're an Anarchist, aren't you?" And the answer would be: "I'm not an Anarchist in the sense of the word you mean"—as if there could be two meanings of the word "Anarchist!" Peter would say, "You believe in violence, do you not?" And then the fellow would become impertinent: "It is you who believe in violence, look at my face that you have smashed." Or Peter would say, "You don't like this government, do you?" And the answer would be, "I always liked it until it treated me so badly"—all kinds of evasions like that, and there would be a stenographer taking it down, and unless Peter could get something into the record that was a confession, it would not be possible to deport that Red. So Peter would fall upon him and "tender him up" until he would answer what he was told to answer; or maybe Peter would prepare an interview as he wanted it to be, and the detectives would grab the man's hand and make him sign it; or maybe Peter would just sign it himself.

These were harsh methods, but there was no way to help it, the Reds were so cunning. They were secretly undermining the government, and was the government to lie down and admit its helplessness? The answer of 100% Americanism was thundered from every wood and templed hill in the country; also from every newspaper office. The answer was "No!" 100% Americanism would find a way to preserve itself from the sophistries of European Bolshevism; 100% Americanism had worked out its formula: "If they don't like this country, let them go back where they come from." But of course, knowing in their hearts that America was the best country in the world, they didn't want to go back, and it was necessary to make them go.

Peter was there for that purpose, and his devoted wife was by his side, egging him on with her feminine implacability. Gladys had always been accustomed to refer to these people as "cattle," and now, when she smelled them herded together in these office rooms for several weeks, she knew that she was right, and that no fate could be too stern for them. Presently with Peter's help she discovered another bomb-plot, this time against the Attorney-General of the country, who was directing these wholesale raids. They grabbed four Italian Anarchists in American City, and kept them apart in special rooms, and for a couple of months Peter labored with them to get what he wanted out of them. Just as Peter thought he had succeeded, his efforts were balked by one of them jumping out of the window. The room being on the fourteenth story, this Italian Anarchist was no longer available as a witness against himself. The incident set the parlor Bolsheviks all over the country to raging, and caused David Andrews to get some kind of court injunction, and make a lot of inconvenience to Guffey's office.

However, the work went on; the Reds were gradually sorted out, and some who proved not to be Reds were let go again, and others were loaded onto special Red trains and taken to the nearest ports. Some of them went in grim silence, others went with furious cursings, and yet others with wailings and shriekings; for many of them had families, and they had the nerve to demand that the government should undertake to ship their families also, or else to take care of their families for them! The government, naturally, admitted no such responsibility. The Reds had no end of money for printing seditious literature, so let them use it to take care of their own!

In these various raids and examinations Peter of course met a great many of the Reds whom he had once known as friends and intimates. Peter had been wont to imagine himself meeting them, and to tremble at the bare idea; but now found that he rather enjoyed it. He was entirely delivered from that fear of them, which had formerly spoiled his appetite and disturbed his sleep. He had learned that the Reds were poor creatures who did not fight back; they had no weapons, and many of them did not even have muscles; there was really nothing to them but talk. And Peter knew that he had the power of organized society behind him, the police and the courts and the jails, if necessary the army with its machine guns and airplanes and poison gas. Not merely was it safe to pound these people, to tread on their toes and spit in their eyes; it was safe also to frame up anything on them, because the newspapers would always back you up, and the public would of course believe whatever it read in its newspapers.

No, Peter was no longer afraid of the Reds! He made up his mind that he was not even afraid of Mac, the most dangerous Red of them all. Mac was safely put away in jail for twenty years, and although his case had been appealed, the court had refused to grant a stay of sentence or to let him out on bail. As it happened, Peter got a glimpse into Mac's soul in jail, and knew that even that proud, grim spirit was breaking. Mac in jail had written a letter to one of his fellow-Reds in American City, and the post-office authorities had intercepted the letter, and Guffey had shown it to Peter. "Write to us!" Mac had pleaded. "For God's sake, write to us! The worst horror of being in jail is that you are forgotten. Do at least let us know that somebody is thinking about us!"

So Peter knew that he was the victor, he was "top dog." And when he met these Reds whom he had been so afraid of, he took pleasure in letting them feel the weight of his authority, and sometimes of his fist. It was amusing to see the various ways in which they behaved toward him. Some would try to plead with him, for the sake of old times; some would cringe and whine to him; some would try to reason with him, to touch his conscience. But mostly they would be haughty, they would glare at him with hate, or put a sneer of contempt on their faces. So Peter would set his "bulls" to work to improve their manners, and a little thumb-bending and wrist-twisting would soon do the work.

Section 83

Among the first load to be brought in was Miriam Yankovich. Miriam had joined the Communist Party, and she had been born in Russia, so that was all there was to her case. Peter, knew, of course that it was Miriam who had set Rosie Stern after him and brought about his downfall. Still, he could not help but be moved by her appearance. She looked haggard and old, and she had a cough, and her eyes were wild and crazy. Peter remembered her as proud and hot-tempered, but now her pride was all gone—she flung herself on her knees before him, and caught hold of his coat, sobbing hysterically. It appeared that she had a mother and five young brothers and sisters who were dependent upon her earnings; all her money had been consumed by hospital expenses, and now she was to be deported to Russia, and what would become of her loved ones?

Peter answered, what could he do? She had violated the law, they had her membership card in the Communist Party, and she had admitted that she was alien born. He tried to draw away, but she clung to him, and went on sobbing and pleading. At least she ought to have a chance to talk with her old mother, to tell her what to do, where to go for help, how to communicate with Miriam in future. They were sending her away without allowing her to have a word with her loved ones, without even a chance to get her clothing!

Peter, as we know, had always been soft-hearted towards women, so now he was embarrassed. In the handling of these cattle he was carrying out the orders of his superiors; he had no power to grant favors to any one, and he told Miriam this again and again. But she would not listen to him. "Please, Peter, please! For God's sake, Peter! You know you were once a little in love with me, Peter—you told me so—"

Yes, that was true, but it hadn't done Peter much good. Miriam had been interested in Mac—in Mac, that most dangerous devil, who had given Peter so many anxious hours! She had brushed Peter to one side, she had hardly been willing to listen to what he said; and now she was trying to use that love she had spurned!

She had got hold of his hand, and he could not get it away from her without violence. "If you ever felt a spark of love for a woman," she cried, "surely you cannot deny such a favor—such a little favor! Please, Peter, for the sake of old times!"

Suddenly Peter started, and Miriam too. There came a voice from the doorway. "So this is one of your lady friends, is it?" And there stood Gladys, staring, rigid with anger, her little hands clenched. "So this is one of your Red sweethearts, one of your nationalized women?" And she stamped her foot. "Get up, you hussy! Get up, you slut!" And as Miriam continued to kneel, motionless with surprise, Gladys rushed at her, and clutched two handfuls of her heavy black hair, and pulled so that Miriam fell prone on the floor. "I'll teach you, you free lover!" she screamed. "I'll teach you to make love to my husband!" And she dragged Miriam about by that mop of black hair, kicking her and clawing her, until finally several of the bulls had to interfere to save the girl's life.

As a matter of fact Gladys had been told about Peter's shameful past before she married him; Guffey had told her, and she had told Peter that Guffey had told her, she had reminded Peter of it many, many times. But the actual sight of one of these "nationalized women" had driven her into a frenzy, and it was a week before peace was restored in the Gudge family. Meantime poor Peter was buffeted by storms of emotion, both at home and in his office. They were getting ready the first Red train, and it seemed as if every foreign Red that Peter had ever known was besieging him, trying to get at him and harrow his soul and his conscience. Sadie Todd's cousin, who had been born in England, was shipped out on this first train, and also a Finnish lumberman whom Peter had known in the I. W. W., and a Bohemian cigar worker at whose home he had several times eaten, and finally Michael Dubin, the Jewish boy with whom he had spent fifteen days in jail, and who had been one of the victims of the black-snake whippings.

Michael made no end of wailing, because he had a wife and three babies, and he set up the claim that when the "bulls" had raided his home they had stolen all his savings, two or three hundred dollars. Peter, of course, insisted that he could do nothing; Dubin was a Red and an alien, and he must go. When they were loading them on the train, there was Dubin's wife and half a hundred other women, shrieking and wringing their hands, and trying to break thru the guards to get near their loved ones. The police had to punch them in the stomachs with their clubs to hold them back, and in spite of all these blows, the hysterical Mrs. Dubin succeeded in breaking thru the guards, and she threw herself under the wheels of the train, and they were barely able to drag her away in time to save her life. Scenes like this would, of course, have a bad effect upon the public, and so Guffey called up the editors of all the newspapers, and obtained a gentleman's agreement that none of them would print any details.

All over the country the Red trains were moving eastward, loaded with "wobblies" and communists, pacifists and anarchists, and a hundred other varieties of Bolsheviks. They got a shipload together and started them off for Russia—the "Red Ark" it was called, and the Red soap-boxers set tip a terrific uproar, and one Red clergyman compared the "Red Ark" to the Mayflower! Also there was some Red official in Washington, who made a fuss and cancelled a whole block of deportation orders, including some of Peter's own cases. This, naturally, was exasperating to Peter and his wife; and on top of it came another incident that was still more humiliating.

There was a "pink" mass meeting held in American City, to protest against the deportations. Guffey said they would quite probably raid the meeting, and Peter must go along, so as to point out the Reds to the bulls. The work was in charge of a police detective by the name of Garrity, head of what was called the "Bomb Squad"; but this man didn't know very much, so he had the habit of coming to Peter for advice. Now he had the whole responsibility of this meeting, and he asked Peter to come up on the platform with him, and Peter went. Here was a vast audience—all the Red fury which had been pent up for many months, breaking loose in a whirlwind of excitement. Here were orators, well dressed and apparently respectable men, not in any way to be distinguished from the born rulers of the country, coming forward on the platform and uttering the most treasonable sentences, denouncing the government, denouncing the blockade against Russia, praising the Bolshevik government of Russia, declaring that the people who went away in the "Soviet Ark" were fortunate, because they were escaping from a land of tyranny into a land of freedom. At every few sentences the orator would be stopped by a storm of applause that broke from the audience.

And what was a poor Irish Catholic police detective to make of a proposition like that? Here stood an orator declaring: "Whenever any form of government becomes destructive to these ends, it is the right of the people to alter or to abolish it, and to institute new government, laying its foundations on such principles and organizing its powers in such form, as to them shall seem most likely to effect their safety and happiness." And Garrity turned to Peter. "What do you think of that?" he said, his good-natured Irish face blank with dismay.

Peter thought it was the limit. Peter knew that thousands of men all over America had been sent to prison for saying things less dangerous than that. Peter had read many sets of instructions from the office of the Attorney-General of the United States, and knew officially that that was precisely the thing you were never under any circumstances permitted to say, or to write, or even to think. So Peter said to Garrity: "That fellow's gone far enough. You better arrest him." Garrity spoke to his men, and they sprang forward on the platform, and stopped the orator and placed him and all his fellow-orators under arrest, and ordered the audience out of the building. There were a couple of hundred policemen and detectives on hand to carry out Garrity's commands, and they formed a line with their clubs, and drove the crowd before them, and carted the speakers off in a patrol wagon. Then Peter went back to Guffey's office, and told what he had done—and got a reception that reminded him of the time Guffey had confronted him with the letter from Nell Doolin! "Who do you think that was you pinched?" cried Guffey. "He's the brother of a United States senator! And what do you think he was saying? That was a sentence from the Declaration of Independence!"

PETER COULDN'T "GET IT"; PETER was utterly lost. Could a man go ahead and break the law, just because he happened to be a brother of a United States senator? And what difference did it make whether a thing was in the Declaration of Independence, if it was seditious, if it wasn't allowed to be said? This incident brought Guffey and the police authorities of the city so much ridicule that Guffey got all his men together and read them a lecture, explaining to them just what were the limits of the anti-Red activities, just who it was they mustn't arrest, and just what it was they couldn't keep people from saying. For example, a man couldn't be arrested for quoting the Bible.

"But Jesus Christ, Guffey," broke in one of the men, "have all of us got to know the Bible by heart?"

There was a laugh all round. "No," Guffey admitted, "but at least be careful, and don't arrest anybody for saying anything that sounds as if it came from the Bible."

"But hell!" put in another of the men, who happened to be an ex-preacher. "That'll tie us up tighter than a jail-sentence! Look what's in the Bible!"

And he proceeded to quote some of the things, and Peter knew that he had never heard any Bolshevik talk more outrageous than that.

It made one realize more than ever how complicated was this Red problem; for Guffey insisted, in spite of everything, that every word out of the Bible was immune. "Up in Winnipeg," said he, "they indicted a clergyman for quoting two passages from the prophet Isaiah, but they couldn't face it, they had to let the fellow go." And the same thing was true of the Declaration of Independence; anybody might read it, no matter how seditious it was. And the same thing was true of the Constitution, even tho the part called the Bill of Rights declared that everybody in America might do all the things that Guffey's office was sending them to jail for doing!

This seemed a plain crazy proposition; but Guffey explained it as a matter of politics. If they went too far, these fellows would go out and capture the votes from them, and maybe take away the government from them, and where would they be then? Peter had never paid any attention to politics before this, but both he and Gladys realized after this lecture that they must broaden their view-point. It was not enough to put the Reds in jail and crack their skulls, you had to keep public sympathy for what you were doing, you had to make the public understand that it was necessary, you had to carry on what was called "propaganda," to keep the public aware of the odiousness of these cattle, and the desperate nature of their purposes.

The man who perceived that most clearly was the Attorney-General of the country, and Guffey in his lecture pointed out the double nature of his activities. Not merely was the Attorney-General breaking up the Communist and the Communist Labor parties and sending their members to jail; he was using the funds of his office to send out an endless stream of propaganda, to keep the country frightened about these Red plots. Right now he had men in American City working over the data which Guffey had collected, and every week or two he would make a speech somewhere, or would issue a statement to the newspapers, telling of new bomb plots and new conspiracies to overthrow the government. And how clever he was about it! He would get the pictures of the very worst-looking of the Reds, pictures taken after they had been kept in jail for weeks without a shave, and with the third degree to spoil their tempers; and these pictures would be spread on a sheet with the caption: "MEN LIKE THESE WOULD RULE YOU." This would be sent to ten thousand country newspapers all over the nation, and ninety-nine hundred would publish it, and ninety-nine million Americans would want to murder the Reds next morning. So successful had this plan proven that the Attorney-General was expecting to be nominated for President by means of it, and all the agencies of his department were working to that end.

The same thing was being done by all the other agencies of big business all over the country. The "Improve America League" of American City was publishing full-page advertisements in the "Times," and the "Home and Fireside Association" of Eldorado was doing the same thing in the Eldorado "Times," and the "Patriot's Defense Legion" was doing the same thing in the Flagland "Banner." They were investigating the records of all political candidates, and if any of them showed the faintest tinge of pink, Guffey's office would set to work to rake up their records and get up scandals on them, and the business men would contribute a big campaign fund, and these candidates would be snowed under at the polls. That was the kind of work they were doing, and all Guffey's operatives must bear in mind the importance of it, and must never take any step that would hamper this political campaign, this propaganda on behalf of law and order.

Section 85

Peter went out from this conference a sober man, realizing for the first time his responsibilities as a voter, and a shepherd to other voters. Peter agreed with Gladys that his views had been too narrow; his conception of the duties of a secret agent had been of the pre-war order. Now he must realize that the world was changed; now, in this new world made safe for democracy, the secret agent was the real ruler of society, the real master of affairs, the trustee, as it were, for civilization. Peter and his wife must take up this new role and make themselves fit for it. They ought of course not be moved by personal considerations, but at the same time they must recognize the fact that this higher role would be of great advantage to them; it would enable them to move up in the world, to meet the best people. Thru five or six years of her young life Gladys had sat polishing the fingernails and fondling the soft white hands of the genteel; and always a fire of determination had burnt in her breast, that some day she would belong to this world of gentility, she would meet these people, not as an employee, but as an equal, she would not merely hold their hands, but would have them hold hers.

Now the chance had come. She had a little talk with Guffey, and Guffey said it would be a good idea, and he would speak to Billy Nash, the secretary of the "Improve America League"; and he did so, and next week the American City "Times" announced that on the following Sunday evening the Men's Bible Class of the Bethlehem Church would have an interesting meeting. It would be addressed by an "under cover" operative of the government, a former Red who had been for many years a most dangerous agitator, but had seen the error of his ways, and had made amends by giving his services to the government in the recent I. W. W. trials.

The Bethlehem Church didn't amount to very much, it was an obscure sect like the Holy Rollers; but Gladys had been shrewd, and had insisted that you mustn't try to climb to the top of the mountain in one step. Peter must first "try it on the dog," and if he failed, there would be no great harm done.

But Gladys worked just as hard to make a success of this lecture as if they had been going into real society. She spent several days getting up her costume and Peter's, and she spent a whole day getting her toilet ready, and before they set out she spent at least an hour putting the finishing touches upon herself in front of a mirror, and seeing that Peter was proper in every detail. When Mr. Nash introduced her personally to the Rev. Zebediah Muggins, and when this apostle of the second advent came out upon the platform and introduced her husband to the crowded working-class audience, Gladys was so a-quiver with delight that it was more a pain than a pleasure.

Peter did not do perfectly, of course. He lost himself a few times, and stammered and floundered about; but he remembered Glady's advice—if he got stuck, to smile and explain that he had never spoken in public before. So everything went along nicely, and everybody in the Men's Bible Class was aghast at the incredible revelations of this ex-Red and secret agent of law and order. So next week Peter was invited again—this time by the Young Saints' League; and when he had made good there, he was drafted by the Ad. Men's Association, and then by the Crackers and Cheese Club. By this time he had acquired what Gladys called "savvaa fair"; his fame spread rapidly, and at last came the supreme hour—he was summoned to Park Avenue to address the members of the Friendly Society, a parish organization of the Church of the Divine Compassion!

This was the goal upon which the eyes of Gladys had been fixed. This was the time that really counted, and Peter was groomed and rehearsed all over again. Their home was only a few blocks from the church, but Gladys insisted that they must positively arrive in a taxi-cab, and when they entered the Parish Hall and the Rev. de Willoughby Stotterbridge, that exquisite almost-English gentleman, came up and shook hands with them, Gladys knew that she had at last arrived. The clergyman himself escorted her to the platform, and after he had introduced Peter, he seated himself beside her, thus definitely putting a seal upon her social position.

Peter, having learned his lecture by heart, having found out just what brought laughter and what brought tears and what brought patriotic applause, was now an assured success. After the lecture he answered questions, and two clerks in the employ of Billy Nash passed around membership cards of the "Improve America League," membership dues five dollars a year, sustaining membership twenty-five dollars a year, life membership two hundred dollars cash. Peter was shaken hands with by members of the most exclusive social set in American City, and told by them all to keep it up—his country needed him. Next morning there was an account of his lecture in the "Times," and the morning after there was an editorial about his revelations, with the moral: "Join the Improve America League."

That second morning, when Peter got to his office, he found a letter waiting for him, a letter written on very conspicuous and expensive stationery, and addressed in a woman's tall and sharp-pointed handwriting. Peter opened it and got a start, for at the top of the letter was some kind of crest, and a Latin inscription, and the words: "Society of the Daughters of the American Revolution." The letter informed him by the hand of a secretary that Mrs. Warring Sammye requested that Mr. Peter Gudge would be so good as to call upon her that afternoon at three o'clock. Peter studied the letter, and tried to figure out what kind of Red this was. He was impressed by the stationery and the regal tone, but that word "Revolution" was one of the forbidden words. Mrs. Warren Sammye must be one of the "Parlor Reds," like Mrs. Godd.

So Peter took the letter to McGivney, and said suspiciously, "What kind of a Red plot is this?"

McGivney read the letter, and said, "Red plot? How do you mean?"

"Why," explained Peter, "it says 'Daughters of the American Revolution.'"

And McGivney looked at him; at first he thought that Peter was joking, but when he saw that the fellow was really in earnest, he guffawed in his face. "You boob!" he said. "Didn't you ever hear of the American Revolution? Don't you know anything about the Fourth of July?"

Just then the telephone rang and interrupted them, and McGivney shoved the letter to him saying, "Ask your wife about it!" So when Gladys came in, Peter gave her the letter, and she was much excited. It appeared that Mrs. Warring Sammye was a very tip-top society lady in American City, and this American Revolution of which she was a daughter was a perfectly respectable revolution that had happened a long time ago; the very best people belonged to it, and it was legal and proper to write about, and even to put on your letterheads. Peter must go home and get himself into his best clothes at once, and telephone to the secretary that he would be pleased to call upon Mrs. Warring Sammye at the hour indicated. Incidentally, there were a few more things for Peter to study. He must get a copy of the social register, "Who's Who in American City," and he must get a history of his country, and learn about the Declaration of Independence, and what was the difference between a revolution that had happened a long time ago and one that was happening now.

So Peter went to call on the great society lady in her grey stone mansion, and found her every bit as opulent as Mrs. Godd, with the addition that she respected her own social position; she did not make the mistake of treating Peter as an equal, and so it did not occur to Peter that he might settle down permanently in her home. Her purpose was to tell Peter that she had heard of his lecture about the Red menace, and that she was chairman of the Board of Directors of the Lady Patronesses of the Home for Disabled War Veterans in American City, and she wanted to arrange to have Peter deliver this lecture to the veterans. And Peter, instructed in advance by Gladys, said that he would be very glad to donate this lecture as a patriotic contribution. Mrs. Warring Sammye thanked him gravely in the name of his country, and said she would let him know the date.

Peter went home, and Gladys made a wry face, because the lecture was to be delivered before a lot of good-for-nothing soldiers in some hall, when it had been her hope that it was to be delivered to the Daughters themselves, and in Mrs. Warring Sammye's home. However, to have attracted Mrs. Warring Sammye's attention for anything was in itself a triumph. So Gladys was soon cheerful again, and she told Peter about Mrs. Warring Sammye's life; one picked up such valuable knowledge in the gossip at the manicure parlors, it appeared.

Then, being in a friendly mood, Gladys talked to Peter about himself. They had mounted to a height from which they could look back upon the past and see it as a whole, and in the intimacy and confidence of their domestic partnership they could draw lessons from their mistakes and plan their future wisely. Peter had made many blunders—he must surely admit that. Did Peter admit that? Yes, Peter did. But, continued Gladys, he had struggled bravely, and he had the supreme good fortune to have secured for himself that greatest of life's blessings, the cooperation of a good and capable woman. Gladys was very emphatic about this latter, and Peter agreed with her. He agreed also when she stated that it is the duty of a good and capable wife to protect her husband for the balance of their life's journey, so that he would be able to avoid the traps which his enemies set for his feet. Peter, having learned by bitter experience, would never again go chasing after a pretty face, and wake up next morning to find his pockets empty. Peter admitted this too. As this conversation progressed, he realized that the tour of triumph his life had become was a thing entirely of his wife's creation; at least, he realized that there would be no use in trying to change his wife's conviction on the subject. Likewise he meekly accepted her prophecies as to his future conduct; he would bring home his salary at the end of each week, and his wife would use it, together with her own salary, to improve the appearance and tone of both of them, and to aid them to climb to a higher social position.

Peter, following his wife's careful instructions, has already become more dignified in his speech, more grave in his movements. She tells him that the future of society depends on his knowledge and his skill, and he agrees to this also. He has learned what you can do and what you had better not do; he will never again cross the dead-line into crime, or take chances with experiments in blackmail. He will try no more free lance work under the evil influence of low creatures like Nell Doolin, but will stand in with the "machine," and bear in mind that honesty is the best policy. So he will steadily progress; he will meet the big men of the country, and will go to them, not cringing and twisting his hat in his hands, but with quiet self-possession. He will meet the agents of the Attorney-General aspiring to become President, and will furnish them with material for their weekly Red scares. He will meet legislators who want to unseat elected Socialists, and governors who wish to jail the leaders of "outlaw" strikes. He will meet magazine writers getting up articles, and popular novelists looking for local Red color.

But Peter's best bid of all will be as a lecturer. He will be able to travel all over the country, making a sensation. Did he know why? No, Peter answered, he was not sure he did. Well, Gladys could tell him; it was because he was romantic. Peter didn't know just what this word meant, but it sounded flattering, so he smiled sheepishly, showing his crooked teeth, and asked how Gladys found out that he was romantic. The reply was a sudden order for him to stand up and turn around slowly.

Peter didn't like to get up from his comfortable Morris chair, but he did what his wife asked him. She inspected him on all sides and exclaimed, "Peter, you must go on a diet; you're getting ombongpoing!" She said this in horrified tones, and Peter was frightened, because it sounded like a disease. But Gladys added: "You can not be a romantic figure on a lecture platform if you've got a bay-window!"

Peter found it interesting to be talked about, so he asked again why Gladys thought he was romantic. There were several reasons, she said, but the main one was that he had been a dangerous criminal, and had reformed, which pleased the church people; he had made a happy ending by marriage, which pleased those who read novels.

"Is that so?" said Peter, guilelessly, and she assured him that it was. "And what else?" he asked, and she explained that he had known intimately and at first hand those dreadful and dangerous people, those ogres of the modern world, the Bolsheviks, about whom the average man and woman learned only thru the newspapers. And not merely did he tell a sensational story, but he ended it with a money-making lesson. The lesson was "Contribute to the Improve America League. Make out your checks to the Home and Fireside Association. The existence of your country depends upon your sustaining the Patriot's Defense Legion." So the fame of Peter's lecture would spread, and the Guffeys and Billy Nashes of every city and town in America would clamor for him to come, and when he came, the newspapers would publish his picture, and he and his wife would be welcomed by leaders of the best society. They would become social lions, and would see the homes of the rich, and gradually become one of the rich.

Gladys looked her spouse over again, as they started to their sleeping apartment. Yes, he was undoubtedly putting on "ombongpoing"; he would have to take up golf. He was wearing a little American flag dangling from his watch chain, and she wondered if that wasn't a trifle crude. Gladys herself now wore a real diamond ring, and had learned to say "vahse" and "baahth." She yawned prettily as she took off her lovely brown "tailor-made," and reflected that such things come with ease and security.

Both she and Peter now had these in full measure. They had lost all fear of ever finding themselves out of a job. They had come to understand that the Red menace is not to be so easily exterminated; it is a distemper that lurks in the blood of society, and breaks out every now and then in a new rash. Gladys had come to agree with the Reds to this extent, that so long as there is a class of the rich and prosperous, so long will there be social discontent, so long will there be some that make their living by agitating, denouncing and crying out for change. Society is like a garden; each year when you plant your vegetables there springs up also a crop of weeds, and you have to go down the rows and chop off the heads of these weeds. Gladys' husband is an expert gardener, he knows how to chop weeds, and he knows that society will never be able to dispense with his services. So long as gardening continues, Peter will be a head weedchopper, and a teacher of classes of young weedchoppers.

Ah, it was fine to have married such a man! It was the reward a good woman received for helping her husband, making him into a good citizen, a patriot and an upholder of law and order: For always, of course, those who own the garden would see that their head weedchopper was taken care of, and had his share of the best that the garden produced. Gladys stood before her looking-glass, braiding her hair for the night, and thinking of the things she would ask from this garden. She and Peter had earned, and they would demand, the sweetest flowers, the most luscious fruits. Suddenly Gladys stretched wide her arms in an ecstasy of realization. "We're a Success, Peter! We're a Success! We'll have money and all the lovely things it will buy! Do you realize, Peter, what a hit you've made?"

Peter saw her face of joy, but he was a tiny bit frightened and uncertain, because of this unusual sharing of the honors. So Gladys was impelled to affection, mingled with pity. She held out her arms to him. "Poor, dear Peter! He's had such a hard life! It was cruel he didn't have me sooner to help him!"

And then Gladys reflected for a moment, and was moved to another outburst. "Just think, Peter, how wonderful it is to be an American! In America you can always rise if you do your duty! America is the land of the free! Your example of a poor boy's success ought to convince even the fool Reds that they're wrong—that any boy can rise if he works hard! Why, I've heard it said that in America the poorest boy can rise to be President! How would you like to be President, Peter?"

Peter hesitated. He doubted if he was equal to that big a job, but he knew that it would not please Gladys for him to say so. He murmured, "Perhaps—some day—"

"Anyhow, Peter," his wife continued, "I'm for this country! I'm an American!"

And this time Peter didn't have to hesitate. "You bet!" he said, and added his favorite formula—"100%!"

A little experimenting with the manuscript of "100%" has revealed to the writer that everybody has a series of questions they wish immediately to ask: How much of it is true? To what extent have the business men of America been compelled to take over the detection and prevention of radicalism? Have they, in putting down the Reds, been driven to such extreme measures as you have here shown?

A few of the incidents in "100%" are fictional, for example the story of Nell Doolin and Nelse Ackerman; but everything that has social significance is truth, and has been made to conform to facts personally known to the writer or to his friends. Practically all the characters in "100%" are real persons. Peter Gudge is a real person, and has several times been to call upon the writer in the course of his professional activities; Guffey and McGivney are real persons, and so is Billy Nash, and so is Gladys Frisbie.

To begin at the beginning: the "Goober case" parallels in its main outlines the case of Tom Mooney. If you wish to know about this case, send fifteen cents to the Mooney Defense Committee, Post Office Box 894, San Francisco, for the pamphlet, "Shall Mooney Hang," by Robert Minor. The business men of San Francisco raised a million dollars to save the city from union labor, and the Mooney case was the way they did it. It happened, however, that the judge before whom Mooney was convicted weakened, and wrote to the Attorney-General of the State to the effect that he had become convinced that Mooney was convicted by perjured testimony. But meantime Mooney was in jail, and is there still. Fremont Older, editor of the San Francisco "Call," who has been conducting an investigation into this case, has recently written to the author: "Altogether, it is the most amazing story I have ever had anything to do with. When all is known that I think can be known, it will be shown clearly that the State before an open-eyed community was able to murder a man with the instruments that the people have provided for bringing about justice. There isn't a scrap of testimony in either of the Mooney or Billings cases that wasn't perjured, except that of the man who drew the blue prints of Market Street."

To what extent has the detection and punishment of radicalism in America passed out of the hands of public authorities and into the hands of "Big Business?" Any business man will of course agree that when

"Big Business" has interests to protect, it must and will protect them. So far as possible it will make use of the public authorities; but when thru corruption or fear of politics these fail, "Big Business" has to act for itself. In the Colorado coal strike the coal companies raised the money to pay the state militia, and recruited new companies of militia from their private detectives. The Reds called this "Government by Gunmen," and the writer in his muckraking days wrote a novel about it, "King Coal." The man who directed the militia during this coal strike was A. C. Felts of the Baldwin-Felts Detective Agency, who was killed just the other day while governing several coal counties in West Virginia.

You will find this condition in the lumber country of Washington and Oregon, in the oil country of Oklahoma and Kansas, in the copper country of Michigan, Montana and Arizona, and in all the big coal districts. In the steel country of Western Pennsylvania you will find that all the local authorities are officials of the steel companies. If you go to Bristol, R. I., you will find that the National India Rubber Company has agreed to pay the salaries of two-thirds of the town's police force.

In every large city in America the employers' associations have raised funds to hold down the unions and smash the Reds, and these funds are being expended in the way portrayed in "100%." In Los Angeles the employers' association raised a million dollars, and the result was the case of Sydney R. Flowers, briefly sketched in this story under the name of "Sydney." The reader who wishes the details of this case is referred to Chapter LXVI of "The Brass Check." Flowers has been twice tried, and is about to be tried a third time, and our District-Attorney is quoted as saying that he will be tried half a dozen times if necessary. At the last trial there were produced a total of twenty-five witnesses against Flowers, and out of these nineteen were either Peter Gudges and McGivneys, or else police detectives, or else employees of the local political machine. A deputy United States attorney, talking to me about the case, told me that he had refused to prosecute it because he realized that the "Paul letter," upon which the arrest had been based, was a frame-up, and that he was quite sure he knew who had written it. He also told me that there had been formed in Los Angeles a secret committee of fifty of the most active rich men of the town; that he could not find out what they were doing, but they came to his offices and demanded the secret records of the government; and that when he refused to prosecute Flowers they had influence enough to have the governor of California telegraph to Washington in protest. Questioned on the witness stand, I repeated these statements, and the deputy United States attorney was called to the stand and attributed them to my "literary imagination."

In the old Russian and Austrian empires the technique of trapping agitators was well developed, and the use of spies and "under cover" men for the purpose of luring the Reds into crime was completely worked out. We have no English equivalent for the phrase "agent provocateur," but in the last four years we have put thousands of them at work in America. In the case against Flowers three witnesses were produced who had been active among the I. W. Ws., trying to incite crime, and were being paid to give testimony for the state. One of these men admitted that he had himself burned some forty barns, and was now receiving three hundred dollars a month and expenses. At the trial of William Bross Lloyd in Chicago, charged with membership in the Communist party, a similar witness was produced. Santeri Nourteva, of, the Soviet Bureau in New York, has charged that Louis C. Fraina, editor of the "Revolutionary Age," was a government agent, and Fraina wrote into the platform of the Communist party the planks which were used in prosecuting and deporting its members. On December 27, 1919, the chief of the Bureau of Investigation of the Department of Justice in Washington sent to the head of his local bureau in Boston a telegram containing the following sentences: "You should arrange with your under cover informants to have meetings of the Communist Party and Communist Labor Party held on the night set. I have been informed by some of the bureau officers that such arrangements will be made." So much evidence of the activity of the provocateur was produced before Federal Judge G. W. Anderson that he declared as follows: "What does appear beyond reasonable dispute is that the Government owns and operates some part of the Communist Party."

It appears that Judge Anderson does not share the high opinion of the "under cover" operative set forth by the writer of "100%." Says Judge Anderson: "I cannot adopt the contention that Government spies are any more trustworthy, or less disposed to make trouble in order to profit therefrom, than are spies in private industry. Except in time of war, when a Nathan Hale may be a spy, spies are always necessarily drawn from the unwholesome and untrustworthy classes. A right-minded man refuses such a job. The evil wrought by the spy system in industry has, for decades, been incalculable. Until it is eliminated, decent human relations cannot exist between employers and employees, or even among employees. It destroys trust and confidence; it kills human kindliness; it propagates hate."

To what extent have the governmental authorities of America been forced to deny to the Reds the civil rights guaranteed to good Americans by the laws and the constitution? The reader who is curious on this point may send the sum of twenty-five cents to the American Civil Liberties Union, 138 West 13th Street, New York, for the pamphlet entitled, "Report upon the Illegal Practices of the United States Department of Justice," signed by twelve eminent lawyers in the country, including a dean of the Harvard Law school, and a United States attorney who resigned because of his old-fashioned ideas of law. This pamphlet contains sixty-seven pages, with numerous exhibits and photographs. The practices set forth are listed under six heads: Cruel and unusual punishments; arrests without warrant; unreasonable searches and seizures; provocative agents; compelling persons to be witnesses against themselves, propaganda by the Department of Justice. The reader may also ask for the pamphlet entitled "Memorandum Regarding the Persecution of the Radical Labor Movement in the United States;" also for the pamphlet entitled "War Time Prosecution and Mob Violence," dated March, 1919, giving a list of cases which occupies forty pages of closely printed type. Also he might read "The Case of the Rand School," published by the Rand School of Social Science, 7 East Fifteenth Street, New York, and the pamphlets published by the National Office of the Socialist Party, 220 South Ashland Blvd., Chicago, dealing with the prosecutions of that organization.

To what extent has it been necessary to torture the Reds in prison in America? Those who are interested are advised to write to Harry Weinberger, 32 Union Square, New York, for the pamphlet entitled "Twenty Years Prison," dealing with the case of Mollie Steimer, and three others who were sentenced for distributing a leaflet protesting against the war on Russia; also to the American Civil Liberties Union for the pamphlet entitled "Political Prisoners in Federal Military Prisons," also the pamphlet, "Uncle Sam: Jailer," by Winthrop D. Lane, reprinted from the "Survey;" also the pamphlet entitled "The Soviet of Deer Island, Boston Harbor," published by the Boston Branch of the American Civil Liberties Union; also for the publications of the American Industrial Company, and the American Freedom Foundation, 166 West Washington St. Chicago.

There may be some reader with a sense of humor who asks about the brother of a United States senator being arrested for reading a paragraph from the Declaration of Independence. This gentleman was the brother of United States Senator France of Maryland, and curiously enough, the arrest took place in the city of Philadelphia, where the Declaration of Independence was adopted. There may be some reader who is curious about a clergyman being indicted and arrested in Winnipeg for having quoted the prophet Isaiah. The paragraph from the indictment in question reads as follows: "That J. S. Woodsworth, on or about the month of June, in the year of our Lord one thousand nine hundred and nineteen, at the City of Winnipeg, in the Province of Manitoba, unlawfully and seditiously published seditious libels in the words and figures following: 'Woe unto them that decree unrighteous decrees, and that write grievousness which they have prescribed; to turn aside the needy from judgment, and to take away their right from the poor of my people that widows may be their prey and that they may rob the fatherless. . . And they shall build houses and inhabit them, and they shall plant vineyards and eat the fruit of them. They shall not build and another inhabit, they shall not plant and another eat; for as the days of a tree are the days of my people, and mine elect shall long enjoy the work of their hands.'"

There has been reference in this book to the Centralia case. No one can consider that he understands the technique of holding down the Reds until he has studied this case, and therefore every friend of "Big Business" should send fifty cents, either to the I. W. W. Headquarters, 1001 West Madison Street, Chicago, or to the "Liberator," New York, or to the "Appeal to Reason," Girard, Kansas, for the booklet, "The Centralia Conspiracy," by Ralph Chaplin, who attended the Centralia trial, and has collected all the details and presents them with photographs and documents. Many other stories about the I. W. W. have been told in the course of "100%." The reader will wish to know, are these men really so dangerous, and have the business men of America been driven to treat them as here described. The reader may again address the I. W. W. National Headquarters for a four-page leaflet with the quaint title, "With Drops of Blood the History of the Industrial Workers of the World has Been Written." Despite the fact that it is a bare record of cases, there are many men serving long terms in prison in the United States for the offense of having in their possession a copy of this leaflet, "With Drops of Blood." But the readers of this book, being all of them 100% Americans engaged in learning the technique of smashing the Reds, will, I feel sure, not be interfered with by the business men. Also

I trust that the business men will not object to my reprinting a few paragraphs from the leaflet, in order to make the public realize how dangerously these Reds can write. I will, of course, not follow their incendiary example and spatter my page with big drops of imitation blood. I quote:

"We charge that I. W. W. members have been murdered, and mention here a few of those who have lost their lives:

"Joseph Michalish was shot to death by a mob of so-called citizens. Michael Hoey was beaten to death in San Diego. Samuel Chinn was so brutally beaten in the county jail at Spokane, Washington, that he died from the injuries. Joseph Hillstrom was judicially murdered within the walls of the penitentiary at Salt Lake City, Utah. Anna Lopeza, a textile worker, was shot and killed, and two other Fellow Workers were murdered during the strike at Lawrence, Massachusetts. Frank Little, a cripple, was lynched by hirelings of the Copper Trust at Butte, Montana. John Looney, A. Robinowitz, Hugo Gerlot, Gustav Johnson, Felix Baron, and others were killed by a mob of Lumber Trust gunmen on the Steamer Verona at the dock at Everett, Washington. J. A. Kelly was arrested and re-arrested at Seattle, Washington; finally died from the effects of the frightful treatment he received. Four members of the I. W. W. were killed at Grabow, Louisiana, where thirty were shot and seriously wounded. Two members were dragged to death behind an automobile at Ketchikan, Alaska.

"These are but a few of the many who have given up their lives on the altar of Greed, sacrificed in the ages-long struggle for Industrial Freedom.

"We charge that many thousands of members of this organization have been imprisoned, on most occasions arrested without warrant and held without charge. To verify this statement it is but necessary that you read the report of the Commission on Industrial Relations wherein is given testimony of those who know of conditions at Lawrence, Massachusetts, where nearly 900 men and women were thrown into prison during the Textile Workers' Strike at that place. This same report recites the fact that during the Silk Workers' Strike at Paterson, New Jersey, nearly 1,900 men and women were cast into jail without charge or reason. Throughout the northwest these kinds of outrages have been continually perpetrated against members of the I. W. W. County jails and city prisons in nearly every state in the Union have held or are holding members of this organization.

"We charge that members of the I. W. W. have been tarred and feathered. Frank H. Meyers was tarred and feathered by a gang of prominent citizens at North Yakima, Washington. D. S. Dietz was tarred and feathered by a mob led by representatives of the Lumber Trust at Sedro, Wooley, Washington. John L. Metzen, attorney for the Industrial Workers of the World, was tarred and feathered and severely beaten by a mob of citizens of Staunton, Illinois. At Tulsa, Oklahoma, a mob of bankers and other business men gathered up seventeen members of the I. W. W., loaded them in automobiles, carried them out of town to a patch of woods, and there tarred and feathered and beat them with rope.

"We charge that members of the Industrial Workers of the World have been deported, and cite the cases of Bisbee, Arizona, where 1,164 miners, many of them members of the I. W. W., and their friends, were dragged out of their homes, loaded upon box cars, and sent out of the camp. They were confined for months at Columbus, New Mexico. Many cases are now pending against the copper companies and business men of Bisbee. A large number of members were deported from Jerome, Arizona. Seven members of the I. W. W. were deported from Florence, Oregon, and were lost for days in the woods, Tom Lassiter, a crippled news vender, was taken out in the middle of the night and badly beaten by a mob for selling the Liberator and other radical papers.

"We charge that members of the I. W. W. have been cruelly and inhumanly beaten. Hundreds of members can show scars upon their lacerated bodies that were inflicted upon them when they were compelled to run the gauntlet. Joe Marko and many others were treated in this fashion at San Diego, California. James Rowan was nearly beaten to death at Everett, Washington. At Lawrence, Massachusetts, the thugs of the Textile Trust beat men and women who had been forced to go on strike to get a little more of the good things of life. The shock and cruel whipping which they gave one little Italian woman caused her to give premature birth to a child. At Red Lodge, Montana, a member's home was invaded and he was hung by the neck before his screaming wife and children. At Franklin, New Jersey, August 29, 1917, John Avila, an I. W. W., was taken in broad daylight by the chief of police and an auto-load of business men to a woods near the town and there hung to a tree. He was cut down before death ensued, and badly beaten. It was five hours before Avila regained consciousness, after which the town 'judge' sentenced him to three months at hard labor.

"We charge that members of the I. W. W. have been starved. This statement can be verified by the conditions existing in most any county jail where members of the I. W. W. are confined. A very recent instance is at Topeka, Kansas, where members were compelled to go on a hunger strike as a means of securing food for themselves that would sustain life. Members have been forced to resort to the hunger strike as a means of getting better food in many places. You are requested to read the story written by Winthrop D. Lane, which appears in the Sept. 6, 1919, number of 'The Survey.' This story is a graphic description of the county jails in Kansas.

"We charge that I. W. W. members have been denied the right of citizenship, and in each instance the judge frankly told the applicants that they were refused on account of membership in the Industrial Workers of the World, accompanying this with abusive remarks; members were denied their citizenship papers by judge Hanford at Seattle, Washington, and judge Paul O'Boyle at Scranton, Pennsylvania.

"We charge that members of the I. W. W. have been denied the privilege of defense. This being an organization of working men who had little or no funds of their own, it was necessary to appeal to the membership and the working class generally for funds to provide a proper defense. The postal authorities, acting under orders from the Postmaster-General at Washington, D. C., have deliberately prevented the transportation of our appeals, our subscription lists, our newspapers. These have been piled up in the post offices and we have never received a return of the stamps affixed for mailing.

"We charge that the members of the I. W. W. have been held in exorbitant bail. As an instance there is the case of Pietro Pierre held in the county jail at Topeka, Kansas. His bond was fixed at $5,000, and when the amount was tendered it was immediately raised to $10,000. This is only one of the many instances that could be recorded.

"We charge that members of the I. W. W. have been compelled to submit to involuntary servitude. This does not refer to members confined in the penitentiaries, but would recall the reader's attention to an I. W. W. member under arrest in Birmingham, Alabama, taken from the prison and placed on exhibition at a fair given in that city where admission of twenty-five cents was charged to see the I. W. W."

Finally, for the benefit of the reader who asks how it happens that such incidents are not more generally known to the public, I will reprint the following, from pages 382-383 of "The Brass Check," dealing with the "New York Times," and its treatment of the writer's novel, "Jimmie Higgins":

"In the last chapters of this story an American soldier is represented as being tortured in an American military prison. Says the 'Times':

"'Mr. Sinclair should produce the evidence upon which he bases his astounding accusations, if he has any. If he has simply written on hearsay evidence, or, worse still, let himself be guided by his craving to be sensational, he has laid himself open not only to censure but to punishment.'

"In reply to this, I send to the 'Times' a perfectly respectful letter, citing scores of cases, and telling the 'Times' where hundreds of other cases may be found. The 'Times' returns this letter without comment. A couple of months pass, and as a result of the ceaseless agitation of the radicals, there is a congressional investigation, and evidence of atrocious cruelties is forced into the newspapers. The 'Times' publishes an editorial entitled, 'Prison Camp Cruelties,' the first sentence of which reads: 'The fact that American soldiers confined in prison-camps have been treated with extreme brutality may now be regarded as established.' So again I write a polite letter to the 'Times,' pointing out that I think they owe me an apology. And how does the 'Times' treat that? It alters my letter without my permission. It cuts out my request for an apology, and also my quotation of its own words calling for my punishment! The 'Times,' caught in a hole, refuses to let me remind its readers that it wanted me 'punished' for telling the truth! 'All the News that's Fit to Print!'"

A Note About the Author

Upton Sinclair (1878–1968) was an American writer from Maryland. Though he wrote across many genres, Sinclair's most famous works were politically motivated. His self-published novel, *The Jungle*, exposed the labor conditions in the meatpacking industry. This novel even inspired changes for working conditions and helped pass protection laws. *The Brass Check* exposed poor journalistic practices at the time and was also one of his most famous works. As a member of the socialist party, Sinclair attempted a few political runs but when defeated he returned to writing. Sinclair won the Pulitzer Prize in 1943 for Fiction. Several of his works were made into film adaptations and one earned two Oscars.

A Note from the Publisher

Spanning many genres, from non-fiction essays to literature classics to children's books and lyric poetry, Mint Edition books showcase the master works of our time in a modern new package. The text is freshly typeset, is clean and easy to read, and features a new note about the author in each volume. Many books also include exclusive new introductory material. Every book boasts a striking new cover, which makes it as appropriate for collecting as it is for gift giving. Mint Edition books are only printed when a reader orders them, so natural resources are not wasted. We're proud that our books are never manufactured in excess and exist only in the exact quantity they need to be read and enjoyed.

Discover more of your favorite classics with Bookfinity™.

- Track your reading with custom book lists.
- Get great book recommendations for your personalized Reader Type.
- Add reviews for your favorite books.
- AND MUCH MORE!

Visit **bookfinity.com** and take the fun Reader Type quiz to get started.

Enjoy our classic and modern companion pairings!

Printed in the USA
CPSIA information can be obtained
at www.ICGtesting.com
JSHW022219140824
68134JS00018B/1153

9 781513 269887